WORLD MAP

PACIFIC
OCEAN

NORTH
AMERICA

CARIBBEAN
SEA

SOUTH
AMERICA

ATLA
OCE

PACIFIC
OCEAN

ARCTIC OCEAN

EUROPE

ASIA

PACIFIC
OCEAN

AFRICA

OCEANIA

INDIAN
OCEAN

ANTARCTICA

開口就會
旅遊英語

實踐大學應用外語系專任講師
黃 靜 悅
Danny O. Neal ◎著

TRAVEL ENGLISH

五南圖書出版公司 印行

麥克魯漢（Marshall McLuhan）於上世紀六〇年代首度提出了「地球村」的概念，當時他原本用這個新名詞來說明電子媒介對於人類未來之衝擊，實不亞於古騰堡（Johann Gutenberg）印刷術對西方文明的影響；曾幾何時，「地球村」在今天有了新的涵義：天涯若比鄰！

現代科技進步昌明，往昔「五月花」號上的新教徒花了六十幾天，歷經千辛萬苦才橫渡大西洋，今日搭乘超音速飛機只要四個多小時就可完成；網際網路的普及，世界上任何角落發生的事情對千里以外的地方都會有不可思議的影響，亦即所謂「蝴蝶效應」；語言文字的互通理解；東方的「博愛」和西方的「charity」使得普天下心懷「人溺己溺」之心的信徒，都能為營造開創一個由愛出發、以和為貴的世界而一起努力！這一切都說明了一個事實：人與人之間不再因距離、時空、障礙和誤解而「老死不相往來」！

當然，在這一片光鮮亮麗的外表下，隱憂依然存在。「全球化」（Globalization）對第三世界的人而言，竟成為新帝國主義和資本主義的同義字！造成這種誤解，甚至於扭曲的主要原因是對不同於自己的文化、風俗、傳統及習慣的一知半解；是不是用法文就顯得比較文明？使用義大利文就會比較熱情？德文，富哲理？英文，有深度？而美語，就「財大氣粗」？是不是有一套介紹書籍，雖不一定包含了所有相關的資訊，但至少是對那些想要知道或了解異國風物的好

奇者，能有所幫助的參考工具書？

　　放眼今日的自學書刊，林林總總，參差不齊。上者，艱澀聱牙或孤芳自賞；下者，錯誤百出或言不及意！想要找兼具深度和廣度的語言學習工具書，實屬不易。現有本校應用外語學系黃靜悅和唐凱仁兩位老師，前者留學旅居國外多年，以國人的角度看外國文化；後者則以外國人的立場，以其數十年寄居臺灣的經驗，兩人合作撰寫系列叢書，舉凡旅遊、日常生活、社交、校園及商務應用，提供真實情境對話，佐以「實用語句」、「字句補給站」讓學習者隨查隨用，並穿插「小叮嚀」和「小祕訣」，提供作者在美生活的點滴、體驗與心得等的第一手資訊。同時，「文化祕笈」及「旅遊資訊站」更為同類書刊中之創舉！

　　學無止境！但唯有輔以正確的學習書籍，才能收「事半功倍」之效。本人對兩位老師的投入與努力，除表示敬意，特此作序說明，並冀望唐黃兩位老師在教學研究之餘，再接再厲，為所有有志向學、自我提昇的學習者，提供更精練、更充實的自學叢書。

前實踐大學　校長

張光正

　　學習外語的動機不外乎外在（instrumental）及內在（intrinsic）兩類：外在動機旨在以語言作為工具，完成工作任務；內在動機則是希望透過外語學習達成自我探索及自我實現的目標。若人們在語言學習上能有所成，則此成就也必然是雙方面的；一方面完成工作任務而得到實質上的利益報償，另一方面則因達成溝通、了解對方文化及想法而得到豐富的感受。

　　現今每個人都是地球公民中的一員，而語言則是自我與世界的連結工具。今日網路科技的發展在彈指間就可以連結到我們想要的網站，人類的學習心與天性因刺激而產生對未知的好奇心及行動力，使我們對於異國語言文化自然產生嚮往；增進對這個世界的了解已不是所謂的個人特色或美德，而是身處現代地球村的每個人都該具備的一種責任與義務！

　　用自己的腳走出去、用自己的眼睛去看、用自己的心靈去感受世界其他國家人們的生活方式、用自己學得的語言當工具，與不同國家的人們交談；或許我們的母語、種族、膚色、性別不同，或許我們的衣著、宗教信仰、喜好以及對事情的看法、做法不同，但人與人之間善意的眼神、微笑、肢體動作、互相尊重、善待他人的同理心，加上適切的語言，對世界和平、國際友邦間相互扶持的共同渴望，使我們深深體會到精彩動人的外語學習旅程其實是自我發現的旅程！只有自己親自走過的旅程、完成過的任務、通過的關卡、遇到的人們、累積的智慧經驗、開拓的視野、體驗過的人生，才是無可替代的真實感受。世界

有多大、個人想為自己及世人貢獻的事有多少，學習外語完成自我實現內在動機的收穫就有多豐富！

今日有機會將自己所學與用腳走世界、用心親感受的經驗交付五南出版社出版叢書，誠摯感謝前實踐大學張光正校長慨為本叢書作序、前鄧景元主編催生本系列書，眾五南夥伴使本書順利完成，及親愛的家人朋友學生們的加油打氣。若讀者大眾能因本系列叢書增進英語文實力，並為自己開啟一道與世界溝通的大門，便是對作者最大的回饋與鼓勵！

願與所有立志於此的讀者共勉之。

作者　黃靜悅　謹誌

特點圖示

頁碼

172

單元標題

5.17 駕駛——高速公路標示
Driving—Highway Signs

Dialog 1　對話1

A: 這裡速限是多少？

A: What is the speed limit here?

B: 我不知道。

B: I don't know.

依不同情境模擬對話

A: 找一個路旁有數字的標誌。

A: Look for a sign along the road with a number on it.

B: 那邊，看那邊，I-95。哇！那可真快。

B: There. Look there. I-95. Wow! That's fast.

A: 不，不是，那不是速限標誌。

A: No, no. That's not a speed limit sign.

B: 不是嗎？那是什麼？

B: It's not? What is it?

Word Bank　字庫

重要單字解釋

toll [tol] n. 通行費，過路費
change [tʃendʒ] n. 零錢
toll ticket n. 回數票
pass card n. 通行卡
refundable [rɪ'fʌndəbl] adj. 可退費的

基本對話
機場與飛機
入境
住宿
交通
餐飲
觀光
購物
郵電
銀行
麻煩事
回國

 Useful Phrases 實用語句 ➤ 各式場景常用句子

1. 這是收費公路嗎？
   Is this a toll road?
2. 我要回數票。
   I need toll tickets.

 Tips 小祕訣 ➤ 快速適應美國旅遊生活的妙方

　　收費公路在美東比美西普遍。有些地段你會收到一張計費票，千萬別弄丟，行駛到某一路段時會有收費亭，必須停車依票繳費。在其他公路上有些是機器收費，要你丟零錢進去桿子才會拉起放行。美西舊金山灣區則有許多收費橋樑 (toll bridge)，有的是單向收費。在許多收費站有不同收費方式的車道，不要走錯了。回數票 (toll ticket) 及電子卡 (e-card) 是當地居民會用的，至於觀光客就走現金 (cash)、找零 (change) 或不找零 (no change) 車道吧。

 Language Power 字句補給站 ➤ 補充相關單字

◆ 常見交通標誌 Common Traffic Signs

northbound	北向
southbound	南向
exit 12	12 號出口
San Diego 60 miles	距聖地牙哥 60 英里
stop	停車

Cultural Tips 文化祕笈 ➤ 介紹美國風俗文化

重要交通標誌 Important Traffic Signs

no U turn 禁止迴轉　　　　　one way 單行道

目錄

Unit 3 入境 Arrivals

Unit 4 住宿 Accommodations

Unit 5 交通 Transportation

Unit 6 餐飲
Food and Drinks

Unit 7 觀光 Sightseeing

Unit 8 購物 Shopping

Unit 9 郵電
Mail and Telephones

附錄 Appendices

字句補給站 Language Power

Unit 1　Basic Expressions

基本對話

臺灣是世界上少數對外國遊客極為友善的地方,但當我們到國外旅遊時,除了想賺錢的小販、店家或捎客外,西方人常因為不確定能否溝通而未必對亞洲遊客友善。每個文化有其對待外來遊客的方式,時間、場合、印象、修養及心情等則造成個人差異。在適當安全的情況下,主動說「Hi」自我介紹,打破隔閡會讓旅遊更自在。聊些天氣、景點、交通、食物等輕鬆的話題以表達友善,也可獲得當地資訊。記住避免個人隱私或政治、宗教等敏感議題。別擔心別人聽不懂你說什麼,重複地將自己的意思清楚表達就對了。當你聽不懂時,請別人重複剛說的話,別猶豫。在路上巧遇,點頭微笑招呼或寒暄兩句,也是基本禮貌。

基本對話

機場與飛機

入境

住宿

交通

餐飲

觀光

購物

郵電

銀行

麻煩事

回國

1.1 打招呼及問候
Greetings

Dialog 1 對話1

A: 嗨，你好嗎？

A: Hi, how are you today?

B: 好啊，你呢？

B: Just fine. And you?

A: 我也很好。

A: I feel fine, too.

B: 今天在忙些什麼呢？

B: What are you up to today?

A: 沒什麼，只是稍微觀光一下。

A: Not much, just a little sightseeing.

B: 聽起來不錯，要拍些照片喔。

B: Sounds good. Take some pictures.

A: 我一定會的。

A: I'll do that for sure.

Word Bank 字庫

sightseeing ['saɪt,siɪŋ] n. 觀光

Notes 小叮嚀

　　在美國及加拿大，人們碰面打招呼多半較為輕鬆不正式。歐洲人也大多如此，保持微笑、自我介紹及聊點小事。注意對方是否有事要忙，別耽誤太久。進出公共場所時，為下一位進出的陌生人拉住門再離開，以免門忽然打到別人。有人提重物進出時稍微幫忙提抬物品，也是基本禮貌。將心比心即可，若冷漠不在乎，會被認為是無禮的。完整版請見附錄「不可不知的美國文化祕笈」之「小寒暄大學問」。

　　旅行者雖對自身安全需要警戒，但也必須表現友善，在飯店進電梯、用早餐、導遊接送等經常需與其他國籍旅客相處，應該主動打招呼微笑，最好以當地語言或至少以英語說 Hi, (everyone)/good morning，使用適當的肢體語言，化解陌生的尷尬。國人被教導「不要跟陌生人說話」的防禦觀念要看狀況，在該打招呼的時候卻沉默以對會被解讀成「不友善」或「沒禮貌」。旅行時個人行為代表國民外交，給他國人民友善的第一個好印象就從打招呼開始。

Dialog 2 對話2

A: 嘿，你好嗎？

A: Hey! How are you doing?

B: 啊，真驚訝！我很好。

B: Wow! What a surprise! I'm fine.

A: 你要去那裡呢？

A: Where are you going?

B: 一個本地歷史悠久之處。

B: To a local historical site.

基本對話

機場與飛機

入境

住宿

交通

餐飲

觀光

購物

郵電

銀行

麻煩事

回國

A: 我好幾天沒見到你了。

A: I haven't seen you in a couple of days.

B: 我知道，我最近都自己亂跑。

B: I know. I've been running around by myself.

A: 很棒喔，你喜歡自由行。

A: Great! You like independent traveling.

B: 是啊。

B: Yes, I do.

 Word Bank 字庫

local ['lokḷ] adj. 本地的，當地的
historical [hɪs'tɔrɪkḷ] adj. 歷史的
couple ['kʌpḷ] n. 一對；幾個
run around 到處去
independent [ˌɪndɪ'pɛndənt] adj. 獨立的

Useful Phrases 實用語句

● 問候 **To greet**
（一般來說，**meet** 用在初次見面，**see** 用在以後的碰面）

1. 好久不見。

   Long time no see.

2. 見到你真好。(已認識對方，不正式)

   It's so good to see you.

3. 真高興認識你。(初次見面，不正式)

   I'm so happy to meet you.

4. 很高興認識你。(初次見面，較正式)

   I'm very pleased to meet you.

5. 認識你真好。(初次見面，較正式)

It's nice to make your acquaintance.

6. 久仰大名。

I've heard a lot about you.

7. 你好嗎？(初次見面，正式)

How do you do?

8. 你好嗎？(一般)

How are you?

9. 你好嗎？(一般，較不正式)

How are you doing?

10. 最近好嗎？(一段時間未見面)

How have you been (lately)?

11. 怎麼樣啊？(一般，較不正式)

How's it going?

12. 一切可好？(一般，較不正式)

How are things?

13. 在忙什麼？(較不正式)

What are you up to?

14. 最近在忙什麼？

What have you been up to?

15. 有何新鮮事？(不正式)

What's up? / What's new?

16. 嗨，那邊的人！(不正式)

Hi, there!

● 應答 To respond

1. 你也好嗎？(當問句為 How do you do?)

How do you do?

2. 還可以。

OK. / All right.

3. 還不錯。

Not bad.

4. 還好。

Just fine.

5. 好極了。

Couldn't be better.

基本對話

機場與飛機

入境

住宿

交通

餐飲

觀光

購物

郵電

銀行

麻煩事

回國

基本對話
機場與飛機
入境
住宿
交通
餐飲
觀光
購物
郵電
銀行
麻煩事
回國

6. 沒什麼。

   Not much. / Nothing much.

7. 老樣子。

   Same old (thing).

8. (一樣) 忙碌。

   Busy (as ever).

● 其他寒暄語 Small talk

1. 工作如何啊?

   How's work?

2. 學校好嗎?

   How's school?

3. 小孩好嗎?

   How are the children?

4. 波士頓天氣如何?

   How's the weather in Boston?

5. 那個新案子進展如何?

   How's that new project going?

6. 今天交通有點塞。

   The traffic is kind of slow today.

7. 你平時做何消遣?

   What do you usually do in your free time?

Notes 小叮嚀

臺灣在世界地圖上是很小的一點,儘管臺灣製造 (Made in Taiwan) 的各類產品在世界經濟上表現優異,但許多外國人士卻未必知道臺灣在哪裡或將所有出國的亞洲人都當作日本人;因為發音類似,將臺灣誤認為泰國 (Thailand),或在曾經收容了許多難民的歐美國家被當作越南人 (Vietnamese)、柬埔寨人 (Cambodian) 也很常見。許多人一輩子的活動範圍仍僅限於自己的國家,對外國了解有限。萬一碰到外國人士問了好笑的問題,不要生氣反諷,要有耐性回答。外國人很難了解亞洲人有何差別,如同亞洲人看老外都差不多,或許你是他們第一個(或極少數)碰到的外國人。隨著地球村、網際網路、新興市場崛起及各國國民身為世界公民的自覺,情況應該會慢慢改變。

1.2 道別
Farewells

Dialog 1 對話1

A: 你搭的車幾點會到呢？

A: So what time will your ride get here?

B: 應該隨時會到。

B: Should be here any moment.

A: 那麼別擔心禮貌問題了，有必要就離開吧。

A: Well, don't worry about being polite. Take off when you have to.

B: 好的，謝謝，我不想要沒禮貌。

B: OK, thanks. I don't want to be rude.

A: 沒問題的。

A: No problem.

B: 嘿，巴士來了，我得走了。

B: Hey, the bus is here. I've got to run.

A: 再見。

A: See you later.

基本對話
機場與飛機
入境
住宿
交通
餐飲
觀光
購物
郵電
銀行
麻煩事
回國

基本對話

機場與飛機

入境

住宿

交通

餐飲

觀光

購物

郵電

銀行

麻煩事

回國

Word Bank 字庫

ride [raɪd] n. 搭乘
polite [pə'laɪt] adj. 禮貌的
take off 離開
rude [rud] adj. 粗魯的

Tips 小祕訣

　　道別通常是很不正式的，除非是非常正式的場合，否則無需特別注意說什麼道別語。倒是要注意表現禮貌，道別後再離開。必須離開時，可以說明理由。例如：
It's getting late. 有點晚了。
I need to pick up my laundry. 我得去取衣服。
I've got to go. / I have to go. / I've got to get going. 我得走了。

Dialog 2 對話2

A: 這景點很棒，很高興你邀我來。

A: It was a great viewing spot. I'm so glad you invited me.

B: 我很慶幸你樂在其中。

B: I'm happy you enjoyed it.

A: 下次我們要日落時在那裡。

A: Next time we must be there at sunset.

B: 那一定會很好玩，我們下週去吧！

B: That would be fun. Let's do it next week!

A: 好，就這麼說定了，我會打電話給你。

A: OK. It's set. I'll call you.

B: 我迫不及待了呢。

B: I can't wait.

 Word Bank 字庫

> viewing spot n. 景點
> invite [ɪn'vaɪt] v. 邀請
> sunset ['sʌn,sɛt] n. 日落

 Useful Phrases 實用語句

1. 再見。

   See you (later). / Later. / So long. / Catch you later.

2. 別變陌生人。(保持聯絡。)

   Don't be a stranger.

3. 朋友再見了。(西班牙文)

   Adiós, amigo.

4. 寶貝再見了。[(西班牙文) 阿諾電影經典句 (宜謹慎使用)。]

   Hasta la vista, baby.

5. 保重。

   Take care.

6. 放輕鬆。

   Take it easy.

7. 說定了。

   It's set.

8. 我迫不及待。

   I can't wait.

基本對話 機場與飛機 入境 住宿 交通 餐飲 觀光 購物 郵電 銀行 麻煩事 回國

9. 很高興與你談話。

It's been good talking with you.

10. 保重，下次再來。

Take care, and come again.

11. 直到下次碰面了。(再見了。)

Until we meet again.

 Tips （小祕訣）

外語道別語很常見 (如國人常講日語 Sayonara!)，尤其美國西語人口不在少數，使用外語可能令人感覺俏皮、好玩或親切，但對於非該語言背景、不熟的人與長輩，應避免使用為宜。在美國常用的外語道別語如下：

西班牙語 Spanish— *Adiós*! [ˌɑdɪˋos] 再見 (goodbye)!
法語 French —*Au revoir*! [o r(ə)vwar] 再見 (goodbye)!
義大利語 Italian—*Ciao*![tʃau] 哈囉 / 嗨及再見 (hello/hi, and goodbye)!

It's a deal! 是 It's set. 的另一說法。更簡單些，直接問 Deal? 即可，回答也是 Deal!。另外常用的 Promise? 以及回答 Promise!，是「保證」的意思。

1.3 道謝
Thanking

 Dialog 1 （對話1）

A: 你問了鮑伯週末會來與我們聚會嗎？

A: Did you ask Bob about coming with us this weekend?

B: 我問了。

B: Yes, I did.

A: 他怎麼說呢？

A: What did he say?

B: 他說他一定會來。

B: He said he'd come for sure.

A: 好極了！多謝你打電話給他。

A: Great! Thanks a lot for calling him.

Dialog 2　(對話2)

A: 這裡就是你問起的餐廳。

A: Here is that restaurant you asked about.

B: 哇！我們來得真快。

B: Wow, we got here quick.

A: 嗯，我知道你真的很想嘗試這裡有名的肋排。

A: Well, I know you really want to try the famous ribs here.

B: 當然了，再次謝謝你是這麼一個好的主人。

B: I sure do. Thanks again for being such a good host.

A: 這是我的榮幸。

A: My pleasure.

Word Bank　(字庫)

rib [rɪb] n. 肋骨
host [host] n. 主人
pleasure ['plɛʒɚ] n. 愉悅

機場與飛機

入境

住宿

交通

餐飲

觀光

購物

郵電

銀行

麻煩事

回國

 Useful Phrases 實用語句

● 道謝 To thank

1. 非常謝謝你。

   Thank you very much.

2. 多謝。

   Thanks a lot.

3. 十二萬分感謝。

   Thanks a million.

4. 我很感激。

   I'm grateful. / I really appreciate it.

5. 謝謝，我非常感激這件事。

   Thanks, I appreciate this a lot.

6. 謝謝你做了那件事。

   Thanks for doing that.

7. 謝謝你所有的幫忙。

   Thanks for all your help.

8. 為每件事謝謝你。

   Thanks for everything.

● 應答 To respond

1. 不客氣。

   You're welcome.

2. 當然的事。

   Sure.

3. 當然的事，我很開心能幫忙。

   Sure. I'm glad I could help.

4. 沒問題。

   No problem.

5. 那沒什麼。

   It was nothing.

6. 隨時都樂意幫忙。

   Any time.

基本對話

7. 樂意之至。

My pleasure.

1.4 道歉
Apologies

 Dialog 1 對話1

A: 抱歉我遲到了，我遇到塞車了。

A: Sorry I'm late. I got stuck in traffic.

B: 沒關係。

B: That's all right.

A: 我以後不會再犯了，真抱歉。

A: I won't let it happen again. I'm really sorry.

B: 算了，沒什麼大不了的。

B: Forget it. It's no big deal.

 Tips 小祕訣

stick (黏；阻塞) 的三態為「stick-stuck-stuck」，是不規則變化。

 Dialog 2 對話2

A: 喔，你來了。你發生什麼事了？

A: Oh, there you are. What happened to you?

機場與飛機

入境

住宿

交通

餐飲

觀光

購物

郵電

銀行

麻煩事

回國

基本對話

機場與飛機

入境

住宿

交通

餐飲

觀光

購物

郵電

銀行

麻煩事

回國

B: 我必須為昨天沒來道歉。

B: I must apologize for not being here yesterday.

A: 你昨天怎麼了？你在哪兒呢？

A: What happened to you yesterday? Where were you?

B: 我必須去醫院。

B: I had to go to the hospital.

A: 為什麼？

A: Why?

B: 我生病了去醫院，我告訴導遊了。

B: I got sick and went to a hospital. I told our tour guide.

A: 我想他忙到忘了告訴我們。

A: I guess he was too busy to tell us.

 Useful Phrases 實用語句

1. 我希望你接受我的道歉。

   I hope you accept my apology.

2. 抱歉我今晚沒辦法來。

   Sorry, but I can't make it tonight.

3. 請原諒我做了這件事。

   Please forgive me for this.

4. 算了。

   Forget it.

5. 沒什麼大不了的。

   It's no big deal.

6. 很遺憾聽到這件事。

I'm sorry to hear that.

1.5 同意與附和
Agreeing and Responding to Agree

 Dialog 1 對話1

A: 你認為他說的對嗎？

A: Do you think what he said is right?

B: 我不確定。

B: I'm not sure.

A: 我想至少值得我們考慮。

A: I think it's at least worth considering.

B: 我同意。

B: I agree with that.

A: 你認為我們今天該再和他談談嗎？

A: Do you think we ought to talk to him again today?

B: 是啊。

B: Yes, I do.

 Dialog 2 對話2

A: 你想吃些什麼？

A: What do you want to eat?

基本對話

機場與飛機

入境

住宿

交通

餐飲

觀光

購物

郵電

銀行

麻煩事

回國

B: 你有何建議嗎？ → **B:** Do you have any suggestions?

A: 我知道有家不錯的墨西哥餐廳。 → **A:** I know of a good Mexican restaurant.

B: 我不會反對這個選擇。 → **B:** I won't argue about that choice.

A: 他們也有不錯的啤酒。你覺得呢？ → **A:** They have good Mexican beer, too. What do you say?

B: 走吧！ → **B:** Let's hit the road!

Word Bank 字庫

at least 至少
worth [wɝθ] prep. 值得
consider [kən'sɪdɚ] v. 考慮
ought to 應該
suggestion [sə'dʒɛstʃən] n. 建議
argue ['argju] v. 爭論
choice [tʃɔɪs] n. 選擇

Useful Phrases 實用語句

● 徵求同意 **Asking for Approval**

1. 你同意嗎？

   Do you agree?

2. 你覺得呢？

   What do you say?

● 肯定的應答 Agreeing

1. 我同意。

   I agree with that.

2. 我不會反對它。

   I wouldn't argue about it.

3. 聽來不錯。

   Sounds good to me.

4. 我想你是對的。

   I believe you are right.

5. 好主意。

   Good idea.

6. 好，我會做這件事。

   OK, I'll do it.

7. 沒問題。

   No problem.

● 不太確定的應答 Responding to Uncertainty

1. 這個我不確定。

   I'm not sure about this.

2. 我們考慮一下吧。

   Let's think about it.

3. 我們晚點再問。

   Let's ask again later.

基本對話

機場與飛機

入境

住宿

交通

餐飲

觀光

購物

郵電

銀行

麻煩事

回國

1.6 確認
Confirmation

 Dialog 1 （對話1）

A: 不好意思，請問這是我們今晚聚會的會議室嗎？

A: Excuse me. Is this the room we should meet in tonight?

B: 不是，沿著走廊一直走，在住宿登記櫃臺的對面。

B: No, it's not. That room is down the hall and across from the check-in desk.

A: 有兩個紅色大門的那間嗎？

A: The one with two large red doors?

B: 對，就是那間。

B: Yes. That's the one.

 Word Bank （字庫）

hall [hɔl] n. 走廊，門廳
across [əˈkrɔs] prep. 在對面
check-in desk n. 住宿登記櫃臺

 Tips （小祕訣）

「Excuse me.」(不好意思、對不起) 用於必須打斷別人、引人注意、請問事情時；「I'm sorry.」(對不起) 則用於道歉時。

Dialog 2 （對話2）

A: 嗨，我怎麼幫你呢？

A: Hi. How can I help you?

B: 明天的旅遊還有名額嗎？

B: Are there still seats available for tomorrow's tour?

A: 有的。

A: Yes, there are.

B: 行程是從早上 7 點開始嗎？

B: Does the tour start at 7:00 in the morning?

A: 沒錯。

A: That's right.

B: 我可以就在這裡買票嗎？

B: Can I buy tickets right here?

A: 當然，沒問題。

A: Sure, no problem.

Word Bank 字庫

seat [sit] n. 座位

available [ə'veləbl] adj. 空著的，可用的

基本對話

機場與飛機

入境

住宿

交通

餐飲

觀光

購物

郵電

銀行

麻煩事

回國

基本對話

機場與飛機

入境

住宿

交通

餐飲

觀光

購物

郵電

銀行

麻煩事

回國

📖 Useful Phrases 實用語句

1. 這樣對嗎？

   Is this right?

2. 我們走對方向嗎？

   Are we going in the right direction?

1.7 請求說明
Asking for Clarification

Dialog 1 對話1

A: 明天 7 點半碰面。

A: We'll meet at 7:30 tomorrow.

B: 你是說早上或晚上的 7 點半呢？

B: Do you mean 7:30 a.m. or p.m.?

A: 我指的是晚上。

A: I mean p.m.

B: 那我們在飯店大廳還是其他地方碰面呢？

B: So we'll meet at the hotel lobby, or elsewhere?

A: 抱歉，我該說清楚，我們在停車場碰面。

A: Sorry. I should make things clear. We'll meet at the parking lot.

Dialog 2 對話2

A: 不好意思，我不懂菜單上的一些東西。

A: Excuse me. I don't understand something on the menu.

B: 是什麼問題呢？

B: What is your question?

A: 標準早餐包括咖啡及馬芬蛋糕嗎？

A: Does the standard breakfast include coffee and a muffin?

B: 是的，如果在 10 點前點餐的話，否則就沒有了。

B: Yes, if you order before 10:00 a.m., otherwise they are not.

A: 只有包含一杯咖啡嗎？

A: Is only one cup of coffee included?

B: 不，續杯都是免費的。

B: No. Refills are always free.

✎ Word Bank 字庫

a.m. / p.m. 早上 / 晚上
lobby ['lɑbɪ] n. 大廳，門廊
make things clear 說清楚，弄清楚
menu ['mɛnju] n. 菜單
standard ['stændəd] adj. 標準的
include [ɪn'klud] v. 包含
muffin ['mʌfɪn] n. 馬芬蛋糕
order ['ɔrdə] v. 點餐
otherwise ['ʌðə,waɪz] adv. 否則
refill ['ri,fɪl] n. 再裝滿

基本對話

機場與飛機

入境

住宿

交通

餐飲

觀光

購物

郵電

銀行

麻煩事

回國

 Useful Phrases 實用語句

1. 這個我不確定。

   I'm not sure about this.

2. 請再解釋一次。

   Please explain it again.

3. 很抱歉，我只是想確定我了解。(接著提出問題)

   I'm sorry. I just want to make sure I understand.

4. 抱歉打擾你，你是說…嗎？

   Sorry to bother you, but did you say...?

 Tips 小祕訣

1.「question」指的是要問的問題，「problem」則是指造成的問題，兩者別混淆了。

2.「Do you mean...?」(你是指…？) 用在要問清楚時。聽不懂或不知道怎麼做時不要著急，冷靜地請對方重述或示範給你看，這也是出門在外學習的機會。

1.8 請求重述
Requesting Repetition

 Dialog 1 對話1

A: 您可以告訴我荷曼博物館的地址嗎？

A: Could you please tell me the address of the Holman Museum?

B: 當然，北七街1254號。

B: Of course. It's 1254 North Seventh Avenue.

A: 您是說北七街1254號嗎？

A: Did you say 1254 North Seventh Avenue?

B: 是的，沒錯。

B: Yes. That's right.

A: 真感謝您。

A: Thank you so much.

 Dialog 2 （對話2）

A: 洗手間在哪裡？

A: Where are the restrooms?

B: 沿著走廊走下去，穿過盡頭右手邊的那扇門，然後在左邊的門上找標示。

B: Go down this hall. Go through the swinging doors at the end on the right. Then look for the signs on the doors to your left.

A: 好的。你說洗手間的門在右邊嗎？

A: OK. Did you say the restroom doors will be on the right?

B: 不，在左邊。

B: No. They'll be on your left.

A: 在我穿過這扇門之後嗎？

A: After I pass through the swinging doors?

基本對話
機場與飛機
入境
住宿
交通
餐飲
觀光
購物
郵電
銀行
麻煩事
回國

B: 是的，正確。

B: Yes, that's correct.

A: 謝謝。

A: Thanks.

 Word Bank 字庫

museum [mju'zɪəm] n. 博物館
avenue ['ævə,nju] n. 大街，大道
swinging door n. 向內外推開可自動關上的門

 Useful Phrases 實用語句

1. 請您重講一次好嗎？(could 較客氣)

   Could you repeat that, please?

2. 請你重講一次好嗎？(can 較直接)

   Can you repeat that, please?

3. 請再說一次好嗎？(音調提高請求重述)

   Pardon? / May I beg your pardon?

4. 你是說…嗎？

   Did you say…?

5. 請再說一次。

   Say that again, please.

6. 請再說一遍。

   Say once more, please.

7. 可以請你說慢點嗎？

   Could you say that more slowly, please?

基本對話

機場與飛機

入境

住宿

交通

餐飲

觀光

購物

郵電

銀行

麻煩事

回國

Notes 小叮嚀

　　即使是同地方、同種族、說相同語言的人，也會請對方重述或說清楚點，何況是在國外呢！所以聽不懂時不需要裝懂，可以請對方重述或說慢點，但不要只說「What?」，這樣顯得無禮。說「Excuse me?」聲調上揚即表示沒聽清楚，或是使用上列實用語句。

1.9 請求幫忙
Asking for Favors

Dialog 1 對話1

A: 嘿，山姆，你可以幫我個忙嗎？

A: Hey, Sam. Can you do a small favor for me?

B: 或許吧，是什麼忙呢？

B: Maybe. What is it?

A: 我需要幫忙搬動這些行李箱。

A: I need help moving these suit-cases.

B: 喔，好，你要放在哪裡？

B: Oh, OK. Where do you want to put them?

A: 放在那邊吧。

A: Let's put them over there.

基本對話

機場與飛機

入境

住宿

交通

餐飲

觀光

購物

郵電

銀行

麻煩事

回國

 Dialog 2 (對話2)

A: 傑瑞，我需要幫忙。

A: Jerry, I need a favor.

B: 需要幫什麼忙呢，珍？

B: What do you need, Jane?

A: 呃，我租的車子在修車廠裡，所以我需要人載。

A: Well, my rental car is in the shop, so I need a ride.

B: 我可以幫你，而且無論如何我還欠你個人情。

B: I can do that for you. Besides, I owe you a favor anyway.

A: 為什麼？

A: For what?

B: 你不記得了嗎？兩天前你載過我。

B: Don't you remember? You gave me a ride a couple of days ago.

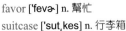 Word Bank (字庫)

favor ['fevɚ] n. 幫忙
suitcase ['sut‚kes] n. 行李箱
shop [ʃɑp] n. 修車廠(= auto shop)
besides [bɪ'saɪdz] adv. 此外，而且
a couple of days n. 兩天(= two days)

Useful Phrases 實用語句

1. 你可以幫我一分鐘嗎？

   Can you help me out a minute?

2. 你可以幫我忙嗎？

   Would you lend me a hand?

3. 不好意思，我需要人幫點忙。

   Excuse me. I need a little favor done.

1.10 請求許可
Asking for Permission

Dialog 1 對話1

A: 我現在離開可以嗎？

A: Would it be all right if I left now?

B: 可以。你另外有約嗎？

B: Yes. Do you have another appointment?

A: 是的，在此鎮的另一邊。我可以使用電話嗎？

A: Yes, I do. It's across town. Can I use the phone?

B: 當然，就在這裡。

B: Sure, of course. It's in here.

A: 抱歉這麼叨擾。

A: Sorry to be such a bother.

B: 沒關係的。

B: Forget about it.

基本對話　機場與飛機　入境　住宿　交通　餐飲　觀光　購物　郵電　銀行　麻煩事　回國

Word Bank 字庫

appointment [ə'pɔɪntmənt] n. 約會
bother ['bɑðə-] n. 叨擾，打擾

Tips 小祕訣

1.「Would it be all right if I left now?」是客氣的用法，用過去式「would」及「left」，是種假設的口氣。若被拒絕，彼此不會尷尬。

2.「appointment」指的是職業或商業上的約定，如「an appointment with Mr. Carson」(與卡森先生的約定會面)，或「a doctor's appointment」(看醫生的約診)；男女朋友間的約會則用「date」。

Dialog 2 對話2

A: 我可以把這些東西留在這裡嗎？

A: Is it acceptable for me to leave these things here?

B: 我想可以，讓我先把其他東西挪開。

B: I think so. Let me move these other things first.

A: 你確定沒問題？

A: Are you sure it's no problem?

B: 我確定。

B: I'm certain.

A: 我還想放一件在行李保管處。

A: I would also like to put one in luggage storage.

B: 我現在就收走它，替你放進去。 ▶ **B:** I'll take it now and put it in for you.

A: 太好了，謝謝。 ▶ **A:** Terrific. Thanks.

Word Bank 字庫

acceptable [ək'sɛptəbḷ] adj. 可接受的
leave [liv] v. 放置，留下
certain ['sɝtən] adj. 確定的
luggage ['lʌɡɪdʒ] n. 行李
storage ['storɪdʒ] n. 保管，存放
terrific [tə'rɪfɪk] adj. 極好的

Useful Phrases 實用語句

○ **請求許可 To ask for permission**

1. 這可以嗎？
   Is this OK?

2. 我們可以現在進去嗎？
   May we go in now?

3. 我可以用這個嗎？
   Can I use this?

4. 我可以把這個留在這裡嗎？
   May I leave this here?

5. 我可以問一個問題嗎？
   May I ask a question?

○ **應答 To respond**

1. 我確定。(肯定)
   I'm certain.

基本對話

機場與飛機

入境

住宿

交通

餐飲

觀光

購物

郵電

銀行

麻煩事

回國

基本對話

機場與飛機

入境

住宿

交通

餐飲

觀光

購物

郵電

銀行

麻煩事

回國

2. 我確定。(肯定)

   I'm sure.

3. 肯定的。(肯定)

   Positive.

4. 我不很確定。(不太確定)

   I'm not really sure.

5. 我不那麼確定。(不太確定)

   I'm not so sure.

6. 恐怕不行。(客氣的否定)

   I'm afraid not.

7. 你大概不能。(客氣的否定)

   You probably can't.

Unit 2　Airport and Aircraft

機場與飛機

　　出門旅行盡量不要帶太多東西，長途旅行更是要輕便。近來機場安檢越趨嚴格，旅客需隨時準備出示登機證及護照。美國執行嚴格的反恐飛航安檢，不管是國際或國內航班，所有行李都會被打開檢查，所以必須提早報到。除非使用運輸安全管理 TSA 核可的鎖，行李可以被打開受檢，否則不要上鎖，以免安檢時被破壞。出國務必按照託運與隨身行李之規定打包，可攜式電子產品的鋰電池及備用鋰電池限放置隨身行李，勿託運。如果不知道要去的地方或如何使用設備、需要協助等，可以到詢問臺查詢，或詢問空服員。在國際航班機上多配有會說多國語言的服務人員，多數機場也在機場出口處提供免費小冊子協助旅客。

基本對話

機場與飛機

入境

住宿

交通

餐飲

觀光

購物

郵電

銀行

麻煩事

回國

2.0 機票及通關流程
Ticketing and Customs

機票是你遨遊世界的入場券，當然要了解它的內容囉！直接對照第 35 頁的圖及說明，這一點也不難。智慧型手機上之應用程式 (app) 也有航空公司的軟體可供購買機票。

 Notes 小叮嚀

機票條件：

機票價格隨淡旺季需求而改變，網路發達後，直接在航空公司網站訂票與在票務網訂購票價可能已經相當接近，宜比較其他條件後再選擇。旺季時人口多的國家之主要都會，票務網站的機票不但一天可能出現好幾個價格，甚至秒殺搶票(比輸入速度)都來不及。購買機票一定要先了解其限制，無論是早鳥票 (early bird special)、廉價航空 (budget airlines) 或紅眼航班 (redeye flights)，越便宜的促銷機票限制越多。拿到機票後要確認英文名字拼法正確無誤。除了有效日期的限制外，其他常見的限制：不可轉讓 (non-endorsable)、不可退票 (non-refundable) 及不可更改行程 (non-reroutable)。

以信用卡購買機票，務必帶著該信用卡以備航空公司報到時確認，開票後儘早完成劃位及個人餐點需求。自廉價航空興起搭機各項服務需額外收費的潮流後，現在有些非廉價航空也跟進，將某些座位或服務加價。本章所提之搭機服務以一般航空機票為主。

行李打包：

因為旅客託運行李發生物品被盜情事屢見不鮮 (先進國家也一樣)，有價值物品應隨身攜帶，不要託運。航空公司為開源節流，允許之行李重量經常下修，行李打包要依照各國駐我國代表處 (或其外交部) 及航空公司之最新公告打包，經濟艙託運行李 (記得掛上行李識別) 不超過20公斤(有些航程為23公斤)，隨身行李不超過7公斤，隨身之膏、膠、液態類每瓶限100毫升，全數不超過1公升，集中放在一個透明夾鏈袋內。不可攜帶打火機或高壓噴霧劑 (如：髮膠、肌肉痠痛劑或防蚊劑) 及任何農產品及含乳、肉、蛋類食品 (如：肉燥泡麵、肉鬆、月

餅、鳳梨酥、蛋黃酥…等)，如果非帶中藥不可，要帶著英文處方箋及藥單，以免引起外國海關誤會。可攜帶常用藥品 (個人藥品及醫師處方)，否則許多藥品在國外需醫生處方。如果外國海關不了解你攜帶的物品及其來源是什麼，又沒有標籤可供判斷，可能會被拘留查問。任何名牌物品及電腦軟體等都必需是合法真品。任何刀類或鐵製品 (如：指甲剪、指甲油 (含揮發物)、銼刀、小剪刀、鐵製刀叉筷、自拍棒等)，須放置於託運行李，不可隨身攜帶。出境安檢時如果有上類品項會當場被要求丟棄或扣留，入境時如被外國海關查到未申報之管制物品 (有申報並不表示海關就會允許攜入)，則遭監禁或巨額罰款皆有可能。

手機：

　　團體旅遊者，須牢記領隊、導遊手機，個人旅遊者外交部海外緊急聯絡電話亦須隨身攜帶 (請見附錄)。入境外國後打開手機出現外國電信公司名稱即開始國外漫遊，出發前先詢問你的手機業者關於漫遊、收發簡訊及通話費率，以智慧手機軟體傳訊及使用簡訊是最經濟的方式。有通話需求者，買國際預付卡或使用網路電話可節省通話費。為避免收到高昂帳單，出國前請電信業者關掉手機在國外以3G行動上網之功能。手機在遊輪上無法使用 (只能撥打遊輪上昂貴之衛星電話) 需等上岸，在偏遠地區或發展較落後國家也可能完全無訊號。

其他：

　　美國與臺灣電壓的插頭完全相同。到其他國家電源轉換器與轉接插頭先準備好，不要浪費時間到當地找插頭。預防護照、簽證、旅行支票或重要文件遺失，影印2份備用 (1份隨身攜帶，1份放置家人熟悉位置以防萬一)。此外，記得打電話給信用卡公司以利在國外信用卡之使用。出國前應當看看「外交部領事事務局」網站之出國旅遊最新消息，可下載app，並於「旅外國人動態網頁」登錄出國停留資料。

Tips 小祕訣

　　除了網路不發達地區、非網路使用者及某些特定行程的航班持續使用紙本機票外，現今電子機票 (e-ticket) 當道，乘客可以直接在網路上以信用卡或傳真付款後印出購票紀錄及上網選位，

基本對話

機場與飛機

入境

住宿

交通

餐飲

觀光

購物

郵電

銀行

麻煩事

回國

搭乘班機前至櫃臺提示購票所使用之信用卡、身分證明及購票紀錄 (三項任何之一) 登記登機，取得登機證。兩人一起搭機如未預選座位，因反恐之故通常座位會被分開。美國國內機場幾乎全數 (較大的歐洲機場亦) 採用自助登機 (self check-in machine)，近年機器已有中文，將購買電子機票所使用信用卡或 (電子) 護照刷入後資料即顯示出來，機器會問你是否需要託運行李 (如需託運行李，有專人協助託運)，登機證印出，就可直接進入安檢區。有些機場為方便旅客，在機場外人行道上即設有便捷櫃臺 (curbside check-in) 辦理報到及收取行李，省去拖拉大行李至櫃臺的麻煩，但航空公司會收取每件行李若干費用，並須給行李員 (skycap) 小費 (tips)。近來許多航空公司 (含臺灣) 已開放網上預辦登機，即起飛前 24 (或 48) 小時內自行於網路 e-check in 後，自己於家中或辦公室列印登機證 (self-print boarding pass)，手機內有登機證二維條碼 (Quick Response Code, 簡稱 QR Code) 者，亦可直接登機。

機場提供免費之行李推車向來是最基本的服務，旅客付出成本即包含機場服務，但美國機場早已額外對行李推車收費，至少 $3 以上，並持續上漲。有些推車須刷卡才可推出，有些則使用現金，記得隨身攜帶外幣零錢以免要大排長龍換錢租推車，許多歐洲機場也已開始對行李推車收費 (或作為押金) 約 2 歐元。

自原物料及燃油上漲後，美國國內航班餐點已採收費趨勢，各家標準相似，但收費經常調漲 (冷三明治約 $6，米果脆餅類 $3，非酒精飲料目前免費)，金融風暴後美國開始對國內經濟艙乘客 (限重 20 公斤) 收取每人託運行李費用：一件約 $25，兩件約 $35，只允許一個背包及一個上機箱 (須符合尺寸，限重 7 公斤)，國際加國內連結班機不收取，但行李箱須保有該國際航班標籤，並對經濟艙乘客之行李收取昂貴的超重費；如果搭乘廉價航空 (budget airlines) 航班則所有服務，如枕頭、毛毯、影片等，都要額外付費。出發前最好先行上網 (現今許多外國航空公司已建置簡體中文網頁) 了解有關規定與各項收費標準，也可事先查詢外國機場各項服務、位置、動線及通關規定，使旅行更順暢。

 Cultural Tips 文化祕笈

◆ 電子機票收據樣本 E-Ticket Receipt

英文文字經常以省略母音的方式來簡寫。

```
                        ELECTRONIC TICKET
                   PASSENGER ITINERARY/RECEIPT

① NAME: WANG/SHIAOMING MS
                                ② ETKT NBR: 257 16097146358
③ ISSUING AIRLINE: CATHAY PACIFIC AIRWAYS
④ ISSUING AGENT: POLOARIS INTL TAIPEI TW / V1T8AKW
⑤ DATE OF ISSUE: 29MAR15          ⑥ IATA: 54-102757

⑦ BOOKING REFERENCE: KBXJEC/6P     ⑧ BOOKING AGENT: C7A8BP3

                                    TOUR CODE: TW3ALEG368

⑨ DATE AIRLINE⑩   ⑪ FLT ⑫ CLASS ⑬ FARE BASIS  ⑭ STATUS
- - - - - - - - - - - - - - - - - - - - - - - - - - - - - -
   03APR CATHAY PACIFIC AIRWAY401   ECONOMY/M YRT       CONFIRMED
      ⑮ LV: TAIPEI          AT: 1920  DEPART    ⑯
         AR: HONG KONG       AT: 2100  ARRIVE: TERMINAL 1
      ⑰ BAGS: 20K SEAT 65B VALID: UNTIL 03 JUL15
   03APR CATHAY PACIFIC AIRWAY685   ECONOMY/M YRT       CONFIRMED
         LV: HONG KONG       AT: 2150  DEPART: TERMINAL 1
   04APR AR: MUMBAI          AT: 0130
         BAGS: 20K SEAT 57H VALID: UNTIL 03 JUL15
   11APR CATHAY PACIFIC AIRWAY684   ECONOMY/M YRT       CONFIRMED
         LV: MUMBAI          AT: 0240
         AR: HONG KONG       AT: 1110  ARRIVE: TERMINAL 1
         BAGS: 20K          ⑱ VALID: UNTIL 03 JUL15
   11APR CATHAY PACIFIC AIRWAY406   ECONOMY/M YRT       CONFIRMED
         LV: HONG KONG       AT: 1230  DEPART: TERMINAL 1
         AR: TAIPEI          AT: 1415  ARRIVE: TERMINAL 1
         BAGS: 20K SEAT 46H VALID: UNTIL 03 JUL15

⑲ ENDORSEMENTS: NONENDO/NONRERTG/NONREF HKGTPE VLD ON CX/KA.TKT VLD 0D-3M.
  ../          ..VLD TPEHKG ON CX/KA DE

⑳ FARE CALC: TPE CX X/HKG CX BOM Q4.25M939.50CX X/HKG CX TPE Q4.25M939.50N
   UC1887.50END ROE32.2428  XT416IN3880YR ../          ..VLD TPEHKG 0
   N CX/KA DEP 01APR-25JUN15

㉑ FORM OF PAYMENT: INV

㉒ FARE: TWD60858  ㉓ T/F/C: 300TW T/F/C: 182WO T/F/C: 4296XT
㉔ TOTAL: TWD68636


   T/F/C: TAX /FEE /CHARGE

㉕ AIRLINE CODE
   CX - CATHAY PACIFIC AIRWAYS   REF: GPQH7

                    ㉖ NOTICE
   CARRIAGE AND OTHER SERVICES PROVIDED BY THE CARRIER ARE SUBJECT TO
   CONDITIONS OF CONTRACT, WHICH ARE HEREBY INCORPORATED BY REFERENCE.
   THESE CONDITIONS MAY BE OBTAINED FROM THE ISSUING CARRIER.

   WE RECOMMEND THAT YOU CARRY THIS RECEIPT WITH YOU IN CASE YOU MAY BE
   REQUIRED TO SHOW YOUR PROOF OF PURCHASE TO THE IMMIGRATION OR ANY OTHER
   THIRD PARTY.

   ┌─────────────────────────────┐
   │   CATHAY PACIFIC             │
   │ BAG. IDENTIFICATION TAG      │
   │   WANG          BN231        │
   │      CX684/11APR HKG         │
   │ ☐R   CX406/11APR TPE         │
   │ ☐s                           │
   │   DEST - TAIPEI              │
   │   ‖‖‖‖‖‖‖‖‖‖‖‖‖              │
   │   CX280821                   │
   └─────────────────────────────┘
```

基本對話 機場與飛機 入境 住宿 交通 餐飲 觀光 購物 郵電 銀行 麻煩事 回國

❶NAME 名字 (確認與護照相同)

❷ETKT NBR (ticket number) 機票號碼

❸ISSUING AIRLINE 航空公司

❹ISSUING AGENT 開票旅行社

❺DATE OF ISSUE 開票日期

❻IATA (International Air Transport Association)
開票旅行社之「國際航空運輸協會」代號

❼BOOKING REFERENCE 旅行社訂位代號

❽BOOKING AGENT 旅行社訂位人員號碼

❾DATE 日期

❿AIRLINE 航空公司

⓫FLT (flight) 班機號碼

⓬CLASS 艙等 (頭等艙：P/F商務艙：J/C經濟艙：Y/L/M/Q/K)

⓭FARE BASIS 費用基準 (票價種類)

⓮STATUS 機位狀態 (CONFIRMED 已確認)

⓯LV / AR (leave / arrive) 起飛 / 到達

⓰TERMINAL 航站 (號碼)

⓱BAGS 行李 (規定)

⓲VALID UNTIL (有效期至為止)

⓳ENDORESEMENTS 機票使用限制

⓴FARE CALC (fare calculation) 票價計算

㉑FORM OF PAYMENT 付費方式

㉒FARE 票價

㉓T/F/C (tax / fee / charge) 燃料與機場稅

㉔TOTAL 機票總價 (票面價)

㉕AIRELINE CODE: REF 航空公司訂位代碼

㉖NOTICE 備註

◆ 紙本機票樣本 Paper Ticket Sample

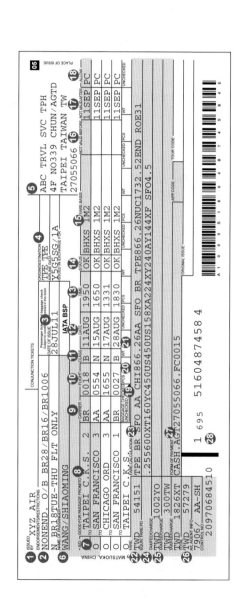

基本對話

機場與飛機

入境　住宿　交通　餐飲　觀光　購物　郵電　銀行　麻煩事　回國

❶ISSUED BY 航空公司名稱

❷ENDORSEMENTS/RESTRICTIONS 機票使用限制

❸DATE OF ISSUE 開票日期

❹ORIGIN / DESTINATION 出發地及目的地

❺PLACE OF ISSUE 開票地點（旅行社）

❻NAME OF PASSANGER 乘客姓名

❼X/O 轉機過境／可以入境

❽GOOD FOR PASSAGE FROM / TO 飛行從／到（依序為城市名、機場名、航站票示）

❾CARRIER 航空公司代號

❿FLIGHT 班機號碼

⓫CLASS 艙等（F：頭等艙，C：商務艙，Y：經濟艙）

⓬DATE 日期

⓭TIME 時間

⓮STATUS 機位狀態（OK：確認，RO：候補）

⓯FARE BASIS 費用基準（票價種類）

⓰NOT VALID BEFORE 機票開始使用日期

⓱NOT VALID AFTER 機票效期

⓲ALLOW 行李限制

⓳BAGGAGE CHECKED 託運行李
UNCHECKED 上機行李

⓴PCS 件數

㉑WT 重量

㉒FARE 原始費用

㉓FARE CALCULATION 費用計算

㉔EQUIV. FARE PD. 費用換算臺幣金額

㉕TAX / FEE / CHARGE 機場稅

㉖TOTAL 機票總價

㉗FORM OF PAYMENT 付款方式

㉘機票號碼

◆ 國際機場出境通關流程 Passing through the Customs

1 到達搭乘班機航廈

2 到達航班報到櫃臺

3 在報到櫃臺劃位及託運行李

（1）確定位子及登機門
（2）確定登機時間
（3）確定行李通過安全檢查

4 進入安全檢查區，通過護照檢查

5 通過人身及攜帶行李安檢

6 進入離境班機閘門等待區

7 注意廣播是否有異動

基本對話
機場與飛機
入境
住宿
交通
餐飲
觀光
購物
郵電
銀行
麻煩事
回國

◆ 機場告示牌 Airport Signs

terminal	航站
gate	登機閘門
concourse	機場大廳
departure	離境
departure board	離境告示牌
arrival	入境
arrival board	入境告示牌
monitor	螢幕
transit / transfer	轉機
quarantine	檢疫
passenger facilities	旅客設施
airline lounges	航空公司候機室
passport / visa check	護照 / 簽證查驗
security check	安全檢查
baggage claim	行李提領處
money exchange	外幣兌換
post office	郵局
duty-free shops	免稅商店
city transportation	市內交通
shuttle bus	接駁巴士
car rentals	租車公司
hotels	旅館
transit hotel	過境旅館
Internet	網路
VIP lounge	貴賓室
take off	起飛
land	降落
delayed	誤點
on time	準時
final call	最後呼叫

2.1 尋找登機閘門
Looking for the Gate

Dialog 對話

(廣播) 請注意,搭乘西北航空 644 班機的旅客,請立刻到 24 號登機門。

(Announcement) Your attention please. Passengers boarding Northwest Flight 644 are requested to proceed immediately to Gate 24.

A: 對不起,請問 24 號登機門在哪?

A: Excuse me. Where is Gate 24?

B: 搭手扶梯到二樓後右轉。

B: Take the escalator to level two. Then turn right.

A: 很遠嗎?

A: Is it far?

B: 不會,大約走 5 分鐘。

B: No. About a five minute walk.

Word Bank 字庫

passenger ['pæsṇdʒɚ] n. 乘客
escalator ['ɛskəˌletɚ] n. 手扶梯
level ['lɛvl] n. 樓層

基本對話

機場與飛機

入境

住宿

交通

餐飲

觀光

購物

郵電

銀行

麻煩事

回國

 Useful Phrases 實用語句

1. 走這邊。

   Go to this direction.

2. 上 [下] 樓。

   Go upstairs [downstairs].

3. 右 [左] 轉。

   Turn right [left].

4. 搭乘機場接駁車。

   Take the air shuttle.

5. 請跟我來。

   Follow me, please.

2.2 登機延誤
Boarding Delay

 Announcement 1 廣播1

西北航空 166 班機到洛杉磯的旅客請注意，班機將延誤一小時。造成不便，我們深感抱歉。

Attention passengers on Northwest Flight 166 to Los Angeles. We are sorry to announce that the flight will be delayed one hour. We are sorry for this inconvenience.

Announcement 2　（廣播2）

請注意，任何願意明天登機的旅客，請到櫃臺與西北航空人員洽談，我們提供雙人國際來回機票給任兩位願意明天登機的旅客。

Attention please. Any passenger willing to delay departure until tomorrow, please come to the counter to talk to a Northwest representative. We are offering a free round trip international ticket to any two people that will accept delaying departure until tomorrow.

Tips　（小祕訣）

機場用語較日常用語正式，例如「depart」較「leave」正式。

Dialog　（對話）

A: 你可以告訴我，我的班機情況嗎？

A: Can you tell me about my flight's status?

B: 可以的，請問您搭哪個航班呢？

B: Yes, I can. Which flight are you on?

A: 聯合 755。

A: United Flight 755.

B: 我來替你查，先生。我查到了，這班機將延誤一小時。

B: I'll check for you, sir. I see. Your flight is going to be an hour late.

基本對話

機場與飛機

入境

住宿

交通

餐飲

觀光

購物

郵電

銀行

麻煩事

回國

A: 為什麼？

A: Why?

B: 他們在裝晚到的行李。

B: They're loading late luggage.

 Useful Phrases 實用語句

1. 班機準時嗎？

   Is the flight on time?

2. 班機誤點嗎？

   Is the flight delayed?

3. 何時是新的登機時間？

   When is the new boarding time?

4. 新的登機門在哪兒？

   Where is the new boarding gate?

5. 我們可以有點心或飲料嗎？

   Can we have some snacks or drinks?

6. 因為誤點，你們有發午 [晚] 餐券嗎？

   Do you give lunch [dinner] coupons for the delay?

7. 我需要優待券。

   I need a coupon.

8. 我擔心會延誤銜接班機。

   I'm afraid I'll miss my connecting flight.

9. 請不要忽略我。

   Don't ignore me, please.

10. 我要找經理談。

    I want to talk to the manager.

11. 我需要住宿及餐飲憑證。

    I need hotel and meal vouchers.

Notes 小叮嚀

　　通關手續及機場設備對國外遊客而言，可能讓人感到困惑。碰到旅遊旺季或班機延誤，尤其容易有各種狀況。經過長途飛行後，如須大排長龍等待入關，常會因為身心疲累而失去耐性，此時可詢問地勤人員情況或要求協助以減低焦慮。另外要注意不要讓行李離開視線，也勿接受陌生人委託照顧或攜帶物品，以免惹上麻煩。如果班機延遲嚴重耽誤用餐時間，航空公司通常會發給旅客餐券，若延遲到隔天就需要發給住宿券，因為班機延誤而產生的費用要拿憑證及航空公司延誤證明 (voucher) 以備將來申請理賠之用。

2.3 登機
Boarding

西北航空 166 班機到洛杉磯的旅客請注意，現在在 5 號閘門登機。我們現在請頭等艙、商務艙及需要幫忙或與小孩同行的旅客先行登機。

Attention passengers on Northwest Flight 166 to Los Angeles. Now boarding at Gate 5. We will board First Class, Business Class, and passengers that need assistance, or are traveling with small children, now.

基本對話

機場與飛機

入境

住宿

交通

餐飲

觀光

購物

郵電

銀行

麻煩事

回國

基本對話

機場與飛機

入境

住宿

交通

餐飲

觀光

購物

郵電

銀行

麻煩事

回國

 Announcement 2 廣播2

旅客請注意，現在請第 66 排到 72 排登機。請您登機時將登機證及護照準備好。

Attention passengers. We are now boarding rows 66 through 72. Please have your boarding pass and passport ready as you board.

 Dialog 對話

A: (廣播) 最後呼叫 533 航班到芝加哥，在 33 號登機門登機。

A: (Announcement) Final call for flight 533 to Chicago, boarding at Gate 33.

B: 抱歉，我遲到了。

B: Sorry I'm late.

A: 你的登機證。

A: Your boarding pass, please.

B: 在這邊。

B: Here it is.

A: 你必須託運那個行李，它太大了，不能帶上機。

A: You'll have to check in that bag. It's too big for carry on.

B: 怎麼做呢？

B: How?

A: 留在這裡，我們會貼上標籤。

A: Leave it here. We'll tag it.

B: 我可以登機了嗎？

B: Can I get on now?

A: 是的，請趕快，飛機在等了。

A: Yes, please hurry. The plane is waiting.

Word Bank 字庫

carry on 帶上(機)
tag [tæg] v. 附上標籤
get on 登(機)

2.4 機上入座
To Be Seated

Dialog 1 對話1

A: 先生，歡迎登機。我可以看您的登機證嗎？

A: Welcome aboard, sir. May I see your boarding pass?

B: 當然了。

B: Yes, of course.

A: 您在第27排座位A，請走另一側。

A: You are in aisle 27, seat A. Go to the other side please.

基本對話

機場與飛機

入境

住宿

交通

餐飲

觀光

購物

郵電

銀行

麻煩事

回國

B: 好的。

B: OK.

Dialog 2 （對話2）

A: 你可以幫我把這個放到上面的櫃子裡嗎？

A: Can you help me put this in the overhead bin?

B: 當然。

B: Sure.

Word Bank （字庫）

aboard [ə'bord] adv. 在機上
aisle [aɪl] n. 走道
overhead bin n. 頭頂上方的行李櫃

Notes （小叮嚀）

　　機票開票時可以請旅行社人員先預選座位，或直接在航空公司網路上預選座位。預防飛機噪音 (坐在引擎旁者) 或怕萬一有嬰幼兒搭機不適哭鬧，可自備耳塞。因為從安檢走到登機門通常要一段時間，注意不要在免稅店停留過久而耽誤登機時間。如搭機前在機場免稅店選購物品，可以寄存至回國後再領取。

Dialog 3 （對話3）

A: 對不起，我想你坐到我的位子了。

A: Excuse me. I think you're in my seat.

B: 真的嗎？讓我確定一下，是27排C。

B: Really? Let me check my ticket. It's 27, C.

A: C是靠走道位子，你坐在A，是靠窗戶位子。

A: C is the aisle seat, and you're in A, the window seat.

B: 喔，真抱歉，我馬上挪開。

B: Oh, I'm sorry. I'll move right away.

A: 沒問題。

A: No problem.

 Dialog 4 對話4

A: 不好意思，我坐在15F，我可以和你換位子嗎？

A: Excuse me. I'm in 15F. Is it OK if I change my seat with you?

B: 喔，我看一下。15F，好，沒問題。

B: Oh, let me see. 15F, yeah, no problem.

A: 非常感謝你。

A: Thank you very much.

 Word Bank 字庫

aisle seat n. 靠走道座位
window seat n. 靠窗戶座位

基本對話

機場與飛機

入境

住宿

交通

餐飲

觀光

購物

郵電

銀行

麻煩事

回國

基本對話
機場與飛機
入境
住宿
交通
餐飲
觀光
購物
郵電
銀行
麻煩事
回國

Dialog 5 對話5

A: 不好意思，請問我可以更換座位嗎？

A: Excuse me. Is it OK if I change my seat?

B: 我看看。現在可以，所有乘客都已登機。

B: Let me see. Yes, it is now. All the passengers are on board.

A: 那個靠窗座位是空的嗎？

A: Is that window seat empty?

B: 是的，它是空的。你要換到那裡嗎？

B: Yes, it's available. Would you like to move there?

A: 是的，謝謝。

A: Yes, please.

2.5 機上廣播
Announcements on the Plane

 Announcement 1　廣播1

各位女士、先生午安，西北航空 166 班機歡迎您登機。我們祝您今日飛行愉快，並期待為您服務。請您在座位上時隨時保持繫上安全帶，如需協助請接洽空服員。

Good afternoon ladies and gentlemen. Welcome aboard Northwest Flight 166. We hope you'll enjoy today's flight, and look forward to serving you. Please keep your seatbelt fastened at all times when you are in your seat, and contact a flight attendant if you need assistance.

Announcement 2 （廣播2）

旅客請注意，機長剛開啟了繫上安全帶的指示燈，我們即將經過一些亂流，請坐在座位上繫好安全帶，直到機長熄滅安全帶指示燈。

Passengers, your attention please. The Captain has turned on the fasten seatbelt sign. We are about to pass through some turbulence. Please remain seated with your seatbelt on until the Captain turns off the seatbelt sign.

Announcement 3 （廣播3）

各位午安，這是機長華勒斯的廣播。我們現在北太平洋上空三萬七千呎飛行，我們已飛行3小時，氣象報告說我們到洛杉磯的飛行將一路順暢。空服員即將開始提供今天的第一份餐點，請放鬆享受您的餐點。希望您享受與我們一起飛行，我們期待未來為您服務，謝謝您搭乘西北航空。

Good afternoon everyone. This is Captain Wallace speaking. We are currently cruising at 37,000 feet over the North Pacific. We are about three hours into our flight, and weather reports say we can expect a smooth flight almost all the way to L.A. The flight crew will soon start serving today's first meal, so please sit back and enjoy your meal. I hope you will all enjoy flying with us. We look forward to seeing you again in the future. Thank you for flying Northwest Airlines.

Notes （小叮嚀）

　　在飛機起飛及降落時，絕對不可以使用電子產品 (electronic devices)。通常在飛行途中，可以使用筆記型電腦、數位相機及其他不會發射電波及訊號之電子產品 (須切換至飛航模式下)。留意機上廣播告訴你何時可使用或禁用，若不確定可以詢問空服員。

基本對話

機場與飛機

入境

住宿

交通

餐飲

觀光

購物

郵電

銀行

麻煩事

回國

有些航空公司已推出機上上網服務，但收費不貲且速度過慢，目前僅極少數航空公司免收費。

2.6 使用設備
Using the Facilities

Dialog 1 對話1

A: 我沒有耳機。

A: I don't have any headphones.

B: 在這邊。

B: Here you go.

A: 要插在哪裡？

A: Where do I plug them in?

B: 就在這邊，椅子的扶手上。

B: Right here in the arm of the chair.

A: 音量控制也在這裡嗎？

A: Is the volume control here, too?

B: 是的，就是這個調整盤。

B: Yes, it is. It's this dial here.

Word Bank 字庫

headphone ['hɛd,fon] v. 耳機
plug [plʌg] v. 插入(插座)
volume ['valjəm] n. 音量
dial ['daɪəl] n. 調整盤

Dialog 2 (對話2)

A: 先生，我可以幫你嗎？ → **A:** Can I help you, sir?

B: 洗手間在哪兒呢？ → **B:** Where are the toilets?

A: 中間區有四間，還有四間在後面。 → **A:** There are four at mid section, and four in the back.

B: 好，謝謝。 → **B:** Good. Thanks.

A: 我很樂意幫忙。 → **A:** Happy to help.

Word Bank (字庫)

toilet ['tɔɪlɪt] n. 洗手間
mid [mɪd] adj. 中間的
section ['sɛkʃən] n. 區段

Tips (小祕訣)

機上的洗手間標誌用的是「lavatory」，但口語上不用此字，而是用「bathroom」、「restroom」或「toilet」。洗手間上的標示為「vacant」時，表示沒人。機上洗手間男女不分，一般在外面的洗手間，男士的可以說「men's room」女士的為「ladies' room」。標示也會看到「WC」，但此字也不用於口語。

基本對話

機場與飛機

入境

住宿

交通

餐飲

觀光

購物

郵電

銀行

麻煩事

回國

 Dialog 3 對話3

A: 不好意思，請問怎麼打開洗手間的門？

A: Excuse me. How do you open the door to the bathroom?

B: 我來幫你，先生。這間有人，我們看下一間。

B: Let me help you, sir. This one is occupied. Let's check the next one.

A: 抱歉，我沒注意到。

A: Sorry, I did not notice that.

B: 沒問題。現在推門就開了。

B: No problem. Now just push the door open.

A: 多謝了。

A: Thanks a lot.

B: 還要確定閂上門，不然燈不會亮。

B: Be sure to latch the door, too, or the lights won't come on.

Word Bank 字庫

occupied ['ɑkjə,paɪd] adj. 已占用的，有人的
notice ['notɪs] v. 注意
latch [lætʃ] n., v. 門閂

Notes 小叮嚀

女士們用洗手間需要較多時間，且洗手間數量常不夠而必須排隊。在國外公共場所排隊 (如銀行、洗手間) 是在門口排成一排，輪到哪間空出來就進去，而不是在每間外面等。排隊時要注意別靠別人太近，會使人不舒服。

2.7 機上餐飲
Food and Beverage on the Plane

 Dialog 1 對話1

A: 茶，有人要茶嗎？

A: Tea? Does anyone want tea?

B: 有咖啡嗎？

B: Do you have coffee?

A: 服務員兩分鐘就過來。

A: She'll be by in a couple of minutes.

B: 知道了，謝謝。

B: I see. Thanks.

 Dialog 2 對話2

A: 先生，你要雞肉還是魚呢？

A: Sir, would you like chicken or fish?

基本對話

機場與飛機

入境

住宿

交通

餐飲

觀光

購物

郵電

銀行

麻煩事

回國

B: 我要魚。　　➤　**B:** I'd like fish.

A: 你要喝什麼呢？　　➤　**A:** What would you like to drink?

B: 有果汁嗎？　　➤　**B:** Do you have juice?

A: 有，我們有柳橙、蘋果及番茄汁。　　➤　**A:** Yes. We have orange, apple, and tomato juice.

B: 請給我柳橙汁。　　➤　**B:** Orange juice, please.

A: 好的。　　➤　**A:** OK.

Tips　小祕訣

　　點餐時用「I'd like...」較有禮貌。「I want...」很直接，在速食店較常用。

Useful Phrases　實用語句

1. 我需要再一條餐巾。

   I need another napkin.

2. 我打翻我的飲料了。

   I spilled my drink.

3. 你們有筷子嗎？

   Do you have chopsticks?

4. 這個沒有煮熟。

   This isn't cooked enough.

5. 我想要再一袋花生 [椒鹽脆餅]。

   I'd like to have another bag of peanuts [pretzels].

6. 我可以再要一杯飲料嗎？

   May I have another drink, please?

7. 請給我一杯健怡可樂。

   A diet coke, please.

8. 請再來點咖啡 [茶]。

   More coffee [tea], please.

9. 我想要些糖。

   I'd like some sugar.

10. 你們有奶精嗎？

   Do you have any creamer?

11. 夠了，謝謝。

   No more, thank you.

12. 請別放冰塊。

   No ice, please.

2.8 其他服務
Other Services on the Plane

Dialog 1 對話1

A: 對不起，我有點冷。	**A:** Excuse me. I'm a little cold.
B: 我拿條毯子給你。	**B:** I'll get a blanket for you.

A: 也可以再要一個枕頭嗎？

A: Can I have another pillow, too?

B: 好的，沒問題。

B: Sure, no problem.

Dialog 2 （對話2）

A: (空服員拿著報紙) 要讀點東西嗎？

A: (Flight Attendant with newspapers) Something to read?

B: 你們有汽車雜誌嗎？

B: Do you have any car magazines?

A: 有，我去拿一本給你。

A: Yes, we do. I'll get one for you.

B: 喔，謝謝。

B: Oh, thanks.

Dialog 3 （對話3）

A: 對不起，我不舒服。

A: Excuse me. I don't feel well.

B: 怎麼了呢？

B: What is wrong?

A: 我想吐。

A: I want to vomit.

B: 這裡有嘔吐袋。

B: Here is an airsickness bag.

A: 我可能還要一個。

A: I might need another one.

B: 馬上來。

B: Right away.

✏️ Word Bank 字庫

blanket ['blæŋkɪt] n. 毯子
pillow ['pɪlo] n. 枕頭
vomit ['vɑmɪt] v. 嘔吐
airsickness bag n. 嘔吐袋

 Tips 小祕訣

起飛及降落時,為避免因高度變化造成耳朵痛,可以嚼口香糖 (chewing gum) 或吃顆糖果以減低不舒服。有時飛機上會提供,若沒有或忘了帶,可以向空服員要。

 Dialog 4 對話4

A: 你可以告訴我目的地現在是幾點嗎?

A: Can you tell me what time it is at our destination?

B: 好的，現在是早上 8 點。

B: Yes. It's 8:00 a.m.

A: 我們還要多久會到？

A: How long will it be before we arrive?

B: 大約一個半鐘頭後抵達。

B: We'll arrive in about one and a half hours.

Useful Phrases 實用語句

1. 請給我一個枕頭。

   A pillow, please.

2. 請給我入境卡。

   An arrival card, please.

3. 你們有中 [英] 文報紙嗎？

   Do you have any Chinese [English] newspapers?

4. 你們有運動雜誌嗎？

   Do you have any sports magazines?

5. 我可以借枝鉛筆來填字謎嗎？

   May I borrow a pencil for the crossword puzzle?

6. 我不舒服。

   I don't feel well.

7. 我需要再一個袋子。

   I need another bag.

8. 我需要暈機藥。

   I need medicine for air sickness.

9. 我可以在機上用數位相機 [筆記型電腦] 嗎？

   Can I use my digital camera [laptop (computer)] on the plane?

10. 這個餐盤 [耳機] 壞了。

This tray [headphone] is broken.

11. 請收走這個。

Please take this (away).

12. 現在目的地是幾點呢？

What time is it now at our destination?

13. 還要多久會到呢？

How long will it be before we arrive?

14. 我們會準時到嗎？

Will we arrive on time?

Tips 小祕訣

　　機上除提供餐點外，其他服務包含提供止痛藥 (pain killer)、暈機藥 (airsickness medicine)、撲克牌 (poker cards)、小孩玩具 (children's toys)、明信片 (postcards) 等。需要服務時，按機上叫人鈕，空服員就會來幫忙。若是長途飛行，貼心的航空公司會給乘客發放盥洗包 (overnight kit)，內有牙膏、牙刷、棉襪或拖鞋、眼罩、梳子等物品。在機上需要任何東西，只需簡單地說出物品，再加個「請 (please)」就可以了。

2.9 機上免稅商品
In-flight Duty Free

 Announcement 廣播

各位女士、先生，我們的空服員即將過來販售免稅商品。請參考您面前的免稅商品型錄，如有任何要購買的商品，請告知空服員，謝謝。

Ladies and gentlemen, our flight attendants will be coming around with the duty free cart. Please look at the duty free catalog located in front of you, and tell the attendants if there is anything you'd like to buy. Thank you.

基本對話

機場與飛機

入境

住宿

交通

餐飲

觀光

購物

郵電

銀行

麻煩事

回國

Dialog 對話

A: 免稅商品、免稅商品，有人需要嗎？

A: Duty free. Duty free anyone?

B: 有，我要買二瓶威士忌。

B: Yes. I want to get two bottles of whiskey.

A: 你要哪個牌子呢，先生？

A: Which brand do you want, sir?

B: 這個牌子。

B: This one.

A: 總共是 36 元。

A: That will be \$36.

B: 這裡是 40 元。

B: Here's \$40.

A: 我回來時找零給你。

A: I'll be back with your change.

Word Bank 字庫

brand [brænd] n. 牌子
change [tʃendʒ] n. 零錢

Useful Phrases 實用語句

1. 你們還有這個嗎？

   Do you still have this?

2. 我不要這一個。

   I don't want this one.

3. 你們有新的嗎？

   Do you have a new one?

4. 我要買它。

   I'll take it.

5. 總共是…元。

   That will be....

6. 我在哪裡簽名？

   Where do I sign?

7. 如果有問題怎麼辦？

   What can I do if there are problems?

2.10 入出境紀錄及海關申報
Arrival/Departure Record and Customs Declaration

Dialog 對話

A: 不好意思，我需要入境卡。

A: Excuse me. I need an arrival card.

B: 在這裡。

B: Here you are.

A: 我可以也借枝筆嗎？

A: May I borrow a pen, too?

基本對話

機場與飛機

入境

住宿

交通

餐飲

觀光

購物

郵電

銀行

麻煩事

回國

B: 當然，稍等一下，我拿一枝給你。

B: Certainly. Wait a moment. I'll get one for you.

A: 非常謝謝你。

A: Thank you very much.

 Useful Phrases 實用語句

1. 你可以幫我填這個嗎？

   Can you help me fill this out?

2. 我可以借你的筆嗎？

   May I borrow your pen?

3. 班機號碼是什麼呢？

   What is this flight number (designation)?

4. 抱歉，我需要再一張卡。

   Sorry. I need another card.

Cultural Tips 文化祕笈

入出境卡 Arrival / Departure Card

Admission Number

053754856 12

Immigration and
Naturalization Service

I-94
Arrival Record

1 Family Name
YU

2 First (Given) Name
LI-YING

3 Birth Date (Day/Mo/Yr)
08 05 68

4 Country of Citizenship
TAIWAN

5 Sex (Male or Female)
FEMALE

6 Passport Number
M 3 1 1 2 5 5 8

7 Airline and Flight Number
BR 0018

8 Country Where You Live
TAIWAN

9 City Where You Boarded
TAIPEI

10 City Where Visa Was Issued
TAIPEI

11 Date Issued (Day/Mo/Yr)
28 01 15

12 Address While in the United States (Number and Street)
PLAZA HOTEL

13 City and State
SAN FRANCISCO, CA

Departure Number

053754856 12

Immigration and
Naturalization Service

I-94
Departure Record

14 Family Name
YU

15 First (Given) Name
LI-YING

16 Birth Date (Day/Mo/Yr)
08 05 68

17 Country of Citizenship
TAIWAN

See Other Side   ENGLISH   **STAPLE HERE**

基本對話

機場與飛機

入境

住宿

交通

餐飲

觀光

購物

郵電

銀行

麻煩事

回國

基本對話

機場與飛機

入境

住宿

交通

餐飲

觀光

購物

郵電

銀行

麻煩事

回國

入出境卡 (arrival / departure card) 的上聯為入境紀錄 (arrival record)，下聯為出境紀錄 (departure record)，美國又稱為 I-94 或 E (embarkation) / D (disembarkation) card，須以大寫填入全部資料。

❶Family Name 姓
❷First (Given) Name 名
❸Birth Date (Day / Mo / Yr) 出生日 (日/月/年)
❹Country of Citizenship 國籍
❺Sex (Male or Female) 性別 (男或女)
❻Passport Number 護照號碼
❼Airline and Fight Number 航班號碼
❽Country Where You Live 居住國
❾City Where You Boarded 登機城市
❿City Where Visa Was Issued 簽證核發城市
⓫Date Issued (Day / Mo / Yr) 核發日期 (日/月/年)
⓬Address While in the United Sates (Number and Street) 在美地址 (號碼及街名)：填寫旅館名稱、地址或填入「local hotel (當地旅館)」即可
⓭City and State 城市名及州名
⓮-⓱Departure Record 出境紀錄：同❶-❹項，出境時會收回

註：2013 年 5 月開始，美國部分機場已將 I-94 自動化，從航空公司取得旅客資料，旅客不需再手寫表格。

海關申報表 Customs Declaration Form

DEPARTMENT OF THE TREASURY
UNITED STATES CUSTOMS SERVICE

海關申報

19 CFR 122.27, 148.12, 148.13, 148.110, 148.111, 1498; 31 CFR 5316

核准的表格
OMB NO. 1515-0041

每個抵達的旅客或負責的家庭成員一定要提供以下的資料（每個家庭只需要填寫一份申報單）：

1. **姓氏** YU
   名字 LI-YING　　　西方人的中間名

2. **出生日期**　日 08　月 05　年 68

3. 與您一起成行的**家庭成員**有幾位　2

4. (a) 美國**街道地址**（旅館名稱/目的地）
   PLAZA HOTEL
   (b) 城市 SAN FRANCISCO　　(c) 州 CA

5. **護照發照國** TAIWAN

6. **護照號碼** M131112558

7. **居住國家** TAIWAN

8. 此次抵達美國
   之前**到訪的國家** NONE

9. **航空公司/班機號碼**或船隻名稱 BR0018

10. 此次旅行的主要目的是**商務**：　　　　　　　　是　　否 X

11. 本人（我們）有攜帶
   (a) 水果、植物、食物、昆蟲：　　　　　　　　是　　否 X
   (b) 肉類、動物、動物/野生動物產品：　　　　是　　否 X
   (c) 疾病因子、細胞培養物、蝸牛：　　　　　是　　否 X
   (d) 泥土或曾經在農地/牧場/畜牧場待過：　　是　　否 X

12. 本人（我們）曾經接近過牲畜
   （例如觸摸或處理）**牲畜**　　　　　　　　是　　否 X

13. 本人（我們）攜帶超過**美金**
   10,000 元或等值外幣的貨幣或**幣值票據**：　是　　否 X
   （請參閱反面的幣值票據定義）

14. 本人（我們）有**商業用品**：　　　　　　　　是　　否 X
   （銷售物品、招攬訂單用的樣品、或非個人用的物品）

15. **居民**－本人/我們在海外購買或獲得（包括別人給的禮物，但不是郵寄到美國的物品），並攜帶到美國的**所有物品總價值**，包括商業用品，是：　　　　　　　美元

   訪客－所有將留在美國的**所有物品總價值**，
   包括商業用品：　　　　　　　美元　　　O

請詳細閱讀本表格後面的說明。您可以在空格處列出所有需要申報的項目。

本人已閱讀過本表格反面的重要資訊，並做了誠實的申報。

X
_____
（簽名）　　　　　　　　　　　　　日期（日/月/年）

僅限官員使用

Customs Form 6059B Chinese (Traditional) (11/02)

基本對話

機場與飛機

入境

住宿

交通

餐飲

觀光

購物

郵電

銀行

麻煩事

回國

圖為美國財稅局海關申報單 (Customs Declaration Form) 正面，一家人填一張表即可。

表格背面大致說明如下：

「美國海關歡迎各位旅客訪美：如果你被挑中檢查行李，將會被有禮貌地及專業地對待，如果你有疑問，海關人員會回答你的問題。

重要資訊：旅客將留在美國的物品價值若超過100美元則必須申報。」

Notes 小叮嚀

美國對於旅客攜帶物品很嚴謹，除上述申報單上的規定外，還要注意不要攜帶植物乾貨 (如海帶、紫菜)、肉製品或魚肉製品 (如香腸、肉鬆、魚鬆)、調理包、月餅等，以免傳播病菌。緝私犬當場就會讓你現出原形，千萬不要大意。許多華人或越南超市多少都可買到類似的東西，不必冒險從臺灣帶。翻印的東西更是不能攜帶，包括燒錄的音樂光碟，任何牽涉智慧財產權的東西都要是合法的正版。萬一被查到，後果是可以把人嚇呆的超高罰金，還會留下紀錄。如果隨身行李攜帶手提電腦，在安檢時要拿出來受檢，裡面的軟體也必須是正版，雖說查到軟體的機率甚小但並非不可能。因為恐怖攻擊，各國安檢對於手提電腦是很敏感的，電腦的電池可能會被要求卸下，甚至開機檢查 (因此電池務必隨電腦攜帶)，證明不是炸彈。

2.11 降落
Landing

 Announcement 1　廣播1

【降落準備】各位女士、先生，我們再 30 分鐘左右即將降落，請您回到座位上並確定您安全放置上機物品。請確定您的椅背豎直，並繫上安全帶，空服員會來收走您不需要的東西。希望您今日與我們一同飛行愉快，而我們當然樂在為您服務。謝謝您選擇搭乘西北航空。

Ladies and gentlemen, we will be landing in about thirty minutes. Please return to your seats and be sure that all your carry-on things are securely stored. Make sure your seat back is in the full upright position, and fasten your seatbelt. Flight attendants will be coming around to take away any items you do not want. We hope you have enjoyed flying with us today, and we have certainly enjoyed serving you. Thank you very much for choosing Northwest Airlines.

 Word Bank　字庫

land [lænd] v. 降落
upright ['ʌp,raɪt] adj. 豎直的
fasten ['fæsṇ] v. 繫上
seatbelt ['sit,bɛlt] n. 安全帶
tray [tre] n. 機上桌子

 Dialog　對話

A: 先生，我們將要降落了，請把你的桌子收好，椅背豎直。

A: Sir, we are going to land soon. Please put your tray away, and return your seat to the upright position.

B: 好的。

B: OK.

A: 你也要繫上安全帶。

A: You need to fasten your seatbelt, too.

B: 我要把這個放進上頭的櫃子裡。

B: I need to put this in the overhead compartment.

A: 我來幫你放。

A: I'll do that for you.

 Announcement 2　廣播2

【抵達】我們已降落在洛杉磯國際機場，請留在座位上保持安全帶繫好，直到飛機完全停穩且機長熄滅安全帶指示燈。再次謝謝您搭乘西北航空。

We have arrived at Los Angeles International Airport. Please remain seated with your seatbelt fastened until the plane is fully stopped and the Captain has turned off the seatbelt sign. Thank you again for flying Northwest.

2.12 轉機
Transfer Flights

 Announcement 廣播

如果你要轉機，順著指示牌到轉機區，請機場人員協助或指示。

If you are transferring to another flight, follow the signs to the transfer area. Ask airport personnel for assistance or directions.

 Dialog 1 對話1

A: (出示機票) 我要轉機到紐約市。

A: (showing flight ticket) I have a connecting flight to New York City.

B: 好的。

B: OK.

A: 我要靠走道的位子可以嗎？

A: Can I have an aisle seat?

B: 好。(處理中) 這是你的登機證，登機時間是 2 點 20 分，您的座位是 24C，67 號登機門，在你的右手邊。

B: Yes. (processing) Here's your boarding pass. The boarding time is 2:20. You're in 24C, boarding gate 67. It's to your right.

基本對話

機場與飛機

入境

住宿

交通

餐飲

觀光

購物

郵電

銀行

麻煩事

回國

基本對話

機場與飛機

入境　住宿　交通　餐飲　觀光　購物　郵電　銀行　麻煩事　回國

A: 謝謝。

A: Thank you.

Dialog 2　對話2

A: 轉機是在 12 號登機門登機嗎？

A: Does this transfer flight board at Gate 12?

B: 讓我看看。不是喔，你要到 15 號登機門。

B: Let me see. No, it doesn't. You must go to Gate 15.

A: 你確定嗎？機上的女士告訴我在 12 號登機門。

A: Are you sure? The woman on the airplane told me Gate 12.

B: 登機門已被改過了。

B: There has been a gate change.

A: 我懂了，謝謝你告訴我。

A: I understand. Thanks for telling me.

Useful Phrases　實用語句

1. 您的最後目的地是哪兒呢？

   What is your final destination?

2. 我要去哪個登機門呢？

   Which gate should I go to?

3. 登機門號碼已變更。

   The gate number has been changed.

4. 我要到二樓去嗎？

   Do I need to go to level 2?

5. 我必須搭接駁電車嗎？

Should I take the shuttle train?

6. 你要向機場地勤人員報到。

You need to report to the airline ground staff.

7. 人員會安排銜接班機的座位。

The staff will arrange your seat for the connecting flight.

Tips 小祕訣

　　轉機可能讓人困惑，尤其在機場大，人潮多，轉機時間短時更是如此。你若對機場不熟，可以去查出入境告示牌，上面會顯示你要去的登機門。你的空服員也會知道你要到哪裡去登機，也可以問地勤人員，他們甚至會直接帶你過去。若第一站出發時，航空公司沒有收續程機票，把轉機部分的登機證給你，就必須到航空公司轉機櫃臺 (transfer desk) 辦 check in 手續，告訴櫃臺人員「I'd like to receive my boarding pass.」取得登機證。

　　美國國內班機可能只提供飲料及脆餅，而不包含餐點 (登機閘門旁櫃臺登機告示板會顯示 beverages only)。若飛行時間稍長 (超過 2.5 小時或更久一些)，機上可能會提供餐點供旅客購買。

Unit 3 Arrivals

入境

境外飛機到達美國目的地前,旅客要將入出境卡及海關申報表填寫完畢,並將護照、機票與簽證被要求之資料準備好供查驗,機上食物不要帶下機。到達時,首先要尋找入境海關的標示,按照身分種類(美國通常分為 citizens 本國居民、green card 綠卡、non-citizens / visitors 非本國居民),排隊檢查身分入關。移民官員會問你來訪目的、停留多久、是否有親友在美國及住宿地點等資料。之後前往 baggage claim 提領行李,務必確認掛牌是自己的行李。有時海關人員會請你打開行李受檢,如果不需受檢就可走出口直接出關。機場服務臺可提供住宿、交通資訊的小冊子,或是有標示各項服務的櫃臺,包括貨幣兌換處。

3.1 入境準備
Going through Customs

 Dialog 1 對話1

A: 入境海關在哪個方向呢？

A: Which way is arrival customs?

B: 跟著指標吧。

B: Just follow the signs.

A: 我需要先拿行李嗎？

A: Do I need to get my luggage first?

B: 你得先通關。

B: First you have to pass through immigration.

Dialog 2 對話2

A: 不好意思，請問我要排在哪一列？

A: Excuse me. Which line should I get into?

B: 你是這國的公民嗎？

B: Are you a citizen of this country?

A: 不是，我只是來遊覽。

A: No, I'm only visiting.

B: 你要排標示「非本國居民」的行列。

B: You should use the lines marked "non-residents".

A: 知道了，謝謝。　　→　**A:** I see. Thank you.

Dialog 3 （對話3）

A: 對不起，先生，你不可以進去那裡。　→　**A:** Excuse me, sir. You're not allowed to go in there.

B: 喔，對不起，我不知道。　→　**B:** Oh, sorry, I didn't know.

A: 這是限制區，請用另一個出口。　→　**A:** It's a restricted area. Please use the other exit.

B: 謝謝。　　→　**B:** Thanks.

Word Bank （字庫）

arrival customs n. 入境海關

sign [saɪn] n. 指標

immigration [,ɪmə'greʃən] n. 移民關口

line [laɪn] n. 隊伍

citizen ['sɪtəzn̩] n. 公民

mark [mɑrk] v. 標示

non-resident [,nɑn'rɛzədənt] n. 非居民

restricted area n. 限制區

exit ['ɛksɪt] n. 出口

基本對話
機場與飛機
入境
住宿
交通
餐飲
觀光
購物
郵電
銀行
麻煩事
回國

Useful Phrases 實用語句

1. 這地方是對的嗎？

   Is this the right place?

2. 這是隊伍的盡頭嗎？

   Is this the end of the line?

3. 我是觀光客。

   I am a tourist.

Notes 小叮嚀

在機上就要填好入境所需表格 (內容須與簽證申請文件一致)，否則將延誤通關，甚至被請去辦公室面談而耽誤更多時間。反恐及防堵非法移民確實給國際旅客帶來不便，但每個國家賦予第一線海關人員絕對權力處理任何不配合或他們認為有嫌疑的人進入該國，甚至取消簽證、遣返或拘禁。因此旅客無論長途飛行有多麼累，排隊安檢或通關隊伍有多麼長，絕對不可抱怨或顯出怒氣，以免因誤會而招來更大的麻煩。

3.2 海關檢查
Customs and Immigration

Dialog 1 對話1

A: 你來此地做什麼？

A: What are you doing here?

B: 度假。

B: I'm on vacation.

A: 你職業是什麼呢？

A: What do you do?

B: 我在銀行上班。

B: I work at a bank.

A: 你會在紐約待多久呢？

A: How long will you be staying in New York?

B: 兩個禮拜。

B: Two weeks.

A: 你有返程機票嗎？

A: Do you have a return ticket?

B: 有，在這裡。

B: Yes. Here it is.

Dialog 2 對話2

A: 請出示護照。

A: Passport, please.

B: 好的。

B: OK.

A: 你來訪的目的是什麼？

A: What's the purpose of your visit?

B: 我來拜訪一些客戶。

B: I'm visiting some clients.

基本對話

機場與飛機

入境

住宿

交通

餐飲

觀光

購物

郵電

銀行

麻煩事

回國

基本對話

機場與飛機

入境

住宿

交通

餐飲

觀光

購物

郵電

銀行

麻煩事

回國

A: 你會住在哪裡？

A: Where will you be staying?

B: 凱樂飯店。

B: The Kazler Hotel.

A: 現在將你的右手食指放在這裡。

A: Now put your right index finger here.

B: 好。

B: Ok.

A: 請按重一點。(處理中)現在換你的左手食指。

A: Please press harder. (processing) Now your left index finger.

Word Bank 字庫

purpose ['pɝ·pəs] n. 目的
client ['klaɪənt] n. 客戶

Useful Phrases 實用語句

1. 待在紅線後面。

   Stay behind the red line.

2. 你的護照和簽證。

   Your passport and visa, please.

3. 請走過來這裡。

   Please step over here.

4. 你跟誰旅行？

   Who are you traveling with?

5. 我跟 (旅行 / 商業考察) 團。

   I'm with a (tour / business) group.

6. 我跟朋友一起。

   I'm with a friend.

7. 我自己旅行。

   I'll travel by myself.

8. 我來度假。

   I'm on vacation.

9. 我來出差。

   I'm on business.

10. 我住飯店。

    I'll stay at a hotel.

11. 我住朋友那裡。

    I'll stay with friends.

Notes 小叮嚀

　　不要怕英文不好，移民官員問的就是那幾句並以你所填的資料問你 (在臺申辦簽證所填表格與入關文件)。這幾年美國入境海關已增加相當比例少數族裔移民官員及協助人員。雖然長途旅行令你疲憊，隊伍又長，但是過關時記得面帶微笑，直視官員，依照官員指示遞上文件不要緊張或焦躁。過關時的所有行動務必按照指示，等待時不要越線，前面的人英文表達不好也不要趨前幫忙，這是會被斥止的，除非是移民官員要你這麼做。移民官會將入出境卡 (I-94) 的存根 (即出境紀錄) 還給你或釘在護照上，一定要妥為保管，出境時必須繳回。

　　移民局官員最怕外國人滯留不歸或可能從事項目與入境目的不符，所以遊客要準備工作證明 (certificate of employment)、財力證明 (financial statement)、回程機票 (return flight)、旅遊行程 (itinerary) 或其他簽證時使用的資料要帶著備查，並記得自己所帶所填過文件的內容，證明你一定會如期返國。因為你的目的就是旅行觀光，所以即使有朋友在該國，最好別自找麻煩提到親友而橫生枝節引起官員追問更多問題 (除非官員主動問你，那麼就誠實以對)，填寫住宿地點最好就填飯店 (並有其確實地址電話)，別填親友處，問誰來接機「Who's picking you up?」可以回答自己安排「I'll take a taxi / public transportation.」，如果是跟團就回答旅行社安排「I'm with a group.」。總而言之，你就是來觀光的，沒有其他目的，記住不要懵懂回答任何聽不懂的問題。入境歐洲或其他免簽證國家，過關文件 (除上述外，可能被要求住宿資料及旅遊保險證明) 仍須依照要求備齊，才能確保通關順利。

3.3 提領行李
Baggage Claim

 Dialog 1 對話1

A: 你知道 233 航班的行李在哪兒嗎？

A: Do you know where baggage from Flight 233 is?

B: 到 7 號行李轉盤。

B: Go to carousel number 7.

A: 謝謝。

A: Thanks.

 Dialog 2 對話2

A: 你有行李單據嗎？

A: Do you have your baggage claim tickets?

B: 有，在這裡。

B: Yes, I do. Here they are.

A: 兩件嗎？

A: Two pieces?

B: 是的。

B: Yes.

A: 你有要申報什麼嗎？

A: Do you have anything to claim?

基本對話 / 機場與飛機 / 入境 / 住宿 / 交通 / 餐飲 / 觀光 / 購物 / 郵電 / 銀行 / 麻煩事 / 回國

基本對話

機場與飛機

入境

住宿

交通

餐飲

觀光

購物

郵電

銀行

麻煩事

回國

B: 沒有。 ▶ **B:** No, I don't.

A: 好,那請從入境門過去。 **A:** OK then. Please pass through the arrival gates.

Word Bank 字庫

baggage ['bægɪdʒ] n. 行李(= luggage)
carousel ['kærə'sel] n. (行李)轉盤
claim [klem] v. 申報

Useful Phrases 實用語句

1. 我要申報這個 [這些]。

   I need to claim this [these].

2. 我需要申報這個 [這些] 嗎?

   Do I need to claim this [these]?

3. 我沒有東西要申報。

   I have nothing to claim.

4. 把行李從轉盤上拿下來。

   Get the luggage off the carousel.

5. 我有行李確認單。

   I have the baggage claim tickets.

6. 這些是給我客戶 [朋友] 的禮物。

   These are gifts for my clients [friends].

7. 這是我的藥。

   It's my medicine.

8. 這是我的眼藥水。

   It's my eye drops.

Notes 小叮嚀

有些機場出口會檢查行李存根 (baggage identification tag，如電子機票樣本左下方)，確定每位乘客拿到自己的行李無誤才能離開。萬一存根弄丟了，要等到整個班機所有乘客沒有人有任何行李問題才能領取，所以行李存根一定要保管好。

3.4 行李遺失
Missing Luggage

Dialog 對話

A: 我的行李不在這裡。

A: My luggage is not here.

B: 請告訴我你搭乘的班機。

B: Please tell me the flight you were on.

A: 從臺北出發的 355 班機。

A: Flight 355 from Taipei.

B: 知道了，我會告訴行李人員尋找你的行李。

B: I see. OK. I'll tell the baggage handlers to look for it.

A: 我必須到市內開會，不能等。

A: I must go to a meeting in the city. I can't wait.

B: 請給我你會住宿的地點，行李找到後我們會送過去。

B: Please give me the address of where you will be staying. We'll forward it there when we find it.

基本對話 機場與飛機 入境 住宿 交通 餐飲 觀光 購物 郵電 銀行 麻煩事 回國

A: 請告訴我打哪個電話及找誰聯絡，如果我今晚晚點時還沒有行李。

A: Please tell me the phone number and who to contact if I don't have my luggage later tonight.

B: 打這個免付費電話或這邊另一支電話找我，我的名字是瑪麗，或找線上其他人。

B: Call this toll-free number, or this other number here, and ask for me. My name's Mary, or anyone on line.

A: 是24小時服務嗎？

A: Is it 24 hour service?

B: 是的。

B: Yes.

Word Bank 字庫

baggage handler n. 行李人員
forward ['fɔrwəd] v. 遞送
toll-free number n. 免付費電話號碼

Useful Phrases 實用語句

1. 遺失行李部門在哪裡呢？

   Where is the lost luggage department?

2. 這是我的行李確認標籤。

   Here are my luggage tags.

3.5 兌換錢幣
Money Exchange

 Dialog 對話

A: 我想換美金。

A: I want to exchange for U.S. dollars.

B: 要用什麼貨幣換?

B: What are you exchanging?

A: 英鎊。

A: British Pounds.

B: 知道了,沒問題。

B: I see. No problem.

A: 匯率多少呢?

A: What's the exchange rate?

B: 今天的匯率顯示在這邊。

B: Today's rates are shown here.

Word Bank 字庫

exchange [ɪks'tʃendʒ] v., n. 兌換
rate [ret] n. 匯率

基本對話

機場與飛機

入境

住宿

交通

餐飲

觀光

購物

郵電

銀行

麻煩事

回國

基本對話
機場與飛機
入境
住宿
交通
餐飲
觀光
購物
郵電
銀行
麻煩事
回國

3.6 廣播尋人
Paging Someone

 Dialog 對話

A: 我跟朋友約碰面遲到了，您可以幫我廣播找他嗎？

A: I'm late to meet my friend. Could you page him please?

B: 當然可以，什麼名字？

B: Yes, of course. What's the name?

A: 羅伯西蒙。

A: Robert Simon.

B: 我們現在就廣播。

B: We'll make the announcement now.

A: (廣播) 羅伯西蒙，請接任何白色免費話筒。羅伯西蒙，請接任何白色接待話筒。

A: (Broadcast) Robert Simon. Please pick up any white courtesy phone. Robert Simon, a white courtesy phone, please.

 Word Bank 字庫

page [pedʒ] v. 免費話筒呼叫，廣播尋人
announcement [ə'naunsmənt] n. 廣播
courtesy phone n. (機場、大賣場等使用之) 免費接待電話

Useful Phrases 實用語句

1. 我需要廣播尋人。

   I need to page someone.

2. 你可以替我廣播這個嗎？

   Can you announce this for me?

3. 嗨，我想你們在呼叫我。

   Hi, I think you are paging me.

4. 哈囉，我是＿＿＿，你們有呼叫我。

   Hello, I'm ＿＿＿. You paged me.

3.7 交通及住宿查詢
Transportation and Accommodations Inquiries

Dialog 1 對話1

A: 往市區的巴士在哪兒呢？

A: Where is the bus to downtown?

B: 穿過門後左轉。

B: Go through the doors and turn left.

A: 我在哪裡買票呢？

A: Where do I buy a ticket?

B: 同一個地點，你會看到售票亭也在那裡。

B: Same place. You will see the ticket counter there, too.

基本對話
機場與飛機
入境
住宿
交通
餐飲
觀光
購物
郵電
銀行
麻煩事
回國

 Dialog 2　對話2

A: 去飯店的計程車一趟要多少錢呢？

A: What does a taxi ride to the hotel cost?

B: 計程車是跳錶的。

B: Taxis are metered here.

A: 最低收費多少呢？

A: What is the minimum charge?

B: 2 元起跳，之後每 1/4 英里收費 40 分錢。

B: Two dollars at flag drop. It costs $0.40 per quarter mile after that.

Word Bank　字庫

meter ['mitɚ] v. 以儀錶計量
minimum charge n. 最低收費金額
flag drop 起跳
quarter ['kwɔrtɚ] n. 四分之一

 Dialog 3　對話3

A: 你可以告訴我機場旅館資訊服務區在哪兒嗎？

A: Can you tell me where the airport's hotel information area is?

B: 好的，沿著這條走廊一直走，就在盡頭。

B: Yes. Go straight down this corridor. It's at the end.

A: 在左邊或右邊呢？

A: On the left or right?

B: 在右邊，事實上很容易看到。

B: On the right. It's actually very easy to see.

A: 他們那裡可以回答關於飯店交通的問題嗎？

A: Can they answer questions about hotel transportation there?

B: 當然可以。

B: Definitely.

Word Bank 字庫

information area n. 資訊服務區
straight [stret] adv. 一直地
corridor ['kɔrədɚ] n. 走廊

Useful Phrases 實用語句

1. 這班巴士進城嗎？

   Does this bus go to the city?

2. 最近的巴士站在哪兒？

   Where is the nearest bus stop?

3. 下一班巴士幾點呢？

   When is the next bus?

4. 巴士多久來一班呢？

   How often does the bus come?

5. 我可以在哪裡買公車票？

   Where can I buy a bus pass?

基本對話 | 機場與飛機 | 入境 | 住宿 | 交通 | 餐飲 | 觀光 | 購物 | 郵電 | 銀行 | 麻煩事 | 回國

基本對話

機場與飛機

入境

住宿

交通

餐飲

觀光

購物

郵電

銀行

麻煩事

回國

6. 我要準備剛好的零錢嗎？

Do I need to have the exact change?

Tips 小祕訣

為求簡便，「information」常用「info」來代替。平常在資料上看到的「FYI (for your information)」，就是有消息報給你知道的意思。

3.8 飯店接駁車
Hotel Shuttle

Dialog 1 對話1

A: 皇宮飯店。我可以為你服務嗎？

A: Palace Place Hotel. May I help you?

B: 是的，我的名字是卡爾徐，我有訂房。

B: Yes. My name is Carl Hsu. I have a reservation.

A: 是的，徐先生，你的房間已準備好等候你的到來。

A: Yes, Mr. Hsu. Your room is ready for your arrival.

B: 好的。你可以告訴我去哪裡搭飯店接駁車嗎？

B: Good. Can you also tell me where to find the hotel shuttle?

A: 當然可以。你在二號航站的西側嗎？

A: Certainly. Are you at the west end of Terminal 2?

B: 不是。

B: No, I'm not.

A: 請到二號航站的西側找我們的標示。

A: Please go to the west end of Terminal 2 and look for our sign.

B: 標示是什麼顏色呢？

B: What color is the sign?

A: 黃底黑字，你一定不會錯過，你會在左邊看到它。

A: Yellow with black letters. You can't miss it. You'll see it on the left side.

Word Bank 字庫

shuttle ['ʃʌtl̩] n. 定時往返的短程巴士，接駁車
reservation [,rɛzə·'veʃən] n. 預訂
terminal ['tɝmənl̩] n. 航站
miss [mɪs] v. 錯過，遺漏

Tips 小祕訣

　　在主要城市的機場，有時可以見到一整排可以直接打給旅館的電話。拿起話筒直撥旅館電話即可訂房。機場的接待電話 (courtesy phone) 上面列有相關電話分機號碼，可以免費直接撥號給租車公司訂車。旅館或租車公司的接駁巴士通常設在機場出口的人行道上，只要隨著指示就可找到。大機場的租車公司接駁巴士通常不需久等，看到接駁巴士直接揮手上車，不必買票也不需給小費。某些較大的機場可能要上一個樓層去搭接駁電車 (air train) 去租車公司取車，機場會有清楚的指示。

Dialog 2 對話2

A: 不好意思,請問這裡是我搭接駁車去皇宮飯店的地方嗎?

A: Excuse me. Is this where I catch the shuttle to the Palace Place?

B: 可以這麼說,我替你查訂房及開給你一張接駁票。

B: Almost. I'll check your reservation and issue you a shuttle ticket here.

A: 好。接駁車站牌離這裡近嗎?

A: OK. Is the shuttle station close to here?

B: 喔,是的,就在外面。

B: Oh, yes. It's right outside.

A: 我現在可以上車了嗎?

A: Can I get on now?

B: 還沒,下一班車幾分鐘後就到了。

B: Not quite yet. The next one will be here in just a few minutes.

A: 好的,我在那邊等。

A: Fine. I'll wait over there.

B: 請吧,這裡是你的票。

B: Please do, and here is your ticket.

A: 謝謝。

A: Thanks.

Word Bank 字庫

catch [kætʃ] v. 搭上，趕上
issue ['ɪʃju] v. 開出，核發

Dialog 3 對話3

A: 這是去皇宮飯店的接駁車嗎？

A: Is this the shuttle for the Palace Place Hotel?

B: 是的，上來吧，把你的行李放在架子上。

B: Yes, it is. Go ahead and put your luggage on the rack.

A: 這是我的接駁票。

A: Here is my shuttle ticket.

B: 謝謝。(打洞) 你的票。(還票)

B: Thank you. (punching it) Here you go. (giving it back)

A: 要搭多久呢？

A: How long is the ride?

B: 約 20 分鐘。讓自己舒適些，我們要走了。

B: About twenty minutes. Make yourself comfortable. We're about to go.

Word Bank 字庫

rack [ræk] n. 行李架
punch [pʌntʃ] v. 打洞

Useful Phrases 實用語句

1. 我打電話來問我的訂房。

   I'm calling about my reservation.

2. 我的房間準備好了嗎？

   Is my room ready?

3. 接駁巴士在哪裡呢？

   Where is the shuttle bus?

4. 我需要票嗎？

   Do I need a ticket?

5. 走出機場。

   Step outside of the airport terminal.

6. 接駁站牌就在外面。

   The shuttle stop is right outside.

Tips 小祕訣

許多接駁巴士不只為一家飯店服務，搭這類巴士你可能需要票，但有時依然是免費的。上車時要與司機確定飯店名稱及位置，確定所搭的巴士是正確的。搭接駁巴士通常是自己提行李，也有司機會不時幫忙提一下行李，但美國人一般不給接駁巴士司機小費。

Unit 4 Accommodations

住宿

在歐美地區，有各式飯店及汽車旅館，價格依位置及服務而不同。提早預訂通常比當日才找到該飯店住宿的價格便宜。訂房網站常以價格戰作為促銷花招，但對隱藏費用或諸多限制一概不提，有些以極小字體印在背面或需外部連結才能看到。網站裡的房間條件或提供項目，飯店可不一定承認，所以別光看表面價格，打電話或 email 確認免於到了旅館才發現吃悶虧而壞了遊興。以信用卡預訂飯店，當然要記得帶著該信用卡，沒去住宿 (no show) 也沒在允許免費取消期限前取消，該筆住宿費不能退回。有關飯店如何收費及退費 (refund policy) 的規定，在預訂時就要確定。通常飯店對住宿較長時間或經常投宿的旅客有折扣，若有此打算，可跟飯店要求優惠價格。住房時間通常下午 3 點開始，退房時間通常為 11 點或中午。

基本對話

機場與飛機

入境

住宿

交通

餐飲

觀光

購物

郵電

銀行

麻煩事

回國

4.1 詢問空房
Asking for Vacancies

 Dialog 對話

A: 請問你們還有空房間嗎？

A: Do you have any rooms available?

B: 幾個人要住的呢？

B: For how many people?

A: 兩個。

A: Two.

B: 要雙人床還是兩個單人床的房間呢？

B: Do you need a double or twin bed room?

A: 請給我們兩個單人床的。房價是多少呢？

A: A twin, please, and how much is the rate?

B: 80 元稅外加。

B: Eighty dollars plus tax.

A: 好。我們可以要禁菸的房間嗎？

A: Ok. Can we have a non-smoking room?

 Word Bank 字庫

available [ə'veləbl] adj. 空著的，可用的
rate [ret] n. 費率

 Useful Phrases 實用語句

1. 這是聯德飯店嗎？

   Is this the Lander Hotel?

2. 你們有空房嗎？

   Do you have any vacancies?

3. 今天的雙人房要多少錢呢？

   What's today's rate for a double room?

4. 只住今晚。

   For tonight only.

5. 你們允許攜帶寵物嗎？

   Do you allow pets?

6. 飯店裡可以吸菸嗎？

   Is smoking allowed in the hotel?

7. 我幾點可以登記住房？

   What time can I check in?

8. 我幾點要結帳離開飯店？

   What time do I need to check out?

9. 我需要預訂明早去機場的接駁車。

   I need to reserve a shuttle ride to the airport for tomorrow morning.

 Tips 小祕訣

在旅館外若見到「Vacancy」就表示還有空房，「No Vacancy」就表示客滿了。確定要訂房住宿前，可以要求先看房間。雖說每家旅館依條件不同而定價，還是可能有些彈性。如果覺得價格太高或登記住宿時間已經很晚，可以請問櫃臺人員是否有便宜點的可能「Do you have any discounts?」「Do you have any special rate?」，或是有什麼會員可以打折的房價「Do you give a discount for _____ members?」。如果多住幾晚或在淡季住宿，那機會就大的多了。若會常住在相同連鎖飯店，可以在住宿登記時當場申請會員卡，櫃臺人員可給你一張暫時卡，下次住宿連鎖旅館即享有 10% 的折扣，相當實用。

基本對話｜機場與飛機｜入境｜住宿｜交通｜餐飲｜觀光｜購物｜郵電｜銀行｜麻煩事｜回國

4.2 房間樣式及設備
Room Types and Facilities

 Dialog 1 （對話1）

A: 哈囉，泰斯豪頓飯店。

A: Hello. Tice Harlton Hotel.

B: 哈囉，我想了解你們有什麼樣式的房間。

B: Hello. I'd like to know what types of rooms you offer.

A: 好的，我們所有樣式都有。

A: Fine. We have all types of accommodations available.

B: 我們有三個人，二個大人、一個小孩。

B: There are three in my party, two adults, one child.

A: 我們有標準房、豪華房及超級房，都可容納小孩。

A: We have regular, deluxe and superior rooms. All accommodate children.

B: 你們房間有景觀嗎？

B: Do your rooms have views?

A: 我們有令人喜愛的面海港房間，也有面公園景色的房間。

A: We have lovely harbor side rooms, and park view rooms, too.

B: 小孩加床要加價嗎？

B: Is there an extra charge for a children's bed?

基本對話

機場與飛機

入境

住宿

交通

餐飲

觀光

購物

郵電

銀行

麻煩事

回國

A: 豪華房及超級房不必加價，標準房每晚要多加 10 元。

A: Not for deluxe or superior rooms. There is a ten dollar per night charge for regular rooms.

Word Bank 字庫

offer ['ɔfɚ] v. 提供
accommodations [ə,kamə'deʃənz] n. 住宿設備
party ['partɪ] n. 一夥人
adult [ə'dʌlt] n. 成人
regular ['rɛgjələ] adj. 一般的
deluxe [dɪ'lʌks] adj. 豪華的
superior [sə'pɪrɪɚ] adj. 超級的
accommodate [ə'kamə,det] v. 可容納
harbor ['harbɚ] n. 海港
charge [tʃardʒ] n., v 收費，費用

Dialog 2 對話2

A: 你可以告訴我，我們房間有什麼嗎？

A: Can you tell me what is available to us in our room?

B: 有冰箱，內有冷飲及啤酒，以及電視、收音機和電話。

B: There is a refrigerator with cold drinks and beer inside, TV, radio, and telephone.

A: 浴室有洗髮精嗎？

A: Is there shampoo in the bathroom?

B: 有的，還有牙刷、牙膏、香皂及浴帽。

B: Yes, plus toothbrushes, toothpaste, soap, and a shower cap.

基本對話

A: 冰箱裡有冰塊嗎？

A: Is there any ice in the freezer?

機場與飛機

B: 如果你需要，客房服務會送上去。

B: Room service can send some up if you need it.

入境

Word Bank 字庫

refrigerator [rɪˈfrɪdʒə,retə] n. 冰箱
shampoo [ʃæmˈpu] n. 洗髮精
toothbrush [ˈtuθ,brʌʃ] n. 牙刷
toothpaste [ˈtuθ,pest] n. 牙膏
soap [sop] n. 香皂
shower cap n. 浴帽

住宿

交通

Useful Phrases 實用語句

1. 你們的房間有冷氣嗎？
   Are your rooms air-conditioned?

2. 房間大嗎？
   Are your rooms large?

3. 有附早餐嗎？
   Is breakfast included?

4. 何時供應早餐？
   When is breakfast served?

5. 早餐室在哪裡呢？
   Where is the breakfast room?

6. 我們需要上網。
   We need to surf the net.

7. 我們需要多一條毛巾。
   We need an extra towel.

餐飲 觀光 購物 郵電 銀行 麻煩事 回國

8. 我們需要多些衛生紙。

We need more toilet paper.

9. 我需要吹風機。

I need a hair dryer.

Notes 小叮嚀

　　美加 (及多數中南美洲國家) 電壓和臺灣、日本相同,為 110-120 伏特。如果是在五星級飯店,設備當然應有盡有,但住宿也所費不貲。在美國一般的旅館,通常至少會有電視、電話、冷氣等基本設備。在走道也通常備有冰塊機,有些旅館會有投幣式洗衣房 (Laundromat)、游泳池及 jacuzzi (spa) 池,房內有燙衣板、美式咖啡機、冰箱、微波爐、鬧鐘。旅館多有洗髮精、沐浴乳或香皂、吹風機,但牙膏、牙刷、拖鞋為個人用品,旅館不供應,旅客要自備。其他國家電壓為 220 伏特。出國要帶電壓變換器 (power converter) 及 (萬用) 轉接插頭 (adapter),切記使用電器 (如吹風機等) 之電壓轉換 (許多國家明文規定禁用電湯匙),否則電線走火,引起火災!在歐洲因建築物歷史悠久或旅館等級不同,可能會有兩三間房間共用一個浴室的情形。在夏天短暫的歐洲地區,有些四星旅館也可能沒有冷氣。若旅館有保險箱 (safe deposit box) 可以將護照鎖在裡面,只需帶影印的護照出門即可 (不只換外幣要用到),但離開時要記得取出。

Language Power 字句補給站

◆ 旅館房間 Hotel Rooms

lodging, accommodations	住宿
reservation	預訂
vacancy	空房
facilities	設備
concierge	禮賓人員
bellboy	行李員
swimming pool	游泳池

基本對話 機場與飛機 入境 住宿 交通 餐飲 觀光 購物 郵電 銀行 麻煩事 回國

meeting [conference] room	會議室
laundromat	洗衣房
gift shop	禮品部
mail service	郵件服務
wake-up call	叫醒服務
hotel shuttle	旅館接駁車
complimentary breakfast	免費早餐
suite	套房 (包含客廳、臥室、衛浴或／及廚房)
single room	單人房(single bed 單人床)
double room	雙人房(double bed 一張雙人床／queen 標準床／king 加大床／twin beds 兩張成對單人床)
standard	標準房
deluxe	豪華房
bunk beds	上下鋪
camp bed	輕便帆布床
futon	鋪於地板的床墊
extra bed	加床
rollaway	加床 (床底下加輪子可移動或摺疊者)
motel	汽車旅館
hostel	青年旅館
guest house / B&B (bed and breakfast)	民宿
cottage	鄉間小屋
resort	度假屋
villa	別墅
campground	露營區
Don't disturb.	請勿打擾。
Please make up the room. / Maid service.	請整理房間。
remote (control)	遙控器
lamp	燈
faucet	水龍頭
shower head	蓮蓬頭
flush	沖(馬桶)
clog	堵住
drain	排水口
plug	塞子；插頭
socket	插座

4.3 旅館櫃臺登記
Checking into a Hotel

 Dialog 對話

A: 嗨，我要住房。

A: Hi. I want to check in.

B: 你有跟我們預訂嗎？

B: Do you have a reservation with us?

A: 有，我的名字是凱爾楊。

A: Yes, I do. My name is Kyle Young.

B: 是的，楊先生，你訂了一間雙人不吸菸房。

B: Yes, Mr. Young. You reserved a double, non-smoking room.

A: 沒錯。我想要一樓的房間。

A: That's right. I'd like to have a room on the first floor.

B: 我查一下。112號房，這是鑰匙，過了門右轉。

B: Let me check. Room 112. Here's your key. Pass the door and turn right.

A: 謝謝。

A: Thank you.

 Useful Phrases 實用語句

1. 這是我的護照。

   Here's my passport.

基本對話

機場與飛機

入境

住宿

交通

餐飲

觀光

購物

郵電

銀行

麻煩事

回國

2. 我會在大廳等。

   I'll wait in the lobby.

3. 你們的吧臺幾點開？

   What time does your bar open?

4. 我需要一張收據。

   I'll need a receipt, please.

5. 這是旅行社業務員給的已支付證明。

   Here's the voucher from the travel agent.

Cultural Tips 文化祕笈

旅館住宿登記卡 Hotel Registration Card

1. 住宿登記卡

```
Hotel Registration Form

NAME        Li-ying , Yu
ADDRESS          88  Chung Hwa Rd.
CITY   Taipei , Taiwan   STATE _____ ZIP _____
NUMBER OF PEOPLE ___3___
ARRIVAL DATE ___/___/___ DEPARTURE DATE ___/___/___
CREDIT CARD TYPE:  ☑ visa  ☐ master  ☐ other _____
CREDIT CARD NUMBER:  5521-7763-5371-8168
CREDIT CARD SIGNATURE:
CREDIT CARD EXPIRATION DATE: ___06___ (mo) ___18___ (yr)
```

旅館住宿登記卡一般要求提供姓名(name)、住址(address)、住宿
人數(number of people)，以及信用卡的種類(type)、卡號(creadit
card number)、簽名(signature)、有效期限(expiration date)。
另有一些旅館在登記卡上加註印刷非常小的不退款及免責聲明
(此做法有待商榷)，登記住宿時要注意，願意接受才簽名。

2. 住宿登記卡

REGISTRATION		ROOM NO

```
                    REGISTRATION                      ROOM NO _____
  IN                 NO REFUNDS              OUT       RATE: _____
                ADVANCE PAYMENT REQUESTED
  NOTICE TO GUESTS:                                    DATE IN: _____
  This property is privately owned and the management reserves the right to refuse service
  to anyone, and will not be responsible for accidents or injury to guests or for the loss of   DATE OUT: _____
  money, jewelry or valuables of any kind. By signing this contract, I abide to the rules set
  by management to not to conduct any illegal or unlawful activities on premises. Also
  declare the accompanied quest is my Spouse or Boyfriend/Girlfriend or as stated.

  NAME:  Li-ying, Yu

  STREET:  88 Chung Hwa Rd.
            For your protection please give full address
  CITY:  Taipei        STATE: Taiwan  ZIP:

  CAR
  LICENSE:  3UJ3528      STATE:  CA    ZIP:

  DRIVERS
  LICENSE:              STATE:        ZIP:

  MAKE                  NUMBER
  OF CAR: Toyota, Camry  OF PERSONS:  3

  SIGNATURE
  AMTEX, CA 1-800-650-3360
```

Days: SUN MON TUE WED THUR FRI SAT — Rate $ ___ Tax ___ TOTAL DAYS Total ___

上方為旅館聲明不退費 (no refunds)、先付款再住宿 (advanced payment requested)、旅館不負責房客意外傷害或竊盜損失，以及住此旅館願遵守規定不從事非法活動。下方登記旅客 (name)、地址 (address)、車牌 (car license)、駕照 (driver's license)、車款 (make of car)、住宿人數 (number of persons)，並簽名 (signature)。右方表格為房號、住宿日期、天數及費用。旅館報價未含稅，稅後費用才是總價。有些旅館會要求先以信用卡刷一筆費用 (an imprint in advance) 作為預付房費或押金，結帳時多退少補清算費用。

美國有些旅館已經可以用手機感應直接入飯店房間，不必排隊等櫃臺 check in 拿鎖匙。步驟如下：在網路上預訂房間支付信用卡款後，取得 QR Code，選好房間。入住時在旅館櫃臺確認身分及信用卡後，直接用手機感應開房，不用等櫃臺給你鎖匙。離開旅館時，因已經付過款，不需 check out 直接離開，如有使用冰箱飲料零食等，會直接計入信用卡帳單。

4.4 旅館附近地圖
Area Map

Dialog 對話

A: 我需要這地區的地圖。

A: I need a map of the area.

基本對話

機場與飛機

入境

住宿

交通

餐飲

觀光

購物

郵電

銀行

麻煩事

回國

B: 我們這裡有。

B: We have them here.

A: 地圖有包含些什麼？

A: What does it cover?

B: 它包含了一面市區、一面邊遠地區。

B: It covers the city on one side and outlying areas on the other.

A: 我知道了。

A: I see.

B: 它還有里程縮尺、公車路線、公車站及號碼，以及觀光景點的資料。

B: Yes. It also has a scale of miles, bus routes, stops, and numbers, and info about sites.

A: 看起來很棒。

A: It looks very good.

Word Bank 字庫

cover ['kʌvɚ] v. 包含
outlying ['aut,laɪɪŋ] adj. 遠離中心的
scale [skel] n. 比例尺，縮尺
route [rut] n. 路線
site [saɪt] n. 地點

　　選擇治安良好地區的旅館及確認自己旅遊路線的安全，離開旅館務必攜帶旅館名片及附近地圖，以防走丟或必要時之緊急連絡。若要拜訪某處，先查好路線後，請服務人員確認及在地圖上標示旅館正確地點及上下車站名 (及前一站站名)，這是非常重要的。在人生地不熟的國外，旅館在白天及晚上看起來可能完全不同。若需在天黑後找回旅館，不管任合一種交通工具，能結伴同行較好。萬一走丟了、開錯路或坐錯車、下錯站，有同伴較能鎮定且較容易找到回去的路。如果到國土面積大、溫度與時間概念不同的國家要多留意，當地人所謂「就」在前面、「一下子」就到了、有「熱」水、「有點」冷的定義將與國人在臺的亞熱帶小島生活經驗完全不同，誤判可能因此錯用交通工具而有挨餓受凍、疲累困頓之虞。

　　國人對老外的人情味 (hospitality) 在許多國家是天方夜譚，有些人仍有狹隘的偏見 (bias) 或對其他族群的刻板印象 (stereotype)，即使如土生土長的美國總統歐巴馬 (Barack H. Obama) 及許多奮鬥成功的少數族裔 (minorities)，都曾遭遇種族歧視 (racial discrimination)，更何況身處歐美的外國人。貶低中國人的「清客」Chink，或用中國菜的名字嘲笑人，與nigger (黑鬼) 一詞同樣是侮辱 (insult) 語言。所幸觀光客或旅行者在當地時間較短，到當地也有利振興當地經濟，碰到歧視或語言霸凌 (bully) 的情形應當較少。

　　因為遊客在國外被欺生占便宜並非什麼新鮮事，除了謹守財物寄放旅館房間保險箱 (safe box)、出門財不露白、分處藏放現金及使用暗袋 (money belt) 外，人潮擁擠時將背包前背，拉鍊以安全別針固定防止被任意拉開。開發中國家各類掮客群聚機場、車站、飯店或單獨在路上跟隨搭訕攬客，令人不勝其擾，在長途夜車上趁人熟睡竊取財物的小偷更要提防。

　　旅遊安全在人們可以合法擁有槍械但毒品氾濫之地區格外重要。即使是先進國家也有治安惡名昭彰之地，遊客看地圖或照相攝影之舉是羊入虎口，穿金戴銀彰顯名牌者無疑招來被偷拐搶騙、假警臨檢甚至綁架之危險！許多歐洲大都會等在公共場所或交通工具上對落單異性灌迷湯或施行偷騙詐術洗劫財物的人多有所聞，遊客因為疲累鬆懈或有浪漫想法都可能讓自己受害，不得不慎。

基本對話

機場與飛機

入境

住宿

交通

餐飲

觀光

購物

郵電

銀行

麻煩事

回國

4.5 服務詢問——旅館早餐
Requesting Services—Breakfast

Dialog （對話）

A: 我住宿這裡有包含早餐嗎？

A: Does my stay here include breakfast?

B: 有的。

B: Yes, it does.

A: 在哪兒呢？

A: Where is it?

B: 拿這張憑證交給領班。

B: Take this voucher and give it to the *Maitre d'*.

A: 去哪裡的餐廳呢？

A: Where is the restaurant I go to?

B: 從大廳穿過去就是了。

B: Just cross the main lobby.

Word Bank （字庫）

voucher ['vautʃɚ] n. 憑證(如旅行社發出的已支付證明、旅客住宿或用餐的收據)

Maitre d' [ˌmetrə'di, ˌmetR'di] n. (法國高級餐館的) 領班 ([R] 深喉音，類似 [h])

main [men] adj. 主要的

Tips 小祕訣

旅館含早餐費用者,有時會發出 [voucher],有些則報房號或出示鑰匙即可。

有些旅館使用自動感應冰箱 (automated minibars) 及零食盤,但房內不一定有清楚告示。任何飲料零食被移動,即判定消費自動入帳。如自己的飲料食物要使用冰箱,因移動冰箱物品會被計價,應詢問櫃臺。有些旅館提供收費冰箱,房客或可使用保冰袋或冰塊冰鎮自己的食物飲料。結帳時應查看帳單,避免收到莫名又價昂的飲料零食費用。

4.6 服務詢問——網路服務
Requesting Services—Internet Service

 Dialog 對話

A: 你們飯店有無線網路服務嗎?

A: Does your hotel have wireless Internet service?

B: 有的。

B: Yes, it does.

A: 是免費的嗎?

A: Is it free?

B: 是的,住客免費。

B: For guests it is.

A: 在飯店的咖啡廳也可以用嗎?

A: Is it available in the hotel coffee shop, too?

基本對話

機場與飛機

入境

住宿

交通

餐飲

觀光

購物

郵電

銀行

麻煩事

回國

B: 是的。

B: Yes, it is.

Word Bank 字庫

Internet service n. 網路服務
wireless ['waɪrlɪs] adj. 無線的

Useful Phrases 實用語句

1. 我的手提電腦需要一個轉接插頭。

   I need a plug-in adapter for my laptop.

2. 你們有延長線可以借我嗎？

   Do you have an extension cord I can borrow?

3. 這附近有網咖嗎？

   Is there an Internet café nearby?

Notes 小叮嚀

歷年來訂房網站的調查顯示免費快速的無線上網 (Wi-Fi) 服務是所有旅客最希望旅館提供的標準化配備，其重要性遠超過第二名的免費早餐，是旅客選擇住宿時最重要的考慮項目。連鎖汽車旅館房客進住後，通常可以免費登入 Wi-Fi。但有些飯店仍把網路收費當作重要營收工具 (記住飯店「有」提供網路並不表示免費，飯店可能提供不同價格的上網速度，如使用免費網路可能會為龜速所苦)，免費網路也可能僅限於旅館大廳。有些飯店提供房客專用電腦房或商務中心，計時收費。若房客要在房內使用自己的筆記型電腦，可在櫃臺購買 24 小時以上 (1,3 或 6 日) 之預付卡 (prepaid card)，取得一組登入號碼，費用以日計價，每日約 $5-20 美元間 (稅外加)。一組號碼通常允許登錄 (log in) 兩臺電子產品 (如筆電，iPad 或智慧型手機)，如在飯店網頁購買所需小時 (1, 6 或 24 小時)，則只能使用一種產品。因此，以時或以日計價方式不同，登入限制也有差異。

4.7 服務詢問——游泳池
Requesting Services—Swimming Pool

Dialog 對話

A: 飯店游泳池幾點關呢？

A: What time does the hotel pool close?

B: 晚上 9 點關。

B: It closes at 9 p.m.

A: 很早開嗎？

A: Is it open early?

基本對話

機場與飛機

入境

住宿

交通

餐飲

觀光

購物

郵電

銀行

麻煩事

回國

B: 早上 7 點開。

B: It opens at 7 a.m.

A: 那夠早了，謝謝。喔，游泳池有加溫嗎？

A: That's early enough. Thanks. Oh, is the swimming pool heated?

B: 有的，大約74度。

B: Yes, it's about 74 degrees.

 Useful Phrases 實用語句

1. 那裡也有兒童池嗎？

   Is there a children's pool, too?

2. 我需要買泳褲。(男士)

   I need to buy some swim trunks.

3. 我需要買泳衣。(女士)

   I need to buy a swimsuit.

4. 游泳池更衣室在哪裡？

   Where is the pool dressing room?

5. 你們有賣蛙鏡嗎？

   Do you sell swimming goggles?

6. 我想買些游泳用耳塞。

   I want to buy some earplugs for swimming.

7. 請給我一條毛巾。

   I need a towel, please.

Notes 小叮嚀

　　美國游泳池通常並不要求泳客帶泳帽，但夏天早晚游泳都很冷，若不想白天頂著大太陽下水，詢問游泳池是否加溫就很重要了。要游泳時，不要帶房內的毛巾去 (房內與泳池用的毛巾是分開的)，可向旅館櫃臺或泳池邊櫃臺人員拿游泳用的毛巾。

4.8 服務詢問——會議室
Requesting Services—Meeting Room

 Dialog 對話

A: 我需要預訂一間會議室。

A: I need to reserve a meeting room.

B: 我們的飯店有好幾間，你要多大間的？

B: Our hotel has several. What size do you need?

A: 我要對大約 50 人講話。

A: I'll be speaking to about fifty people.

B: 好，也許你會要橡廳。

B: Fine. Perhaps you'd like to use the Oak Room.

A: 我可以看一下嗎？

A: May I see it?

B: 當然。這邊請，跟我來。

B: Of course. This way please. Follow me.

基本對話｜機場與飛機｜入境｜住宿｜交通｜餐飲｜觀光｜購物｜郵電｜銀行｜麻煩事｜回國

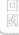

基本對話

機場與飛機

入境

住宿

交通

餐飲

觀光

購物

郵電

銀行

麻煩事

回國

Word Bank 字庫

reserve [rɪ'zɜv] v. 預訂
meeting ['mitɪŋ] n. 會議

4.9 服務詢問──自助洗衣
Requesting Services—Laundromat

Dialog 1 對話1

A: 對不起，我要找自助洗衣店。

A: Excuse me. I'm looking for a Laundromat.

B: 街道左邊大約三個街區左右有一間。

B: There's one about three blocks down on the left side of the street.

A: 謝謝。

A: Thanks.

Dialog 2 對話2

A: 我要換機器用的零錢。

A: Hi. I need change for the machines.

B: 好，你要多少？

B: OK. How much do you want?

A: 要夠用三臺洗衣機及一臺烘乾機。

A: Enough for three washers and a dryer.

B: 我看看，那大約要 5 元。

B: Let's see, that would be about five dollars worth.

A: 這裡是 5 塊錢。

A: Here's five dollars.

B: 你要的硬幣在這裡，每臺洗衣機要 1 元 50 分來使用。

B: And here are the coins you need. Each washing machine needs $1.50 to operate.

A: 那烘衣機呢？

A: What about the dryers?

B: 25 分錢可以烘 15 分鐘。

B: One quarter buys fifteen minutes of drying time.

Dialog 3 對話3

A: 我要買肥皂和柔軟精。

A: I need to buy some soap and softener.

B: 你要多少盒？

B: How many boxes do you need?

A: 三盒。多少錢呢？

A: Three. How much are they?

B: 肥皂是 50 分一盒，柔軟紙也是 50 分一捲。

B: Soap is 50¢ a box. Softener is also 50¢ a roll.

基本對話

機場與飛機

入境

住宿

交通

餐飲

觀光

購物

郵電

銀行

麻煩事

回國

A: 一捲有多少張呢？

A: How many sheets in one roll?

B: 有十張。

B: There are ten.

Tips 小祕訣

　　等級高的旅館有價格不菲的洗衣服務，一般旅館則可能設有投幣式自助洗衣房。若是沒有的話，就要去外面的自助洗衣店。

4.10 客房服務
Room Service

Dialog 對話

A: 哈囉，這裡是客房服務嗎？

A: Hello. Is this room service?

B: 是的，先生。

B: Yes, sir, it is.

A: 我要一瓶本飯店白酒。

A: I'd like a bottle of the hotel's house white wine.

B: 請問你的房號。

B: Your room number, please.

A: 612 號房。

A: Room 612.

B: 我立刻送去。

B: I'll have it sent up immediately.

Notes 小叮嚀

　　原物料與製造國工資高漲，加上金融危機後美國接連採取寬鬆政策大量印鈔的結果，導致美國物價與工資節節上漲，小費行情當然也不例外。住飯店給小費 (tipping) 在西方是很平常的，在美國如果要求行李員服務，應該準備至少每件 2 元，兩件 5 元給行李員 (盡量整數)，許多高檔飯店僅行李一事即須支付兩次小費——一位行李員 (bellhop) 從車上取下行李推到飯店大廳，須給一次小費 (每件 2 元)。房客櫃臺登記入住後，進入房間等待行李送達，另一位行李員從大廳將行李推進房間，需再給一次小費。賭場飯店小費行情一件行李$5，兩件$10。有些普級飯店則會在大門口擺放行李推車(luggage cart) 供客人自行使用。房間續住的話，每房要準備每日 3-5 元的小費 (tips) 給服務人員，放在枕頭上方或床頭櫃電話下就可以。有客房服務的飯店，送餐人員通常獲得至少 5 美元小費。若是禮賓人員 (Concierge) 有代為安排行程、租車、代叫計程車及代訂活動門票，也要記得給小費 (問路、推薦餐廳則不必)。簡單的訂票可以給$5小費，不好訂的票大約在$10-20之間。小費多寡基本上視交代服務的項目難易而定，而給小費是因為得到了好的服務心存感謝 (或希望獲得迅速的服務) 的表示。

　　日、韓、紐、澳與臺灣一樣，傳統上並無小費文化 (意即員工薪資無論多寡由雇主給付，消費即包含「無價」之服務品質)。但美國早就形成根深蒂固的意識 (可說是「制度」)，美國服務業基本時薪過低 (加州為略高州別之一，近年歷經抗爭而有所調高)，是以消費者給小費補貼作為解決方式，業者不但不須提高薪資，許多餐廳還規定抽取或分配小費，導致服務員所剩不多，結果形成無論服務品質良莠，服務員皆期待收到「令人滿意」小費的心態，甚至發生收到小費要倒貼給餐廳或追問消費者為何小費不夠多的奇怪現象！這對不諳小費文化、預算不多、或不認同普通服務卻被期待打賞高額比例小費的消費者 (菜單價格加小費加稅之後才是總金額) 而言，確實是

基本對話 機場與飛機 入境 住宿 交通 餐飲 觀光 購物 郵電 銀行 麻煩事 回國

種負擔。除了外籍旅客,即使是美國本地人,有關小費制度的辯論,行情及如何給小費在網路上的歧見非常多。

　　入境就必須隨俗,即使我們所得比不上旅遊地,也要將此支出包含在預算內 (其他美洲、歐洲、中東國家小費行情略低些)。去小費盛行的地區旅行,在出國時結匯就換一些零錢備用。隨著國際旅行日漸頻繁,原本沒有小費文化 (如亞洲) 的國家也漸漸改變,拜訪前宜先了解,別影響了旅遊興致。如果帳單本身已包含服務費,可以酌量再給或不給。要特別注意的是小費不要給太碎的零錢,會給人不舒服的感受。小費不必給多,但也要遵從當地慣例,不該少給或不給。所謂多給傷己,少給失禮,不給無禮。記得身上要準備一些小鈔,尤其是當面給人的小費要給紙鈔才好。

4.11 疑難排解──換房
Solving Problems—Changing a Room

Dialog 對話

A: 嗨,我想換房。

A: Hi. I would like to have a different room.

B: 有問題嗎,先生?

B: Is there a problem, sir?

A: 是的,我的房間面對街道,太吵了。

A: Yes. Mine faces the street. It's too noisy.

B: 我了解了,我會找間安靜點的給你。

B: I understand. I'll find something quieter for you.

Useful Phrases 實用語句

1. 你們有大一點的房間嗎？

   Do you have a larger room available?

2. 我想要一間比較好的房間。

   I'd like to have a better room.

3. 我想要一間有景觀的房間。

   I'd like a room with a view.

4. 我想再待一晚。

   I want to stay another night.

Notes 小叮嚀

　　雖說服務人員會整理，但是也不要把房間弄得太亂，尤其別把用過的毛巾丟在浴室地上 (可放在浴缸) 或弄得太髒，這是很不應該的。若有小孩同行，要約法三章不要吵到別人，也不能在公共場所亂跑。入境隨俗，不要在遠處就扯開喉嚨呼叫同伴，而是走近再交談。

4.12 疑難排解——燈壞了
Solving Problems—Broken Lamp

Dialog 對話

A: 接待櫃臺。我可以幫你嗎？

A: Reception desk. May I help you?

B: 我房裡的燈壞了。

B: The lamp in my room doesn't work.

基本對話

機場與飛機

入境

住宿

交通

餐飲

觀光

購物

郵電

銀行

麻煩事

回國

A: 抱歉，女士，我會立刻叫房務人員過去修理。

A: Sorry, ma'am. I'll have someone from housekeeping come fix it immediately.

B: 謝謝。

B: Thank you.

Word Bank 字庫

lamp [læmp] n. 燈
housekeeping [ˈhaʊsˌkipɪŋ] n. 房務部門
fix [fɪks] v. 修理

Useful Phrases 實用語句

1. 燈壞了。

   The lamp doesn't work.

2. 咖啡壺壞了。

   The coffee maker doesn't work.

3. 水龍頭漏水。

   The faucet is leaking.

4. 馬桶堵住了。

   The toilet is plugged up.

5. 馬桶不能沖水。

   The toilet won't flush.

6. 排水口堵住了。

   The drain is clogged.

4.13 疑難排解——插頭不合
Solving Problems—Plugs

 Dialog 對話

A: 旅館櫃臺。

A: Front desk.

B: 我的電腦插頭跟這裡的插座不合。

B: My computer's plug-in does not fit the outlet here.

A: 沒問題，我馬上派房務人員送一個轉接插頭過去。

A: No problem. I'll have housekeeping send an adapter to you right now.

Word Bank 字庫

plug [plʌg] n. 插頭
fit [fɪt] v. 符合
outlet ['aʊt,lɛt] n. 插座
adapter [ə'dæptɚ] n. 轉接頭，轉接器

4.14 疑難排解——冷氣太強
Solving Problems—The Air Con

 Dialog 對話

A: 這是房務部門嗎？

A: Is this housekeeping?

基本對話

機場與飛機

入境

住宿

交通

餐飲

觀光

購物

郵電

銀行

麻煩事

回國

基本對話

機場與飛機

入境

住宿

交通

餐飲

觀光

購物

郵電

銀行

麻煩事

回國

B: 是的。

B: Yes, it is.

A: 我房間太冷了。

A: My room is very cold.

B: 你調整過溫度嗎？

B: Did you adjust the temperature?

A: 有，但是沒有用。

A: Yes, I did, but it didn't work.

B: 我會立刻派人去幫你檢查。

B: I'll send someone immediately to check for you.

A: 但是我很快就要出門了。

A: But I must leave very soon.

B: 別擔心，你可以離開，房務人員會處理。

B: Don't worry. You can leave. The housekeepers will take care of it.

Word Bank 字庫

adjust [ə'dʒʌst] v. 調整
temperature ['tɛmprətʃə-] n. 溫度
take care of 處理

4.15 退房
Checking Out

Dialog 1 對話1

A: 我要退房。

A: I need to check out.

B: 好的,先生,請給我鑰匙。

B: Yes, sir. The key, please.

A: 在這邊。

A: Here it is.

B: 我來準備你的收據。

B: I'll prepare your receipt.

Dialog 2 對話2

A: 先生,另有一筆 4 元的市內電話費帳單。

A: Sir, there is an additional \$4.00 charge for local calls.

B: 知道了。還有別的嗎?

B: I see. Anything else?

A: 是的,還有外加的客房服務費用。

A: Yes. There are additional charges for room service.

B: 好,請加到我的信用卡收費。

B: Fine. Please add it to my credit card charges.

基本對話 機場與飛機 入境 住宿 交通 餐飲 觀光 購物 郵電 銀行 麻煩事 回國

基本對話
機場與飛機
入境
住宿
交通
餐飲
觀光
購物
郵電
銀行
麻煩事
回國

A: 沒問題。可以再給我一次你的信用卡嗎？

A: Certainly. May I have your card again?

✎ Word Bank 字庫

check out 退房
receipt [rɪ'sit] n. 收據
additional [ə'dɪʃənl] adj. 另外的，外加的
add [æd] v. 添加

📖 Useful Phrases 實用語句

1. 有其他費用嗎？

   Are there any other charges?

2. 我可以要一份價目表嗎？

   Can I have a price brochure?

3. 這個飯店有其他地點 (連鎖分店) 嗎？

   Does this hotel have other locations?

4. 我想另外訂房。

   I'd like to make another reservation.

Tips 小祕訣

　　有些旅館會收取免付費 1-800 字頭電話的使用費，每通約 50 分錢。若要在外聽旅館房間的答錄機留言，出門前要先問櫃臺是否要有密碼才能聽到。若在外面打電話回旅館聽留言，剛好碰到旅館人員忙碌、不能親自接電話時，你將會聽到一長串語音要密碼，那可就累了。

　　退房後若需寄放行李，可以向行李員接洽，通常旅館可以免費提供寄放行李，行李員會給你暫存行李收據或號碼牌。取回行李時別忘了給小費。

4.16 叫車
Calling for Taxis

 Dialog 1 （對話1）

A: 王牌計程車服務派遣。

A: Ace Taxi Service dispatch.

B: 嗨，我在綠洲飯店，我需要一部計程車。

B: Hi. I'm at the Oasis Hotel. I need a cab.

A: 沒問題，先生。請問您的名字？

A: Certainly, sir. Your name, please?

B: 安迪石。

B: Andy Shih.

A: 好，你的計程車會在5到10分鐘內到達。

A: Very well. Your taxi should arrive within the next five to ten minutes.

B: 謝謝。

B: Thank you.

 Dialog 2 （對話2）

A: 石先生嗎？

A: Mr. Shih?

B: 是的，是我。

B: Yes, that's me.

基本對話

機場與飛機

入境

住宿

交通

餐飲

觀光

購物

郵電

銀行

麻煩事

回國

A: 我是你叫的計程車司機。

A: I'm the driver of the taxi you called for.

B: 嗨,我還有一件行李。

B: Hi. I have a piece of luggage, too.

A: 沒問題,我把它放到後車廂。

A: No problem. I'll put it in the trunk.

B: 請到機場。

B: To the airport, please.

A: 哪個航廈?

A: Which terminal?

B: 第二航廈

B: Number 2.

A: 好的。

A: OK.

Dialog 3 對話3

A: 到那裡要多久呢?

A: How long will it take to get there?

B: 看交通而定,但現在我猜差不多 20 到 30 分鐘。

B: It depends on the traffic, but right now I'd guess about twenty to thirty minutes.

A: 請走最快路線，我擔心會遲到。

A: Please take the fastest route. I'm afraid I'll be late.

B: 好的，沒問題。

B: Sure, no problem.

 Word Bank 字庫

dispatch [dɪ'spætʃ] n. 派遣
cab [kæb] n. 計程車
trunk [trʌŋk] n. 後車廂
route [rut] n. 路線

To the airport, please.

Which terminal?

基本對話

機場與飛機

入境

住宿

交通

餐飲

觀光

購物

郵電

銀行

麻煩事

回國

Unit 5 Transportation

交通

旅行時有許多交通工具可選擇。拜科技之賜,各類交通工具的 app 應運而生。出國前就能查詢時刻表規劃行程。為減少困惑及問路頻率,最好多做功課熟悉當地交通時刻及路線。為服務旅客,各大城市皆有多處旅遊資訊站,提供當地大眾運輸系統,如國內班機、巴士、地鐵、火車的資訊。要找計程車或租車公司機場就有,但租車最好事先上網預訂。如需查詢電話簿,在美可打 411。在旅館內或許可問到如何租腳踏車或摩托車及拿到通常免費的步行地圖。若有搭機行程,最好一開始就安排好,確定行程中的出入境轉機時間,搭機前則要先確認你的班機。

5.1 計程車——停著的計程車
Taxis—Parked Taxi

Dialog　對話

A: 你現在有服務嗎？

A: Are you in service?

B: 有，我剛剛只是在休息一下。

B: Yes. I was just resting a little.

A: 這計程車是跳錶的嗎？

A: Is this taxi metered?

B: 當然。起跳是2元，之後每1/4英里50分錢。

B: Yes, of course. Flag drop is $2, fifty cents a quarter mile after that.

A: 了解了，我們要去這個地址。

A: I see. We want to go to this address.

B: 我看一下。好的，沒問題。

B: Let me see. OK, no problem.

Useful Phrases　實用語句

1. 起跳多少錢？

   What's the flag rate? / What's the initial fare?

2. 有夜間加成嗎？

   Is there night surcharge?

3. 也有計時計費嗎？

   Is it metered by time, too?

基本對話｜機場與飛機｜入境｜住宿｜交通｜餐飲｜觀光｜購物｜郵電｜銀行｜麻煩事｜回國

4. 塞車時每分鐘收費多少？

> How much is charged each minute idle?

5.2 計程車——攔下的計程車
Taxis—Waved Down Taxi

Dialog 對話

A: 我們看秀遲到了，請趕快載我們到那邊。

A: We're late for a show. Please get us there quickly.

B: 沒問題。

B: Certainly.

Notes 小叮嚀

　　紐約大都市的街上就有許多計程車可隨時攔下，但晚上 8 點至早上 6 點會按夜間加成收費。此外公共交通工具也很普遍，算是美國少數大眾運輸比自己開車方便的地方。但在其他都市及城鎮，大部分的人都自己開車，這些地方若要搭計程車就得打電話叫車 (radio taxi)，也可以透過叫車 app。在大都市如紐約，許多計程車司機是移民，英語並非他們的母語，所以要多注意溝通。如果能寫下你要去的地址及隨身攜帶旅館名片或地圖，就可以避免走丟或走冤枉路。

　　有行李時，除了隨身提包，行李讓司機服務不要自己拿，給計程車司機的小費 (tip) 通常是 10-15% 或是讓司機留下找的零錢 (keep the change)。近年寬鬆政策物價攀升，一件小行李的小費約\$3，一到二件大行李約\$5, 二到四件以上大行李約\$10 (含小費)，到賭場的小費通常需要給的較多。

基本對話 / 機場與飛機 / 入境 / 住宿 / 交通 / 餐飲 / 觀光 / 購物 / 郵電 / 銀行 / 麻煩事 / 回國

基本對話

機場與飛機

入境

住宿

交通

餐飲

觀光

購物

郵電

銀行

麻煩事

回國

5.3 計程車——包車遊覽
Taxis—Taxi Tour

Dialog 對話

A: 司機，載兩個人在市內遊覽整天要多少錢？

A: Driver, how much would it cost to drive two people around the city all day?

B: 我載一位乘客收費 100 元，兩位 150 元。

B: I'll take one for $100, two for $150.

A: 真的，這在這城市還不錯。

A: Really, that's not bad for this city.

B: 是的，這是個好價錢。

B: Yes. It's a good price.

A: 我不想今天遊市區，要明天。

A: I don't want to do it today, but tomorrow.

B: 沒問題。你要我幾點來接你？

B: No problem. What time do you want me to pick you up?

A: 早上 9 點在這個旅館好嗎？

A: Is 9 a.m. at this hotel OK?

B: 好。

B: Sure.

Tips 小祕訣

　　若計程車有包車服務，可以跟司機商量價錢，價錢高低因景點是否熱門及交通方便與否而異。

5.4 地下鐵
The Subway

Dialog 1 對話1

A: 哪裡可以買到大眾運輸卡呢？

A: Where can I buy a mass transit card?

B: 在那邊的那個亭子。

B: At that booth over there.

A: (售票員) 我可以幫你嗎？

A: (Man in booth) May I help you?

B: 是的，我要買一張大眾運輸卡。

B: Yes. I'd like to buy a mass transit system card.

A: 好的，我們有不同種類，你需要幾天的？

A: OK. We have different kinds. How many days do you need?

B: 三天。

B: Three days.

基本對話
機場與飛機
入境
住宿
交通
餐飲
觀光
購物
郵電
銀行
麻煩事
回國

Dialog 2 對話2

A: 對不起，小姐，請問月臺的哪一側是往北？

A: Excuse me, miss. Which side of the platform goes north?

B: 你要到另一邊去。你要去哪裡呢？

B: You need to go to the other side. Where are you going?

A: 希爾德斯公園。

A: Hilders Park.

B: 那你要在兩站後轉車。

B: Then you'll need to transfer after two stops.

A: 多謝了。

A: Thanks very much.

Word Bank 字庫

mass transit card n. 大眾運輸卡

booth [buθ] n. 亭子

platform ['plæt,form] n. 月臺

Useful Phrases 實用語句

1. 我可以在哪裡買票呢？

   Where can I buy a ticket?

2. 你可以教我怎麼使用售票機嗎？

   Can you show me how to use the ticket machine?

3. 下一班地鐵何時來？

   When does the next subway train come?

4. 請坐下。

   Please sit down.

5. 沒關係，我站著就好。

   That's OK. I'll stand.

 Tips 小祕訣

地下鐵多有自動售票機，投入金額後取票找零。若無小鈔或零錢買票，旁邊會有零錢兌換機可以找開。有些城市對每張車票的使用時間有限制 (如 90 分鐘)，有些城市則有不同日數的交通票供觀光客選擇 (city pass)，在時限內可以無限制搭乘地鐵及公車。

在車上看到 priority seat 就是禮讓老弱婦孺的座位。在國外許多地區，腳踏車可以帶上地鐵，但是有些地方要為腳踏車買票。

5.5 市區巴士
City Bus

 Dialog 1 對話 1

A: 這是到市區的巴士嗎？

A: Is this the bus to downtown?

B: 是的。

B: Yes, it is.

A: 我現在付錢嗎？

A: Do I pay now?

B: 是的，把硬幣放進這個零錢箱。

B: Yes. Put your coins in this coin box.

基本對話

機場與飛機

入境

住宿

交通

餐飲

觀光

購物

郵電

銀行

麻煩事

回國

基本對話 ｜ 機場與飛機 ｜ 入境 ｜ 住宿 ｜ 交通 ｜ 餐飲 ｜ 觀光 ｜ 購物 ｜ 郵電 ｜ 銀行 ｜ 麻煩事 ｜ 回國

A: 好的。

A: OK.

Dialog 2 對話2

A: 我想要搭巴士到南波士頓。

A: I want to catch a bus to South Boston.

B: 你要搭 17 路到愛國區，然後下車轉搭 21 路公車。

B: You need to get on the 17 to Patriot Circle, then get off and transfer to bus 21.

A: 知道了，謝謝你。

A: I see. Thank you.

Notes 小叮嚀

看到 Exact change. 就是要準備好所需的零錢，不找零的喔！紐約、芝加哥等都會區的巴士班次頻繁，但其他地區則不然。許多歐洲城市的巴士站牌以電子螢幕顯示 (如地鐵站) 等待下班巴士須時多久，通常班次頻繁且到站時間精準。許多車票有時間限制，在第一次開始搭乘時一上車須自行過卡 (validate the ticket)，開始啟用該票。未過卡者，視為逃票，查到當然會有罰款。例如：購買三日票啟用過卡後，可搭任何交通工具，72 小時後自動失效。在義大利威尼斯 (Venice) 搭船跟搭公車一樣，船票使用方式相同。

Dialog 3 對話3

A: 這是我轉 21 路到南波士頓的地方嗎？

A: Is this where I transfer to bus 21 to South Boston?

B: 是的，就是這站。

B: Yes, this is the stop.

A: 公車多久來一班呢？

A: How often does the bus come?

B: 大約每隔 5 分鐘就來一班。

B: It comes about every five minutes.

A: 太棒了。

A: Great.

B: 有一班來了。

B: There's one coming now.

A: 謝謝。

A: Thanks.

 Useful Phrases （實用語句）

1. 我該在哪裡下車？

   Where should I get off?

2. 我下車的前一站站名是什麼？

   What's the name of the bus stop before I get off?

3. 我在哪裡轉車？

   Where do I transfer?

基本對話

機場與飛機

入境

住宿

交通

餐飲

觀光

購物

郵電

銀行

麻煩事

回國

5.6 灰狗巴士
Greyhound

 Dialog 1　對話 1

A: 我要搭巴士到德州達拉斯。

A: I want to take the bus to Dallas, Texas.

B: 好的,到達拉斯的巴士車資是 117 元 50 分,晚上 8 點才會到。

B: OK, the bus to Dallas costs $117.50. It will not arrive until 8 p.m.

A: 你可以現在收我的行李嗎?

A: Can you take my baggage now?

B: 好的,我們這裡會保管行李,並且看它放到車上。

B: Sure. We'll hold it here and see it gets put on the bus.

A: 要搭多久的車呢?

A: How long will the ride take?

B: 20 小時 34 分鐘。

B: Twenty hours and thirty four minutes.

A: 沿途要轉幾次車呢?

A: How many transfers along the way?

B: 這裡到達拉斯之間,你要轉兩次車。

B: You will have to transfer two times between here and Dallas.

Word Bank 字庫

Greyhound ['gre,haund] n. 灰狗巴士
transfer ['trænsfɚ, træns'fɚ] n., v. 轉車

Dialog 2 對話2

A: 各位旅客請上車。
A: Time to board.

B: 這是到德州達拉斯的巴士嗎?
B: Is this the bus to Dallas, Texas?

A: 是的。
A: Yes, it is.

B: 我有座位號碼嗎?
B: Do I have a seat number?

A: 沒有,是先到先坐。讓我查一下你的票。
A: No, it's first come, first serve. Let me check your ticket.

B: 在這裡。
B: Here it is.

A: 好的,你一切就緒,歡迎上車。
A: OK, you're set. Welcome aboard.

B: 車上可以抽菸嗎?
B: Can people smoke on the bus?

A: 車上任何地方都禁菸。

A: No smoking is allowed anywhere on the bus.

 Word Bank 字庫

First come, first serve. 先到先服務。
set [sɛt] adj. 準備好的
allow [əˈlau] v. 允許

 Dialog 3 對話3

A: 達拉斯轉車處，所有到達拉斯的乘客在這裡下車。

A: Dallas Transfer. All those going on to Dallas get off here.

B: 我們會在這裡待多久？

B: How long will we be here?

A: 去達拉斯的巴士半小時後會到這裡。

A: The bus to Dallas will be here in half an hour.

B: 這裡有東西吃嗎？

B: Is there anything to eat here?

A: 當然，站裡有一個點心吧及販賣機。

A: Sure. The station has a snack bar and vending machines.

B: 也有候車室嗎？

B: Is there a waiting lounge, too?

A: 有的。

A: Yes, there is.

Word Bank 字庫

snack bar n. 點心吧
vending machine n. 販賣機
waiting lounge n. 候車室

Tips 小祕訣

　　灰狗巴士為國營，至今已有百年歷史，跨越全美，甚至涵蓋加拿大與墨西哥。灰狗巴士路線也涵蓋整個澳洲大陸，雖不是最快的交通方式，但是價錢合理 (網路早鳥價格更低)，並且可以一睹鄉間景色，巴士清潔、舒適，駕駛員經驗豐富。

Useful Phrases 實用語句

1. 到達拉斯一張車票多少錢？

   How much is a ticket to Dallas?

2. 誰處理轉車行李？

   Who handles the luggage at the transfer?

3. 這趟車程要多久？

   How long is the trip?

4. 我們會在休息區停多少次？

   How many times will we stop at a rest area?

5. 我們多久會在休息區停一次？

   How often will we stop at a rest area?

6. 休息區有東西吃嗎？

   Is there anything to eat at the rest area?

基本對話

機場與飛機

入境

住宿

交通

餐飲

觀光

購物

郵電

銀行

麻煩事

回國

7. 我們可以帶食物及飲料上巴士嗎？

Can we bring food and drinks onto the bus?

8. 巴士上有洗手間嗎？

Is there a toilet on the bus?

9. 我們可以用巴士上的洗手間嗎？

Can we use the restroom on the bus?

10. 到下一個休息區還要多久？

How long will it be before we stop by the next rest area?

5.7 火車
Trains

Dialog 1 對話1

A: 我要一張到西雅圖的車票。

A: I need one ticket to Seattle.

B: 那是個三天的旅程，你要臥鋪嗎？

B: That's a three day trip. Do you want a sleeper?

A: 要多少錢呢？

A: How much does it cost?

B: 單趟 225 元。

B: $225 one way.

Dialog 2 對話2

A: 火車幾點出發到西雅圖呢？

A: What time does the train depart to Seattle?

B: 15 分鐘後出發，今天下午 5 點 43 分到。

B: It will depart in fifteen minutes. It arrives at 5:43 this afternoon.

A: 有餐車嗎？

A: Is there a dining car?

B: 有的，而且搭臥鋪的話，所有餐點全包。

B: Yes, there is, and all meals are included if you have a sleeper.

A: 真的嗎？

A: Really?

B: 還附飲料。

B: Including extra drinks.

Dialog 3 對話3

A: 我去哪裡上車呢？

A: Where do I go to get on the train?

B: 穿過這些大門。

B: Pass through these big doors.

A: 我向誰出示車票呢？

A: Who do I show my ticket to?

B: 服務員會在你上車前查票。

B: The attendants will check it before you board.

基本對話

機場與飛機

入境

住宿

交通

餐飲

觀光

購物

郵電

銀行

麻煩事

回國

146

基本對話

機場與飛機

入境

住宿

交通

餐飲

觀光

購物

郵電

銀行

麻煩事

回國

Word Bank 字庫

sleeper ['slipɚ] n. 臥鋪
dining car n. 餐車

Tips 小祕訣

　　美國國鐵 (Amtrak) 是美國全國性的鐵路系統，旅客可以透過網路、app 或電話查詢及訂票。美國國鐵經過大小城鎮，提供與飛機上類似的服務。

Dialog 4 對話4

A: 餐車開了嗎？

A: Is the dining car open now?

B: 喔，是的，這班車的餐車隨時都開放。

B: Oh, yes. It's open all the time on this run.

A: 也有雞尾酒嗎？

A: Do you have cocktails, too?

B: 我們有各式飲料。

B: We have all types of beverages available.

A: 我們可以在我們的房裡喝酒嗎？

A: Can we drink alcohol in our private rooms?

B: 可以。

B: Yes, you may.

A: 也可以在景觀車內嗎？	**A:** Is it OK in the viewing cars, too?
B: 抱歉，你不可以在大眾區喝酒。	**B:** Sorry, you're not allowed to drink liquor in general passenger areas.

Word Bank 字庫

run [rʌn] n. 路線，班次
cocktail ['kɑk,tel] n. 雞尾酒
beverage ['bɛvərɪdʒ] n. 飲料
private ['praɪvɪt] adj. 私人的
viewing car n. 景觀車
alcohol ['ælkə,hɔl], liquor ['lɪkɚ] n. 酒

Useful Phrases 實用語句

1. 我們什麼時候離開？
   When do we go?
2. 我們什麼時候會到？
   When will we arrive?
3. 我們可以在哪兒用餐呢？
   Where can we eat?

Language Power 字句補給站

◆ 火車 Train

ticket window	售票窗口
train station	火車站
boarding platform	乘車月臺
conductor	車掌
passenger	乘客

基本對話

機場與飛機

入境

住宿

交通

餐飲

觀光

購物

郵電

銀行

麻煩事

回國

基本對話

first class	頭等車廂
coach class	普通車廂
lounge car	休閒車廂
dining car	餐車
sleeper	臥鋪
departure	出發
arrival	抵達
one-way ticket	單程車票
round-trip ticket	來回車票
destination	目的地

機場與飛機

入境

住宿

5.8 船舶
The Ferry

Dialog 對話

交通

餐飲

觀光

購物

郵電

銀行

麻煩事

回國

A: 我們要把車載到對面。

A: We want to take our car to the other side.

B: 那要多 5 元。

B: It costs five dollars more.

A: 你可以告訴我下一班渡輪何時開嗎?

A: Can you tell us when the next ferry leaves?

B: 時刻表上是排在 5 點離開。

B: It's scheduled to leave at 5:00.

A: 到對岸要花多久時間呢?

A: How long does it take to reach the other side?

B: 大約 40 分鐘。

B: About forty minutes.

A: 我們過河時一定要待在自己車裡嗎？

A: Do we have to stay in our car while crossing?

B: 不必，裡面有很多位子，還有一間餐廳。

B: No. There is plenty of seating inside, and a restaurant.

 Word Bank 字庫

ferry ['fɛrɪ] n. 渡輪
schedule ['skɛdʒul] v. 排入時刻表
reach [ritʃ] v. 抵達
cross [krɔs] v. 橫越，橫渡

 Useful Phrases 實用語句

1. 我們在哪裡上船？

   Where do we board?

2. 哪一班渡船去史達坦島呢？

   Which ferry goes to Staten Island?

3. 這是去史達坦島的渡船嗎？

   Is this the ferry to Staten Island?

4. 搭渡船多少錢呢？

   How much does it cost to take the ferry?

5. 渡輪多久來一班呢？

   How often does the ferry come?

6. 我可以要一份渡輪的小冊子嗎？

   Can I have a brochure of the ferry?

7. 我可以要一份時刻表嗎？

Can I have a timetable?

8. 我們到達前有幾站呢？

How many stops are there before we arrive?

9. 你可以告訴我路線嗎？

Can you tell me the route?

10. 渡輪何時回來？

When does the ferry come back?

11. 渡輪最晚幾點從這裡離開？

What time does the last ferry leave from here?

12. 回程渡輪最晚幾點開船？

What time does the last ferry leave to come back?

Tips　小祕訣

　　渡輪有各種大小，有些只搭載乘客，有些也搭載交通工具。在美國及加拿大主要水域，渡輪來往頻繁，不止搭載觀光客、居民，也搭載商業車輛或通勤車輛。

5.9 租車——取車
Car Rental—Picking Up the Rental Car

Dialog 1　對話1

A: 我想要租一輛車。

A: I'd like to rent a car.

B: 你有信用卡嗎？

B: Do you have a credit card?

A: 有。	A: Yes, I do.
B: 你要什麼樣的車？	B: What kind of car do you want?
A: 中型轎車。	A: A mid-size sedan.

 Word Bank 字庫

pick up 領，取
rental car n. 租來的車
mid-size ['mɪd,saɪz] adj. 中型的
sedan [sɪ'dæn] n. 轎車

 Useful Phrases 實用語句

1. 你們有什麼樣的車可租呢？

   What kinds of cars do you have available?

2. 你們的車多老呢？

   How old are your cars?

3. 我可以在另一個城市歸還車子嗎？

   Can I drop it off in a different city?

4. 這是我的國際駕照。

   Here is my international driver's license.

5. 這是我的證件。

   Here is my I.D.

基本對話

機場與飛機

入境

住宿

交通

餐飲

觀光

購物

郵電

銀行

麻煩事

回國

Dialog 2 對話2

A: 我們有預訂。

A: We have a reservation.

B: 請給我你的駕照和信用卡。

B: I need your driver's license and credit card, please.

A: 在這裡。

A: Here you are.

B: 好的,楊先生,大型車兩天。一位或兩位駕駛呢?

B: OK, Mr. Young, a full size car for two days. Is it going to be one or two drivers?

A: 兩位。你們有多收另外駕駛費嗎?

A: Two. Do you charge more for additional drivers?

B: 沒有,但我需要看全部的駕照。

B: No, we don't, but I need to see all the driver's licenses.

A: 在這邊。

A: Here they are.

B: 我們現在有Toyota Camry及 Nissan Altima,你要哪一款?

B: We have Toyota Camry and Nissan Altima right now. Which do you prefer?

A: 我們開過 Toyota Camry,所以這次試試Nissan Altima。

A: We had Toyota Camry before, so we'll try an Altima this time.

Language Power 字句補給站

租車 Car Rental

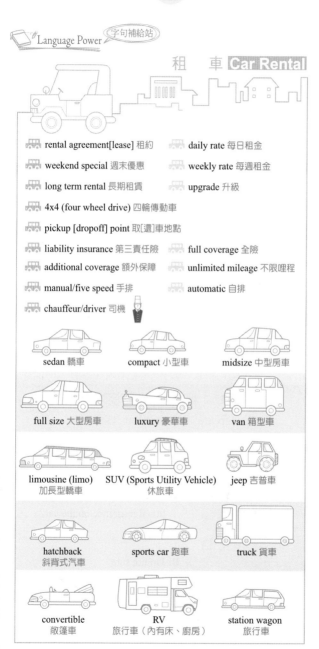

- rental agreement[lease] 租約
- weekend special 週末優惠
- long term rental 長期租賃
- 4x4 (four wheel drive) 四輪傳動車
- pickup [dropoff] point 取[還]車地點
- liability insurance 第三責任險
- additional coverage 額外保障
- manual/five speed 手排
- chauffeur/driver 司機
- daily rate 每日租金
- weekly rate 每週租金
- upgrade 升級
- full coverage 全險
- unlimited mileage 不限哩程
- automatic 自排

sedan 轎車
compact 小型車
midsize 中型房車
full size 大型房車
luxury 豪華車
van 箱型車
limousine (limo) 加長型轎車
SUV (Sports Utility Vehicle) 休旅車
jeep 吉普車
hatchback 斜背式汽車
sports car 跑車
truck 貨車
convertible 敞篷車
RV 旅行車（內有床、廚房）
station wagon 旅行車

基本對話 機場與飛機 入境 住宿 交通 餐飲 觀光 購物 郵電 銀行 麻煩事 回國

Tips 小祕訣

　　如果當地道路左右駕駛習慣不同、看標誌有語言問題、需雪地或結冰的道路開車等情況，國人駕駛習慣恐未能勝任，安全起見應考慮其他交通工具 (各國對我國際駕照態度及注意事項可查詢外交部全球資訊網)。在美國租車必須年滿 21 歲，許多租車公司對 25 歲 (被視為駕駛漸趨安全之年齡) 以下駕駛每日加收昂貴的未足齡費用 (underage surcharge)，並限制可租車種。租車公司常會推出優惠方案，如週末優惠 (weekend special)，或是超過五天就算一星期，適用較便宜的每週租金。即使在機場，並非每一家租車公司都是 24 小時營業，一定要先行確認取還車時間能配合 (早晚) 班機。機場租車較貴 (含機場建設捐等諸多稅賦)，但方便性及車種車況等條件較佳。為避免租到較差的車，可以先看車再簽租車同意書。取車還車時記得要與服務人員一起檢查車況，並確定如何操作雨刷、頭燈、方向燈及後照鏡等。此外在美國租車沒有隔熱貼紙 (tinted glass) 是正常的。許多州即使允許使用，也對一般車輛隔熱貼紙的顏色限制在淺色程度。為方便導航及繳交過路費，可租用 GPS 及 I-Pass (或 E-Pass 各地名稱不一)，或下載離線導航地圖。離開租車公司前不妨向櫃臺要一份地圖。

5.10 租車──租車保險
Car Rental—Rental Car Insurance

Dialog 對話

A: 先生，你的車要多保點險嗎？

A: Sir, would you like to add additional insurance on the car?

B: 我不確定。

B: I'm not sure.

A: 州政府規定至少要保最低限度的意外責任險。

A: The State requires that you have at least minimum liability.

B: 我買這個，我要確定我有合法保障。

B: I'll buy it. I want to make sure I'm legally covered.

A: 這只要每天多加 7 元。

A: It will only cost an additional $7 a day.

B: 它保障什麼呢？

B: What does it cover?

A: 碰撞及傷害。

A: Collision and injury.

✏️ Word Bank 字庫

additional [ə'dɪʃənl] adj. 額外的，外加的
insurance [ɪn'ʃurəns] n. 保險
minimum ['mɪnəməm] a. 最低限的，最少量的
liability [ˌlaɪə'bɪlətɪ] n. 責任
collision [kə'lɪʒən] n. 碰撞
injury ['ɪndʒərɪ] n. 傷害

基本對話

機場與飛機

入境

住宿

交通

餐飲

觀光

購物

郵電

銀行

麻煩事

回國

基本對話 | 機場與飛機 | 入境 | 住宿 | 交通 | 餐飲 | 觀光 | 購物 | 郵電 | 銀行 | 麻煩事 | 回國

Tips 小祕訣

　　租車交易使用信用卡收費，且網路預訂時可能就要支付車子租金，到租車公司領車時再加保險費。出國前可以詢問信用卡公司是否有任何租車優惠及是否提供不需額外付費的保險。租車時如果只買第三責任險 (liability)，即保障因自己過失引起他人身體或財產損失，保障其實是不夠的。如果租車天數不是很長，保費還付得起的話，可以考慮買保費較高但有完全保障的全險 (full coverage insurance)，如此就不必擔心在國外可能發生的任何大小租車意外了。

　　記得除國際駕照 (臺灣的國際駕照其實只是 driving permit 駕駛許可) 外，也要帶本國駕照備查。若有其他駕駛換手開車，可以大為減少開車旅遊的疲累，但有些地區的租車公司因為保險的關係，要求第二駕駛登記於租約上，並收取每日將近 10 美元的另外駕駛費 (additional driver charge)，如此就要再多一筆花費了。

5.11 租車——還車
Car Rental—Dropping Off the Rental Car

Dialog 1 對話1

A: 嗨，我要還車。	A: Hi, I want to return my rental.
B: 請讓我看你的租約。	B: Please let me see your rental agreement form.
A: 在這裡。	A: Here you go.
B: 好，一切看來很好。你把車停哪兒？	B: OK. Everything looks good. Where did you leave the car?

A: 就在外面，鑰匙在裡面。

A: Right out front. The key is in it.

B: 好極了。汽油是滿的嗎？

B: Perfect. Is it full of gas?

A: 是的。

A: Yes, it is.

B: 好的，我們的服務員會處理剩下的事。

B: OK. Our attendants will take care of the rest.

A: 我還需要簽什麼嗎？

A: Do I need to sign anything else?

B: 不必，但要確定取走你所有的物品。

B: No, but make sure you took all your things out of the car.

Dialog 2 (對話2)

A: (租車公司人員) 嗨，你今天好嗎？

A: (Car Rental Clerk) Hi, how're you doing today?

B: 好。

B: Fine.

A: 你要還車嗎？

A: Are you returning your car?

基本對話
機場與飛機
入境
住宿
交通
餐飲
觀光
購物
郵電
銀行
麻煩事
回國

B: 是的。

B: Yes.

A: 好，我檢查一下。

A: Ok. Let me check it.

B: 好的。

B: Sure.

A: (檢查車子及汽油) 很好，這是你的收據，金額和租約上寫的一樣。

A: (checking the car and the gas) Alright. Here's your receipt, same amount as on your rental agreement.

B: 謝謝。

B: Thank you.

✎ Word Bank 字庫

amount [ə'maunt] n. 金額，總額

159

gas 有瓦斯及汽油 (gasoline的簡稱) 的意思。如果要在不同城市還車，要先告知租車公司，在租約上註明，否則可能會被罰款。因為需要處理調度問題，大多數租車公司對甲地租乙地還 (one-way rentals) 收取較貴租金。還車時間要注意不要遲到，否則可能會被加收一天租金。如果取車時為滿油狀態，還車時記得要加滿油，否則不足的汽油部分，租車公司會用較高的費用來計算。有的租車公司以稍低於市面的油價推出跑光汽油案，對大多數不精於計算或不想冒險跑光汽油的消費者而言，其實並不划算。規模大的機場租車公司，還車時一駛入租車公司之停車場內，租車公司人員在掌上電腦內輸入車號，檢查車況及查看汽油，甚至不必看租約，你也不必進辦公室，收據馬上就印出來，非常有效率。

還車時間要注意不要遲到，否則可能會被加收一天租金。美國不僅有不同時區 (共 6 個時區，某些州有兩個)，絕大多數州 (除夏威夷州及亞利桑那州外) 並實行日光節約時間 (daylight saving time, DST)，在三月第二個週日往前撥快 1 小時 (半夜兩點變三點)，十一月第一個週日往後撥慢 1 小時 (半夜兩點變一點)。相鄰的兩個城市如果分屬不同時區，即使只有數哩之遙，也可能因未注意時間差異而耽誤了還車或班機時間。除美國外，歐洲澳洲一樣有地區時差及實施日光節約時間。

5.12 加油——自助加油
At the Gas Station—Self Service

Dialog 1 對話1

A: 我可以幫你嗎，先生？

A: Can I help you, sir?

B: 是的，這個幫浦我沒法加油。

B: Yes. I can't get any gas from this pump.

基本對話 / 機場與飛機 / 入境 / 住宿 / 交通 / 餐飲 / 觀光 / 購物 / 郵電 / 銀行 / 麻煩事 / 回國

基本對話 機場與飛機 入境 住宿 **交通** 餐飲 觀光 購物 郵電 銀行 麻煩事 回國

A: 我來幫你。

A: Let me help you.

B: 我不太清楚怎麼加油。

B: I'm not familiar with pumping gas.

A: 沒問題,大家常覺得滿頭霧水。

A: No problem. People often find it confusing.

B: 是啊,我知道,我學到了幫浦都不大一樣。

B: Yes, I know. I have learned that the pumps are not all the same.

A: 沒錯。

A: That's right.

Word Bank 字庫

pump [pʌmp] n. 幫浦;v. 抽出
familiar [fə'mɪljɚ] adj. 熟悉的
confusing [kən'fjuzɪŋ] adj. 令人困惑的

Tips 小祕訣

　　自助加油有幾個步驟,跟著油臺 (island) 上的指示操作即可:使用信用卡插入刷卡後取出、稍待一下、取下油槍放入加油口、選擇汽油種類、開始按下加油柄加油、結束後印出收據。某些地區的油臺設計會要求輸入居住地的郵遞區號 (zip code) 共五碼才授權加油。外國人的信用卡是在外國發出的,輸入美國郵遞區號可能被拒絕,此時必須到櫃臺刷卡。另一種方式是用現金加油,必須先到櫃臺付錢及告知油臺號碼,櫃臺人員依照加油金額設定後,即可開始加油。

小輔車使用美國的無鉛汽油 (unleaded)，名稱各家不同，分類為普通 (regular，87)、高級 (plus / mid-grade，89)，以及超級 (supreme / premium / v-power，91) 等，當然還有卡車用的柴油 (diesel)，也已改為無鉛。如果加到一定金額，可以較低價格加購洗車，免費洗車幾乎已成絕響。

 Dialog 2 （對話2）

A: (與出納員對話) 請加 20 元汽油。(付 20 元)

A: (talking to the cashier) Twenty dollars of gas, please. (paying $20 cash)

B: 哪一臺加油機？

B: Which pump number?

A: 三號。

A: Number 3.

B: 好。

B: Ok.

(自己加油)

(pumping gas him / herself)

 Useful Phrases （實用語句）

1. 請加 20 元 (汽油)。

   Twenty dollars worth, please.

2. 我要付現。

   I'll pay cash.

3. 我要刷卡。

   I'll charge it.

基本對話

機場與飛機

入境

住宿

交通

餐飲

觀光

購物

郵電

銀行

麻煩事

回國

4. 你們這裡有洗車嗎？

Do you have a car wash here?

Tips 小祕訣

　　加油站多提供類似的服務：加油、清洗擋風玻璃、檢查機油及胎壓。你可以選擇自助式 (self service)，價格較低，或是選擇全套服務 (full service) 請加油站人員幫忙，價格較高。自助加油全部自己來，當然不必給小費。全套服務售價已較高 (因含服務)，傳統上不必給小費，加油站員工也不會期待小費，但是在較富裕的州或大城市，給不給小費要看當地習慣是否已漸改變，依照服務多寡給 1-5 元也算常見。有些州如奧勒岡州，為安全起見並不允許自助加油，所有加油站都是全套服務，該州仍維持不必給小費的習慣。有些加油站的洗手間是上鎖的，只供顧客使用，必須向櫃臺索取鑰匙，使用後歸還。

5.13 加油──全套服務
At the Gas Station—Full Service

Dialog 1 對話1

A: 請加滿超級汽油。

A: Fill it up with premium, please.

B: 付現或刷卡？

B: Cash or charge? / Cash or credit?

A: 刷卡，卡在這裡。

A: Charge. Here's my card.

B: 好，等一下，我現在幫你加油。(加完油) 總共是 $ 27.75。(歸還信用卡) 這是你的卡，先生。

B: OK, just a second. I'll pump your gas in now. (after pumping the gas) It came to $27.75. (retuning the card) Here's your card, sir.

A: 我不用簽任何東西嗎？

A: Don't I need to sign anything?

B: 不用，先生。

B: No, sir.

A: 謝謝。

A: Thanks.

Dialog 2 (對話2)

A: 請你幫我洗擋風玻璃好嗎？

A: Would you please wash my windshield?

B: 當然。

B: Sure.

A: 我還需要請你看一下水及機油。

A: Also, I need the water and oil checked.

B: 好，我會替你檢查那些。

B: OK. I'll take care of those for you.

A: 多謝了。

A: Thanks a lot.

 Word Bank 字庫

premium ['primɪəm] adj. 特優的
charge [tʃɑrdʒ] v. 記帳
windshield ['wɪndˌʃild] n. 擋風玻璃
oil [ɔɪl] n. 機油

 Useful Phrases 實用語句

1. 請加滿。

   Fill it up, please.

2. 普通汽油加滿。

   Fill it up with Regular.

3. 請加 10 元 (汽油)。

   Ten dollars worth, please.

4. 請洗車窗。

   Wash the windows, please.

5. 請檢查機油量。

   Check the oil level, please.

6. 請查看胎壓。

   Check the tire air pressure, please.

5.14 洗車
Car Wash

Dialog 1 對話1

A: 嗨，我要洗車。我怎麼做呢？

A: Hi, I want my car washed. How do I do it?

B: 在這裡付錢，然後開到洗車機入口。

B: Pay here, and then drive over to the entrance of the car wash.

A: 多少錢呢？

A: How much does it cost?

B: 如果只是簡單洗車，是 5 元。

B: If you want a simple car wash, it's $5.

A: 豪華洗車多少錢？

A: How much is a deluxe car wash?

B: 加 2 元。

B: It's two dollars more.

A: 兩者有何差別呢？

A: What's the difference between them?

B: 豪華洗車包含上兩次清潔劑、車底清潔，以及手工擦乾。

B: The deluxe includes double soaping, undercarriage cleaning and hand wipe down.

基本對話

機場與飛機

入境

住宿

交通

餐飲

觀光

購物

郵電

銀行

麻煩事

回國

基本對話
機場與飛機
入境
住宿
交通
餐飲
觀光
購物
郵電
銀行
麻煩事
回國

A: 我要豪華洗車。

A: I'll take the deluxe wash.

Word Bank 字庫

undercarriage [ˈʌndəˌkærɪdʒ] n. 汽車底盤
wipe [waɪp] v. 擦拭

 Dialog 2 對話2

A: 不好意思，你要把天線收起來。

A: Excuse me. You need to remove the antenna.

B: 好的，沒問題，但我不知道怎麼正確進入洗車道。

B: Sure, no problem, but I'm not sure how to enter the car wash correctly.

A: 不必擔心，很簡單的，只要往前慢慢開，直到左前輪滑進夾板內。

A: Don't worry. It's easy. Just pull ahead until the left front tire slips into the clamp.

B: 然後呢？

B: Then what?

A: 然後把車子排到空檔，洗車系統會做剩下的事。

A: Then put the car in neutral, the car washing system will do the rest.

Word Bank 字庫

antenna [æn'tɛnə] n. 天線
pull [pʊl] v. 行駛，滑行
slip [slɪp] v. 滑動
clamp [klæmp] n. 夾板
neutral ['njutrəl] n. 空檔

Useful Phrases 實用語句

1. 我付錢給誰？
   Who do I pay?
2. 我在哪裡付錢？
   Where do I pay?
3. 要多久？
   How long does it take?

Tips 小祕訣

你可以在加油站或洗車店洗車，此外也有人工洗車，近來費用上漲，約在 10-15 美元間。許多高中生或社會人士會以人工洗車的方式來募款，如此所支付的洗車費便是用在成就善事。

5.15 停車 Parking

Dialog 對話

A: 我想在這裡停車。

A: I want to park here.

B: 好，看來你要拿一張票。

B: Fine. Looks like you need to take a ticket.

A: 好，現在呢？

A: OK. Now what?

B: 那個指標說，我們停在任何空位都可以。

B: That sign says we can park in any empty spot.

A: 那簡單。

A: It's pretty easy.

B: 我們怎麼付費呢？

B: How do we pay?

A: 我們離開時在出口付給收費員。

A: We pay the cashier at the exit when we leave.

Word Bank　字庫

spot [spɑt] n. 地點，位置
cashier [kæˈʃɪr] n. 出納員

Notes 小叮嚀

　　停車的地方一定要記牢。許多美國購物中心停車場非常大，還有各個不同的方向和樓層，遊樂場的停車區 (如迪士尼) 更是超大。即使停在市區路邊，因道路不熟，也要特別記住停車位置。停車費在大都市或熱門海灘遊樂區，可能每小時就要 5 到 7 美元。有些停車場提供到某些餐廳或商店消費可抵一小時的優惠，這時要記得請商家在停車卡上蓋章 (Please validate my parking card.)。

5.16 駕駛——收費公路
Driving—Toll Roads

Dialog 1 對話1

A: 嘿，找些零錢，我們快要付過路費了。

A: Hey. Find some change. We have to pay a toll soon.

B: 真的嗎？這是收費道路嗎？

B: Really? This is a toll road?

A: 是啊，我們大約每十英里路就要付一次錢。

A: Yes. We have to pay a toll every ten miles or so.

B: 多少錢呢？

B: How much is it?

A: 75 分。

A: Seventy five cents.

基本對話
機場與飛機
入境
住宿
交通
餐飲
觀光
購物
郵電
銀行
麻煩事
回國

B: 我們可以給 1 元嗎？

B: Can we give them a dollar?

A: 可以，但是不找零。

A: Sure, but we'll get no change.

 Dialog 2 對話2

A: 嗨，我要買一本回數票。

A: Hi, I'd like to buy a book of toll tickets.

B: 我們的系統不用回數票，但你可以買通行卡。

B: There are no tickets for our system, but you can buy a pass card.

A: 通行卡有多少金額的呢？

A: What amounts are they available in?

B: 30 元是最便宜的，其中 10 元可以退費。

B: Thirty dollars is the cheapest. Ten dollars of that is refundable.

A: 只能在主要收費道路使用嗎？

A: Are they good for only the main toll way?

B: 不，你可以在這三州內任何地方使用。

B: No. You can use them anywhere in the Tri-State area.

Word Bank 字庫

toll [tol] n. 通行費，過路費
change [tʃendʒ] n. 零錢
toll ticket n. 回數票
pass card n. 通行卡
refundable [rɪˈfʌndəbl] adj. 可退費的

Useful Phrases 實用語句

1. 這是收費公路嗎？

   Is this a toll road?

2. 我要回數票。

   I need toll tickets.

3. 我要收費公路通行卡。

   I need a toll road pass.

Tips 小祕訣

　　收費公路在美東比美西普遍。有些地段你會收到一張計費票，千萬別弄丟，行駛到某一路段時會有收費亭，必須停車依票繳費。在其他公路上有些是機器收費，要你丟零錢進去桿子才會拉起放行。美西舊金山灣區則有許多收費橋樑 (toll bridge)，有的是單向收費。在許多收費站有不同收費方式的車道，不要走錯了。回數票 (toll ticket) 及電子卡 (e-card) 是當地居民會用的，至於觀光客就走現金 (cash)、找零 (change) 或不找零 (no change) 車道吧。

基本對話

機場與飛機

入境

住宿

交通

餐飲

觀光

購物

郵電

銀行

麻煩事

回國

5.17 駕駛──高速公路標示
Driving—Highway Signs

Dialog 1 對話1

A: 這裡速限是多少？

A: What is the speed limit here?

B: 我不知道。

B: I don't know.

A: 找一個路旁有數字的標誌。

A: Look for a sign along the road with a number on it.

B: 那邊，看那邊，I-95。哇！那可真快。

B: There. Look there. I-95. Wow! That's fast.

A: 不，不是，那不是速限標誌。

A: No, no. That's not a speed limit sign.

B: 不是嗎？那是什麼？

B: It's not? What is it?

A: 那標誌告訴我們現在是在哪條高速公路上。

A: That sign tells us which highway we are on.

B: 喔。

B: Oh.

Word Bank 字庫

speed [spid] n. 速度
limit ['lɪmɪt] n. 限制

 Dialog 2 對話2

A: 我還是不知道在這條高速公路上我們可以開多快。

A: I still don't know how fast we can drive on this highway.

B: 我看到前方另一個標誌了。

B: I see another sign ahead.

A: 我也看到了。是的，那是個速限標誌，寫著 75mph。

A: I see it, too. Yes, that's a speed limit sign. It says, 75 mph.

B: 所以那表示這裡可以開到每小時 75 英里。

B: So that means it's OK to go seventy five miles per hour here.

A: 是的，沒錯。那很好，我們會在兩小時內到達芝加哥。

A: Yes, that's right. That's good. We'll be in Chicago within two hours.

B: 知道了真好。

B: That's nice to know.

Word Bank 字庫

mph n. 每小時英里數 (miles per hour)

基本對話

機場與飛機

入境

住宿

交通

餐飲

觀光

購物

郵電

銀行

麻煩事

回國

Useful Phrases 實用語句

1. 那個標誌說什麼？(what's 是 what is / has 之縮寫，把 what's 當作 what does 是文法不當，卻經常聽到的隨性口語。)

   What's that sign say?

2. 找里程標示。

   Look for the mileage signs.

Cultural Tips 文化祕笈

重要交通標誌 Important Traffic Signs

no U turn 禁止迴轉

one way 單行道

caution 小心

yield 讓

speed limit 速限

car pool lane 共乘車道

Tips 小祕訣

　　每個州 (甚至每個郡或市) 都有自己的交通法規。到最近的類似監理處的機動車輛部門 (Department of Motor Vehicles，簡稱 DMV) 去拿一份駕駛手冊，可以幫自己很快了解當地的交通標誌及駕駛法規。如果在美國看到重型機車行駛高速公路，別太驚訝，這是合法的 (臺灣也已開放重機行駛快速道路)，小型摩托車並不常見，但一般而言不騎上高速公路就可以。各州對摩托車大小、行駛規定不盡相同，一般人也少用普通機車代步。

Language Power 字句補給站

◆ 常見交通標誌 Common Traffic Signs

northbound	北向
southbound	南向
exit 12	12 號出口
San Diego 60 miles	距聖地牙哥 60 英里
stop	停車
crosswalk	行人穿越道
rest stop	休息站
rest area	休息區
men working	人員工作中
construction ahead	前方施工
do not pass	禁止超車
school zone	學校區域
lights on	開燈
tunnel	隧道
ramp	斜坡；高速公路引道
overpass	高架橋；天橋
underpass	橋下通道；地下道
no parking	禁止停車
4 way stop	四面停車
do not enter	禁止進入
no left turn	禁止左轉
no right turn	禁止右轉
slow	慢行

基本對話

機場與飛機

入境

住宿

交通

餐飲

觀光

購物

郵電

銀行

麻煩事

回國

基本對話

機場與飛機

入境

住宿

交通

餐飲

觀光

購物

郵電

銀行

麻煩事

回國

toll station	收費站
tollbooth	收費亭
exact change	不找零車道
change lane	找零車道
electronic pass lane / e-lane	電子掃描收費道
ticket only	回數票車道
gas, food and lodging ahead	前有加油站、用餐及住宿
recreation area	休閒遊樂區
scenic area	景觀區
scenic route	風景路線

5.18 駕駛——警察攔停
Driving—Stopped by Police

Dialog 1 （對話1）

A: 有輛警車在我們後面閃紅藍燈。

A: There is a police car behind us with its red and blue lights flashing.

B: 真的嗎？那表示我們必須停車。

B: Really? That means we have to stop the car.

A: 好，我要在這寬點的地方靠邊停車。（等待警察走到車子）

A: OK. I'll pull over here where it's wider. (waiting for the officer to come up to the car)

C: 午安，我可以看你的駕照嗎？

C: Good afternoon. May I see your driver's license, please?

A: 在這裡，警察先生。

A: Here it is, officer.

基本對話

機場與飛機

入境

住宿

交通

餐飲

觀光

購物

郵電

銀行

麻煩事

回國

C: 你有行照嗎？

C: Do you have the registration for this car?

A: 我不認為我有，這是租來的車。

A: I don't think so. It's a rental car.

C: 知道了，我可以看一下你的租賃契約嗎？

C: I see. May I see your rental agreement?

A: 好的，在這裡。

A: Sure. Here it is.

Word Bank 字庫

flash [flæʃ] v. 閃爍
pull over 開到路邊
registration [ˌrɛdʒɪˈstreʃən] n. 登記

Dialog 2 對話2

A: 警察先生，我做錯什麼了嗎？

A: Did I do something wrong, officer?

B: 你在過橋時超車。

B: You passed a car while crossing the bridge.

A: 那是違法的嗎？

A: Is that illegal?

基本對話

機場與飛機

入境

住宿

交通

餐飲

觀光

購物

郵電

銀行

麻煩事

回國

B: 在本州是的，你要小心那個 (規定)。

B: It is in this State. You have to be careful about that.

A: 我不知道那樣不行。

A: I didn't know it's not all right.

B: 好，這次我只給你口頭警告。

B: OK, I'm only going to give you a verbal warning this time.

A: 真感謝你。

A: Thank you very much.

B: 小心開車，還有我建議你注意本地的開車規定。

B: Drive carefully, and I suggest you check out the local driving regulations.

 Word Bank 字庫

illegal [ɪ'ligl̩] adj. 違法的
verbal ['vɝbl̩] adj. 口頭的
warning ['wɔrnɪŋ] n. 警告
suggest [sə'dʒɛst] v. 建議
regulation [ˌrɛgjə'leʃən] n. 規定

Useful Phrases 實用語句

1. 這是我的駕照。

   Here's my license.

2. 我可以知道是什麼問題嗎？

   May I ask what the problem is?

179

3. 我從外國來，拜訪這城市一週。

I'm from another country. I'm visiting the city for a week.

4. 抱歉，警察先生，我現在起會更小心。

Sorry, officer. I'll be more careful from now on.

5. 我要怎樣繳罰款？

How do I pay the fine?

5.19 駕駛──救護車
Driving—Ambulance

Dialog 對話

A: 不好了，我們又要被警察攔車了。
A: Oh, no! We're being stopped by the police again.

B: 我不敢相信，今天兩次了。
B: I can't believe it. That's twice today.

A: 真難以相信，但你聽到警笛聲，而且就在我們後面。
A: It is hard to believe, but you can hear the siren, and it's right behind us.

B: 上次我們很幸運，警察只給我們口頭警告。
B: We were lucky last time. That officer only gave us a verbal warning.

A: 我知道，我們這次肯定會拿到罰單了。
A: I know. We'll get a ticket for sure this time.

B: 在那裡停車。
B: Pull the car over there.

基本對話 機場與飛機 入境 住宿 交通 餐飲 觀光 購物 郵電 銀行 麻煩事 回國

A: 嘿！它超過去了。

A: Hey! It has just passed us.

B: 那不是警車，是救護車。

B: That's not a police car, that's an ambulance.

A: 還好我們靠邊停車，擋他們的路是違法的。

A: It's a good thing we pulled over. It's illegal to stay in their way.

Word Bank 字庫

ambulance ['æmbjələns] n. 救護車
siren ['saɪrən] n. 警笛聲
stay in the way 擋路

Notes 小叮嚀

碰到救護車或消防車從後面來，一定要馬上靠邊停或減低速度行駛在慢車道上，不可擋路。詳見附錄「不可不知的美國文化祕笈」之「美國駕駛須知」。

5.20 行李寄放
Luggage Storage

 Dialog 1 對話1

A: 我要把這兩個袋子寄放三天。

A: I need to store these two bags for three days.

B: 好,每日收費是 7 元再加稅。	**B:** OK. The charge per day is \$7 plus tax.
A: 了解了。我現在付嗎?	**A:** I understand. Do I pay now?
B: 不用,回來取袋子時再付。	**B:** No. You pay when you pick up your bags.
A: 請問你們的營業時間?	**A:** What are your hours?
B: 早上 8 點到晚上 10 點。請給我看些證件。	**B:** 8 a.m. to 10 p.m. I'll need to see some ID, please.
A: 我的護照可以嗎?	**A:** Is my passport good enough?
B: 當然。(查驗護照) 你還要簽這份同意書及帶著這個號碼牌。	**B:** Sure. (checking ID) You'll also need to sign this agreement, and keep this number tag.

基本對話

機場與飛機

入境

住宿

交通

餐飲

觀光

購物

郵電

銀行

麻煩事

回國

Notes 小叮嚀

　　住宿飯店在旅客退房後,大多可以提供免費的暫存行李服務。除此之外,機場或地鐵車站也有收費的寄放行李處。各地收費不一,但是短期的以小時計算,較長期的以天計算。記住要問到提領行李的時間,免得錯過了。另外,暫存行李總是有風險的,記得不要把貴重東西留在寄放的行李內。

Dialog 2 對話2

A: 哈囉，我要領回我寄放的行李。

A: Hello. I want to pick up my stored luggage.

B: 請讓我看你的號碼牌。

B: Let me see your number tag, please.

A: 在這裡。

A: Here.

B: 請給我看你的證件。

B: I need to see your ID, please.

A: 在這裡。

A: Here it is.

B: (查驗證件) 好，我去拿你的袋子。

B: (checking ID) OK. I'll get your bags.

A: 謝謝。

A: Thanks.

B: 袋子在這邊。

B: Here they are.

A: 總共多少錢呢？

A: What's the total cost?

基本對話

機場與飛機

入境

住宿

交通

餐飲

觀光

購物

郵電

銀行

麻煩事

回國

B: 含稅是22元78分。 → **B:** It comes to \$22.78 with tax.

 Useful Phrases　實用語句

1. 我要寄放行李。

   I need to store luggage.

2. 我可以寄放行李在這兒嗎？

   Can I store baggage here?

3. 我要領回我寄放的袋子。

   I want to claim my stored bags.

4. 行李寄放處幾點開 [關] 門。

   What time does the baggage storage open [close]?

Unit 6 Food and Drinks

餐飲

在美國，供應傳統美國菜的餐廳到處都是，速食店也到處都有。如同其他移民普遍的國際都會一樣，美國有多種族裔，所以有多種餐廳提供具民族風味的菜肴，在大城市特別是如此，且餐廳的布置及服務也較複雜。最普遍的異國菜餐廳是中國菜、義大利菜及墨西哥菜。遊客們對不熟悉的菜肴可以請服務生描述菜色、招牌菜、做法及推薦佳肴。在小城鎮，餐廳選擇及菜色樣式就簡單多了。雖說菜色及價錢多受制於季節及食材取得之難易，多數的餐廳都希望提供令人滿意的服務。除了速食店及自助餐，其他餐廳都要給小費。

基本對話 | 機場與飛機 | 入境 | 住宿 | 交通 | 餐飲 | 觀光 | 購物 | 郵電 | 銀行 | 麻煩事 | 回國

6.1 餐廳種類——飯店餐廳
Restaurant Types—Hotel Restaurant

Dialog 對話

A: 請把這（餐費）計入我房間。

A: I want to charge this to my room, please.

B: 好的，女士，沒問題。您的大名及房號？

B: Yes, ma'am, no problem. What is your name and room number?

6.2 餐廳種類——咖啡廳
Restaurant Types—Coffee Shop

Dialog 1 對話1

A: 請給我一杯拿鐵。

A: I'd like a *latte*, please.

B: 你要什麼尺寸的？

B: What size do you want?

A: 你們有什麼尺寸的？

A: What sizes do you have?

B: 我們有小、中、大，請看這邊。

B: We have short, tall, and *grande*. Look here.

A: 中杯就好了。

A: Tall is fine.

B: 你要加糖嗎？

B: Do you want sugar added?

A: 不用了，謝謝。

A: No, thank you.

B: 這邊用還是帶走？

B: Is it for here or to go?

A: 這邊用。

A: For here.

✏️ Word Bank 字庫

latte ['latɛ , la'tɛ] n. 拿鐵(義大利文)
tall [tɔl] adj. 中杯的
grande ['grandɛ] adj. 大杯的(義大利文)

 Dialog 2 對話2

A: 你們有無線連線嗎？

A: Do you have wireless access here?

B: 有。

B: Yes, we do.

A: 要多少錢呢？

A: How much does it cost?

基本對話

機場與飛機

入境

住宿

交通

餐飲

觀光

購物

郵電

銀行

麻煩事

回國

基本對話 | 機場與飛機 | 入境 | 住宿 | 交通 | 餐飲 | 觀光 | 購物 | 郵電 | 銀行 | 麻煩事 | 回國

B: 免費，但是我必須給你連線密碼。

B: It's free, but I'll have to give you the access code.

Word Bank 字庫

wireless ['waɪrlɪs] adj. 無線的
access ['æksɛs] n. 連線
code [kod] n. 密碼

Useful Phrases 實用語句

1. 這邊用還是帶走？
   (Is it) for here or to go?
2. 請給我冰咖啡。
   Ice coffee, please.
3. 請給我糖球。
   Liquid sugar, please.
4. 奶精在哪裡？
   Where is the cream?
5. 我喝黑的 (咖啡)。
   I drink it black.

Tips 小祕訣

　　在許多國家，咖啡是極受歡迎的飲料。在美國，普通咖啡 (regular coffee) 既普遍又廉價，許多地方都可以免費續杯。一般而言，美國人習慣喝熱咖啡，冰咖啡在餐廳或速食店並不是那麼普遍。在餐廳裡，服務生會過來問是否再來些咖啡，或咖啡喝一半冷掉了，是否要再倒一些熱咖啡進去「Do you want to warm it up?」。

　　近年有些美國連鎖咖啡盛行義大利風，以商業手法或義大利文為杯子尺寸命名，short/small, tall/medium, *grande*/large, *venti*/extra large。商業命名是經營手法，但有時名不符實，如 medium 稱為 tall（比 short 高），*grande* 給消費者覺得大（*grande* 義法西葡文皆同），而 *venti* ['vɛntɪ] 超大杯，意為「20」盎司，但義大利並不用盎司為單位。

6.3 餐廳種類──網路咖啡店
Restaurant Types—Internet Café

 Dialog 對話

A: 嗨，我需要上網。	**A:** Hi. I need to get onto the Internet.
B: 沒問題，挑這裡任何一臺你想用的電腦。	**B:** No problem. Choose any computer here you want to use.
A: 抱歉，我要知道費用多少。	**A:** Sorry, I need to know how much it costs.
B: 我們最低收費 5 元。	**B:** We charge a minimum of \$5.
A: 那抵用多少時間？	**A:** How much time does that buy?
B: 半小時，之後是每小時 2 元。	**B:** Half an hour. After that it costs \$2 per hour.

6.4 餐廳種類——速食店
Restaurant Types—Fast Food Restaurant

 Dialog 1 （對話1）

A: 我可以幫你嗎？

A: May I help you?

B: 我要一個漢堡、薯條及一杯可樂。

B: I want a hamburger, fries and a coke.

A: 你要什麼大小的漢堡呢？

A: What size hamburger do you want?

B: 大的。

B: Large.

A: 這裡用還是帶走？

A: Is this for here or to go?

B: 帶走。

B: To go.

A: 好的，你的餐點馬上就好。

A: OK. Your order will be ready soon.

 Word Bank 字庫

hamburger ['hæmbɚgɚ] n. 漢堡
fries [fraɪz] n. 薯條(= French fries)

 Dialog 2 （對話2）

A: 不好意思，我可以多要些紙巾嗎？

A: Excuse me. May I have more napkins?

B: 它們在調味品那邊。

B: They are over there with the condiments.

A: 那要多些番茄醬呢？

A: What about some more ketchup?

B: 也在那邊。

B: It's over there, too.

Word Bank （字庫）

napkin ['næpkɪn] n. 紙巾
condiment ['kɑndəmənt] n. 調味品
ketchup ['kɛtʃəp] n. 番茄醬

 Useful Phrases （實用語句）

1. 我要多點些薯條。

   I want to order more fries.

2. 我要再點一個漢堡。

   I want to order another burger.

3. 我要的是套餐，不是單點漢堡。

   I'd like a meal, not just a hamburger.

4. 請不要放洋蔥。

   No onions, please.

基本對話

機場與飛機

入境

住宿

交通

餐飲

觀光

購物

郵電

銀行

麻煩事

回國

5. 你們有什麼口味的冰淇淋？

What flavor of ice cream do you have?

6.5 餐廳種類──中國餐館
Restaurant Types—Chinese Restaurant

Dialog 對話

A: 嘿，你看，我們的餐點有幸運餅。

A: Hey, look. We got fortune cookies with our meal.

B: 真的耶，我們打開吧。

B: Really? Let's open them.

A: 這真是在西方的中國餐館可愛的習俗。

A: This is a cute Chinese restaurant custom here in the West.

B: 是啊，我也這麼想。

B: Yes, I think so, too.

A: 你的幸運餅寫什麼？

A: What does your cookies fortune say?

Word Bank 字庫

fortune cookie n. 幸運餅
custom ['kʌstəm] n. 習俗，慣例

Tips 小祕訣

判斷中餐館是否道地，只要看上門的客人就知道了。除了華人聚集的大城市，海外的中國餐館多數已加入當地人的口味，因此感覺不中不西。這類中國餐廳經常菜肴都是酸甜 (sweet and sour) 口味以迎合老外，在國外的白米飯也幾乎都是乾硬的泰國米，廚師也不一定是華人。但人在國外，將就些吧！帶老外到中國餐館用餐時，可以告訴餐廳不要放味精 (MSG)，許多老外對味精過敏。在美國的中國餐館用餐後要結帳時，服務生會送來幸運餅 (fortune cookies)，內有處事格言或運勢預測，後又加入樂透明牌。許多老外到了中國大陸或臺灣，才知道原來這只是海外中國餐館吸引顧客的手法。另一個特點是海外的中國餐館皆在戶外懸掛紅燈籠，很好辨識。

6.6 選擇餐廳
Choosing a Restaurant

Dialog 1 對話1

A: 你知道有什麼好餐廳嗎？

A: Do you know of any good restaurants?

B: 這條街直走有一家不錯。

B: There is a good one down the street.

A: 是什麼名字呢？

A: What is its name?

B: 我不記得，但是它的義大利食物很棒。

B: I don't remember, but it has great Italian food.

基本對話

機場與飛機

入境

住宿

交通

餐飲

觀光

購物

郵電

銀行

麻煩事

回國

Dialog 2 對話2

A: 你們這裡有中國菜嗎？

A: Do you serve Chinese food here?

B: 有，我們西式及中式菜肴都有。

B: Yes, we have both Western and Chinese dishes.

A: 我可以先看菜單嗎？

A: May I see the menu first?

B: 當然，請等一下。

B: Sure, just a minute.

Word Bank 字庫

serve [sɝv] v. 提供服務

dish [dɪʃ] n. 菜肴，一道菜

Useful Phrases 實用語句

1. 我可以看菜單嗎？

   May I see the menu?

2. 我想看甜點單。

   I'd like to see the dessert menu.

3. 這裡有吸菸區嗎？

   Is there a smoking section here?

4. 我們要等多久呢？

   How long will we have to wait?

5. 我們晚點會回來。

   We'll come back later.

6.7 餐廳訂位
Making a Reservation at a Restaurant

 Dialog 對話

A: 哈囉,豐月餐廳。

A: Hello. Harvest Moon Restaurant.

B: 哈囉,我想預訂今晚的位子。

B: Hello. I'd like to make a reservation for tonight.

A: 好的。你們會有幾位?

A: Very well. How many will be in your party?

B: 我們會有七位。

B: There will be seven of us.

A: 你們幾點會到呢?

A: And what time will you arrive?

B: 大約 7 點。

B: Around seven.

A: 沒問題,我們期待見到你們。

A: All right. We look forward to seeing you.

Word Bank 字庫

look forward to 期待

基本對話

機場與飛機

入境

住宿

交通

餐飲

觀光

購物

郵電

銀行

麻煩事

回國

基本對話

機場與飛機

入境

住宿

交通

餐飲

觀光

購物

郵電

銀行

麻煩事

回國

Useful Phrases 實用語句

1. 你們今晚有任何空位嗎？

   Do you have any tables available for tonight?

2. 我想訂位。

   I'd like to make a reservation.

3. 我想預訂明天的位子。

   I want to make a reservation for tomorrow.

4. 今晚有現場演奏嗎？

   Is there live music tonight?

5. 今晚有收娛樂費嗎？

   Is there a cover charge for tonight?

Tips 小祕訣

　　cover charge 通常是在有表演節目的餐廳或夜店，在餐點服務之外，對每人額外收取的費用，可以稱為表演費、節目費或娛樂費。如果在夜店只有飲料或點心的服務，並無太多餐點可供應時，此收費可能包含了免費附贈飲料及小點心。

6.8 餐廳內——帶位
Inside the Restaurant—Getting Seated

Dialog 1 對話1

A: 歡迎光臨。幾位呢？

A: Welcome. How many?

B: 兩位，謝謝。

B: Table for two, please.

A: 好的。吸菸還是不吸菸呢？

A: Very good. Smoking or non-smoking?

B: 不吸菸。

B: Non-smoking.

A: 你們要靠窗的位子嗎？

A: Would you like a window seat?

B: 好，麻煩你。

B: Yes, please.

Dialog 2 (對話2)

A: (服務生) 您這裡坐得舒適嗎？

A: (Waiter) Are you comfortable?

B: 可以，這裡很好。

B: Yes, this is nice.

A: 菜單在這裡。

A: Here are your menus.

B: 謝謝。

B: Thank you.

A: 您要先點個飲料嗎？

A: Would you like to order a drink first?

基本對話　機場與飛機　入境　住宿　交通　餐飲　觀光　購物　郵電　銀行　麻煩事　回國

基本對話

機場與飛機

入境

住宿

交通

餐飲

觀光

購物

郵電

銀行

麻煩事

回國

B: 我要一杯瑪格麗特。

B: I'd like a *margarita*.

 Word Bank 字庫

comfortable ['kʌmfə·təbl] adj. 舒適的

margarita [ˌmɑrɡə'ritɑ] n. 瑪格麗特(一種墨西哥飲料,含有龍舌蘭 *tequila*、碎冰、萊姆汁 lime juice,杯口有一圈鹽巴)

 Useful Phrases 實用語句

1. 我們想坐外面陽臺。

   We'd like to sit out on the terrace.

2. 我們想在外面平臺用餐。

   We'd like to eat out on the deck, please.

3. 我們要先去吧臺。

   We'll go to the bar first.

4. 我們可以看飲料邊單嗎?

   May we see your drink list?

5. 我們想先喝飲料。

   We'd like our drinks first.

6. 我們想邊喝飲料邊用晚餐。

   We want our drinks with our dinner.

7. 我們要晚點喝飲料。

   We'll have drinks later.

8. 我們今晚不想喝飲料 [雞尾酒]。

   We don't want any drinks [cocktails] tonight.

Notes 小叮嚀

　　到餐廳用餐要等候帶位，不要逕自入內，想坐在哪個區 (侍者不同) 坐下前就表明，不要自己隨便換位，引起原侍者可能因失去桌位服務之小費收入而不悅。餐廳禁菸已漸成趨勢，許多地區的餐廳全面禁菸 (smoke free)。西方文化裡把喝湯擺第一，且習慣上點菜前會先點個冷飲或咖啡。

　　到餐廳，慣例是先點飲料，再點餐，點水要付費。因為水龍頭就有水，美國自來水可生飲喝，餐桌上點水上來的必然是需付費的礦泉水。

6.9 餐廳內——點餐
Inside the Restaurant—Ordering Meals

 Dialog 1 對話1

A: 這裡是您的飲料。您準備點餐了嗎？

A: Here are your drinks. Are you ready to order?

B: 今日特餐是什麼呢？

B: What is today's special?

A: 雞肉袋餅加摩雷醬汁。

A: Chicken *fajitas*, with *mole* sauce.

B: 還有包含什麼呢？

B: What else is included?

A: 這餐點包含湯或沙拉及一杯飲料。

A: The meal includes soup or salad and a drink.

基本對話 機場與飛機 入境 住宿 交通 餐飲 觀光 購物 郵電 銀行 麻煩事 回國

Word Bank 字庫

fajita [fə'hitɑ] n. (墨西哥)袋餅(內有生菜、番茄、紅蘿蔔絲、洋蔥絲、起司及肉條)

mole sauce n. 摩雷醬汁(一種墨西哥沾醬,由豆子、薑、巧克力、香辛料做成)

soup [sup] n. 湯

salad ['sæləd] n. 沙拉

Dialog 2 對話2

A: 我要點牛排。
A: I would like to order a steak.

B: 你要幾分熟?
B: How do you want it cooked?

A: 我要五分熟。
A: I'd like it medium rare.

B: 你要牛排醬嗎?
B: Do you want steak sauce?

A: 要。
A: Yes, I do.

B: 你要配馬鈴薯泥還是烤馬鈴薯?
B: Do you want mashed or baked potato with that?

A: 烤的。
A: Baked.

Tips （小祕訣）

　　在臺灣常點五分熟牛排的人，到美國點牛排如果說：「I'd like my steak medium, please.」(我想要我的牛排五分熟)，端上來的多半已是七分熟了。我們的三、五、七分熟到美國可能是五、七、九分的熟度，因此要點 medium rare 才能享受到我們所謂五分熟的口感。以下列出煎牛排的簡短說法與煎熟的顏色程度，作為大致的參考標準：

Blue rare / Very rare, please. 二分熟 (外層快炙，內層紅色為溫肉)

Rare, please. 三分熟 (外層灰咖啡色，最內層紅色，其餘粉紅色)

Medium rare, please. 五、六分熟 (外層咖啡色，最內層粉紅色，
　　　　　　　　　　其餘粉紅至咖啡色)

Medium, please. 七分熟 (外層咖啡色，最內層有些粉紅色，其餘
　　　　　　　　少數粉紅至咖啡色)

Medium well, please. 八、九分熟 (幾乎全部是咖啡色，肉汁已收
　　　　　　　　　　乾)

Well-done, please. 全熟 (全部是咖啡色，味道乾澀)

Dialog 3 （對話3）

A: 我要菜單上的六號餐，但不要太辣。

A: I want number 6 on the menu, but not very spicy.

B: 沒問題。要不要來個開胃菜？

B: Certainly. Would you like an appetizer?

A: 好，我點(炸)烏賊。

A: Yes. I'll have the calamari.

B: 好的。要喝什麼嗎？

B: Very well. Anything to drink?

基本對話

機場與飛機

入境

住宿

交通

餐飲

觀光

購物

郵電

銀行

麻煩事

回國

A: 你們有啤酒嗎？ → **A:** Do you have beer?

B: 有的，我們有精選微釀 (啤酒)。 → **B:** Yes, we have a selection of micro brews.

A: 你們有啤酒單嗎？ → **A:** Do you have a list of your beers?

B: 有，我去拿給你。 → **B:** Yes. I'll get it for you.

✏️ Word Bank 字庫

spicy ['spaɪsɪ] adj. 辣的
appetizer ['æpə,taɪzə-] n. 開胃菜
calamari ['kælə,mɛrɪ] n. 烏賊(通常是炸的)
selection [sə'lɛkʃən] n. 精選品
micro ['maɪkro] adj. 微小的
brew [bru] n. 釀製酒

📖 Useful Phrases 實用語句

1. 您準備點餐了嗎？
   Are you ready to order?
2. 請再給我們一分鐘。
   Please give us another minute.
3. 今日特餐是什麼呢？
   What is today's special?
4. 本店特餐是什麼呢？
   What is the house special?
5. 這裡什麼受歡迎呢？
   What's popular here?

6. 你建議我們試什麼呢？
   What do you recommend we try?
7. 你們有兩人套餐嗎？
   Do you have set meals for two?
8. 你們有供應雞尾酒嗎？
   Do you serve cocktails?
9. 我可以看一下飲料單嗎？
   May I see the drink list?
10. 請描述一下這種啤酒。
    Please describe this beer.
11. 我想要再來一杯這個。
    I'd like another one of this.

Notes 小叮嚀

　　基本餐桌禮儀不可忽略，紳士行為在世界各國存在，在平權社會同樣被期待 (含各種場合)，沒有紳士習慣的男士必須學習。為女士開門，為最鄰近自己的女士拉椅子都是被期待的行為。有些人用餐前要先祈禱 (say grace)，別急著開動。喝湯勿低頭就碗，吃麵包要先撕成小片，要有「公筷母匙」的概念。用餐時不要先聞食物，否則美國人會感到受冒犯。

　　用餐時有刺或骨頭，千萬不要直接從嘴裡吐在盤子上，要用叉子接著，放到盤子旁邊，不可放在餐桌上，也不可以打嗝，在美國這都是失禮的。萬一打嗝，要道歉說 Excuse me. 再加上解釋 I ate too much. 在人前打哈欠、伸懶腰、打噴嚏、打嗝這些動作都要表示抱歉及解釋。

　　要擤鼻涕、剔牙、補妝都要去洗手間，才不會無禮。別人道歉時可以說沒關係 (It's OK.)，(上帝) 保佑你 (God)B/bless you.或保重 (Take care.) 另外，要拿遠處的食物或調味料，必須請別人傳過來 (例如Please pass the salt.) 而不是自己伸長手臂去拿。要拿餐盤上最後一片食物時，必須先問別人是否需要，才不會失禮。(在法國若將麵包沾醬料完全吃完，主人會很高興，但在埃及留一小口表示不貪心。)

　　刀叉擺放也要注意，如將刀叉各擺在5及7點鐘位置，表示仍在進食。兩者擺在5點鐘位置為用餐完畢，兩者都在7點鐘位置表示食物不合胃口或不好吃，可能會讓廚師很難過。

　　對外國餐飲文化或社交禮儀 (social etiquette) 不了解，可請教當地人或宴請餐聚之主人、賓客，有助於拉近距離，是實用又有趣的話題。

基本對話　機場與飛機　入境　住宿　交通　餐飲　觀光　購物　郵電　銀行　麻煩事　回國

Language Power 字句補給站

食物及餐廳
Food and Restaurants ①

waiter 服務生

waitress 女服務生

terrace 陽台

menu 菜單

juice 果汁

tea 茶

coffee 咖啡

appetizers 開胃菜

entree 主菜

dessert 甜點

sauce 醬汁

steak 牛排

fish fillet 魚排

cocktail 雞尾酒

chowder 濃湯

soup 湯

salad 沙拉

salad dressing 沙拉醬

食物及餐廳
Food and Restaurants ②

butter 奶油　　　　jam 果醬　　　　jelly 果凍

 for here 這裡用　　　　 to go 帶走

 side order 附加餐點　　　 refill 續杯

 margarine 人工奶油　　 MSG 味精

◆ 常見西餐烹調方式 Common Cooking Methods

baked	烤的
broiled	燒烤的
fried	油煎的，炸的
deep fried	油炸的
boiled	煮的
sautéed	嫩煎的

6.10 餐廳內——點酒
Inside the Restaurant—Ordering Wine

Dialog 對話

A: 服務生，我們要一瓶酒。

A: Waiter. We would like a bottle of wine.

基本對話

機場與飛機

入境

住宿

交通

餐飲

觀光

購物

郵電

銀行

麻煩事

回國

B: 好，你要什麼呢？

B: Certainly. What would you like?

A: 你有任何推薦嗎？

A: Do you have any recommendations?

B: 我們有一種不錯的本店酒，一紅一白。

B: We have a good house wine. A red and a white.

A: 我們試試白酒，還有請給兩個冰酒杯。

A: We'll try the white. Two chilled glasses, too, please.

B: 馬上來，女士。

B: Right away, ma'am.

Word Bank 字庫

recommendation [ˌrɛkəmɛnˈdeʃən] n. 推薦
chilled [tʃɪld] adj.(冰) 冷的

Tips 小祕訣

　　葡萄酒類分紅酒 (red wine)、白酒 (white wine)、甜 (sweet) 及不甜 (dry) 等種類。

6.11 餐廳內──點甜點
Inside the Restaurant──Ordering Desserts

 Dialog 對話

A: 你們有什麼派呢？

A: What kind of pie do you have?

B: 我們有蘋果、草莓、水蜜桃、檸檬、藍莓及巧克力奶油。

B: We have apple, strawberry, peach, lemon, blueberry, and chocolate cream.

A: 我要一片藍莓派。

A: I'd like a piece of blueberry pie.

B: 你要加冰淇淋嗎？

B: Do you want it *à la mode*?

A: 是的。

A: Yes.

Word Bank 字庫

dessert [dɪ'zɝt] n. 甜點
strawberry ['strɔbɛrɪ] n. 草莓
peach [pitʃ] n. 水蜜桃
blueberry ['blu,bɛrɪ] n. 藍莓
à la mode [,alə'mod] adj. 加冰淇淋的 (法語)

基本對話

機場與飛機

入境

住宿

交通

餐飲

觀光

購物

郵電

銀行

麻煩事

回國

6.12 餐廳內——侍者招呼
Inside the Restaurant—Service Satisfaction

 Dialog 1 （對話1）

A: 您喜歡您的餐點嗎？

A: Are you enjoying your meal?

B: 是的，不錯。

B: Yes, it's good.

A: 來份甜點嗎？

A: How about dessert?

B: 不了，謝謝，我飽了。

B: No, thanks. I'm full.

Dialog 2 （對話2）

A: 您喜歡您的餐點嗎？

A: Are you enjoying your meal?

B: 是的，不錯。

B: Yes, it's good.

A: 來份甜點嗎？

A: How about dessert?

B: 你們有什麼呢？

B: What do you have?

A: 讓我拿甜點單給你看。

A: Let me show you the dessert menu.

Dialog 3 對話3

A: 這裡是免費招待的馬鈴薯脆片及莎莎醬。

A: Here is your complimentary chips and salsa.

B: 謝謝。我可以多要些水嗎？

B: Thank you. Can I have more water?

A: 當然，我馬上過來。

A: Sure. I'll be right back.

Word Bank 字庫

> complimentary [ˌkɑmpləˈmɛntərɪ] adj. 贈送的
> chips [tʃɪps] n. 馬鈴薯脆片
> salsa [ˈsɑlsə] n. 莎莎醬

Dialog 4 對話4

A: 您喜歡您的餐點嗎？

A: Are you enjoying your meal?

B: 是的，不錯。我可以要多點水嗎？

B: Yes, it's good. Can I have more water, please?

A: 當然。

A: Yes, of course.

基本對話

機場與飛機

入境

住宿

交通

餐飲

觀光

購物

郵電

銀行

麻煩事

回國

基本對話
機場與飛機
入境
住宿
交通
餐飲
觀光
購物
郵電
銀行
麻煩事
回國

B: 我還需要再一份紙巾。

B: I need another napkin also.

A: 我會拿一份給你。你還要什麼別的嗎？

A: I'll get you one. Do you want anything else?

B: 我決定也來個甜點。

B: I've decided I want a dessert, too.

A: 讓我也拿甜點單來給你。

A: Let me bring the dessert menu to you also.

 Useful Phrases 實用語句

1. 請加點水。

   More water, please.

2. 請多點沾醬。

   More dipping sauce, please.

3. 請多給點脆片。

   More chips, please.

4. 請給我一根吸管。

   I need a straw, please.

5. 你們有筷子嗎？

   Do you have chopsticks?

6. 我掉了叉子，請再給我一支。

   I dropped my fork. I need another one, please.

7. 服務生，我打翻了我的飲料。

   Waiter, I spilled my drink.

8. 可以請你收走這個嗎？

   Would you take this, please?

9. 我們要一份點心帶走。

We want a dessert to go.

10. 我們的帳單,麻煩你。

Our bill, please.

 Language Power 字句補給站

醬　料　**Sauces**

salt 鹽巴	pepper 胡椒
ketchup 番茄醬	sugar 糖
steak sauce 牛排醬	mustard 芥茉醬
sweet and sour sauce 甜酸醬	barbecue sauce 烤肉醬
salsa 莎莎醬	guacamole 酪梨醬

餐　具　**Eating Utensils**

knife 刀子

fork 叉子

spoon 湯匙

straw 吸管

plate 盤子

saucer 碟子

glass 玻璃杯

cup 杯子

steak knife 牛排刀

butter knife 奶油刀

napkin 紙巾

基本對話

機場與飛機

入境

住宿

交通

餐飲

觀光

購物

郵電

銀行

麻煩事

回國

6.13 餐廳內——多餘食物打包
Inside the Restaurant—Taking Extra Food Home

 Dialog 對話

A: 我們要帶剩餘的食物回家。

A: We'd like to take the leftover food home.

B: 好的，先生。

B: Yes, sir.

A: 可以外加一些醬料嗎？

A: Is it possible to get some extra sauce?

B: 稍等一下，我去問。

B: Just a moment. I'll go ask.

 Word Bank 字庫

leftover ['lɛft,ovɚ] adj. 吃剩的
extra ['ɛkstrə] adj. 額外的，外加的

 Useful Phrases 實用語句

1. 這些請用盒子裝起來。

   Please box these up.

2. 我想另外點餐帶走。

   I'd like to place an extra order to go.

基本對話 機場與飛機 入境 住宿 交通 餐飲 觀光 購物 郵電 銀行 麻煩事 回國

基本對話 機場與飛機 入境 住宿 交通 **餐飲** 觀光 購物 郵電 銀行 麻煩事 回國

Tips 小祕訣

　　要將多餘食物帶回家，也可以直接問可否給一個 bag 或 doggy bag，意指剩菜是要給小狗吃的。如果要外帶，直接說食物加 to go 就可以了，例如：「A chicken salad to go.」或「A cheeseburger to go.」或「A coffee to go.」。

6.14 餐廳內──買單
Inside the Restaurant—Paying the Bill

Dialog 1 對話1

A: 你想我們該留多少小費呢？帳單是 30 元 50 分。

A: How much do you think we should leave for a tip? Our bill is $30.50.

B: 不，你看，已經有 10% 的服務費了。

B: No. Look. There is already a 10% service charge.

A: 好，那我們就不必給小費了。

A: OK, then we don't need to tip.

Tips　小祕訣

　　有些服務生因為希望拿到較好的小費而頻獻殷勤，但不必因此而受影響，按自己感受給小費就好。若是餐廳為吃到飽的自助式 buffet，有提供少許服務如倒咖啡、收盤子等，就酌量給小費。至於機場、學校等自己拿餐盤點餐結帳的自助式 cafeteria 及速食店，因為服務都是自己來，就不必給小費了。有些歐洲地區的餐廳會收取少許的餐具費，侍者為你倒杯水解渴亦須加收茶水費，而一般餐廳用餐的小費為 10%，另須加稅。在澳洲的餐廳不必給小費。

　　金融風暴美國大量印鈔的結果使得小費支出也被迫攀升，在一般的美國餐廳用餐，點餐金額外尚有稅金及小費才是全部支出，現今行情服務普通之午餐小費 (tips) 約為消費額的 15%，若是在較高檔 (upscale) 或優質服務的餐廳晚餐約為 20% 的小費。同桌人數較多的話，要多給一些，許多餐廳註明 6 人以上帳單直接加收服務費 18-23%。如果帳單已含某百分比的服務費 (service charge)，就視情況酌量再給一些或不給也可以。然而卻有越來越多的美國餐廳口徑一致，不管消費者感受如何，直接在菜單上註明餐點加稅收外，另加收 18% 之服務費 (18% gratuity added)，用餐時碰到大多數餐廳皆如此，消費者也只能無奈接受。

　　近年有些餐廳已在餐桌上擺設 self check-out 螢幕供消費者自行按步驟刷卡結帳，小費則直接留在桌上即可。

Dialog 2　對話2

A: 我們要走了，帳單在哪裡呢？

A: We need to go. Where is the bill?

B: 服務生放在桌子這裡。

B: The waiter left it here on the table.

A: 我們看一下。總共 54 元，我們應該留 10% 的小費。

A: Let's see. It comes to $54. We should leave a 10% tip.

基本對話
機場與飛機
入境
住宿
交通
餐飲
觀光
購物
郵電
銀行
麻煩事
回國

B: 我認為服務生的服務特別好，我們該多給點小費。

B: I think the waiter's service was especially good. I think we ought to tip more.

A: 好，我留 15%，那是多少錢呢？

A: OK, I'll leave 15%. How much is that?

B: 大約 8 元。

B: About eight dollars.

A: 我有 5 元紙鈔，你有 1 元的紙鈔嗎？

A: I've got a five dollar bill. Do you have any ones?

B: 有，這裡有 3 塊錢。

B: Yes, here is three bucks.

A: 好，我們搞定了。

A: Good. We got it covered.

✎ Word Bank 字庫

bill [bɪl] n. 帳單；鈔票
tip [tɪp] n. 小費；v. 給小費
buck [bʌk] n. (俚語)美元

📖 Useful Phrases 實用語句

1. 這裡有收服務費嗎？

   Is there a service charge here?

2. 服務費是多少呢？

   How much is the service charge?

3. (這是小費) 謝謝。(給小費時其實說謝謝就可以了)

   (Here's your tip.) Thank you.

4. 我們來分攤小費。

   Let's split the tip.

Notes 小叮嚀

> 小費是留給服務生的，所以這部分最好不要刷卡而是給現金，只要將小費留在桌上就可以了，但記得不要給過於零碎的小費。

Language Power　字句補給站

基本對話
機場與飛機
入境
住宿
交通
餐飲
觀光
購物
郵電
銀行
麻煩事
回國

Traditional Restaurant Sample Menu
(傳統餐廳菜單範例)

Appetizers 開胃菜

- Potato skins with cheese　馬鈴薯皮加起司
- Buffalo wings 炸雞翅加特製醬料
- Calamari (炸) 烏賊
- Deep fried mushrooms 炸香菇
- French Fries 炸薯條
- Onion Rings 洋蔥圈
- Chips and salsa 脆片與莎莎沾醬

Breakfast 早餐

- *Breakfast Meat Lovers Special* 愛肉者早餐特餐
  sausage, bacon and ham, with hash browns, eggs and toast 香腸、培根和火腿加油炸刨絲馬鈴薯塊、蛋及土司

- *Breakfast Fajitas* 早餐袋餅
  Mexican fajitas prepared with potatoes and grated cheese 墨西哥袋餅加馬鈴薯及刨絲起司

- *Pancake Stacks* 鬆餅層
  one, two, or three pancakes with real butter, syrup and bacon or sausage 一片、兩片或三片鬆餅加奶油、糖蜜、培根或香腸

- *Eggs* 蛋
  two halves English muffin topped with poached eggs, sauce and served with hash browns 對半分開之英式馬芬(杯形鬆餅)，上加白煮蛋、醬汁及油炸刨絲馬鈴薯塊

- *Vegetarian Breakfast* 素食者早餐
  grilled vegetables, fresh fruit and yogurt served with whole wheat toast and orange juice 烤蔬果、新鮮水果及優格，配全麥土司及柳橙汁

Traditional Restaurant Sample Menu
(傳統餐廳菜單範例)

- *French Toast 法國土司*

  three pieces served with syrup and butter 三片法國土司加上楓糖漿及奶油

Lunch Selections 午餐

- *House Burger / House Cheese Burger / House Bacon Cheese Burger* 本店漢堡 / 本店起司漢堡 / 本店培根起司漢堡

  special burgers served with French fries, and a drink 特別漢堡加炸薯條及飲料

- *Garden Burger 蔬菜漢堡*

  a burger made of fresh vegetables and a meatless burger patty 由新鮮蔬菜加無肉之漢堡餡做成

- *Club Sandwich 總匯三明治*

  smoked chicken, bacon, lettuce and tomatoes in a sandwich sliced into four sections served with potato chips 三明治由燻雞、培根、生菜、番茄做成，切成四份，外加薯條

- *Meat or vegetable lasagna 肉或蔬菜千層麵*

  a choice of Italian style lasagna served hot with garlic bread 熱騰騰的義大利千層麵加大蒜麵包

- *Hot Turkey Sandwich 熱火雞三明治*

  a hot turkey sandwich topped with gravy and served with a salad and fries 熱火雞三明治加上肉汁，外加沙拉及薯條

- *Fish and Chips 魚及薯條*

  deep fried fish and fries served with a special sauce 炸魚及薯條加上特別醬料

基本對話

機場與飛機

入境

住宿

交通

餐飲

觀光

購物

郵電

銀行

麻煩事

回國

基本對話

機場與飛機

入境

住宿

交通

餐飲

觀光

購物

郵電

銀行

麻煩事

回國

Traditional Restaurant Sample Menu
(傳統餐廳菜單範例)

Soups 湯

- Vegetable soup 蔬菜湯
- Corn soup 玉米濃湯
- Clam chowder 文蛤巧達濃湯 (以蛤肉、馬鈴薯等煮成之濃湯)
- Minestrone 義大利蔬菜什錦濃湯 (以當季食材如豆類、紅蘿蔔、番茄、洋蔥、西洋芹等什錦蔬菜及義大利麵類煮成的一種雜菜濃湯)

Salads 沙拉

- *Green Garden Salad* 青菜沙拉

  fresh picked vegetables, sliced, with your choice of dressing 鮮採蔬菜切片加上任你挑選之沙拉醬

- *Chicken Salad* 雞肉沙拉

  fried chicken strips over mixed greens, bacon pieces, ham and dressing 炸雞肉條加什錦蔬菜、培根碎片、火腿及沙拉醬

- *Mexican Salad* 墨西哥沙拉

  lettuce, tomato, salsa, taco chips, olives, and beef with a special dressing 生菜、番茄、莎莎醬、玉米片、橄欖及牛肉與特別的沙拉醬汁

Dinner Selections 晚餐

- *Stir Fry Chicken* 炒雞肉

  grilled chicken, oriental vegetables, served with a sauce 烤雞、亞洲蔬菜配醬汁

- *Salmon* 鮭魚

  a thick slice of fresh salmon served with a baked potato, salad, and dinner rolls 厚片新鮮鮭魚配烤馬鈴薯、沙拉及麵包捲

Traditional Restaurant Sample Menu
(傳統餐廳菜單範例)

- *T-Bone Steak* 丁骨牛排

  a thick slice of steak served with a baked potato, vegetables, and a salad 厚片牛排配烤馬鈴薯、蔬菜及沙拉

- *Sirloin Steak* 沙朗牛排

  same as above, but a sirloin 同上，但用沙朗牛排

- *Pork Loin Steak* 豬排 (腰肉)

  same as above, but a pork loin 同上，但用豬排 (腰肉)

Drinks 飲料

- coffee / tea (tea bags) / milk / fruit juices, including tomato juice

  咖啡 / 茶 (茶包) / 牛奶 / 果汁，包括番茄汁

- soft drinks—Coca Cola or Pepsi /Sprite / Root Beer / ginger ale/ ice tea / other flavors

  汽水類─可口可樂或百事可樂 / 雪碧 / 露比 (沙士) / 薑汁汽水 / 冰紅茶 / 其他口味

- beer and wine (in many, but not all restaurants)

  啤酒及酒 (多數餐廳供應)

- cocktails (in many, but not all restaurants)

  雞尾酒 (多數餐廳供應)

Desserts 點心

- ice cream (vanilla, chocolate, strawberry)

  冰淇淋 (香草、巧克力、草莓)

- apple pie, banana pie, chocolate pie, lemon pie, pie à la mode 蘋果派、香蕉派、巧克力派、檸檬派、冰淇淋派

- cheese cake, blueberry cake

  起司蛋糕、藍莓蛋糕

基本對話

機場與飛機

入境

住宿

交通

餐飲

觀光

購物

郵電

銀行

麻煩事

回國

基本對話
機場與飛機
入境
住宿
交通
餐飲
觀光
購物
郵電
銀行
麻煩事
回國

Fast Food Menu (速食菜單)

Meals 餐點

- Hamburger / Cheeseburger /Bacon Cheeseburger (in quarter pound and half pound sizes) 漢堡/起司漢堡/培根起司漢堡(1/4磅及1/2磅)
- Chicken Burger 雞肉漢堡
- Fish Burger 魚堡
- Vegetarian Burger 素食漢堡
- French Fries 薯條
- Tater Tots 薯餅
- Fried Chicken 炸雞
- Chicken Nuggets 炸雞塊
- Hot Dogs 熱狗

Salads 沙拉

- Chicken Salad 雞肉沙拉
- Caesar Salad 凱撒沙拉
- Garden Salad 田園沙拉
- Salad Dressing 沙拉醬 (Thousand Island 千島醬，Italian 義大利醬，oil and vinegar 油醋醬)

Breakfast 早餐

- Croissant Sandwiches 可頌三明治
- Pancakes with Sausage 鬆餅加香腸

Soups 湯

- Corn Soup 玉米濃湯

Beverages 飲料

- Cola 可樂
- Fanta 芬達
- Sprite 雪碧
- Orange juice 柳橙汁
- Ice Tea 冰紅茶
- Coffee 咖啡
- Hot Chocolate 熱巧克力
- Milkshakes 奶昔 (vanilla, chocolate, strawberry 香草、巧克力、草莓)

Desserts 甜點

- Banana Split 香蕉船
- Pie 派

Unit 7　Sightseeing

觀光

從自然奇景、世界遺產到國際大都會或小鎮風光，觀光活動包羅萬象。在美國，觀光選擇可以從簡單的市區散步到在大峽谷底部騎一整天驢子，你想得到的觀光活動在美國都有可能，導覽行程可以從參觀工廠到葡萄園，可以從完全免費到好幾千元不等。旅行者看世界上每個地方都是獨一無二的，無論當地的物質條件如何，所以身在當地要把握時間體會難得的到訪，千萬不要掃興地拿別的地方來批評該地才好。各國旅遊資訊除書籍及網路資料外，在旅館或當地的觀光局、旅遊資訊中心、商會都有娛樂或觀光機會可尋。

基本對話 | 機場與飛機 | 入境 | 住宿 | 交通 | 餐飲 | 觀光 | 購物 | 郵電 | 銀行 | 麻煩事 | 回國

7.1 旅遊資訊
Travel Information

 Dialog 1 對話1

A: 你可以告訴我哪裡可以得到觀光資訊嗎？

A: Can you tell me where I can get some sightseeing information?

B: 我們飯店這兒有很多小冊子。

B: We have many brochures here at the hotel.

A: 是免費的嗎？

A: Are they free?

B: 是的，看看吧。

B: Yes, they are. Have a look.

Word Bank 字庫

brochure [bro'ʃur] n. 小冊子

Dialog 2 對話2

A: 我想找更多關於這裡的參觀地點。

A: I'd like to find out more about places to visit here.

B: 火車站附近有個遊客服務中心。

B: There is a tourist information center near the train station.

A: 那有多遠？

A: How far away is that?

B: 差不多走路五分鐘的路程。

B: About a five minute walk.

A: 那裡有人可以幫忙我安排旅程嗎？

A: Can someone there help me arrange a tour?

B: 我確定他們至少可以替你聯絡上適當的人。

B: I'm sure they can at least connect you to the right people.

A: 他們何時關門呢？

A: When do they close?

B: 它開到午夜。

B: It's open until midnight.

 Word Bank 字庫

tourist information center n. 遊客服務中心
arrange [ə'rendʒ] v. 安排
connect [kə'nɛkt] v. 連接
midnight ['mɪd,naɪt] n. 午夜，半夜 12 點

 Useful Phrases 實用語句

1. 我需要一些觀光資料。

   I need some sightseeing information.

基本對話

2. 遊客服務中心在哪裡呢？

   Where is the tourist information center?

3. 你可以告訴我聯絡誰嗎？

   Can you tell me who to contact?

4. 你們幾點開 [關] 門呢？

   What time do you open [close]?

5. 你們有小冊子嗎？

   Do you have any brochures?

6. 我可以拿這些嗎？

   May I take these?

機場與飛機

入境

住宿

交通

餐飲

7.2 詢問行程
Asking about Tours

觀光

Dialog 1　對話1

A: 我想找個市區觀光之旅。	**A:** I'd like to find about a tour of the city.
B: 我們有好幾個選擇。	**B:** We have several choices.
A: 哪一個是半天的呢？	**A:** Which takes half a day?
B: 我們有兩個，一個包含在河畔的餐廳午餐。	**B:** We have two. One includes lunch at a riverside restaurant.
A: 那聽來很好。	**A:** That sounds nice.

購物

郵電

銀行

麻煩事

回國

Word Bank 字庫

tour of the city n. 市區觀光之旅
riverside ['rɪvə‚saɪd] n. 河畔

Dialog 2 對話2

A: 你們有紅木州立公園一日遊嗎？

A: Do you have a one day tour to Redwood State Park?

B: 我們可以替你安排。

B: We can arrange that for you.

A: 有什麼交通工具可用呢？

A: What transportation is available?

B: 接駁車會來載你。

B: A shuttle bus will take you.

A: 費用是多少？

A: What is the cost?

B: 全天行程價是 27 元 50 分。

B: The whole day trip price is $27.50.

Dialog 3 對話3

A: 這裡有導覽的行程嗎？

A: Are there any guided tours available here?

基本對話

機場與飛機

入境

住宿

交通

餐飲

觀光

購物

郵電

銀行

麻煩事

回國

基本對話

機場與飛機

入境

住宿

交通

餐飲

觀光

購物

郵電

銀行

麻煩事

回國

B: 有，公園有解說導覽，每半個小時開始。

B: Yes, the park has guided tours, and they start every half hour.

A: 我在哪裡買票呢？

A: Where do I buy a ticket?

B: 行程是免費的。

B: The tours are free.

A: 他們在哪兒開始呢？

A: Where do they start?

B: 我來告訴你。

B: Let me show you.

Word Bank 字庫

guided tour n. 導覽行程

Useful Phrases 實用語句

1. 你們有市區觀光嗎？
   Do you have city tours?

2. 行程是多久呢？
   How long is the tour?

3. 何時開始呢？
   When does it start?

4. 多少人參加這個團呢？
   How many people are in the group?

5. 他們何時會來接我？

   When will they pick me up?

6. 我們會在宮殿花園待多久？

   How long will we stay at the Palace Garden?

7. 你是導遊嗎？

   Are you the tour guide?

8. 這是我們行程的集合地點嗎？

   Is this where we should gather for the tour?

9. 下一個行程何時開始呢？

   When does the next tour begin?

10. 我們可以參加下一個行程嗎？

    Can we join the next tour?

11. 有自由參觀的行程嗎？

    Are there free tours?

12. 你們有中文的小冊子嗎？

    Do you have a Chinese brochure available?

Notes 小叮嚀

有些景點或博物館、國會大廈等，基於安全或其他理由，不一定開放自由參觀，有固定的導覽時間或人數限制，必須先買票或預約才能參觀。

7.3 買地圖
Buying a Map

Dialog 對話

A: 我需要一份市區地圖。

A: I need a map of the city.

基本對話

機場與飛機

入境

住宿

交通

餐飲

觀光

購物

郵電

銀行

麻煩事

回國

基本對話

機場與飛機

入境

住宿

交通

餐飲

觀光

購物

郵電

銀行

麻煩事

回國

B: 我們這兒櫃臺有。

B: We have them here at the counter.

A: 哪個最好呢？

A: Which one is best?

B: 我認為這個最好，但是也最貴。

B: I think this one is, but it's also the most expensive.

A: 我拿這個了。你們也有餐廳指南嗎？

A: I'll take it. Do you also have a restaurant guide?

B: 有，也是剛剛才出版，所以包含所有最新的地方。

B: We do. It just came out, too, so it has all the latest places included.

A: 我還想知道你們是否有任何本地的雜誌。

A: I also wonder if you have any magazines that are local.

B: 有兩本，在那邊的架子上。

B: There is a couple. They are over there on the racks.

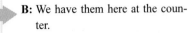 Word Bank 字庫

latest ['letɪst] adj. 最新的
rack [ræk] n. 架子

Tips 小祕訣

Google 地圖提供了極大的便利，但在國外離線使用有其難度及限制。使用導航機亦須先有外國圖資，未必盡如人意。出國前可先下載智慧型手機應用程式離線地圖以供使用，但使用紙本地圖仍有其必要。地圖種類分為「city map」(城市地圖)、「state map」(州地圖 (USA))，和「road map」(道路地圖)。州地圖對遊客而言是最方便的，因為上面有標示關於主要城市、食物、加油站及住宿 (lodging) 的地點，還有公園、露營地、風景名勝及緊急電話等，以及關於州的資訊。

在治安不佳慣於欺生之地，用手機或平板甚至紙本查看旅遊書或地圖等於羊入虎口。避免被偷搶，應先查好地圖及保持警覺。

7.4 請飯店櫃臺人員幫忙
Asking the Concierge

Dialog 對話

A: 可以幫我們買今晚的歌劇票嗎？

A: Is it possible to get tickets for the opera tonight?

B: 我會幫你們處理，多少人要去？

B: I'll take care of it for you. How many will be going?

A: 三個人要去。

A: Three of us want to go.

B: 我會立刻去辦。

B: I'll see to it immediately.

A: 你會打電話給我們嗎？

A: Will you call us?

基本對話

機場與飛機

入境

住宿

交通

餐飲

觀光

購物

郵電

銀行

麻煩事

回國

B: 給我一小時時間，之後可以任何時候來問我。

B: Give me an hour. Then anytime after that, ask for me.

✎ Word Bank 字庫

opera ['apərə] n. 歌劇
see to 照料，負責

7.5 百老匯表演
Broadway Show

 Dialog 1 對話1

A: 我們今晚要看什麼表演呢？

A: What show do you want to see tonight?

B: 我不知道，有這麼多可以選。

B: I don't know. There are so many to choose from.

A: 是啊，我們或許該看些評論。

A: Yes, there are. Maybe we should look at some reviews.

B: 好主意，我們也該打電話查一下有沒有票及價錢。

B: Good idea. We need to call and check on ticket availability and prices, too.

A: 對，受歡迎的秀很快就賣完了，我們可能來不及買某些票。

A: Yes. Popular shows sell out quickly. We might be too late for some.

B: 也有很棒的非百老匯秀。

B: There are great off-Broadway shows also.

A: 是，那倒是真的，想得好！

A: Yes, that's true. Good thinking!

Word Bank 字庫

review [rɪ'vju] n. 評論

off-Broadway ['ɔf 'brɔdwe] n. 非百老匯

Tips 小祕訣

　　不管英文程度如何，在紐約旅遊就不要錯過百老匯現場歌舞劇表演，還有非百老匯表演，可以換個口味。只要在街頭或旅館拿到表演節目單 (playbill)，就可以依據節目資訊及劇評來選擇這些表演，當然出發前就做功課是最好的。訂票方式有電話及網路訂票，但會有手續費。如果人已在紐約，不妨到購票處現場買票。去看表演時衣著要注意，不要因為旅遊在外而太休閒隨便，適當的衣著是對現場表演者的尊重。

Dialog 2 對話2

A: 現在是中場時間，我們到外面劇院大廳去喝一杯吧。

A: It's intermission time. Let's go out into the theater lobby and get a drink.

B: 聽來不錯，我也有點餓了。

B: That sounds good. I'm hungry, too.

A: 我確定他們也有些點心可吃。

A: I'm sure they'll have something to snack on also.

基本對話

機場與飛機

入境

住宿

交通

餐飲

觀光

購物

郵電

銀行

麻煩事

回國

B: 你覺得這場表演到目前為止如何？

B: What do you think of the show so far?

A: 很有娛樂性，我很喜歡。

A: It's really entertaining. I'm enjoying it very much.

B: 演得好而且燈光很特別。

B: The acting is good and the lighting is very special.

A: 你以前有看過百老匯表演嗎？

A: Have you seen any Broadway shows before?

B: 有，但每次來好像都是新上演的。

B: Yes, but every time I go, it seems new.

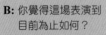 Word Bank 字庫

intermission [ˌɪntə·ˈmɪʃən] n. 中場休息
snack on 當點心吃
entertaining [ˌɛntə·ˈtenɪŋ] adj. 有娛樂性的
lighting [ˈlaɪtɪŋ] n. 舞臺燈光

7.6 博物館——買票
Museums—Buying Tickets

 Dialog 1 對話1

A: 我們必須各區分別買票嗎？

A: Do we have to buy a ticket for each part of the museum?

B: 不必，你只要在入口買一張票就可以了。

B: No, you don't. You just buy one ticket at the entrance.

A: 那柯威爾收藏區呢？

A: What about the Caldwell collection?

B: 喔，抱歉，是的，我忘了，那裡有另外的票要買。

B: Oh, sorry, yes, I forgot. There is a special ticket you have to buy for that.

A: 在哪兒買呢？

A: Where do I get it?

B: 收藏室入口旁，我來指給你看。

B: Next to the entrance of the collections' room. Let me show you there.

🖋 Word Bank 字庫

collection [kə'lɛkʃən] n. 收藏

Tips 小祕訣

　　博物館通常都要收門票，票價依名氣及規模大小而定。多數博物館會有紀念品 (souvenirs) 可買，如明信片 (postcard) 或複製藝術品 (museum replicas) 等。有些人則是反向操作，先買明信片，再給工作人員看，詢問怎麼找到該藝術品。這在時間有限而博物館超大的情形下，確不失為妙招。

基本對話

機場與飛機

入境

住宿

交通

餐飲

觀光

購物

郵電

銀行

麻煩事

回國

Dialog 2 (對話2)

A: 歡迎光臨廉威爾博物館。

A: Welcome to the Lanwell Museum.

B: 謝謝。這裡是售票窗口嗎?

B: Thank you. Is the ticket window here?

A: 進入我們的博物館不用收費。

A: There is no charge to enter our museum.

B: 真好!

B: How nice!

A: 我們會問訪客是否考慮捐款。

A: We do ask people to consider giving a donation.

B: 多少呢?

B: How much?

A: 任何金額都好。

A: Any amount is fine.

Word Bank (字庫)

ticket window n. 售票窗口

donation [do'neʃən] n. 捐款

基本對話 | 機場與飛機 | 入境 | 住宿 | 交通 | 餐飲 | 觀光 | 購物 | 郵電 | 銀行 | 麻煩事 | 回國

Tips 小祕訣

　　多數博物館收取門票，但有些則是要求參觀者捐款，金額不拘，通常在 1 至 5 美元之間。別忘記，博物館通常在星期一關門。

7.7 博物館——租用導覽設備
Museums—Renting Audio Guides

Dialog 1 對話1

A: 這地方有語音導覽可以用嗎？

A: Is there any audio guide information available for this place?

B: 有的，你可以付費租借語音導覽機。

B: Yes, you can rent an audio guide for a fee.

A: 費用多少呢？

A: How much is the fee?

B: 3 塊錢。

B: Three dollars.

A: 使用簡單嗎？

A: Is it easy to use?

B: 是的，就像遙控器一樣。只要看展示品上的編號，然後按下號碼。

B: Yes, it's like a remote control. Just look at the number of the display then press the number.

基本對話 | 機場與飛機 | 入境 | 住宿 | 交通 | 餐飲 | **觀光** | 購物 | 郵電 | 銀行 | 麻煩事 | 回國

| A: 聽來不錯，謝謝。 | A: Sounds good. Thanks. |

Word Bank 字庫

audio ['ɔdɪ,o] adj. 聲音的
fee [fi] n. 費用
remote control n. 遙控器
display [dɪ'sple] n. 展示品

Dialog 2 對話2

A: 這個導覽機壞了。	A: This player does not work.
B: 怎麼了？	B: What's wrong?
A: 我不知道，剛才還好好的，然後就壞了。	A: I don't know. It was OK, but then it quit working.
B: 沒問題，我拿另一個給你。	B: No problem. Let me get you another one.
A: 你們也有這裡的書面介紹嗎？	A: Do you also have a written guide for here?
B: 我們有 2 塊錢一份的。	B: We have one you can buy for $2.

A: 它有照片嗎？

A: Does it have some pictures?

B: 有的，它有一些很棒的照片。

B: Yes, it has some excellent photos.

Word Bank 字庫

quit [kwɪt] v. 停止
written ['rɪtn̩] adj. 書面的

Useful Phrases 實用語句

1. 我需要語音導覽機。
   I need an audio guide.
2. 怎樣開機呢？
   How do you turn it on?
3. 也有樓面圖嗎？
   Is there a floor map, too?

Tips 小祕訣

　　許多觀光地區及博物館備有小型地圖及簡介，另有語音導覽可供租借，費用通常為 3 至 5 元，有些博物館出租 iPod (約 5 元) 導覽或提供 app 下載到手機導覽。除了會員外，有些博物館會給學生及教師折扣，如果有這些身分，不妨出國前申請國際學生證或教師證備用。在美國免費出租採取押金，而非押證件的方式，因為抵押證件有侵犯個資之嫌。

基本對話

機場與飛機

入境

住宿

交通

餐飲

觀光

購物

郵電

銀行

麻煩事

回國

基本對話
機場與飛機
入境
住宿
交通
餐飲
觀光
購物
郵電
銀行
麻煩事
回國

7.8 小鎮嘉年華
County Fair

 Dialog 對話

A: 我們去小鎮嘉年華吧。

A: Let's go to the county fair.

B: 那是什麼？

B: What's that?

A: 小鎮嘉年華是為期一週的市集，有很多東西可看。

A: County fairs are big weeklong fairs with lots of things to see.

B: 像什麼呢？

B: Like what?

A: 動物、藝術、歌唱及舞蹈表演、產品介紹、競賽等等。

A: Animals, art, singing and dancing performances, product demonstrations, competitions, etc.

B: 好像有很多看頭。

B: It sounds like there is a lot to see.

A: 也有很多事可做。可以玩遊戲、贏獎品及乘坐大嘉年華遊樂設施。

A: A lot to do, too. There are games to play, prizes to win, and big carnival rides.

B: 會很貴嗎？

B: Is it expensive?

A: 不算貴，通常每人 5 到 6 元，但遊樂區內有些東西要另外付費。

A: No, not really. It usually costs five or six dollars per person, but you have to pay extra for some things inside the fair grounds.

Tips 小祕訣

　　美國夏天到處可見小鎮嘉年華，這是美國傳統的一部分，每個小鎮都會舉辦。規模大點、有錢點的城鎮，嘉年華規模較大，提供人們食物及多樣娛樂，是全家的好去處。州嘉年華的規模更大，也是在夏天舉辦，吸引更多的人潮。嘉年華的收費視規模大小及地點而定。

Language Power 字句補給站

◆ 小鎮嘉年華 County Fairs

farm animals	農場動物
art show	藝術表演
singing performance	唱歌表演
rodeo	牛仔競技表演
carnival rides	乘坐嘉年華遊樂設施
product show	產品展示
growers competition	農產品競賽
cotton candy	棉花糖
corn dogs	脆皮熱狗 (麵糊裹熱狗後油炸)
carnival games	嘉年華遊戲

基本對話

機場與飛機

入境

住宿

交通

餐飲

觀光

購物

郵電

銀行

麻煩事

回國

基本對話
機場與飛機
入境
住宿
交通
餐飲
觀光
購物
郵電
銀行
麻煩事
回國

7.9 賭城
Gambling (Las Vegas)

Dialog 1 對話1

A: 我們該去哪個賭場呢？

A: Which casino should we go to?

B: 很難講，拉斯維加斯這裡有這麼多賭場。

B: Hard to say. There are so many in Las Vegas.

A: 我還想看場秀。

A: I want to see a show, too.

B: 呃，大的賭場都有秀。

B: Well, all the major casinos have shows.

A: 對耶，而且飲料免費。

A: Right, and drinks are free.

B: 只有在賭博時才免費。

B: Only while you are gambling.

Dialog 2 對話2

A: 不好意思，我們需要拉霸 (吃角子老虎) 的代幣。

A: Excuse me. We need some tokens for the slot machines.

B: 你要多少？

B: How many do you want?

A: 200 元等值。	**A:** Two hundred dollars worth.
B: 好,把你的錢放在盤子上,然後滑到窗戶下。	**B:** OK. Just put your money in the tray and slide it under the window.
A: 在這裡。	**A:** Here you are.
B: 這裡是你的代幣,祝你好運。	**B:** And here are your tokens. Good luck.
A: 謝謝。	**A:** Thanks.

✎ Word Bank 字庫

> gamble ['gæmbl] v. 賭博
> casino [kə'sino] n. 賭場
> token ['tokən] n. 代幣
> slot machine n. 拉霸 (吃角子老虎)
> worth [wɜθ] n. 等值的量
> tray [tre] n. 盤子,托盤

📖 Useful Phrases 實用語句

1. 我們來賭博。

   Let's gamble.

2. 你喜歡玩 21 點嗎?

   Do you like to play Blackjack?

基本對話

機場與飛機

入境

住宿

交通

餐飲

觀光

購物

郵電

銀行

麻煩事

回國

3. 我們去賭城的大街 (拉斯維加斯賭場林立的大街) 吧。

Let's go to the Strip.

4. 我們去黃金峽谷 (在拉斯維加斯市內)。

Let's go to Glitter Gulch.

Language Power 字句補給站

◆ 賭博 Gambling

deck (of cards)	一副紙牌
shuffle	洗牌
cut the deck	切牌
deal	發牌
dealer	發牌員
chip	圓形籌碼
Blackjack (21)	21點
Keno	基諾 (一種似樂透賭博遊戲,使用號碼彩球及紙牌)
Roulette Table	輪盤桌
Poker	撲克牌

7.10 國家公園
National Parks

Dialog 對話

A: 嗨,歡迎光臨優勝美地國家公園。

A: Hi. Welcome to Yosemite National Park.

B: 謝謝,入園費是多少呢?

B: Thank you. How much is the entry fee?

A: 入園一日券每輛車是 15 元。

A: A day pass to the park costs $15 per carload.

B: 我要待五天。

B: I want to stay for five days.

A: 這樣的話，你應該買一星期長的通行證 40 元。

A: In that case you should buy a weeklong pass for $40.

B: 可以用多久呢？

B: How long is it good for?

A: 七天六夜。

A: Six nights, seven days.

Word Bank 字庫

entry ['ɛntrɪ] n. 進入，入場
carload ['kɑr,lod] n. 車載量
pass [pæs] n. 通行證，入場券

Tips 小祕訣

　　像其他多數地方一樣，國家公園也是要收費的。收費標準各地不同，但多在 10 到 25 元間。美國國家公園也推出年票 (annual pass) 每張80元，一年內可暢遊美國各州的國家公園，非常划算。

7.11 動物園
The Zoo

 Dialog 對話

A: 嗨，動物園開到很晚嗎？

A: Hi. Is the zoo open very late?

B: 今天開到下午6點。

B: It's open until 6 p.m. today.

A: 也有可愛動物區嗎？

A: Is there a petting zoo, too?

B: 有，在西區。

B: Yes, there is. It's on the west side.

A: 要另外收費嗎？

A: Is there an extra charge?

B: 平日不必。

B: Not on weekdays.

A: 我們可以在那兒拍照嗎？

A: Can we take pictures there?

B: 可以，但請不要用閃光燈。

B: Yes, but please don't use flash.

 Word Bank 字庫

petting zoo n. 可愛動物區 (可以撫摸擁抱動物之區域)
flash [flæʃ] n. 閃光燈

7.12 遊樂園
Amusement Park

 Dialog 1 對話1

A: 嗨，我們要四張票。

A: Hi. We want tickets for four.

B: 我們有半日通行證及全日通行證。

B: We have half day and full day passes.

A: 全日票可以讓我們做什麼呢？

A: What does the all day pass allow us to do?

B: 跟半日票一樣，但你可以待到關門時間。

B: It's the same as the half day pass, but you can stay until closing time.

A: 你們幾點關閉園區呢？

A: What time do you close the park?

B: 園區在晚上 11 點 30 分關。

B: The park closes at 11:30 p.m.

A: 通行證可以乘坐每樣東西及進入園區所有地方嗎？

A: Does the pass allow us to ride and enter everything in the park?

基本對話 | 機場與飛機 | 入境 | 住宿 | 交通 · 餐飲 | 觀光 | 購物 | 郵電 | 銀行 | 麻煩事 | 回國

B: 是的，除了明日世界。它要多花每人2塊半。

B: Yes, except Future Land. It costs $2.50 per person more.

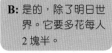

Word Bank 字庫

ride [raɪd] v. 乘坐

Dialog 2 對話2

A: 票務員告訴我，我們應該讀這些警語。

A: The ticket agent told me we should read these warnings.

B: 警語說些什麼呢？

B: What do the warnings say?

A: 大部分是關於健康考量。

A: Mostly they are about health considerations.

B: 喔，好，我知道了。我健康沒問題。

B: Oh, OK, I see. I have no problem with my health.

Word Bank 字庫

agent ['edʒənt] n. 經銷人，代辦人
consideration [kənsɪdə'reʃən] n. 考量

Useful Phrases 實用語句

1. 這是坐那個的隊伍嗎？
   Is this the line for that ride?

2. 隊伍從哪裡開始排的？
   Where does the line start?

3. 小孩可以坐這個嗎？
   Can children ride this one?

4. 一日券可以做什麼？
   What does a day pass allow us to do?

5. 入場券包含乘坐遊樂設施嗎？
   Does the pass include the rides?

7.13 騎馬
Horse Ride

 Dialog 對話

A: 我們這裡海邊有馬可以騎。

A: We have rides available here on the beach.

B: 我們從沒有騎過馬。

B: We've never ridden horses before.

A: 那沒問題，我們的馬很溫馴。

A: That's no problem. Our horses are very tame.

B: 我了解，要多少錢呢？

B: I see. How much does it cost?

基本對話

機場與飛機

入境

住宿

交通

餐飲

觀光

購物

郵電

銀行

麻煩事

回國

A: 我們有個四小時 25 元的騎馬行程。

A: We have a four hour beach ride for \$25.

 Word Bank 字庫

ride [raɪd] n. 騎馬；v. 騎乘
tame [tem] adj. 溫馴的

 Useful Phrases 實用語句

1. 我要一匹溫馴的馬。

   I want a tame horse.

2. 我以前從未騎過馬。

   I've never ridden a horse before.

3. 我的馬鞍有點鬆。

   My saddle feels loose.

4. 請查看我的馬鞍。

   Please check my saddle.

7.14 美國印地安原住民保留區
Native American Indian Reservations

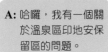 Dialog 對話

A: 哈囉，我有一個關於溫泉區印地安保留區的問題。

A: Hello. I have a question about the Warm Springs Indian Reservation.

B: 什麼問題呢？

B: What is your question?

A: 進入保留區需要任何許可證或特別許可嗎？

A: Do I need any permits or special permission to go into the reservation?

B: 不用，保留區是對大眾開放的，但有些部分有時候是限制區。

B: No, you don't. The reservations are open to the public, although there are some parts of the reservation that are restricted at times.

A: 為什麼呢？

A: Why?

B: 有些地區被住在那裡的族人認為是特別的，有時候舉行特別的活動，只有當地族人能參加。

B: Some places are considered very special by the tribe that lives there, and sometimes special events take place that only the tribe members can attend.

A: 我知道了，謝謝你提供的資訊。

A: I see. Thanks for the information.

 Word Bank 字庫

permit ['pɜ·mɪt] n. 許可證
permission [pɚ'mɪʃən] n. 許可
reservation [ˌrɛzɚ'veʃən] n. 保留區
tribe [traɪb] n. 部落
attend [ə'tɛnd] v. 參加，出席

基本對話

機場與飛機

入境

住宿

交通

餐飲

觀光

購物

郵電

銀行

麻煩事

回國

Tips 小祕訣

印地安原住民保留區在美國各地都有，在許多保留區你可以看到他們開設的賭場。有些保留區是休閒度假區，任何人都可以去打高爾夫、游泳、騎馬及從事其他休閒活動。有的地方會標榜教授部落生活，遊客也可以買到許多原住民的食物及別緻的手工藝品。

7.15 海邊——詢問規定
The Coastline/Beach—Asking about Rules

Dialog 對話

A: 嗨，我有個關於這裡規定的問題。

A: Hi. I have a question about the rules here?

B: 是什麼問題呢？

B: What is your question?

A: 可以撿拾海邊的貝殼嗎？

A: Is it all right to collect seashells from the beach?

B: 可以的，也可以在指定的區域挖蛤。

B: Yes, it is. It's also OK to dig for clams in designated areas.

A: 撿拾漂流木呢？

A: What about picking up driftwood.

B: 不行，這個海灘不可以，也不可以生火。

B: No, not at this beach. No fires allowed, either.

基本對話

機場與飛機

入境

住宿

交通

餐飲

觀光

購物

郵電

銀行

麻煩事

回國

Word Bank 字庫

collect [kə'lɛkt] v. 收集，採集
seashell ['si,ʃɛl] n. 貝殼
dig [dɪg] v. 挖
clam [klæm] n. 蚌，蛤
designated ['dɛzɪg,netɪd] adj. 指定的
driftwood ['drɪft,wud] n. 漂流木

Notes 小叮嚀

　　在美國旅遊，多數地區是對大眾開放的，但是先確定一下總是比較保險。另外一種情形是，遊客可能必須穿越私人道路或土地才能到達某個海邊或河岸。通常遊客會看到「Private property. Don't Trespass.」(私人土地，不可侵入) 的標誌，在這種情形下，旅客必須獲得許可才行，侵入私人土地的結果可能讓主人覺得安全受威脅而拿槍對以對或是報警處理。

7.16 海邊——海灣遊船
The Coastline/Beach—Bay Cruise

Dialog 對話

A: 我們可以在這裡買遊船票嗎？

A: Can we buy tickets for a cruise on the bay here?

B: 可以的。

B: Yes, you can.

A: 有晚上的遊船嗎？

A: Are there any evening cruises?

基本對話

B: 有，我們在 7 點登船，7 點半開航。

→ **B:** Yes. We board at 7:00 p.m., and set sail at 7:30.

機場與飛機

A: 船上有晚餐嗎？

→ **A:** Is dinner available on board?

入境

B: 當然，船票包含一頓精緻五菜餐。

→ **B:** Certainly. A fine five course meal is included in the price.

住宿

交通

餐飲

Word Bank 字庫

> cruise [kruz] n. 航遊
> bay [be] n. 海灣
> set sail 開航
> fine [faɪn] adj. 精緻的

觀光

Notes 小叮嚀

> 歐美地區早晚氣溫變化較大，即使夏季遊河或出海到附近小島一遊，都必須帶件外套備用。晚上看夜景風大，若氣溫降到 15 度左右，甚至需要厚重外套、帽子、圍巾才足夠保暖。

購物

郵電

銀行

7.17 海邊——租水上摩托車
The Coastline/Beach—Jet Ski Rental

麻煩事

Dialog 對話

A: 我們想要租一些水上摩托車。

→ **A:** We want to rent some jet skis.

回國

B: 我們有很多，看這邊。

B: We have many. Look over here.

A: 太好了，多少錢呢？

A: Great. How much does it cost?

B: 30 元四小時或 50 元整天。

B: \$30 for four hours, or \$50 for the day.

A: 我們以前沒使用過，會有問題嗎。

A: We've never used one before. Is that a big problem?

B: 一點也不會，我們會給你免費上一堂課。

B: Not at all. We'll give you a lesson free.

A: 要多久呢？

A: How long will that take?

B: 只要10到15分鐘。

B: Only ten to fifteen minutes.

7.18 海邊——游泳
The Coastline/Beach—Swimming

 Dialog 對話

A: 嗨，這裡游泳安全嗎？

A: Hi. Is it safe to swim here?

基本對話

機場與飛機

入境

住宿

交通

餐飲

觀光

購物

郵電

銀行

麻煩事

回國

B: 你要小心暗流。

B: You must be careful of the undertow.

A: 會很危險嗎？

A: Is it very dangerous?

B: 可能會。

B: It can be.

A: 我會游泳，但不是很棒。

A: I can swim, but not great.

B: 這裡有很多救生員，你就待在標示的區域內。

B: There are many lifeguards here. Just stay in the marked areas.

A: 那些區域安全嗎？

A: Are those areas safe?

B: 比其他海邊游泳區安全多了。

B: They are much safer than other parts of the beach for swimming.

Word Bank 字庫

undertow ['ʌndə‚to] n. 暗流
lifeguard ['laɪf‚gɑrd] n. 救生員
marked [mɑrkt] adj. 標示出的

Useful Phrases 實用語句

1. 這裡可以游泳嗎？

   Is it OK to swim here?

2. 這裡有救生員嗎？

   Is there a lifeguard here?

3. 我們需要救生衣。

   I need a life vest.

4. 我們需要一些救生圈及浮板。

   We need some rubber tubes [float rings] and kick boards.

5. 我們需要蛙鞋。

   We need some fins.

6. 我們來找一些浮潛用具吧。

   Let's get some snorkeling equipment.

Notes 小叮嚀

海邊游泳在許多地方是安全的，但必須小心強浪，並避免到海水溫度低的地方游泳。在美東佛羅里達 (Florida)、路易斯安那 (Louisiana) 或喬治亞州 (Georgia) 的颶風 (hurricane) 季節，要特別注意氣象報告，即使颶風還在數百里外，颶風已帶來強烈海邊暗流。到海邊游泳最好先問旅館及查看當地氣象及水域狀況，並選擇有救生員的海邊。

7.19 海邊——海上垂釣
The Coastline/Beach—Sports Fishing

Dialog 對話

A: 我要買釣魚執照。

A: I want to buy a fishing license.

基本對話

機場與飛機

入境

住宿

交通

餐飲

觀光

購物

郵電

銀行

麻煩事

回國

B: 你要哪種釣魚呢？

B: What type of fishing are you going to do.

A: 我要搭鮭魚船出海。

A: I want to go out on a salmon boat.

B: 這樣的話你應該去碼頭。

B: In that case you should go to the docks.

A: 為什麼？

A: Why?

B: 你可以向賣衣服及裝備的店家買執照。

B: You can buy the license from the outfitter.

A: 那其他需要的設備呢？

A: What about the other equipment I need?

B: 他們會有你所需的任何設備。

B: They'll have everything you need.

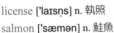

Word Bank 字庫

license ['laɪsn̩s] n. 執照
salmon ['sæmən] n. 鮭魚
dock [dɑk] n. 碼頭
outfitter ['aut.fɪtɚ] n. 販售衣服及裝備的用品店
equipment [ɪ'kwɪpmənt] n. 設備

 Useful Phrases 實用語句

1. 我想買一張釣魚證。

   I'd like to buy a fishing license.

2. 我需要一些釣魚設備。

   I need some fishing equipment.

3. 我需要一些魚餌。

   I need some bait.

4. 這張釣魚證可以用多久？

   How long will this license last?

 Tips 小祕訣

在美國，釣魚及打獵不僅要看季節、準備需要的裝備，還需要證件。對旅客而言，找專門的教練是較方便的選擇，因為他們可以提供所需資料及裝備，並給予你所需要的指導。

7.20 夜生活——外出
Nightlife—Going Out

 Dialog 對話

A: 晚上有哪個地方好去呢？

A: Where is a good place to go at night?

B: 你是指外出進城嗎？

B: You mean go out on the town?

A: 是的。

A: Yes.

基本對話　機場與飛機　入境　住宿　交通　餐飲　觀光　購物　郵電　銀行　麻煩事　回國

基本對話 機場與飛機 入境 住宿 交通 餐飲 觀光 購物 郵電 銀行 麻煩事 回國

B: 那要看你想做什麼。

B: It depends on what you want to do.

A: 這附近有沒有好的爵士酒吧呢？

A: Are there any good jazz bars around here?

B: 當然，而且它們幾乎整晚都開著。

B: Sure, and they stay open almost all night.

A: 有節目費嗎？

A: Any cover charge?

B: 有，但收費不高。

B: Yes, but it's not high.

Notes 小叮嚀

　　晚上外出最好結伴，並且走在燈光明亮的地方。在美國除了少數大都市有精彩的夜生活外，許多中小型城市在市區的商業中心下班後，可能像空城一樣。有些城市有住在市區的貧窮人口或少數無家可歸的流浪漢徘迴在便利商店門口，因此夜晚在市區要格外當心。

Useful Phrases 實用語句

1. 這裡的夜生活怎樣呢？

   What's the nightlife like here?

2. 你可以給我們推薦一間夜店嗎？

   Can you recommend a club to us?

3. 節目費是多少呢？

   What's the cover charge?

4. 快樂時光是什麼時候呢？

When's happy hour?

 Tips 小祕訣

有表演的餐廳可能在餐點費用外，外加節目費。快樂時光 (happy hour) 指的是下班後 4 點到 8 點的時段，店家為商業促銷，啤酒可能特別便宜或買一送一 (two for one) 並贈送爆米花或脆餅等 finger food 的小點心。星期五的 happy hour 較其他日子熱絡，人們說 TGIF (Thank God It's Friday) 感謝上帝，隔天是週末不必上班。

7.21 夜生活——爵士夜店
Nightlife—Jazz Club

 Dialog 1 對話1

A: 歡迎光臨「來享薩 (克斯風)」，每人娛樂費 5 元。

A: Welcome to "Let's Have Sax". There's a five dollar cover charge per person.

B: 這裡是 10 元。

B: Here's ten dollars.

A: 拿著這個 (入場券)，你可以免費喝兩杯飲料。

A: Take this (entry coupon). You can get two free drinks with it.

B: 這裡有跳舞嗎？

B: Is there dancing here?

A: 有的，9 點以後。

A: Yes, there is, after nine o'clock.

基本對話

機場與飛機

入境

住宿

交通

餐飲

觀光

購物

郵電

銀行

麻煩事

回國

262

 Dialog 2 對話2

A: 我們可以坐哪兒呢？

A: Where can we sit?

B: 哪裡都可以，先來先坐。

B: Anywhere you like. It's first come, first serve.

A: 這裡可以吸菸嗎？

A: Can you smoke here?

B: 我們有吸菸區在那邊。

B: We have a smoking section over there.

A: 好。

A: Good.

B: 我們這裡也賣各種牌子的香菸。

B: We sell all brands of cigarettes here, too.

Dialog 3 對話3

A: 我們想用這 (入場券) 換兩杯飲料。

A: We'd like to exchange this (entry coupon) for two drinks.

B: 好，你們要喝什麼呢？

B: OK. What do you want to have?

A: 你們有飲料單嗎？

A: Do you have a drink list?

B: 有,但實際上這些券只能點啤酒或汽水。

B: Yes, but actually these coupons are only good for beer or soft drinks.

A: 了解了,好,兩杯啤酒,但是請送飲料單過來。

A: I see. OK, two beers, please, but please bring a drink list.

B: 沒問題,我馬上連飲料一起帶過去。

B: No problem. I'll be right back with your drinks.

Dialog 4 對話4

A: 我們來跳舞吧。

A: Let's dance.

B: 我不是個會跳舞的人。

B: I'm not a good dancer.

A: 沒關係,你隨便怎麼跳都行。

A: It doesn't matter, you just move anyway you want.

B: 希望我不會踩到別人。

B: I hope I don't step on anybody.

A: 如果這樣,只要微笑及說抱歉。

A: If you do, just smile and say sorry.

B: 好,走吧。

B: OK, let's go.

基本對話

機場與飛機

入境

住宿

交通

餐飲

觀光

購物

郵電

銀行

麻煩事

回國

基本對話
機場與飛機
入境
住宿
交通
餐飲
觀光
購物
郵電
銀行
麻煩事
回國

Tips 小祕訣

　　大都市的夜生活提供另一個了解當地生活及文化的管道，例如在紐約，夜生活各式各樣，多采多姿。中型城市也有不錯的選擇。在熱鬧的場所排隊，或到看來不錯的地方逛逛，每個人覺得有趣好玩的想法不盡相同，不妨讓自己嘗試接受不同的體驗。有些夜店 (在臺灣也是) 會推出淑女之夜及快樂時光，提供各式的音樂、舞步，若對跳舞沒興趣的人，來此坐坐、喝東西、聊天，也是輕鬆的夜晚娛樂方式。

　　小城鎮的夜生活當然比不上大城市的五光十色，但也有一些酒吧可以喝點東西。有些地方可以聽當地樂團現場演奏或有舞池可以跳舞，這些地方多在 9 點或 10 點打烊。此外還有二十四小時的便利商店及電影院或影片出租店，最後就是汽車旅館內的電影頻道了。相較之下，美加人民比我們要早睡早起的多。

Useful Phrases 實用語句

1. 我們想點些食物及飲料。

   We'd like some food and drinks.

2. 請再多些飲料。(請再來一杯。)

   More drinks, please.

3. 我要續杯。

   I'd like a refill.

4. 你有火柴嗎？

   Do you have any matches?

5. 我需要打火機。

   I need a lighter.

6. 洗手間在哪裡？

   Where is the bathroom [restroom]?

7. 這裡有公共電話嗎？

   Is there a pay phone here?

Notes 小叮嚀

在美國，購買香菸必須年滿 18 歲 (少數州已提高到19
歲)，買酒需年滿 21 歲。進入酒吧 (pub, tavern)、夜店 (club)、
賭場 (casino) 等場所，要帶證件 (如駕照、護照) 備查，證明已
超過合法年紀 21 歲，如果沒帶證件是進不去的。除非是很明
顯的情形，西方人通常很難猜對東方人的年紀。事實上，供應
酒精飲料的場所幾乎都要查看每位顧客的證件，不論他們看起
來年紀如何。在美國，商家或其他場所要求查看證件是常有的
事，使用支票也是要看證件的，所以不必多猜疑。喝酒後絕不
可駕車，在美國酒駕的處罰是非常嚴重的。

7.22 夜生活——脫口秀俱樂部
Nightlife—Comedy Club

Dialog 對話

A: 你今晚想去脫口秀
俱樂部嗎？

A: Do you want to go to a comedy
club tonight?

B: 我很喜歡喜劇，笑
一笑很有趣。

B: I like comedy a lot. It's fun to
laugh.

A: 我也是，但我想可
能有個問題。

A: Me too, but I think there might
be a problem.

B: 什麼問題？

B: What's that?

A: 很多笑話都跟他們
本身的文化有關。

A: A lot of the jokes are based in
the culture they come from.

基本對話

機場與飛機

入境

住宿

交通

餐飲

觀光

購物

郵電

銀行

麻煩事

回國

B: 是啊，沒錯，我們可能不懂哪裡好笑。

B: Yes. Right. We may not understand what is funny about them.

A: 好吧，我們可以晚餐時再想一想。

A: Well, we can think it over during dinner.

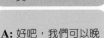 Tips 小祕訣

脫口秀俱樂部在大都市的夜生活較常見。詼諧的脫口秀輪番上臺之餘，可能會有一些好笑的短劇穿插。

7.23 參加晚宴
Showing Up for Dinner

 Dialog 1 對話1

A: 嗨，歡迎，見到你真好。

A: Hi, welcome. It's so nice to see you.

B: 謝謝，見到你也很棒。

B: Thank you. It's nice to see you, too.

A: 請進，我幫你弄杯飲料。

A: Come in and let me fix you a drink.

B: 讓我先把這禮物給你。

B: First let me offer you this gift.

A: 喔，真好！你真的不必 (準備禮物)。	**A:** Oh! How nice! You really shouldn't have.
B: 這是我的榮幸。	**B:** It's really my pleasure.
A: 真謝謝你。	**A:** Thank you very much.

 Word Bank 字庫

fix [fɪks] v. 準備(餐食)
shouldn't have 不必(做某事)

 Notes 小叮嚀

　　美國人的用餐時間與臺灣相似，如果受邀到美國人家裡晚餐，不一定要帶東西去，但不要遲到也不要早到。晚個十分鐘沒問題，但主人會期待客人準時。如果想帶禮物，很多人會帶一瓶好酒，如果不確定主人是否喝酒，或許可以帶甜點。如果是和主人一起看球賽、烤肉，可以帶個六瓶裝啤酒。記住開車時可以把酒放在車內，但是車子裡面不可有已開瓶的酒。

　　某些歐洲 (中南美、中東) 國家用餐時間較晚 (與氣候、日落時間有關)，午餐可能1-2點開始，3-4點結束，晚餐8-10甚至11點開始，10-12點或更晚結束。因為用餐時間晚了許多，先吃些點心再赴約以免餓過頭而狼吞虎嚥，通常當地習慣慢慢吃飯喝酒聊天，晚餐多含社交目的而少談公事 (與午餐的商業目的不同)，入境隨俗，了解當地人對時間的概念與社交文化，不要急著走，否則會顯得只為一頓飯來而失禮。

基本對話

機場與飛機

入境

住宿

交通

餐飲

觀光

購物

郵電

銀行

麻煩事

回國

Dialog 2　對話2

A: 我要感謝你們邀我來晚餐。

A: I want to thank you for inviting me to dinner.

B: 我們很高興你能來。

B: We are happy you could come.

A: 我希望改天能回請你們。

A: I hope I can return the favor sometime.

B: 別操心這個了，歡迎你隨時來。

B: Don't worry about it. You're welcome here anytime.

A: 真感謝你們。

A: Thank you so much.

Word Bank　字庫

favor ['fevə] n. 恩惠

sometime ['sʌm,taɪm] adv. 在未來某時，日後

Useful Phrases　實用語句

1. 這是我為今天晚餐買的東西。

   Here is something I brought for tonight's dinner.

2. 我買了一瓶酒。

   I brought a bottle of wine.

3. 謝謝你邀請我來。

   Thanks for inviting me.

4. (今晚) 很好玩。

It's been fun.

5. 晚餐很棒。

The dinner was great.

6. 希望很快可以再聚會。

I hope we can do it again soon.

Tips 小祕訣

一般而言，美國人不會要客人進門前脫鞋，除非家裡裝了昂貴的地毯，或外面下雪或下雨有泥巴之類的情形。到別人家中作客受到招待，別忘了要寫張感謝卡 (thank-you card) 致謝，或改天回請對方。

7.24 問路
Asking for Directions

Dialog 對話

A: 不好意思，你可以告訴我最近的提款機在哪裡嗎？

A: Excuse me. Can you tell me where the nearest ATM machine is?

B: 好的，那邊的超市裡有一臺提款機。

B: Yes. There is an ATM in the supermarket right over there.

A: 真多謝。

A: Thanks very much.

B: 記得明天是假日，所以今天提款吧。

B: Remember that tomorrow is a holiday, so get money today.

基本對話　機場與飛機　入境　住宿　交通　餐飲　觀光　購物　郵電　銀行　麻煩事　回國

| A: 知道了，謝謝你告訴我。 | A: I see. Thanks for telling me. |

 Useful Phrases 實用語句

1. 最近的便利商店在哪裡呢？

   Where is the nearest convenience store?

2. 附近有好的餐廳嗎？

   Is there a good restaurant nearby?

3. 你可以告訴我銀行在哪裡嗎？

   Can you tell me where the bank is?

4. 博物館在這個方向嗎？

   Is the museum in this direction?

5. 我在找遊客服務中心。

   I'm looking for the tourist information center.

6. 是跟哪一條路交叉呢？

   What's the cross street?

7. 錯不了的！(即目標很明顯)

   You can't miss it!

Language Power 字句補給站

◆ 問路 Directions

go straight	直走
go down [up] the street	沿街一直走
go five blocks	走五個街區
turn left [right]	左 [右] 轉
walk through	穿越
walk past	走經過
go back	走回
cross the street	穿越街道
walk across the street	過馬路
wrong way	走錯

in front of	在前面
on the left [right]	在左 [右] 邊
across from	對面
behind	在後面
next to	在旁邊
between	在兩者之間
not far	不遠
very near	很近
a long way away	非常遠
about a ten minute walk	約走十分鐘的路程
look for (name of a landmark)	尋找 (地標名稱)

7.25 拍照
Taking Photos of People

Dialog 1　對話1

A: 不好意思，我可以拍一張你們的全體照嗎？

A: Excuse me. May I take a photo of all of you?

B: 為什麼呢？

B: What is it for?

A: 是為了我的旅遊剪貼簿。

A: Just for my travel scrapbook.

B: 這是個好主意。

B: That's a nice idea.

A: 我要它幫我記住這次旅行。

A: I want it to help me remember this trip.

基本對話

機場與飛機

入境

住宿

交通

餐飲

觀光

購物

郵電

銀行

麻煩事

回國

B: 好的，沒問題，拍下你全部想拍的吧。

B: OK, sure, take all you want.

Word Bank 字庫

photo ['foto] n. 照片 (= photograph)

scrapbook ['skræp,buk] n. 剪貼簿

Notes 小叮嚀

要拍他人照片最好要經過人家同意再拍，有些人並不喜歡被陌生人拍照 (回教徒因信仰與風俗，對拍照特別敏感)，或是被閃光燈打擾，頻繁自拍的行為也容易惹人反感。除了軍事區、海關、機場、港口、碼頭、邊防(包含軍警人員) 等，因國家安全餘慮，禁止拍照外，博物館、展覽館 (涉及文物保護與版權)、寺廟 (涉及宗教) 等地多數不可拍照 (No photography)，有些則必須在禁用閃光燈 (No flash) 下拍攝。

Dialog 2 對話2

A: 我有足夠時間在我們走之前拍些照片嗎？

A: Do I have enough time to take some pictures before we go?

B: 我們再 20 分鐘要上巴士。

B: We are going to board the buses in twenty minutes.

A: 我會在那之前回來。

A: I'll be back before then.

Dialog 3 對話3

A: 不好意思，請問你可以幫我們拍張照嗎？

A: Excuse me. Would you please take a picture of us?

B: 當然可以，你這相機怎麼用呢？

B: Sure. How do you use this camera?

A: 很簡單，只要瞄準並按這個鈕。

A: It's simple. Just aim and press this button.

B: 知道了。你們準備好了嗎？

B: I see. Are you ready?

A: 等一下。好，可以拍了。

A: Wait a moment. OK. Go ahead.

B: 好，說「起司」(笑一個)。

B: OK. Say "cheese".

A: 起司。(喀擦)

A: Cheese. (click)

Word Bank 字庫

aim [em] v. 瞄準
press [prɛs] v. 按，壓
button ['bʌtn̩] n. 按鈕

274

 Useful Phrases 實用語句

1. 請你替我們照相好嗎？

   Would you take our picture, please?

2. 按下這個鈕。

   Press this button.

3. 只要瞄準及拍攝。

   Just point and shoot.

4. 我們用閃光燈吧。

   Let's use the flash.

5. 閃光燈沒亮。

   It didn't flash.

6. 請多照一張。

   Please take one more.

7. 讓我幫你照一張。

   Let me help you take a picture.

8. 我們得回去了。

   We have to get back now.

9. 我們上巴士吧。

   Let's get on the bus.

Unit 8 Shopping

購物

美國到處都有購物機會，大城市提供流行及設計的貨品，小城鎮有當地的貨品及手工藝品，購物通常有包裝(大多免費)及運送(大多要收費)服務。原住民居住地可見到原住民製作的首飾、捕夢網、沙畫等手工藝品；較鄉下的城鎮，有牛仔衣、帽、馬靴等。美國購物商場營業時間到晚上9點，周日到7點。有午休習慣的歐洲國家(如希臘、西班牙、義大利)，午休時間約2-3小時(1:00-4:00間)，歐洲許多商店甚至在10分鐘前就不讓客人進入，以準時在6或7點關門，週末也不營業，街道只剩餐廳酒吧營業，七、八月是歐洲人度假旺季，許多商店根本不開門。中南美洲治安不佳，除了餐館外，商店(與西班牙一樣)皆在6點左右打烊。夜市可說是東南亞及中東地區特有的文化。

基本對話
機場與飛機
入境
住宿
交通
餐飲
觀光
購物
郵電
銀行
麻煩事
回國

8.1 超市——尋找物品
Supermarket—Looking for Something

Dialog 對話

A: 哪裡是農產品區呢？

A: Where is the produce department?

B: 在 1 號走道。

B: It's on Aisle 1.

A: 你們這裡也有熟食區嗎？

A: Do you have a deli here, too?

B: 有，在後面 10 號走道底。

B: Yes, we do. It's located in the back, at the end of Aisle 10.

A: 我有折價券，我要把折價券給誰？

A: I have a coupon book. Who do I give the coupons to?

B: 給你的收銀員。

B: Give them to your cashier.

A: 謝謝。

A: Thanks.

8.2 超市——結帳
Supermarket—Checkout

Dialog 1 對話1

A: 先生,你可以來這裡結帳。

A: Sir. You can come here to check out.

B: 真的嗎?這裡沒人排隊。

B: Really? There is nobody in this line.

A: 這是快速結帳通道。

A: This is the express lane.

B: 那是什麼意思呢?

B: What does that mean?

A: 如果你買九項以下且付現,就可以使用快速結帳通道。

A: If you have nine items or less, and are paying cash, you can use the express lane.

B: 很方便呢。

B: Very convenient.

A: 你要紙袋還是塑膠袋?

A: Do you want a paper or plastic bag today?

B: 塑膠袋,謝謝。

B: Plastic, please.

基本對話

機場與飛機

入境

住宿

交通

餐飲

觀光

購物

郵電

銀行

麻煩事

回國

基本對話

機場與飛機

入境

住宿

交通

餐飲

觀光

購物

郵電

銀行

麻煩事

回國

Tips 小祕訣

農產品秤重貼上標價後再結帳，或是在櫃臺結帳時再秤重。通常推車都是推到外面停車場放東西後再歸位。有些超市有貼心的裝箱員，幫忙裝箱及幫忙老人、婦女或購買大量物品的人推車或提東西。有些超市已使用 self check-out 通道，讓消費者自行刷卡結帳。

Dialog 2 對話2

A: 我有這些物品的一些折價券。

A: I have some coupons for some of these items.

B: 好，交給我，我來核對。

B: OK. Give them to me. I'll check them.

A: 好，謝謝你。

A: OK, thank you.

B: 沒問題。你要我們裝箱員幫你把這些東西提出去嗎？

B: Sure, no problem. Would you like one of our box boys to help you carry these things out for you?

A: 不，沒關係，我自己提。

A: No, that's OK. I'll carry them.

B: 祝你有美好的一天。

B: Have a nice day.

A: 你也是，再見。

A: You, too. Bye.

 Language Power 字句補給站

◆ 超市 Supermarket

produce	農產品
dairy	乳製品
meat department	肉類區
canned goods	罐頭商品
instant foods	速食
frozen foods	冷凍食品
breakfast cereal	早餐麥片
household items	家用品
home pharmacy	家用藥品
beverages	飲料
beers and wines	啤酒及葡萄酒 [水果酒]
snacks	零食
candy and sweets	糖果類
deli	熟食
baked goods	烘焙食品
checkout counter	結帳櫃臺
express lane/line	快速結帳通道
self check-out	自行結帳
cashier	收銀員
grocery cart	超市購物推車

8.3 購物商場──詢問商品
Shopping Mall—Asking about Goods

 Dialog 1 對話1

A: 這件夾克多少錢？

A: How much is this jacket?

B: 125 元。

B: It costs $125.

基本對話
機場與飛機
入境
住宿
交通
餐飲
觀光
購物
郵電
銀行
麻煩事
回國

A: 它是皮革做的嗎？

A: Is it made of leather?

B: 是的。

B: Yes.

Word Bank 字庫

jacket ['dʒækɪt] n. 夾克
leather ['lɛðɚ] n. 皮革

Tips 小祕訣

　　在美國的商場購物，如果售貨員不忙碌的話，會主動招呼你，問你需要找什麼或是否需要幫忙「Hi, how are you? How can I help you? Are you looking for anything today?」，如果有需要幫忙就可以直接問。如果只是逛逛，就說「Thank you. I'm just looking.」或簡單地說「Just looking」就可以了。到法國商店，要主動跟店員打招呼。簡單說聲「嗨」都好，否則會被視為不禮貌。

Dialog 2 對話2

A: 我喜歡這件毛衣，但我想要別的顏色。

A: I like this sweater, but I want a different color.

B: 讓我看看我們有哪些其他顏色？

B: Let me see what other colors we have.

A: 我想這尺寸也有點太小。

A: I think the size is too small, too.

B: 讓我也查一查尺寸吧。

B: Let me check on that, too.

 Word Bank 字庫

sweater ['swɛtɚ] n. 毛衣

check on 查對

 Useful Phrases 實用語句

1. 這是什麼材質做的？

   What material is this made of?

2. 我可以試穿它嗎？

   May I try it on?

3. 更衣室在哪裡？

   Where is the change room?

4. 它太小 [大] 了。

   It's too small [big].

5. 我想試另一件。

   I want to try another one.

6. 我要這兩件。

   I'll take these two.

7. 會縮水嗎？

   Will it shrink?

8. 會褪色嗎？

   Will the color fade?

9. 可以烘乾嗎？

   Can I put it in a dryer?

10. 這必須乾洗嗎？

    Should this be dry cleaned?

基本對話

機場與飛機

入境

住宿

交通

餐飲

觀光

購物

郵電

銀行

麻煩事

回國

　　美國及加拿大的衣服尺寸比亞洲標準尺寸要大，買衣服最好要試穿。一般尺寸標示有XXL (double extra large) 超超大、XL (extra large) 超大、L (large) 大、M (medium) 中、S (small) 小、XS (extra small) / Petité 超小，以及 F (free size / one size fits all) 不分尺寸。一個在亞洲穿大號衣服的人，在美國可能買中號才合身。各地尺寸對照請見附錄「衣服及鞋子尺寸」。

Language Power 字句補給站

◆ 衣物質料 Clothing Materials

wool	羊毛
cotton	棉
silk	絲
leather	皮革
angora	安哥拉羊毛
cashmere	喀什米爾羊毛織品
denim	丹寧布 (牛仔褲布料)
flannel	法蘭絨
velvet	絲絨
polyester	聚酯纖維
nylon	尼龍
rayon	嫘縈 (人造絲)
Lycra	萊卡
acetate	醋酸纖維
acrylic	亞克力纖維

8.4 購物商場——結帳
Shopping Mall—Payment

Dialog 1 (對話1)

A: 這條（結帳櫃臺）太慢了。

A: This line is too slow.

B: 我們可以過去那條，看起來快一點。

B: We can go to that one. It seems faster.

A: 他們這兒週末真的需要多些收銀員。

A: Really, they need more cashiers here on the weekends.

B: 看，那邊剛開了另一個收銀機。我們過去那邊吧！

B: Look. They just opened another register. Let's go over there.

Word Bank (字庫)

register ['rɛdʒɪstə-] n. 收銀機

Notes (小叮嚀)

即使新開了結帳櫃臺，美國人也不會搶排隊，還是要照順序來。

基本對話

機場與飛機

入境

住宿

交通

餐飲

觀光

購物

郵電

銀行

麻煩事

回國

Dialog 2 （對話2）

A: 總共是 5 塊錢又 78 分，謝謝。

A: That will be $5.78, please.

B: 真的嗎？標示的價錢是 5 塊錢 25 分。

B: Really? The price on it says $5.25.

A: 那是因為本州的銷售稅。

A: It's because of the sales tax in this state.

B: 稅是多少呢？

B: How much is the tax?

A: 10%。

A: 10%.

B: 每個州都一樣嗎？

B: Is it the same in every state?

A: 不是，各州不同，而且某些州沒有銷售稅。

A: No. It varies from state to state, and some don't have a sales tax.

B: 謝謝你告訴我這個。

B: Thanks for telling me about this.

基本對話　機場與飛機　入境　住宿　交通　餐飲　觀光　購物　郵電　銀行　麻煩事　回國

Notes 小叮嚀

　　美國大部分的州都課銷售稅，但每州稅率不同，且哪些物品課多少稅也不同，例如有些州食品免稅。所以購物結帳時，都要在標示的金額上外加一筆銷售稅。若不明白帳單的金額，可以請問結帳人員。出國前可以先查一下拜訪天數較長的地方稅率是多少，對當地消費會比較了解，各地的觀光局、旅遊資訊中心、商會也都會有這類資料。阿拉斯加 (Alaska)、德拉威 (Delaware)、蒙大拿 (Montana)、新罕布夏 (New Hampshire) 及奧勒岡 (Oregon) 等州，都免課銷售稅，雖然如此，有些市或郡除了州稅外還可另課市稅或郡稅。

　　除了德州 (Texas) 與路易斯安納州 (Louisiana) 幾個地方外，須持外國護照、90 天內有效往返機票辦理退稅外，美國可以說並沒有為外籍觀光客退稅的制度。許多歐洲地區加值型營業稅 (value added taxes, VAT) 為消費稅的一種 (多數在 10-20% 間，北歐稅率達驚人之 25%)，觀光大國對外籍旅客達到某購物金額之退稅優惠，早已行之有年，臺灣也已加入此行列。

Dialog 3 對話3

A: 這要付現、開支票，還是刷卡呢？

A: Will this be cash, check or credit card?

B: 我要付現。

B: I'll pay cash.

A: 好，你需要收據嗎？

A: Fine. Do you need a receipt?

B: 要，謝謝。

B: Yes, please.

基本對話 | 機場與飛機 | 入境 | 住宿 | 交通 | 餐飲 | 觀光 | 購物 | 郵電 | 銀行 | 麻煩事 | 回國

Dialog 4 對話4

A: 我可以用信用卡付帳嗎？

A: May I pay by credit card?

B: 當然，沒問題。

B: Sure, no problem.

A: 你們接受什麼卡呢？

A: Which cards do you accept?

B: 我們接受各大信用卡。

B: We accept all major credit cards.

Word Bank 字庫

check [tʃɛk] n. 支票

Tips 小祕訣

　　美國人找錢時算錢的方法很不一樣，是把你買的東西價錢加上找你的錢等於你付出的錢。例如你買了一支熱狗 $3.50，而你付了 20 元，這時找錢的人會邊數錢如下：Here's your change.（接著先給你零錢 50 分）Four,（再給你一張 1 元鈔）five,（再給一張 5 元鈔）ten,（再給一張 10 元鈔）and twenty。這樣加起來等於收到的 20 元，就不會多找或少找，這與我們直接扣掉找 16 塊半的方式完全不同。

8.5 購物商場——退換貨
Shopping Mall—Exchanges and Refunds

Dialog 1 (對話1)

A: 我昨天買了這個，但我需要更換。

A: I bought this yesterday, but I need to exchange it.

B: 你有收據嗎？

B: Do you have the receipt?

A: 我有。

A: Yes, I do.

B: 它有什麼問題呢？

B: What is wrong with it?

A: 它太小了。

A: It's too small.

B: 好，我找個大一點的給你。

B: OK. I'll find a bigger one for you.

Dialog 2 (對話2)

A: 嗨，我幾天前在這裡買了這支腕錶，但現在它壞了。

A: Hi. I bought this wristwatch here a few days ago, but now it's not working.

B: 是的，我記得你，讓我看一下手錶。

B: Yes, I remember you. Let me have a look at the watch.

A: 在這裡。

A: Here you are.

B: 我會檢查一下看是什麼問題。

B: I'll check it to see what the problem is.

A: 那會要多久呢？

A: How long will that take?

B: 喔，別擔心這支錶，我現在馬上換別支給你。

B: Oh, don't worry about this watch. I'll give you a different one right now.

A: 我可以要相同的款式及顏色嗎？

A: Can I have the same style and color?

B: 好的，沒問題。

B: Yes, no problem.

Notes 小叮嚀

　　每個州政府對商店及貨品的退換規定不一，顧客不一定每樣購物都可退換，最好在購買前就問清楚，尤其是購買貴重的東西，更要注意收據上有關更換或退錢的規定。一般而言，美國商店會願意協助顧客解決購物問題。

　　美國的夏季大拍賣 (summer sale) 是在勞動節長週末做最後 Labor Day Sale，冬季大拍賣 (winter sale) 是在聖誕節過後做 Christmas Sale。若是在季末特價時購買買一送一 (buy one get one free) 的物品，恐怕難以更換或退貨，而標有恕不退貨 (All sales are final.) 的拍賣品就更不可能更換或退貨了。

Dialog 3 對話3

A: 我要退錢，我買的這支錶不準。

A: I want to get a refund. This watch I bought does not keep time.

B: 你有收據嗎？

B: Do you have the receipt?

A: 有，在這邊。

A: Yes. Here it is.

B: 通常像這種情形我們提供更換。

B: Usually we offer an exchange in cases like this.

A: 知道了。你們有另一支完全像這支的錶嗎？

A: I see. Do you have another watch exactly like this one?

B: 我們好像沒有了，所以我現在退錢給你吧。

B: It looks like we don't, so I'll give you a refund right now.

A: 謝謝。

A: Thank you.

Useful Phrases 實用語句

1. 我昨天買了這個，這是我的收據。

   I bought this yesterday. Here's my receipt.

2. 我這個要退錢。

   I want a refund for this.

3. 這是收據，你可以查看購買日期。

   Here is the receipt. You can check the date of purchase.

基本對話

機場與飛機

入境

住宿

交通

餐飲

觀光

購物

郵電

銀行

麻煩事

回國

4. 它損壞了。

It's damaged.

5. 這商品壞了。

This product is broken.

6. 我不喜歡這個顏色。

I don't like this color.

7. 它的尺寸不對。

It's the wrong size.

8. 這衣服有瑕疵。

This clothing is flawed.

9. 我要把這換一個不一樣的。

I want to exchange this for a different one.

8.6 購物商場——會員卡
Shopping Mall—Membership

Dialog 對話

A: (櫃臺收銀員)你今天有帶會員卡嗎？

A: (Cashier) Do you have your membership card today?

B: 我沒有會員卡。

B: I don't have a membership card.

A: 你要今天成為會員嗎？

A: Would you like to become a member today?

B: 當會員有用嗎？

B: Is it useful to be a member?

A: 你所有購物都有 10% 的折扣，而且可以累積點數換贈品。	**A:** You get 10% off on all purchases, plus points towards free gifts.
B: 我要怎樣成為會員？	**B:** How do I become a member?
A: 很簡單，只要填這張申請表然後交回給我。	**A:** It's easy. Just fill out this application and give it back to me.
B: 我什麼時候會拿到卡呢？	**B:** When will I get the card?
A: 只要幾分鐘處理你的申請，之後你就會拿到卡了。	**A:** It takes just a few minutes to process your application. Afterward you'll get your card.

Useful Phrases 實用語句

1. 可以打折嗎？

   Is it possible to get a discount?

2. 如果買兩份，可以打折嗎？

   If I buy two of them, is it possible to get a discount?

Notes 小叮嚀

　　殺價文化在許多開發中國家盛行，但在美國購物中心或商店買東西是不殺價的，殺價可能會招來異樣眼光，因為那不是美國人的消費習慣，除非是在跳蚤市場或車庫拍賣。某些場所如果辦了會員卡就有 10% 的折扣 (有些地方接受觀光客以國外地址辦理)，但是辦卡可能要等一下子。美國的折扣標示若為 30% off，就是臺灣的七折，別搞混了。

基本對話

機場與飛機

入境

住宿

交通

餐飲

觀光

購物

郵電

銀行

麻煩事

回國

8.7 購物商場——延長保固
Shopping Mall—Extended Warranty

 Dialog 對話

A: 你要買延長保固嗎？

A: Would you like to buy extended warranty protection?

B: 那是什麼呢？

B: What is that?

A: 是保障你不必額外付費的特別服務契約。

A: It is a special service contract that protects you against extra charges.

B: 抱歉，我不懂。

B: Sorry, I don't understand.

A: 如果你的數位相機在一年保固後故障，你將不必付修理費。

A: If your digital camera breaks after one year, you won't have to pay for repairs.

B: 延長保固的期限多久呢？

B: How long is the extended warranty good for?

A: 五年。

A: Five years.

Word Bank 字庫

extended [ɪk'stɛndɪd] adj. (時間)延長的

warranty ['wɔrəntɪ] n. 擔保

contract ['kɑntrækt] n. 契約

Useful Phrases 實用語句

1. 你們這個有提供延長保固嗎？

   Do you offer an extended warranty for this?

2. 這保固保障什麼？

   What does the warranty cover?

3. 延長保固合約多久呢？

   How long is the extended contract for?

4. 保固是全世界性的還是只有在美國呢？

   Is the warranty worldwide or only in the States?

5. 有這個一年保固在臺灣修理是免費嗎？

   Is the repair free in Taiwan with this one year warranty?

6. 在臺灣可以去哪兒修理呢？

   Where can I go to repair it in Taiwan?

Tips 小祕訣

在美國買較高單價的電器用品時，售貨員都會問你要不要在保固期限外加保「故障修理險」，保障在保固期限外故障修理的高額費用，但是對一般觀光客而言，這種保險是用不到的。

基本對話

機場與飛機

入境

住宿

交通

餐飲

觀光

購物

郵電

銀行

麻煩事

回國

基本對話

機場與飛機

入境

住宿

交通

餐飲

觀光

購物

郵電

銀行

麻煩事

回國

8.8 購物商場——運回家
Shopping Mall—Shipping It Home

 Dialog 對話

A: 我真喜歡你們這裡做的椅子。

A: I really like the chairs you make here.

B: 謝謝。你有興趣買一張嗎？

B: Thank you. Are you interested in buying one?

A: 我想買四張，但我住國外。

A: I'd like to have four, but I live overseas.

B: 那沒問題，我們可以把東西寄運給你。

B: That's no problem. We can ship them to you.

A: 那麼我對你們目錄裡看到的這些最有興趣。

A: Well, I'm most interested in these I see in your catalog.

B: 我們目前沒有那些的庫存，但是我們可以做。

B: We don't have any of those in stock right now, but we can make them.

A: 那要多久呢？

A: How long would that take?

B: 三週，然後就會寄給你。

B: Three weeks, then we'll send them to you.

Word Bank 字庫

ship [ʃɪp] v. 運送
overseas ['ovɚ'siz] adv. 國外地
catalog ['kætəlɔg] n. 目錄

Useful Phrases 實用語句

1. 你可以運送這個 [這些] 嗎？
   Can you ship this [these]?
2. 運費多少？
   How much is shipping?
3. 多久會到？
   When will it [they] arrive?

8.9 精品暢貨中心
Outlet Center

Dialog 對話

A: 我們去這個折扣購物中心吧。

A: Let's go to this outlet center.

B: 我沒去過折扣購物中心，那裡真的好嗎？

B: I've never been to an outlet. Is it any good?

A: 折扣購物中心可以用很好的價錢買名牌商品。

A: Outlet stores have very good prices on famous name brand items.

B: 那裡有什麼樣的東西呢？

B: What sorts of things do they have?

A: 應有盡有，鞋子、衣服、禮物、高爾夫球具等等。

A: Almost everything. Shoes, clothing, gift items, golf equipment, whatever.

B: 我想我們會在那兒待好一下子。

B: I think we'll be there a long time.

A: 也許吧。我知道這些複合商場有的很大，甚至有用餐的地方。

A: Maybe. I know some of these complexes are pretty big, and even have places to eat.

Word Bank 字庫

brand [brænd] n. 牌子
sort [sɔrt] n. 種類
complex ['kɑmplɛks] n. 複合設施

Notes 小叮嚀

美國的折扣購物中心規模相當龐大，雖多設在城外，交通較不方便，但因折扣便宜，在週末還是吸引大量人潮前往。

Language Power 字句補給站

衣 服 Clothing

sweater 毛衣　　jacket 夾克　　coat 外套

slacks 寬鬆休閒長褲　　jeans 牛仔褲　　pants 長褲

shorts 短褲　　(hooded) sweatshirt (有兜帽的)運動衫　　shirt 襯衫

gloves 手套　　mittens 連指手套　　scarf 圍巾

socks 短襪　　hat 帽子　　sneakers 運動鞋

boots 靴子　　belt 皮帶　　tie 領帶

基本對話
機場與飛機
入境
住宿
交通
餐飲
觀光
購物
郵電
銀行
麻煩事
回國

衣 服 Clothing②

skirt 裙子

blouse 女上衣

tank top 男女背心

stockings 襪

swimsuit 泳衣

nightwear 睡衣

pajamas
睡衣（上衣及長褲）

dress 洋裝

T-shirt T恤

sandals 涼鞋

high heels 高跟鞋

flip flops 人字拖鞋

stocking cap
無帽緣軟帽

baseball cap 棒球帽

bandana 頭巾

8.10 車庫拍賣
Garage Sale

 Dialog （對話）

A: 我們停一下，他們正在車庫拍賣。(查看一臺咖啡機) 我想買這臺咖啡機，它可以用嗎？

A: Let's stop here. They're having a garage sale. (checking on a coffee maker) I'd like to buy this coffee maker. Does it work?

B: 可以的，讓我展示給你看。

B: Yes, it does. Here, let me show you.

A: 看來還可以使用。

A: It looks like it works fine.

B: 是的，它還很好，只是我在比賽時得到一臺新的。

B: Yes, it's very good. I'm selling it because I won a new one in a contest.

A: 你很幸運。你這個要賣多少錢？

A: You are lucky. How much do you want for this one?

B: 價錢應該在上面，在這裡。

B: The price should be on it. There it is.

A: 12 元。我有 10 元，你接受嗎？

A: $12. I've got ten on me. Will you accept that?

基本對話

B: 當然，快要收攤了，我想趕快賣掉。

B: Sure. It's almost time to stop the sale for the day, and I want to get rid of this stuff.

機場與飛機

A: 太好了，謝謝。

A: Great. Thanks.

入境

 Word Bank 字庫

contest ['kantɛst] n. 比賽
get rid of 擺脫掉

住宿

交通

 Tips 小祕訣

車庫拍賣和庭院拍賣 (yard sale) 在美國是一樣的，都是把家裡不用的東西 (常擺在車庫內) 拿出來放在車庫或庭院便宜賣，時間通常是在週末。這類拍賣可以殺價，要收的時候去最便宜，識貨的話還可能找到寶藏或收集品。當地報紙會刊登哪裡有拍賣的消息。

餐飲

觀光

購物

8.11 跳蚤市場
Flea Market

郵電

 Dialog 對話

銀行

A: 我讀到明天露天展場有跳蚤市場。

A: I read about a flea market going on at the fairgrounds tomorrow.

麻煩事

B: 我不知道那是什麼。

B: I don't know what that is.

回國

A: 就像庭院拍賣，但大多了。

A: It's like a yard sale, but it's much bigger.

B: 多大呢？

B: How big?

A: 那裡大概有超過上百個攤位。

A: There might be as many as one hundred sellers there.

B: 真的嗎？那一定有很多東西拍賣。

B: Really? There must be a lot of stuff there for sale.

A: 是啊，上千個新舊東西。

A: Yes. Thousands of things new and used.

B: 東西便宜嗎？

B: Are things cheap?

A: 是的，就像車庫或庭院拍賣。

A: Yes, just like a garage or yard sale.

Useful Phrases 實用語句

1. 這可以用嗎？

   Does this work?

2. 你有另一個嗎？

   Do you have another one of these?

3. 這怎麼使用呢？

   How does this work?

基本對話

機場與飛機

入境

住宿

交通

餐飲

觀光

購物

郵電

銀行

麻煩事

回國

4. 這個多久了？

   How old is this?

5. 我願意付 15 元買它。

   I'll give you fifteen dollars for it.

6. 你願意少收點嗎？

   Will you take less?

7. 你願意算我便宜點嗎？

   Will you give me a better/lower price?

8. 讓我考慮一下。

   Let me think about it.

9. 我晚點再來。

   I'll come back later.

Tips 小祕訣

　　跳蚤市場 (又稱 swap meet) 世界各地都有，更是美國文化的一部分。有些跳蚤市場有上百攤之多，新舊貨都有，大部分人是去找好的二手貨。和車庫或庭院拍賣一樣，跳蚤市場多數是在週末才有，當地報紙或布告欄會有這類拍賣的地點、時間等消息。

　　除了跳蚤市場外，喜好收集者可以在古董及收集品雜誌 (Antiques & Collectables) 或網站得知何處、何時、有何主題的收藏品可購買或拍賣 (auction)。如果購買物品需要郵寄，先付郵寄費用後，店家也多半願意幫忙寄運商品。

8.12 購買相機電池及底片
Buying Batteries and Film for the Camera

Dialog 1 對話1

A: 我需要數位相機的電池。

A: I need batteries for my digital camera.

B: 你的相機用哪一型的？

B: What type does your camera use?

A: 3A。

A: Triple A.

B: 你要多少個？

B: How many do you want?

A: 我需要額外的，所以我要買十個。

A: I need extras, so I'll buy ten.

Dialog 2 對話2

A: 我要買一些底片。

A: I need to buy some film.

B: 你要哪一種？

B: What type do you want?

A: 一捲36張、35釐米、一百、彩色的底片。

A: A roll of thirty-six shot, 35 mm, 100, color film.

B: 好，還要什麼別的嗎？

B: OK. Anything else?

A: 是的，我還要兩捲35釐米的黑白底片。

A: Yes. I also want two rolls of 35 mm black and white film.

基本對話　機場與飛機　入境　住宿　交通　餐飲　觀光　購物　郵電　銀行　麻煩事　回國

基本對話 機場與飛機 入境 住宿 交通 餐飲 觀光 購物 郵電 銀行 麻煩事 回國

Word Bank 字庫

battery ['bætərɪ] n. 電池
film [fɪlm] n. 底片
roll [rol] n. 捲
shot [ʃɑt] n. 拍攝

Tips 小祕訣

　　雖然數位相機已取代傳統相機，生產底片的柯達 (Kodak) 也已結束，但並不意味人們在數位時代只用數位相機。除了某些攝影師外，Lomo (graphy) 相機愛好者仍然使用傳統實體底片拍照才能產生特殊的 Lomo 照片風格。

8.13 購買音樂
Buying Music

Dialog 對話

A: 嗨，我可以幫你找什麼嗎？

A: Hi, may I help you find something?

B: 我要買 Scan Rats 的 CD。

B: I want to buy a CD by the Scan Rats.

A: 你知道你要的專輯名稱嗎？

A: Do you know the name of the CD you want?

B: 不知道，但我知道有「她熱情無敵」這首歌。

B: No, but I know it has the song "She's Hot and Beyond."

A: CD是照樂團名字的字母順序排列的。

A: The CD's are in alphabetical order by band name.

B: 太好了，那我到 S 區去找就是了。

B: Great, I'll just look for it in the S section then.

Word Bank 字庫

alphabetical [,ælfə'bɛtɪkl̩] adj. 字母的
order ['ɔrdɚ] n. 順序

8.14 購買禮物
Buying Gifts

Dialog 對話

A: 你需要幫忙嗎？

A: Do you need some help?

B: 我需要買禮物給我一個朋友。

B: I need to buy a gift for a friend of mine.

A: 你的朋友喜歡什麼？

A: What does your friend like?

B: 他喜歡戶外活動。

B: He enjoys outdoor activities.

基本對話 機場與飛機 入境 住宿 交通 餐飲 觀光 購物 郵電 銀行 麻煩事 回國

基本對話

機場與飛機

入境

住宿

交通

餐飲

觀光

購物

郵電

銀行

麻煩事

回國

A: 知道了，我們有一系列精選的運動錶。

A: I see. We have a fine selection of sports watches.

B: 他喜歡健行，你們有附羅盤的嗎？

B: He likes hiking. Do you have one with a compass?

A: 好幾個，請看看吧。

A: Several. Have a look.

Word Bank 字庫

selection [sə'lɛkʃən] n. 選集
hiking ['haɪkɪŋ] n. 健行
compass ['kʌmpəs] n. 羅盤

Useful Phrases 實用語句

1. 我考慮看看。
   I'll think about it.

2. 這個超出我的預算。
   It's beyond my budget.

3. 我要包裝這個。
   I'd like this wrapped.

4. 這要小心包裝。
   This needs to be carefully wrapped.

5. 這容易破，我要安全地把它裝箱。
   This is fragile. I need it boxed securely.

6. 我可以寄放在這裡晚點來拿嗎？
   Can I leave it here, and pick it up later?

Tips 小祕訣

在美國，除非特別指定包裝材料或樣式，多數商家有提供免費包裝服務。

8.15 買特產
Shopping for Locally Made Things

Dialog 對話

A: 我想要買此地的特產。

A: I'd like to buy something that is a specialty of this place.

B: 我不知道那可以問誰。

B: I wonder whom we can ask about that.

A: 我想我們可以問飯店裡的人。

A: I guess we can ask the people at the hotel.

B: 是啊，我們也可以聯絡本地的商會。

B: Sure. We could also contact the local Chamber of Commerce.

A: 那是個好主意，他們會有關於旅遊、購物及住宿的資料。

A: That's a good idea. They'll have information about tours, shopping, and accommodation.

Word Bank 字庫

specialty ['spɛʃəltɪ] n. 特產
Chamber of Commerce n. 商會

基本對話

機場與飛機

入境

住宿

交通

餐飲

觀光

購物

郵電

銀行

麻煩事

回國

基本對話｜機場與飛機｜入境｜住宿｜交通｜餐飲｜觀光｜購物｜郵電｜銀行｜麻煩事｜回國

Useful Phrases 實用語句

1. 你們有觀光資料嗎？

   Do you have any tourist information?

2. 哪裡可以買到此地的特產呢？

   Where can we get some specialty products of this place?

3. 我們可以拿這些小冊子嗎？

   Can we take one of these brochures?

Tips 小祕訣

現在許多地區、州或城市有特產商店，銷售當地特有商品。這些特產多是手工製作的，包括藝術品、手工藝品、服裝、糖果、玩具及許多適合當紀念品的商品。商店可以包裝這些物品並附上特產商品的資訊，各地旅遊局及商會也樂於提供免費資訊，增加商機。

Where can we get some specialty products of this place?

We can ask the people at the hotel.

Unit 9 Mail and Telephones

郵電

貼好郵票的信件直接交給旅館櫃臺即可。明信片的郵票如果在外面沒買到，就必須到郵局去買。喜歡收集郵票的人，可以在郵局買到特殊主題的郵票。如果買的東西太多太重不好帶上飛機，可以先到郵局寄回。郵局有各式大小的箱子，可以購買後打包，但要注意易碎物品打包要小心，郵局有特殊打包材料確保易碎品運送安全無虞。美國郵局開門時間一般為週一到週五早上 8 點到下午 5 點，週六早上 9 點到中午，週日及重要假日休息。

基本對話 | 機場與飛機 | 入境 | 住宿 | 交通 | 餐飲 | 觀光 | 購物 | 郵電 | 銀行 | 麻煩事 | 回國

9.1 郵寄
Mailing

 Dialog 1 （對話1）

A: 不好意思，我可以在哪裡買郵票呢？

A: Excuse me. Where can I buy stamps?

B: 有一臺郵票販賣機在那裡。

B: There is a stamp machine over there.

A: 郵筒在那兒呢？

A: Where is the mailbox?

B: 在那裡。

B: It's over there.

A: 我看到兩個投遞口在上面。

A: I see two slots on it.

B: 上方那個是市內郵件的，底下那個是市外的。

B: The top one is for in town letters, the bottom one for out of town.

 Word Bank （字庫）

stamp machine n. 郵票機
slot [slɑt] n. 狹長縫，投遞口

Dialog 2 對話2

A: 我想寄這些明信片到臺灣。

A: I'd like to mail these postcards to Taiwan.

B: 每張郵資是70分，你需要幾張郵票？

B: The postage is \$0.70 each. How many stamps do you need?

A: 五張。什麼時候會到呢？

A: Five. When will they arrive?

B: 七至十天後。

B: In seven to ten days.

Dialog 3 對話3

A: 我要把這個包裹寄到國外。

A: I need to send this package overseas.

B: 寄到哪裡呢？

B: Where to?

A: 香港。

A: Hong Kong.

B: (稱包裹重量)郵資是 5.75 元。

B: (weighing the package) The postage will cost \$5.75.

A: 是快遞郵件嗎？

A: Is that express mail?

基本對話

機場與飛機

入境

住宿

交通

餐飲

觀光

購物

郵電

銀行

麻煩事

回國

基本對話 / 機場與飛機 / 入境 / 住宿 / 交通 / 餐飲 / 觀光 / 購物 / 郵電 / 銀行 / 麻煩事 / 回國

B: 不是，快遞郵件要多 2 元。

B: No. Express mail will cost you \$2 more.

Word Bank 字庫

postcard ['post,kɑrd] n. 明信片
postage ['postɪdʒ] n. 郵資
package ['pækɪdʒ] n. 包裹
weigh [we] v. 秤重
express mail n. 快遞郵件

Useful Phrases 實用語句

1. 我要把這個寄到國外。

   I need this sent overseas.

2. 我要為這個包裹保險。

   I need to insure this package.

3. 郵資是多少呢？

   How much is the postage?

4. 何時會到呢？

   When will it arrive?

5. 最快的是哪一種郵寄方式？

   What is the quickest kind of mail?

6. 最便宜的是哪一種郵寄方式？

   What's the cheapest kind of mail?

Language Power 字句補給站

◆ 郵政 Postal Service

sea mail	海運
registered [certified] mail	掛號郵件
bulk rate	大宗郵件費率

book rate	印刷品費率
stamp	郵票
stamp machine	郵票機
mailbox	郵筒
mailman	郵差
package, parcel	包裹
postcard	明信片
scale	秤
postage	郵資
postmark	郵戳
zip code	郵遞區號

◆ 美國郵遞種類 United States Postal Services

1. Domestic mail 國內郵件

1 Express Mail	快遞郵件
overnight guaranteed envelopes	保證隔天送達
2 Priority Mail	限時郵件
two to three day envelopes	2～3天送達
3 First Class Mail	一級郵件
(regular cards and letters) two or three days to deliver	(普通卡片及信件) 2～3 天送達

2. International mail 國際郵件

1 Global Express Guaranteed	全球保證快遞
one to three days	1～3天送達
2 Global Express Mail	全球快遞
three to five days	3～5天送達
3 Global Airmail	航空信件
four to ten days	4～10天送達
4 Global Economy Letter Post	航空經濟郵件
(cheapest for heavier things) four to six weeks	(較重物品的最便宜方式) 4～6 週送達

基本對話

機場與飛機

入境

住宿

交通

餐飲

觀光

購物

郵電

銀行

麻煩事

回國

基本對話

機場與飛機

入境

住宿

交通

餐飲

觀光

購物

郵電

銀行

麻煩事

回國

9.2 旅館電話
Hotel Calls

 Dialog 1 (對話1)

A: (打給旅館總機) 哈囉,我想打市內電話。

A: (calling Hotel Operator) Hello. I'd like to make a local call.

B: 先撥 9 即可,先生。

B: Just dial nine first, sir.

A: 謝謝。

A: Thanks.

 Dialog 2 (對話2)

A: (打給旅館總機) 我如何用旅館電話打回我的國家呢?

A: (calling Hotel Operator) How do I call my country on my hotel room phone?

B: 先撥外線號碼 19,再撥你要通話國家的國碼,然後是你要打的號碼。

B: First dial 19 for an open line, then dial the country code number of the country you want to call and then the number you want to call.

A: 知道了,謝謝。

A: I understand. Thank you.

B: 不客氣，總機會在電話結束後打給你，告訴你費用。

B: You are welcome. The hotel operator will call you after the call is finished to tell you about the charge.

A: 好，謝謝。

A: Ok. Thanks.

Useful Phrases 實用語句

1. 怎麼撥出呢？

   How do you dial out?

2. 我想撥國外。

   I want to dial overseas.

3. 市內電話怎麼收費呢？

   How much do you charge for a local call?

4. 打免付費電話旅館要收費嗎？

   Do you charge for a toll free call?

Tips 小祕訣

　　旅館電話上貼有怎麼打電話的說明，按照說明操作即可。例如美國打回臺北的直撥電話為：011 (國際碼) -886 (國碼) -2 (臺北區域號碼去 0) - 電話號碼。旅館通常要先撥外線號碼，再開始撥國際碼。

基本對話

機場與飛機

入境

住宿

交通

餐飲

觀光

購物

郵電

銀行

麻煩事

回國

9.3 長途電話
Long Distance Calls

 Dialog 對話

A: 怎麼打長途電話呢？

A: How do you dial long distance?

B: 撥 1，再撥三位數區域號碼，然後是你要通話的人的七位數號碼，就可以了。

B: Just dial 1, then the three digit area code, then the seven digit number of the person you want to talk to.

A: 我怎麼查區域號碼呢？

A: How do I find out the area code?

B: 你可以查電話簿的區域號碼地圖，包括全美各地，或者你可以打電話問查號臺。

B: You can look at the area code map of a phone book. It covers all of America, or you can call Directory Assistance.

A: 知道了，謝謝。

A: I got it. Thanks.

打長途及國際電話在晚上較晚時段及週末便宜，有些長途電話卡也很划算。要注意的是，打電話給美國人的時間最好在早上 9 點到晚上 9 點之間。

9.4 對方付費電話
Collect Calls

Dialog 對話

A: (撥0)接線生。我可以幫你嗎？

A: (dialing 0) Operator. May I help you?

B: 我想打對方付費電話。

B: I'd like to place a collect call.

A: 請問哪個城市及電話號嗎。

A: Which city and number please?

B: 芝加哥，號碼是855-2229。

B: Chicago, the number is 855-2229.

A: 我要說是誰打的電話呢？

A: Who should I say is calling please?

B: 雪莉徐。

B: Sherry Hsu.

A: 好，請稍待。

A: OK. Please stand by.

Tips　小祕訣

使用公用電話時，撥 0 可與接線生通話或請求協助。當你打對方付費電話，接線生會問對方是否願意接這通你打來的付費電話。例如：「This is telephone operator. Will you accept a collect call from Sherry Hsu?」（這是接線生，你願意接雪莉徐打來的付費電話嗎？）

「Yes, I will.」（好的，我願意。）

「Thank you.」（謝謝。）接著對打電話的人說「Go ahead.」（請說吧。）

9.5 查號臺
Directory Assistance

 Dialog 1　對話1

A: 查號臺。

A: Directory assistance.

B: 我要查 Brandso 公司的電話。

B: I would like the telephone number for the Brandso Company.

A: 它在市內嗎，先生？

A: Is that in the city, sir?

B: 是的。

B: Yes, it is.

A: 請稍待…號碼是786-4433。

A: One moment please... The number is 786-4433.

B: 786-4433。

B: 786-4433.

A: 是的,沒錯。

A: Yes, that's right.

Dialog 2 (對話2)

A: (撥411)查號臺。請問你要查哪個城市?

A: (dialing 411) Directory assistance. Which city, please?

B: 費城。

B: Philadelphia.

A: 你要通話的對象名字是?

A: Name you're calling?

B: 預算租車公司。

B: Budget Rental Cars.

A: 我這裡顯示兩個地點,一個在機場附近,一個在市區。

A: I show two locations. One near the airport, and one downtown.

B: 請給我機場那個。

B: The airport location, please.

A: 號碼是456-9900。

A: The number is 456-9900

B: 456-9900。

B: 456-9900.

A: 是的,正確。

A: Yes, that is correct.

B: 謝謝。

B: Thanks.

Useful Phrases 實用語句

1. (問查號臺) 義大利的國碼是什麼?

   (asking Directory Assistance) What is the country code for Italy?

2. (問查號臺) 帕摩納海灘的區域號碼是什麼?

   (asking Directory Assistance) What is the area code for Pomona Beach?

9.6 公用電話
Pay Phone

Dialog 1 對話1

A: 我需要零錢打公用電話。

A: I need change for the pay phone.

B: 好，你需要多少？

B: Sure. How much do you need?

A: 我需要 2 元的 25 分錢。

A: I need $2 worth the quarters.

B: 沒問題。

B: No problem.

Dialog 2 （對話2）

A: 這裡有公用電話嗎？

A: Is there a pay phone here?

B: 當然，在那兒。

B: Sure, it's over there.

A: 我需要零錢來使用它嗎？

A: Do I need change to use it?

B: 它接受硬幣及電話卡。

B: It will take coins or phone cards.

A: 我可以在哪裡買電話卡呢？

A: Where can I buy a phone card?

B: 去收銀員那兒。

B: Go to the cashier.

基本對話　機場與飛機　入境　住宿　交通　餐飲　觀光　購物　郵電　銀行　麻煩事　回國

基本對話 機場與飛機 入境 住宿 交通 餐飲 觀光 購物 郵電 銀行 麻煩事 回國

Dialog 3 對話3

A: 嗨，我在公用電話打的。

A: Hi. I'm calling from a pay phone.

B: 真高興有你消息。

B: Good to hear from you.

A: 你可以來接我嗎？

A: Can you come pick me up?

B: 你在哪兒呢？

B: Where are you?

A: 靠近第一大道及松樹路的轉角。

A: Near the corner of First Avenue and Pine Street.

B: 好，留在公用電話邊，我很快就到那兒。

B: OK. Stay by the pay phone, I'll be there soon.

Useful Phrases 實用語句

1. 哪裡有公用電話？

   Where is a pay phone?

2. 我需要零錢打電話。

   I need change for the phone.

3. 我要買張電話卡。

   I need to buy a phone card.

4. 你們賣國際電話卡嗎？

   Do you sell international phone cards?

5. 我需要用電話簿。

I need to use a phone book.

6. 你們有本地的電話簿嗎？

Do you have a local phone book?

7. 我會在電話亭等你。

I'll wait for you at the phone booth.

Tips 小祕訣

現在手機普遍，一般人已較少使用到公用電話，但旅客們就用得上了，出國前可以先買國際電話預付卡或租用國際漫遊上網，但須留意陷阱。使用臺灣手機傳簡訊回國的花費很小 (出國前可先問電信公司如何計費)，且直接撥號傳訊即可，不需加撥其他號碼。若要用零錢打公用電話，25 分、10 分及 5 分都可以用；拿起話筒先撥號，話筒裡的電腦總機會告訴你要投多少錢，如果是打當地號碼，通常需投幣 50 分，可以通話十五分鐘；接通後電腦總機會提醒你剩下多少時間可以通話，你也可以在通話時繼續投錢。多數美國公用電話可以接聽，如果沒零錢了，可以告訴對方公用電話號碼，請對方打來。公用電話上也有地址，需要時可以用來聯絡。公用電話下方有列出如何打長途電話 (先撥 1 再撥三碼區號及電話號碼) 及報修或緊急電話等資料。越來越多國家 (如美國、巴西) 已將有些公用電話加設熱點 (hotspot)，並將電話亭加個板子或坐位，提供 wi-fi 上網服務，有些 (如法國) 則採取革命性做法 (但尚在實驗階段)，以平板觸控螢幕汰換舊電話，提供電話與網路服務。無論如何，對出國旅行者都是一大便利。要注意的是在任何公共熱點或設備傳輸資料，皆須考量網路安全。

基本對話

機場與飛機

入境

住宿

交通

餐飲

觀光

購物

郵電

銀行

麻煩事

回國

基本對話 ｜ 機場與飛機 ｜ 入境 ｜ 住宿 ｜ 交通 ｜ 餐飲 ｜ 觀光 ｜ 購物 ｜ 郵電 ｜ 銀行 ｜ 麻煩事 ｜ 回國

Language Power 字句補給站

◆ 公用電話說明 Pay Phone Illustration

有些公用電話是民營的，費率可能稍高，不同電話公司的面板也會有些差異，廣告也不同。公用電話上會註名費率、免費電話和使用方法。

❶COIN SLOT 投幣口 (5分、10分、25分)

　COIN RELEASE 退幣鈕

❷Local Calls... No Time Limit! 50 ¢

　市內電話不限時間一律50分錢

❸Call Anywhere else in the USA! Only 50 ¢

　打美國任何其他地區只要50分錢

　1 - area code - number

　1 - 區域碼 - 號碼

❹No Coins?? Call COLLECT! 1-877-xxx

　沒零錢嗎？打對方付費電話1-877-xxx

❺Call Anywhere else in the World! Only \$1.00

　打世界任何其他地區只要一塊錢

　Taiwan - 4 minutes 臺灣可講 4 分鐘

　China - 8 minutes 中國大陸可講 8 分鐘

❻650-877-7917 本機號碼

❼INSERT FACE-UP AND REMOVE

　朝上插入或取出

　INSERT CALLING OR CREDIT CARD

　插入電話卡或信用卡

❽USE COMPUTER TO DIAL WITH PAYPHONE ON HOOK. TOLL
FREE AND CALLING CARD CALLS ONLY.

　左方 data port 可連接電話接頭使用電腦，只限撥打免付費電話或使
用電話卡。

❾(聯絡電話)

　★SBC Pacific Bell SBC 太平洋電話公司

　★Pay Phone Owner / Operator 本機所有者 / 接線生

　★Pay Phone Refund / Repair 退錢 / 維修電話

　★Local Calls 市內電話

　　Deposit Coins Before Calling 先投幣再撥號

　　Change Not Provided 不找零

　★Coin Calls 投幣電話

　　Within this Area Code 本區域碼內

　　Outside this Area Code 本區域碼外

　★For Emergency HELP Dial 9-1-1 緊急電話直撥911

　★Operator / Assistance 接線生

　　SBC Pacific Bell Service Area 區內

　　Outside this Service Area 外地

　★Directory / Assistance 查號臺

SBC Pacific Bell Service Area 區內

- Additional Charges Apply 有外加費用

Outside this Service Area 外地

★Calling Cards and Collect Calls
   用記帳電話卡或對方付費

❿1151 HUNTINGTON AVE. SAN BRUNO
   本話機地址

9.7 電話卡
Telephone Cards

Dialog 1　對話1

A: 我要買張電話卡。

A: I need to buy a phone card.

B: 我們有一種可用 60 分鐘的。

B: We have one good for sixty minutes.

A: 多少錢呢？

A: How much is it?

B: 10 元。

B: Ten dollars.

A: 我要如何使用它 呢？

A: How do I use it?

B: 用法說明在背面。

B: The instructions are on the back.

Dialog 2 (對話2)

A: 這張電話卡時間用完了，我需要另一張。

A: This phone card is out of minutes. I need another one.

B: 你可以加值，用舊卡加買分鐘便宜50%。

B: You can add value. Just buy more minutes for that card for 50% less.

A: 知道了，好的，我會這麼做。

A: I see. OK, I'll do it.

Word Bank (字庫)

instructions [ɪn'strʌkʃənz] n. 用法說明
value ['vælju] n. 價值

Tips 小祕訣

電話卡正面

電話卡背面

出國前可以先在臺灣購買國際電話預付卡 (international pre-paid card)。也可以到當地的超市或加油站購買電話卡打公用電話，比較划算，有不同面額可選，而且用完加值 (add value) 還可有折扣。此外在中國城或墨西哥人開的商店裡，也可以買到便宜的國際電話卡 (如上圖)，公用電話或旅館電話皆可使用。買卡時要比較何種電話卡在該州使用或打回特定國家較好用、通話分鐘數 (如 900 或 1000 分鐘)、通話品質，以及開卡後的使用期限 (如三個月或半年)。電話卡的缺點是要打很多號碼：根據電話卡背面通話步驟，先打免付費通話號碼 (toll free access number) 1-800-xxx (有中文語音的號碼可選)，再打 PIN 密碼 (密碼需塗開才顯示)，再打 1 及目的地區號及號碼 (destination number)，本地號碼也是一樣的撥法。電話卡上及通話語音會告訴你步驟及剩下的分鐘數，撥通後會告訴你所撥號碼可通話的時間。買這類電話卡可以向店家殺價，面額有 $10、$15、$20、$25 幾種，通常面額的半價就可成交。

短期到美國出差者可在臺灣購買預付卡(如T-Mobile)加值，抵達美國後將 sim 卡插入手機，填入 IMEI 手機序號 (International Mobile Equipment Identity 即手機身分號碼，每支手機只需填入一次)，選擇自動或手動搜尋 T-Mobile 訊號，即可以當地費率通話或上網，也可在美國購買或加值預付卡。

9.8 電話對話
Telephone Conversation

 Dialog 1 對話1

A: 午安，艾許佛博物館。我怎麼幫你呢？

A: Good afternoon. Ashford Museum. How may I help you?

B: 博物館幾點開？

B: What time does the museum open?

A: 我們上午 10 點開，下午 7 點關。

A: We open at 10:00 in the morning, and close at 7:00 p.m.

B: 你們星期六有開嗎？

B: Are you open on Saturday?

A: 有，但我們那天 5 點關。

A: Yes, but we close at 5:00 on that day.

基本對話

機場與飛機

入境

住宿

交通

餐飲

觀光

購物

郵電

銀行

麻煩事

回國

基本對話 機場與飛機 入境 住宿 交通 餐飲 觀光 購物 郵電 銀行 麻煩事 回國

A: 哈囉。

A: Hello.

B: 哈囉，吉姆在嗎？

B: Hello. Is Jim there?

A: 抱歉，他不在。

A: Sorry, he's not.

B: 他什麼時候會回來？

B: When will he be back?

A: 我不確定。

A: I'm not sure.

B: 我可以留言嗎？

B: Can I leave a message?

A: 好的，沒問題。

A: Yes, no problem.

Dialog 3 對話3

A: 哈囉，王牌旅遊。

A: Hello. Ace Travel.

B: 哈囉，傑瑞在嗎？

B: Hello. Is Jerry there?

A: 抱歉，他不在。

A: No, I'm sorry, he isn't.

B: 請告訴他史登迪勒打電話來。

B: Please tell him Stan Dillard called.

A: 迪勒先生，有問題嗎？

A: Is there a problem, Mr. Dillard?

B: 是的，是關於我的機票。

B: Yes, it's about my airline ticket.

A: 他有你的號碼嗎？

A: Does he have your number?

B: 他有。

B: Yes, he does.

A: 他一回來，我就告訴他回電給你。

A: I'll tell him to call you as soon as he returns.

基本對話

機場與飛機

入境

住宿

交通

餐飲

觀光

購物

郵電

銀行

麻煩事

回國

Useful Phrases 實用語句

1. 我想留言。

   I'd like to leave a message.

2. 我會再打給你。

   I'll call you back. / I'll get back to you. / I'll call you later.

3. 請稍待。

   Please hold.

4. 請等一下。

   One moment, please.

5. 撥分機號碼。

   Dial the extension number.

6. 掛斷重撥。

   Hang up the phone and redial.

7. 我被掛斷了。

   I got cut off.

Unit 10 Banks

銀行

對遊客而言，銀行是提供旅行支票兌現及換小鈔的地方，尤其如果身上只有大鈔的話，通常商店是沒有辦法找開的。50 元及 100 元鈔票除銀行外，市面上幾乎沒人使用，提款機也只提供 20 元以下的小鈔。提款機是另一方便工具，可以隨時直接從自己國家的銀行帳戶內提錢。美國銀行營業時間為週一至週五早上 9 點至下午 5 點，但有些銀行為服務顧客，平常日晚上及週六早上也有營業。在歐洲，許多觀光地區都有銀行及外幣兌換中心方便遊客，甚至有些郵局也有外幣兌換的服務，但是營業時間可能因當地的午睡習慣而關閉數小時。

基本對話
機場與飛機
入境
住宿
交通
餐飲
觀光
購物
郵電
銀行
麻煩事
回國

10.1 兌換錢幣
Money Exchange

 Dialog （對話）

A: 我要換一些錢。

A: I'd like to exchange some money.

B: 好，你持有什麼貨幣？

B: Sure. What currency do you have?

A: 歐元。

A: Euros.

B: 多少錢？

B: How much?

A: 300 歐元。今天的匯率是多少？

A: 300 euros. What's the rate today?

B: 就在這邊。

B: It's right here.

A: 知道了。你們收多少佣金呢？

A: I see. How much do you charge for the commission?

Word Bank 字庫

currency ['kɜ·ənsɪ] n. 貨幣
euro ['juro] n. 歐元
commission [kə'mɪʃən] n. 佣金

Notes 小叮嚀

　　在國外銀行兌換外幣時，務必先問清楚遊戲規則再兌換，數錢才發現就來不及了。別被較高牌價所蒙蔽，通常都是暗藏玄機的。兌換 100 元美金或歐元以下的手續費通常較高，可以先問若換多少美金 [歐元] 可以拿回多少歐元 [美金]，滿意結果再兌換。換錢時必須帶身分證明，護照影本即可。

10.2 找開大鈔
Breaking Up Bills

Dialog 對話

A: 我想找開這些百元鈔。

A: I'd like to break these $100 bills.

B: 好，你這裡有多少錢？

B: OK, how much have you got here?

A: 500 元。

A: Five hundred dollars.

B: 你想要怎麼找開呢？

B: How do you want to break them?

基本對話

機場與飛機

入境

住宿

交通

餐飲

觀光

購物

郵電

銀行

麻煩事

回國

A: 四張50，其他的 20。

A: Four fifties, and the rest twenties.

B: 好的，那就是四張 50 和十五張 20。

B: All right, that will be 4 fifties and 15 twenties.

A: 沒錯。

A: That's right.

 Useful Phrases 實用語句

1. 我要找開一張百元鈔。

   I need to break a hundred.

2. 我想買些旅行支票。

   I want to buy some traveler's checks.

3. 哪裡有提款機呢？

   Where is an ATM machine?

10.3 旅行支票兌現
Cashing Traveler's Checks

 Dialog 對話

A: 我想將旅行支票兌現。

A: I'd like to cash traveler's checks.

B: 什麼面額的呢？

B: What denomination?

A: 我想要兑現兩張 100 元的支票。

A: I want to cash two one hundred dollar checks.

B: 好的，請確定它們都簽名了。

B: OK. Please make sure they are signed.

Word Bank 字庫

cash [kæʃ] v. 兑現
traveler's check n.旅行支票
denomination [dɪ,namə'neʃən] n. 面額

Notes 小叮嚀

　　旅行支票的其中一欄必須在使用時當面簽名。旅支的面額較大時，可以先去銀行換些小鈔，否則一般商店很可能會找不開。

Useful Phrases 實用語句

1. 你們有兑現旅行支票嗎？
   Do you cash traveler's checks?
2. 我想要兑現一張支票。
   I'd like to cash a check.
3. 請給我 10 元及 20 元的鈔票。
   I'd like tens and twenties, please.
4. 我在哪兒簽名呢？
   Where do I sign?

基本對話

機場與飛機

入境

住宿

交通

餐飲

觀光

購物

郵電

銀行

麻煩事

回國

基本對話 / 機場與飛機 / 入境 / 住宿 / 交通 / 餐飲 / 觀光 / 購物 / 郵電 / 銀行 / 麻煩事 / 回國

10.4 支票掛失
Reporting Missing Traveler's Checks

 Dialog 對話

A: 我遺失了我的旅行支票。

A: I've lost my traveler's checks.

B: 請給我你的名字及一張有照片的證件。

B: Please give me your name and a picture ID.

A: 我的名字是卡爾吳，我證件在這裡。

A: My name is Carl Wu. Here is my ID.

B: 謝謝你，吳先生，我立刻把支票取消。

B: Thank you, Mr. Wu. I'll have them canceled immediately.

A: 那新支票呢？

A: What about new ones?

B: 我馬上發給你。

B: I'll issue them to you now.

 Notes 小叮嚀

　　務必將旅行支票的號碼記錄下來，並與支票分開存放，萬一遺失有紀錄可尋，才有辦法掛失。

Unit 11 Hassles

麻煩事

出門在外，每個人都可能碰到麻煩。出國前就查好駐外辦事處電話號碼 (可下載外交部旅外安全 app) 或當地警局號碼 (旅館會有)，減低在國外旅行時碰到意外求助無門的狀況發生。美國緊急求救電話是 911，記得出門要帶旅館名片及駐外辦事處電話號碼，大部分的人都願意協助在外旅行的人找路或給予適當的幫忙。

基本對話

機場與飛機

入境

住宿

交通

餐飲

觀光

購物

郵電

銀行

麻煩事

回國

11.1 迷路
Getting Lost

Dialog 對話

A: 對不起，我迷路了，我在尋找彼得森建築物。

A: Excuse me. I'm lost. I'm looking for the Peterson Building.

B: 你要往另一頭走大約六個街區。

B: You need to go the other way about six blocks.

A: 它在這條街上嗎？

A: Is it on this street?

B: 是的，它會在你右邊，你要找一尊女人的雕像。

B: Yes. It will be on your right. Look for a statue of a woman.

A: 雕像是在那棟面前嗎？

A: Is the statue in front of it?

B: 不盡然，但如果你經過雕像，你就走過頭了。

B: Not quite, but if you go past it, you've gone too far.

A: 好，知道了，謝謝。

A: OK. Got it. Thanks.

Word Bank 字庫

statue ['stætʃu] n. 雕像

Notes 小叮嚀

　　如果走丟了，找人問路就好。可以拿出圖片或寫下要去的名稱及地址，請問別人怎麼去，大多數人都會幫忙，但要注意美國大城市中有些區域並不安全。

　　如果路邊無人可問而必須敲門問當地居民時，注意自己的言行，不要讓別人覺得有危險，當然不可以在別人屋外探頭探腦，屋內的人可能報警。要問路敲門或按門鈴就好，裡面的人出來時要說「Sorry to bother you.」(對不起打擾你了)，並往後站一些，減低別人的壓力。到一個地區拜訪時，要知道哪裡治安不佳別去，就更別提在那裡問路了。雖說大部分地區是安全的，但諮詢當地旅遊中心治安資訊也是必要的。

11.2 遺失護照
Lost Passport

Dialog 對話

A: 我找不到我的護照。

A: I can't find my passport.

B: 你有找過你的袋子裡嗎？

B: Did you look in your day bag?

A: 我已找過每個地方，不見了，我弄丟了！

A: I've looked everywhere. It's gone. I lost it!

B: 我們最好聯絡離我們最近的領事館。

B: We'd better contact our nearest embassy.

基本對話

機場與飛機

入境

住宿

交通

餐飲

觀光

購物

郵電

銀行

麻煩事

回國

A: 對，我需要立刻把它換新的。

A: Right. I'll need to get it replaced immediately.

B: 那裡的人也可以發給你暫時的文件。

B: The people there can issue you a temporary document, too.

A: 我最好馬上打電話給他們。

A: I'd better call them right now.

✎ Word Bank 字庫

embassy ['ɛmbəsɪ] n. 領事館
replace [rɪ'ples] v. 代替，更換
temporary ['tɛmpə,rɛrɪ] adj. 暫時的
document ['dɑkjəmənt] n. 文件

📢 Notes 小叮嚀

護照遺失要趕快聯絡最近的領事館或駐當地的代表處，他們會告訴你該怎麼處理接下來的事。不怕一萬只怕萬一，行前要準備好護照影本、機票影本、照片，還有記下信用卡卡號及遺失緊急電話，記得和正本分開放置。

11.3 失物認領
Lost and Found

Dialog 1 對話1

A: 我弄丟了皮夾。

A: I lost my wallet.

343

B: 你有去失物招領處嗎？
B: Did you go to the Lost and Found?

A: 在哪裡呢？
A: Where is it?

B: 沿著走廊一直走，靠近雙門處。
B: It's down the hallway, near the double doors.

Word Bank 字庫

wallet ['wɑlɪt] n. 皮夾
hallway ['hɔl,we] n. 走廊

Dialog 2 對話2

A: 嗨，這是失物招領處嗎？
A: Hi. Is this the Lost and Found?

B: 是的。
B: Yes, it is.

A: 我弄丟了皮夾。
A: I've lost my wallet.

B: 你何時弄丟的？
B: When did you lose it?

基本對話

機場與飛機

入境

住宿

交通

餐飲

觀光

購物

郵電

銀行

麻煩事

回國

A: 昨天下午。

A: Yesterday afternoon.

B: 昨天有兩個皮夾被交過來。

B: Two wallets were turned in yesterday.

A: 我該怎麼做？

A: What should I do?

B: 你要對我形容一下你的皮夾。

B: You'll have to describe it to me.

Word Bank 字庫

turn in 遞交
describe [dɪ'skraɪb] v. 描述

Useful Phrases 實用語句

1. 我想要把這個交給失物招領處。

   I want to give this to the Lost and Found.

2. 我想有人弄丟了這個。

   I think someone lost this.

3. 有人發現我的皮夾嗎？

   Did someone find my wallet?

4. 是個黑色的皮夾。

   It's a black wallet.

5. 裡面有兩張信用卡、大約 300 元，以及我的駕照。

   There were two credit cards, about $300, and my driver's license inside.

11.4 報警
Reporting to the Police

 Dialog 1 （對話1）

A: 我要報案。

A: I want to report a crime.

B: 發生什麼事了，先生？

B: What happened, sir?

A: 有人偷了我的錢包。

A: Someone stole my wallet.

B: 你可以形容一下那個人嗎？

B: Can you describe the person?

A: 可以。他是個十幾歲的青少年，有點高有點瘦。

A: Yes. He's a teenager, kind of tall and thin.

B: 在何時何地發生的呢？

B: When and where did this happen?

 Word Bank （字庫）

report [rɪ'port] v. 告發
crime [kraɪm] n. 罪行

基本對話　機場與飛機　入境　住宿　交通　餐飲　觀光　購物　郵電　銀行　麻煩事　回國

基本對話
機場與飛機
入境
住宿
交通
餐飲
觀光
購物
郵電
銀行
麻煩事
回國

Useful Phrases 實用語句

1. (打電話) 這是警局嗎？

   (calling) Is this the police?

2. 我被攻擊了。

   I was assaulted.

3. 我要報告緊急事件。

   I want to report an emergency.

4. 警員會很快過來嗎？

   Will an officer come soon?

5. 派一輛救護車來。

   Send an ambulance.

Dialog 2 對話2

A: 那麼你發生了什麼事呢？

A: So what happened to you?

B: 那時我正站在巴士站，突然間那名持刀男子抓住我。

B: I was standing at the bus stop when suddenly that man with a knife grabbed me.

A: 你可以描述他嗎？

A: Can you describe him?

B: 可以。他穿著黑皮衣和牛仔褲，金髮、藍眼，比我高。

B: Yes. He was wearing a black leather coat, and jeans. He had blond hair and blue eyes. He was taller than me.

A: 他的髮型呢？

A: How about his hair style?

B: 短髮，不，等等，是中長度，看起來髒髒的。

B: It was short, no wait, it was average length, and it looked dirty.

A: 你還注意到別的嗎？

A: Did you notice anything else?

B: 是的，他有一顆門牙斷掉。

B: Yes. He had a broken front tooth.

A: 好的，請坐在這裡放輕鬆，如果你還想到什麼就告訴我。

A: OK. Just sit here and relax. If you think of anything else let me know.

✎ Word Bank 字庫

grab [græb] v. 抓住
average ['ævərɪdʒ] adj. 一般的，中等的

Tap! Tap! Tap!

I want to report a crime.

◆ 描述某人特徵 Describing Someone

性 別 (sex)	★男 (male)　★女 (female)
年 齡 (age)	★年輕 (young)　★中年 (middle-aged)　★老年 (old)
身 高 (height)	★高 (tall)　　★中等 (average)　★矮 (short)
體 重 (weight)	★重 (heavy)　★中等 (average)　★瘦 (thin)
髮 色 (hair color)	★金 (blond)　★紅 (red)　★褐 (brown)　★黑 (black)
膚 色 (skin color)	★白 (white)　★黃 (yellow)　★深 (dark)　★黑 (black)
衣 著 (clothing)	★夾克 (jacket)　★短褲 (shorts)　★牛仔褲 (jeans) ★靴子 (boots)　★帽子 (hat)
身 材 (body build)	★瘦小 (small)　★中等 (average)　★胖 (heavy-set)
人 種 (race)	★白人 (Caucasian / white)　★亞洲人 (Asian) ★黑人 (African-American / black) ★西班牙裔 (Hispanic)
眼睛顏色 (eye color)	★藍 (blue)　★綠 (green)　★褐 (brown)
髮 型 (hairstyle)	★長 (long)　★中等 (medium)　★短 (short) ★捲 (curly)　★波浪 (wavy)　★直 (straight) ★及肩 (shoulder-length)
外貌特徵 (special features)	★疤痕 (scars)　★刺青 (tattoos)　★留鬍子 (facial hair) ★鬍髭 (mustache)　★鬍鬚 (beard) ★鬢角 (sideburns)　★山羊鬍 (goatee)

基本對話　機場與飛機　入境　住宿　交通　餐飲　觀光　購物　郵電　銀行　麻煩事　回國

11.5 租車出問題
Rental Car Trouble

Dialog 對話

A: 哈囉,行動租車。

A: Hello. Action Rental.

B: 哈囉,我是史丹利王,我昨天向你們租車。

B: Hello. I'm Stanley Wang. I rented a car from you yesterday.

A: 是的,王先生,我怎麼幫你呢?

A: Yes, Mr. Wang, how can I help you?

B: 車子發不動,拋錨了。

B: The car won't start. It broke down.

A: 請告訴我你的位置。

A: Please give me your location.

B: 我在松樹街及卡爾德街轉角的一家商店。

B: I'm at a store on the corner of Pine Street and Calder.

A: 我立刻派拖吊車及另一輛車過去。

A: I'll have a tow truck and another car dispatched to you immediately.

B: 好極了,謝謝。

B: Great. Thanks.

基本對話

機場與飛機

入境

住宿

交通

餐飲

觀光

購物

郵電

銀行

麻煩事

回國

基本對話

機場與飛機

入境

住宿

交通

餐飲

觀光

購物

郵電

銀行

麻煩事

回國

Word Bank 字庫

start [stɑrt] v. 發動
break down 故障
dispatch [dɪ'spætʃ] v. 派遣

Useful Phrases 實用語句

1. 我的輪胎沒氣了。

   I have a flat tire.

2. 我需要一輛拖吊車。

   I need a tow truck.

3. 我需要一架千金頂及一支螺絲扳手。

   I need to use a jack and a lug wrench.

4. 我需要一位技師。

   I need a mechanic.

5. 打開引擎蓋 [後車廂]。

   Open the hood [trunk].

Notes 小叮嚀

　　租來的車通常有良好的保養，故障的機率不高。取車還車時記得要與服務人員一起檢查車況及操作基本配備。

Language Power 字句補給站

汽車 **Cars**

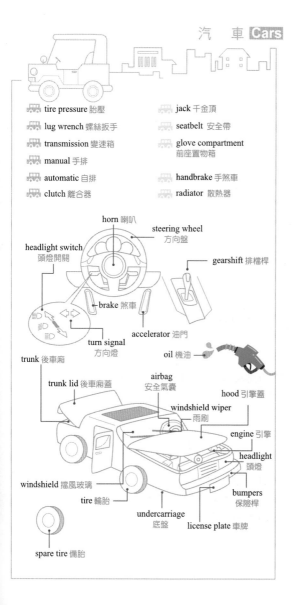

- tire pressure 胎壓
- lug wrench 螺絲扳手
- transmission 變速箱
- manual 手排
- automatic 自排
- clutch 離合器

- jack 千金頂
- seatbelt 安全帶
- glove compartment 前座置物箱
- handbrake 手煞車
- radiator 散熱器

horn 喇叭
steering wheel 方向盤
headlight switch 頭燈開關
gearshift 排檔桿
brake 煞車
turn signal 方向燈
accelerator 油門
oil 機油
trunk 後車廂
trunk lid 後車廂蓋
airbag 安全氣囊
hood 引擎蓋
windshield wiper 雨刷
engine 引擎
headlight 頭燈
windshield 擋風玻璃
tire 輪胎
bumpers 保險桿
undercarriage 底盤
license plate 車牌
spare tire 備胎

基本對話 | 機場與飛機 | 入境 | 住宿 | 交通 | 餐飲 | 觀光 | 購物 | 郵電 | 銀行 | 麻煩事 | 回國

11.6 生病——看醫生
Feeling Sick—Seeing a Doctor

Dialog 1 對話1

A: 我要看醫生。

A: I'd like to see a doctor.

B: 你有預約嗎？

B: Do you have an appointment?

A: 沒有，我來拜訪你們國家，但我生病了。

A: No, I'm visiting your country. I feel ill.

B: 告訴我怎麼了。

B: Tell me what is wrong.

A: 我胃痛，而且感覺頭很暈。

A: I have a stomachache, and I feel very dizzy.

B: 知道了，我來聯絡急診室。

B: I see. Let me call the emergency room.

Word Bank 字庫

ill [ɪl] adj. 生病的
stomachache ['stʌmək͵ek] n. 胃痛
dizzy ['dɪzɪ] adj. 頭暈的
emergency room n. 急診室

Tips 小祕訣

看病的「預約」用 appointment，doctor's appointment 即「約診」，「牙科約診」則為 dental appointment。

Dialog 2 對話2

A: 哈囉，我是安得斯醫生。

A: Hello. I'm Dr. Anders.

B: 哈囉，醫生。

B: Hello, doctor.

A: 我要替你檢查，先請坐這裡。

A: I'm going to examine you. First, please sit here.

B: 我感覺糟透了。

B: I feel terrible.

A: 護士告訴我你覺得病懨懨的。

A: The nurse told me you feel very sick.

B: 是啊，今天早上我吐了兩次。

B: Yes. This morning I threw up twice.

A: 我要量你的體溫。

A: I'm going to take your temperature.

基本對話

機場與飛機

入境

住宿

交通

餐飲

觀光

購物

郵電

銀行

麻煩事

回國

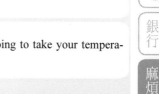

基本對話 機場與飛機 入境 住宿 交通 餐飲 觀光 購物 郵電 銀行 麻煩事 回國

Word Bank 字庫

examine [ɪgˈzæmɪn] v. 檢查
terrible [ˈtɛrəbl] adj. 極糟的
throw up 嘔吐

Tips 小祕訣

看醫生時，如何告訴醫生問題呢？只要說 I have... ，
例如：

I have a headache. 我頭痛。
I have a toothache. 我牙痛。
I have a backache. 我背痛。
I have sore eyes. 我眼睛酸痛。
I have sore legs [muscles]. 我腿 [肌肉] 酸痛。
I have a sore throat. 我喉嚨痛。
I have a cough. 我咳嗽。
I have a runny nose. 我流鼻水。
I have dizziness. 我頭暈。
I have a rash. 我起疹子。

Dialog 3 對話3

A: 我想你感冒了。　　**A:** I think you have the flu.

B: 知道了。　　**B:** I see.

A: 你今晚需要住院。　　**A:** You need to stay at the hospital overnight.

基本對話

機場與飛機

入境

住宿

交通

餐飲

觀光

購物

郵電

銀行

麻煩事

回國

B: 真的？這麼嚴重嗎？

B: Really? Is it so serious?

A: 你嚴重脫水，而且體溫太高。

A: You are badly dehydrated, and your temperature is much too high.

B: 我現在該怎麼辦？

B: What should I do now?

A: 護士會帶你去你的房間。

A: A nurse will take you to your room.

Word Bank 字庫

flu [flu] n. 流行性感冒
overnight ['ovə-'naɪt] adv. 整夜
dehydrate [di'haɪ,dret] v. 脫水

 Dialog 4 對話4

A: 早安，你今天感覺如何？

A: Good morning. How do you feel today?

B: 早安，醫生，我感覺好多了。

B: Good morning, doctor. I feel much better now.

A: 很好，你很快可以離開，我開個處方給你。

A: Good. You can leave soon. I have a prescription for you.

基本對話
機場與飛機
入境
住宿
交通
餐飲
觀光
購物
郵電
銀行
麻煩事
回國

B: 我可以去哪裡配藥呢？

B: Where can I get it filled?

A: 一樓有間藥局。

A: There is a pharmacy on the first floor.

Word Bank 字庫

prescription [prɪ'skrɪpʃən] n. 處方
fill [fɪl] v. 填滿
pharmacy ['fɑrməsɪ] n. 藥局

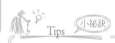
Tips 小祕訣

　　在美國看病通常需要先預約，如果是急診就直接去醫院急診室。歐美的醫療服務是很昂貴的，海外醫療並非普通人可以負擔的。無論到哪個國家，萬一有緊急狀況要包機回國，都是一筆驚人的費用，所以出國前要先了解自己的保險是否有意外醫療及國外就醫的保障(在國外就醫要拿單據，以便回國申起理賠)。在意外發生時又沒有保險的情形下，急診室通常不會拒收病患，但是每個國家情況不同。多數人在遇到危難時，陌生人多半會伸出援手。各地醫療方式雖有不同，但一般檢查都會先量體溫、脈搏、血壓。試著用最簡單的語言及肢體語言向醫護人員表達問題或症狀，如果有經常服用的藥物或過敏的東西(先查好英文怎麼說)，要讓醫師知道。

Useful Phrases 實用語句

1. 這是我第一次來這家醫院。

   This is my first time at this hospital.

2. 我是外地來的。

   I'm from out of town.

3. 我感覺快昏倒了。

   I feel faint.

4. 我需要醫療照顧。

   I need medical attention.

5. 我需要一輛輪椅。

   I need a wheel chair.

6. 我需要點什麼東西來止痛。

   I need something to kill the pain.

7. 喔，好痛！

   Ouch! It hurts very much.

8. 痛死我了！

   The pain is killing me.

9. 我對盤尼西林過敏。

   I'm allergic to penicillin.

10. 這嚴重嗎？

    Is it serious?

11. 我需要打針嗎？

    Do I need a shot?

12. 我需要吃藥嗎？

    Do I need to take medicine?

13. 我必須臥床嗎？

    Should I stay in bed?

14. 我必須留在這裡多久？

    How long will I have to stay here?

15. 我可以離開了嗎？

    Can I leave now?

16. 我可以自己回家嗎？

    Can I go home by myself?

17. 我需要再回來檢查嗎？

    Do I need to come back again?

18. 我要現在預約嗎？

    Do I need to make an appointment now?

基本對話　機場與飛機　入境　住宿　交通　餐飲　觀光　購物　郵電　銀行　麻煩事　回國

基本對話

機場與飛機

入境

住宿

交通

餐飲

觀光

購物

郵電

銀行

麻煩事

回國

19. 我必須取消 [延後] 我的行程 [班機] 嗎？

Should I cancel [postpone] my trip [flight]?

20. 還有什麼我必須知道的嗎？

Is there anything else I should know?

 Language Power　字句補給站

◆ 疾病名稱及症狀 Health Problems

cold	感冒
flu	流行性感冒
ache	痛
pain	痛
burn	燙傷
sunburn	晒傷
heat stroke	中暑
allergy	過敏
bruise	瘀傷
broken bone	骨折
sprain an ankle	扭傷腳踝
symptom	症狀
diarrhea	腹瀉
heartburn	胃酸逆流
fever	發燒
cough	咳嗽
itch	癢
dizzy	暈眩的
throw up	嘔吐
cramp	抽筋
shock	休克
remedy	療法
surgery	手術

◆ 常用藥品 Common Medicine

cold medicine	感冒藥
cough syrup	止咳糖漿
painkiller	止痛藥
burn ointment	燙傷藥膏

sunblock	防晒油
allergy medicine	過敏藥
aspirin	阿斯匹靈
vitamin	維他命
over-the-counter medicine / non-prescription	成藥
bandage	繃帶
Band-Aid	OK繃

11.7 生病——藥局配藥
Feeling Sick—Filling a Prescription

Dialog　對話

A: 哈囉，我需要配藥。

A: Hello. I need to fill a prescription.

B: 沒問題，先生。(配好了)這是你配好的處方，先生。

B: Certainly, sir. (it's ready) Here is your filled prescription, sir.

A: 謝謝你。你能告訴我這藥怎麼吃嗎？

A: Thank you. Can you tell me how to take the medicine?

B: 一天三次飯後，說明寫在標籤這兒。

B: Three times a day after meals. The directions are here on the label.

A: 喔，非常謝謝你。

A: Oh, thank you very much.

B: 不客氣。

B: No problem.

Useful Phrases 實用語句

基本對話
機場與飛機
入境
住宿
交通
餐飲
觀光
購物
郵電
銀行
麻煩事
回國

1. 我需要再拿一次這處方。

   I need this prescription filled again.

2. 我應該多久吃一次這些藥丸呢？

   How often should I take these pills?

3. 這些有副作用嗎？

   Do these have any side affects?

4. 這些會讓我嗜睡嗎？

   Will these make me drowsy?

5. 這些多快會有效？

   How fast will these work?

6. 我可以這兩種一起吃嗎？

   Can I take these two kinds together?

7. 如果漏掉一次要怎麼辦？

   What should I do if I forget to take it once?

8. 如果幾天以後感覺好些要不要繼續吃藥？

   Should I continue to take the medicine if I feel better after a few days?

9. 我該把藥全吃完嗎？

   Should I take all the medicine?

10. 我在吃過敏的藥。

   I'm on medication for my allergies.

Tips 小祕訣

　　需要藥品可去藥局 (pharmacy 或 drug store) 購買，藥劑師可以推薦一些不需醫師處方的成藥，如感冒藥或過敏藥。如果你有醫師處方單，藥劑師會替你配藥，並提供藥物諮詢。

Unit 12 Returning Home

返國搭機 72 小時之前，一定要打電話確認機位，許多航空公司在國外主要城市有中文電話及服務人員。收拾打包時要確定上機行李內沒有不該帶的東西，刀類物品務必放在託運行李內，吸菸者身上不可攜帶打火機。美國託運行李不要上鎖及超重，以免受罰。如果要辦理退稅(歐洲多數國家有退稅，但美國只有極少數地方有)，為避免排隊延誤時間，最好提早報到，要退稅的物品必須帶著備查。入境表格在離境時需繳回，切勿遺失。如果行李箱上有以前的掛牌或貼條，務必清乾淨，只留這次的掛牌，以免行李遺失。如果返國前有發布任何安全警告，更要提早到機場報到，因為更多更詳細的檢查會耗去許多時間。

基本對話
機場與飛機
入境
住宿
交通
餐飲
觀光
購物
郵電
銀行
麻煩事
回國

12.1 回程機位確認
Confirming a Return Flight

Dialog 對話

A: 西北航空。我怎麼幫你呢？

A: Northwest Airlines. How may I help you?

B: 我打電話來確認機位。

B: I'm calling to confirm my flight.

A: 好的，請問你的名字？

A: Fine. Your name, please?

B: 我名字是史丹利王，拼法是S-T-A-N-L-E-Y W-A-N-G。

B: My name is Stanley Wang. That's spelled S-T-A-N-L-E-Y W-A-N-G.

A: 謝謝你。你搭 67 班機，12 日星期二早上 8 點 47 分離境。

A: Thank you. I have you on flight 67, departing Tuesday the 12th at 8:47 a.m.

B: 好的，67 班機，12 日星期二早上 8 點 47 分離境。

B: OK. That's flight 67, departing on Tuesday the 12th at 8:47 a.m.

A: 是的，先生，沒錯。

A: Yes, sir, that is correct.

Notes 小叮嚀

確認機位時也要記得是否已預選座位。

12.2 機位更改
Changing a Flight

 Dialog 1 對話1

A: 西北航空。我可以幫你嗎？

A: Northwest Airlines. May I help you?

B: 是的，我想更改回程機位的離境日期。

B: Yes. I want to change my return flight departure date.

A: 好的，請給我名字及日期。

A: All right. Name and departure date, please.

B: 史丹利王。我搭 67 班機，12 日星期二早上 8 點 47 分離境。

B: Stanley Wang. I'm on flight 67, departing on Tuesday the 12th at 8:47 a.m.

A: 好的，王先生，我這裡有你的資料。你想要何時離境呢？

A: Yes, Mr. Wang. I have your information here. When do you want to depart?

B: 我現在想要 17 日離境。

B: I now want to depart on the 17th.

A: 我看看。好的，我們那天有個空位。

A: Let me see. Yes, we have a seat available on that day.

B: 一樣的離境時間嗎？

B: Same departure time?

基本對話

機場與飛機

入境

住宿

交通

餐飲

觀光

購物

郵電

銀行

麻煩事

回國

基本對話

機場與飛機

入境

住宿

交通

餐飲

觀光

購物

郵電

銀行

麻煩事

回國

A: 是的，早上 8 點 47 分。

A: Yes, 8:47 a.m.

Dialog 2　對話2

A: 美國航空。我怎麼幫你呢？

A: American Airlines. How may I help you?

B: 我要改機位。

B: I need to change my flight.

A: 請告訴我您貴姓。

A: Your last name, please.

B: 李，L-E-E。

B: It's Lee. L-E-E.

A: 你的電腦代號是什麼？

A: What's your reference locator?

B: GKISRG，我跟一個朋友一起旅行。

B: GKISRG. I'm traveling with a friend.

A: 好的，請給我另一位的姓及電腦代號。

A: OK, the other person's last name and reference locator, please.

B: 姓 是 C-H-A-N-G，電腦代號是 KTJHVW。

B: The last name is C-H-A-N-G. The reference locator is KTJH-VW.

A: 你們搭 0554 班機，8 月 15 日。

A: You're on flight 0554, Aug. 15th.

B: 是的，但是我們要改期。我們可以搭 17 日的嗎？

B: Yes, but we need to change the schedule. Can we go on the 17th?

Dialog 3　對話3

A: 我看看。17 日的全滿，18 日可以嗎？

A: Let me see. The 17th is full all day. Is the 18th OK?

B: 好。我們可以搭早上的班機嗎？

B: All right. Can we take the morning flight?

A: 你要早上 7 點還是 9 點 55 分的班機？

A: You want 7 a.m. or the 9:55 flight?

B: 9 點 55 分。我們何時抵達？還有班機號碼是什麼？

B: 9:55. When do we arrive and what's the flight number?

A: 下午 3 點 57 分到，飛行時間四小時，加時差多兩小時，你們搭 1486 班機。

A: 3:57 p.m. The flight is four hours. Add two hours for time zones. You're on flight 1486.

B: 新的電腦代號是什麼？

B: What's the new reference locator?

基本對話　機場與飛機　入境　住宿　交通　餐飲　觀光　購物　郵電　銀行　麻煩事　回國

基本對話

機場與飛機

入境

住宿

交通

餐飲

觀光

購物

郵電

銀行

麻煩事

回國

A: 你的新電腦代號是 George 的 G、Nancy 的 N、William 的 W、Boy 的 B、King 的 K，和 Frank 的 F。

A: Your new locator is G as in George, N as in Nancy, W as in William, B as in Boy, K as in King, and F as in Frank.

B: 我朋友的呢？

B: And my friend's?

A: 是 FUNYZS。

A: It's FUNYZS.

B: 我們可以坐一起嗎？

B: Can we sit together?

A: 是的，你們坐在 25 排 A 跟 B。

A: Yes, you're in 25 A and B.

B: 我們報到登記時會被收取更改機位的手續費嗎？

B: Will we be charged for the change when we check in?

A: 不會，但是記得要早點到機場。

A: No, but remember to arrive at the airport early.

B: 非常謝謝你。

B: Thank you very much.

 Useful Phrases 實用語句

1. 改機位有手續費嗎？

   Is there any service charge for the change?

2. 手續費多少錢？

   How much is the service charge?

3. 週末時你可能必須支付更改機位的手續費。

   On weekends, you may have to pay a service charge for the change.

4. 是否額外收費要看櫃臺人員。

   It depends on the people at the counter whether you are charged extra or not.

5. 你必須付差價。

   You have to pay the price difference.

6. 你的票只能坐N艙，但是已經滿了。

   Your ticket only allows you to take the N class, but it's full.

7. 你的票不允許你搭 Q 艙。

   Your ticket doesn't allow you to take Q class.

12.3 回程機場報到
Checking In for a Return Flight

 Dialog 對話

A: 下一位。早安，先生。	**A:** Next. Good morning, sir.
B: 嗨，我們一起報到。	**B:** Hi. We're checking in together.
A: 好的，請給我你們的護照及機票。	**A:** OK. Your passports and tickets please.

基本對話

機場與飛機

入境

住宿

交通

餐飲

觀光

購物

郵電

銀行

麻煩事

回國

B: 這裡，我們有四件行李要登記託運。

B: Here. We have four pieces of luggage to check in.

A: 請確認填好每件行李的行李掛牌。

A: Be sure to fill out luggage tags for each piece.

B: 掛牌在哪兒呢？

B: Where are the tags?

A: 就在櫃臺上。

A: Right here on the counter.

 Useful Phrases 實用語句

1. 我在哪裡報到呢？

   Where do I check in?

2. 我要掛行李牌。

   I want to tag my luggage.

3. 我有兩件託運行李及一件登機行李。

   I have two pieces to check in and one carry on.

4. 你會給我這趟旅程所有我需要的登機證嗎？

   Will you give me all the boarding passes I will need for this trip?

5. 班機準時嗎？

   Is the flight on time?

6. 登機門在哪個方向呢？

   Which way to the gates?

12.4 安全檢查
Security Check

 Dialog 1 對話1

A: 我們要檢查你的袋子，先生，請過來這邊。

A: We have to search your bags, sir. Please step over here.

B: 什麼問題呢？

B: What is the problem?

A: 沒問題，這只是例行、隨機的檢查。

A: No problem, this is just a routine, random check.

B: 好的。

B: OK.

A: 你有攜帶任何刀具或打火機嗎？

A: Do you have any knives or lighters with you?

B: 不在這裡，我有一把刀在託運行李內。

B: Not here. I have a knife in my check-in luggage.

A: 那沒問題。

A: That is no problem.

Word Bank 字庫

search [sɝtʃ] v. 搜查
routine [ru'tin] adj. 例行的
random ['rændəm] adj. 隨機的

 Dialog 2 對話2

A: 請把袋子放到輸送帶上。
A: Please place your bags on the conveyor.

B: 先生，你要從口袋拿出所有金屬物品。
B: Sir, you'll need to remove anything metal from your pockets.

A: 好的。
A: OK.

B: 把那些物品放到籃子裡。(嗶……)
B: Put those things in this basket. (Beeeeeeeep.)

A: 先生，請過來這裡，我必須要掃描你。
A: Sir, please step over here. I'll have to scan you.

B: 好。
B: OK.

A: 請將手臂離開身體。
A: Please hold your arms away from your body.

B: 好。

B: OK.

A: 請你也把鞋脫掉。

A: Please remove your shoes, too.

 Word Bank 字庫

conveyor [kən'veə-] n. 輸送帶
pocket ['pɑkɪt] n. 口袋
basket ['bæskɪt] n. 籃子
scan [skæn] v. 掃描
remove [rɪ'muv] v. 脫掉，除去

Notes 小叮嚀

　　機場安全人員常會做出許多要求，例如要求你從口袋內拿出所有物品，或是打開袋子的某些拉鍊或夾層，詢問你裡面裝些什麼。萬一你不小心放了任何刀類或其他有安全顧慮而不該帶上機的東西，例如指甲刀、剪刀、水果刀等，被發現時切勿慌亂，否則會引起安全人員緊張。保持鎮定，安全人員會問你一些相關問題，了解你為何會有這東西，然後要你簽名表示物件是你的。這物品將會被分開送往你的目的地，通常在你到達時，這物品也會到達，等你取回。

　　如果不要這麼麻煩，而物品丟掉也不可惜的話，可以直接請安全人員丟棄就行。當然如髮型噴霧罐、撒隆巴斯噴霧罐，是絕對不能帶上飛機的，必須當場丟棄，到當地再買。另外要注意的是，餐點、水果可以帶在機上吃，但吃不完絕不可帶入關。

12.5 購買紀念品
Buying Souvenirs

Dialog 對話

A: 過海關後還有禮品店嗎？

A: Are there any gift shops past customs?

B: 有的。

B: Yes, there are.

A: 也有咖啡廳嗎？

A: Coffee shops, too?

B: 是的，還有餐廳。

B: Yes, and restaurants as well.

Word Bank 字庫

souvenir ['suvə,nɪr] n. 紀念品
as well 另外也，同樣也

Useful Phrases 實用語句

1. 你可以把這個包裝成禮物嗎？
   Can you gift-wrap this?
2. 你可以運送 [郵寄] 這個嗎？
   Can you ship [mail] this?

安檢處前的機場商店並非免稅商店，進入安檢區後才是。

Are there any gift shops past customs?

Yes, there are.

附錄

Appendices

附錄

附錄

1. 不規則變化動詞 Irregular Verbs

現在	過去	過去分詞
be 是	was	been
begin 開始	began	begun
blow 打擊	blew	blown
break 打破	broke	broken
bring 帶來	brought	brought
build 建造	built	built
buy 買	bought	bought
catch 抓住，趕 (巴士)	caught	caught
choose 選	chose	chosen
come 來	came	come
do 做	did	done
drink 喝	drank	drunk
drive 開車	drove	driven
eat 吃	ate	eaten
fall 掉下	fell	fallen
feel 感覺	felt	felt
find 找	found	found
fly 飛	flew	flown
forget 忘記	forgot	forgotten
get 得到	got	gotten
give 給	gave	given
go 去	went	gone
have 有	had	had
hear 聽到	heard	heard
hold 握	held	held
keep 保持	kept	kept
know 知道	knew	known
leave 離開	left	left
lose 遺失	lost	lost
make 做	made	made
meet 遇到	met	met

pay 付款	paid	paid
ride 騎 (馬)，搭 (車)	rode	ridden
run 跑	ran	run
say 說	said	said
see 看	saw	seen
sell 賣	sold	sold
send 寄	sent	sent
sing 唱	sang	sung
sit 坐	sat	sat
sleep 睡	slept	slept
speak 說	spoke	spoken
spend 花 (錢、時間)	spent	spent
stand 站立	stood	stood
swim 游泳	swam	swum
take 拿	took	taken
teach 教	taught	taught
tear 撕	tore	torn
tell 告訴	told	told
think 想	thought	thought
throw 丟	threw	thrown
undertand 了解	understood	understood
wear 穿	wore	worn
write 寫	wrote	written

2. 美國中央情報局世界概況：世界與美國人口資料
CIA - The World Factbook : Population Data (the World and the United States)

A. 世界人口 The World Population

🔹 世界總人口 the World Population：

約 71 億 7 千萬（2014 年 7 月）前 10 大人口國：①中國 China 13.6 億，②印度 India 12.4 億，③美國 United States 3.2 億，④印尼 Indonesia 2.5 億，⑤巴西 Brazil 2.03 億，⑥巴基斯坦 Pakistan 1.96 億，⑦奈及利亞 Nigeria 1.8 億，⑧孟加拉 Bangladesh 1.7 億，⑨蘇俄 Russia 1.4 億，⑩日本 Japan 1.3 億。

🔹 世界人口宗教信仰（Religions）比例：

基督徒 Christians 33.39%	錫克教徒 Sikhs 0.35%
天主教徒 Roman Catholics 16.85%	猶太教徒 Jews 0.22%
新教徒 Protestants 6.15%	大同教 Baha'is 0.11%
東正教徒 Orthodox 3.96%	其他宗教 other religions 10.95%
英國國教徒 Anglicans 1.26%	無信仰者 non-religious 9.66%
回教徒 Muslims 22.74%	無神論者 atheists 2.01%
印度教徒 Hindus 13.8%	（2010 年）
佛教徒 Buddhists 6.77%	

🔹 世界人口語言（Languages）比例：

中文 Mandarin Chinese 11.82%	孟加拉語 Bengali 2.69%
西班牙語 Spanish 5.77%	俄語 Russian 2.33%
英語 English 4.67%	日語 Japanese 1.7%
（北）印度語 Hindi 3.62%	爪哇語 Javanese 1.15%
阿拉伯語 Arabic 3.3%	標準德語 Standard German 1.09%
葡萄牙語 Portuguese 2.83%	（2014 年）

註：1. 將人口數乘上百分比可得人口數。例如：基督徒近 24 億人，回教徒約 16.3 億人，印度教近 10 億人，佛教徒約 4.85 億人。

2. 語言為母語人口 (Native Speaker) 之比例。

3. CIA-The World Factbook，網址為https://www.cia.gov/ibrary/publications/the-world-factbook/，由美國中情局 (Central Intelligence Agency) 發行及更新 (2010 年起資料每週更新)，可以 APP 下載，提供世界及 195 個國家與 72 個政治實體 (共 267) 之檔案查詢，包含簡介、地理、人口、政府、經濟等各方面之統計資料與排名。

B. 美國人口 USA Population

🧍 總人數 (Total Population)：

3 億 1 千 8 百多萬 (2014 年 7 月) 世界第 3 大人口國，僅次於中國與印度

👥 種族 (Ethnic Groups) 比例：

白人 white 79.96%

非洲裔 black 12.85%

亞裔 Asian 4.43%

原住民 Amerindian and Alaska native 0.97%

夏威夷及其他太平洋島民 native Hawaiian and other Pacific islander 0.18%

兩種族以上 two or more races 1.61% (2007 年 7 月)

註：1. 拉丁裔 Hispanic 占美國人口 15.1% (CIA 將此資料分開計算於百分比外另外列表)。

　　2. 白人比例內含中東裔。

🛐 宗教信仰 (Religions) 比例：

基督徒 Christian 78.5%

　新教徒 Protestant 51.3%

　天主教 Roman Catholic 23.9%

　摩門教 Mormon 1.7%

　其他基督教派 other Christian 1.6%

猶太教 Jewish 1.7%

佛教徒 Buddhist 0.7%

回教徒 Muslim 0.6%

其他及未明 other or unspecified 2.5%

不屬於任何宗教派別 unaffiliated 12.1%

無宗教信仰 none 4% (2007 年 7 月)

註：新教徒教派繁多含浸信會 Baptist、衛理會 Methodist、路得會 Lutheran、長老會 Presbyterian、聖公會 Episcopalian、靈恩派 Pentecostal、基督教會 Church of Christ、聯合基督教會 Congregational United Church of Christ、耶和華見證人 Jehovah's Witnesses、神召會 Assemblies of God 等。

語言 (Languages)：

英語 English 79.2%　　　　　　　亞洲及太平洋島語 Asian and Pacific

西班牙語 Spanish 12.9%　　　　　　island 3.3%

其他印歐語 other Indo-European 3.8%　(2011 年)

其他 other 0.9%

3. 度量衡及溫度換算表 Measurement and Temperature Conversion Charts

下載智慧手機度量衡換算應用程式是另一便利

✳ Length / Distance 長度 / 距離

1 centimeter (cm) 公分	= 10 millimeters (mm) 公釐 / 毫米
1 inch 英寸	= 2.54 centimeters (cm) 公分
1 foot 英尺	= 0.3 meters (m) 公里
1 foot 英尺	= 12 inches 英寸
1 yard 碼	= 3 feet 英尺
1 meter (m) 公尺 / 米	= 100 centimeters (cm) 公分
1 meter (m) 公尺 / 米	= 3.28 feet 英寸
1 furlong 弗隆 (1/8 英里)	= 660 feet 英尺
1 kilometer (km) 公里	= 1000 meters (m) 公里
1 kilometer (km) 公里	= 0.62 miles 英里
1 mile 英里	= 5280 ft 英尺
1 mile 英里	= 1.61 kilometers (km) 公里
1 nautical mile 海里	= 1.85 kilometers (km) 公里

✳ Area 面積

1 square foot 平方呎	= 144 square inches 平方吋
1 square foot 平方呎	= 929 square centimeters 平方米
1 square yard 平方碼	= 9 square feet 平方呎
1 square meter 平方米	= 10.7639104 square feet 平方呎
1 Ping 坪 (日本、臺灣)	= 35.58 square feet 平方呎
	3.3 square meters 平方米
1 acre 一英畝	= 43,560 square feet 平方呎
1 hectare 公頃	= 10,000 square meters 平方米
1 hectare 公頃	= 2.47 acres 英畝
1 square kilometer 平方公里	= 100 hectares 公頃
1 square mile 平方哩	= 2.59 square kilometers 平方公里
1 square mile 平方哩	= 640 acres 英畝

✳ Weight 重量

1 milligram (mg) 毫克	= 0.001 grams (g) 公克
1 gram (g) 公克	= 0.001 kilograms (kg) 公斤
1 gram (g) 公克	= 0.035 ounces
1 ounce 盎司	= 28.35 grams (g) 公克
1 ounce 盎司	= 0.0625 pounds 磅
1 pound (lb) 磅	= 16 ounces 盎司
1 pound (lb) 磅	= 0.45 kilograms (kg) 公斤
1 kilogram (kg) 公斤	= 1000 grams 公克
1 kilogram (kg) 公斤	= 35.27 ounces 盎司
1 kilogram (kg) 公斤	= 2.2 pounds (lb)
1 short ton 美噸 / 短噸	= 2000 pounds 磅
1 long ton 英噸 / 長頓	= 2240 pounds 磅
1 metric ton 公噸	= 1000 kilograms (kg) 公斤

✳ Volume 容量

1 US fluid ounce 液盎司	≅ 29.57 milliliters (ml) 公撮 / 毫升
1 US pint 品脫	= 0.473 liter 公升 (473ml 毫升)
1 US quart 夸脫	= 2 US pints 品脫
1 liter 公升	= 1000 milliliters (ml) 毫升
1 liter 公升	= 0.24 US gallon 美加侖
1 US gallon 美加侖	= 4 US quarts 夸脫
1 US gallon 美加侖	= 3.76 liters 公升

❈ Temperature Conversion 溫度換算

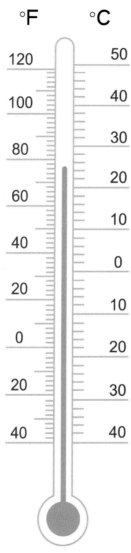

$$°C(Celsius) = (°F - 32) \times \frac{5}{9} \qquad °F(Fahrenheit) = (\frac{9}{5}°C) + 32°$$

4. 衣服及鞋子尺寸 Clothing and Shoe Sizes

　　美國及加拿大的衣服尺寸比亞洲標準尺寸要大，一般尺寸標示有 XXL (double extra large) 超超大、XL (extra large) 超大、L (large) 大、M (medium) 中、S (small) 小、XS (extra small) / Petité 超小，以及 F (free size / one size fits all) 不分尺寸。買衣服最好要試穿。為別人買衣服除了要記得尺寸，還要注意尺寸的差異。一個在亞洲穿大號衣服的人，在美國可能要買中號才合身。

女裝					
日本	7	9	11	13	15
美國	4	6	8	10	12
英國	6	8	10	12	14
法國	36	38	40	42	44
義大利	38	40	42	44	46

男襯衫							
日本	36	37	38	39	40	41	42
美國	14	$14\frac{1}{2}$	15	$15\frac{1}{2}$	16	$16\frac{1}{2}$	17
英國	14	$14\frac{1}{2}$	15	$15\frac{1}{2}$	16	$16\frac{1}{2}$	17
法國	36	37	38	39	40	41	42
義大利	36	37	38	39	40	41	42

買鞋子一定要試穿。鞋子尺寸在美國是以每半號漸增，如 6 號、6 號半、7 號等等。大多數的商店有長度在 5 號到 11 或 12 號間的鞋子，寬度則是以 D 為單位，有 2D (double D) 及 3D (triple D) 的選擇。女鞋與男鞋用同樣的尺寸為單位，當然多數女士適用較小尺寸的鞋子。

男鞋							
日本	24.5	25	25.5	26	26.5	27	27.5
美國	$6\frac{1}{2}$	7	$7\frac{1}{2}$	8	$8\frac{1}{2}$	9	$9\frac{1}{2}$
英國	6	$6\frac{1}{2}$	7	$7\frac{1}{2}$	8	$8\frac{1}{2}$	9
法國	39	40	41	42	43	44	45
義大利	39	40	41	42	43	44	45

女鞋							
日本	22	22.5	23	23.5	24	24.5	25
美國	$4\frac{1}{2}$	5	$5\frac{1}{2}$	6	$6\frac{1}{2}$	7	$6\frac{1}{2}$
英國	3	$3\frac{1}{2}$	4	$4\frac{1}{2}$	5	$5\frac{1}{2}$	6
法國	34.5	35	35.5	36	36.5	37	37.5
義大利	34	35	36	37	38	39	40

5. 美金硬幣及紙鈔 Money in the USA

　　美金在全世界流通，不但是所有旅行者使用最方便的國際貨幣之一，也是除美國外其他國家的國幣，如薩爾瓦多 (El Salvador) 及巴拿馬 (Panama)，許多國家也願意在旅客沒有當地貨幣的情形下以美金交易。有這麼多的使用者，在金融危機後美國又大量印鈔，認識美金的防偽功能變得相當重要。每隔幾年美金紙鈔就增加更多防偽功能，不同面值紙鈔隨著使用年限輪流改版。出國前可先查詢「美國在臺協會」(AIT) 之「新版美鈔防偽辨識」中文說明或 http://www.nowmoney.gov 之英文說明。出國應盡量少用現金大鈔，不但容易失竊及可能找不開外，還會增加找錢而拿到偽幣的風險。

☑ 硬幣 Coins

	Penny 一分幣 (1¢, one cent)
	Nickel 五分幣 (5¢, five cents)
	Dime 十分幣 (10¢, ten cents)
	Quarter 二十五分幣 (25¢, twenty five cents)
另有 Half Dollar 五十分幣 (50¢, fifty cents)，市面少見。	

✔ **紙鈔 Paper Money**

	One Dollar Bill 一元鈔 ($1)
	Five Dollar Bill 五元鈔 ($5)
	Ten Dollar Bill 十元鈔 ($10)
	Twenty Dollar Bill 二十元鈔 ($20)
	Fifty Dollar Bill 五十元鈔 ($50)
	One Hundred Dollar Bill 一百元鈔 ($100)

6. 美國假日 Holidays in the USA

比起歐洲人，美國人的休假時間算是少的。從聖誕節到新年期間是美國的年假，家人們聚在一起享受佳肴、交換禮物或出遊。一年中的休假日並不多，如果有週休二日加上少數放假或補假的星期一，才有 long weekend，許多節日並不休假。

☑ 國定假日 Official Holidays (休假日，遇週末則週一補假)

1. New Year's Day - Jan. 1st 新年 (一月一日)
2. Martin Luther King Day (MLK Day) - 3rd Mon. of Jan. 馬丁路德金恩誕辰 (一月的第三個星期一)
3. President's Day - 3rd Mon. of Feb. 總統紀念日 (二月的第三個星期一)，包括
   Lincoln's Birthday - Feb. 12th 林肯誕辰 (二月十二日)
   Washington's Birthday - Feb. 22nd 華盛頓誕辰 (二月二十二日)
4. Memorial Day - last Mon. of May 陣亡將士紀念日 (五月的最後一個星期一)
5. Independence Day - July 4th 獨立紀念日 / 國慶日 (七月四日)
6. Labor Day - 1st Mon. of Sept. 勞動節 (九月的第一個星期一)
7. Columbus Day - Oct. 12th 哥倫布紀念日 (十月十二日)
8. Veterans Day - Nov. 11th 退伍軍人節 (十一月十一日)
9. Thanksgiving Day - 4th Thurs. of Nov. 感恩節 (十一月的第四個星期四)
10. Christmas - Dec. 25th 聖誕節 (十二月二十五日)

☑ 非國定假日 Non-official Holidays (不休假)

1. Groundhog Day - Feb. 2nd 土撥鼠日 (二月二日)
2. Valentine's Day - Feb. 14th 情人節 (二月十四日)
3. Saint Patrick's Day - Mar. 17th 聖派屈克節 (三月十七日)
4. April Fool's Day - Apr. 1st 愚人節 (四月一日)
5. Easter - A Sun. in Mar. or Apr. 復活節 (春分滿月後的第一個星期天)
6. Mother's Day - 2nd Sun. of May 母親節 (五月的第二個星期天)
7. Father's Day - 3rd Sun. in June 父親節 (六月的第三個星期天)
8. Halloween - Oct. 31st 萬聖節 (十月三十一日)

7. 不可不知的美國文化祕笈
American Cultural Tips You Need to Know

各國文化有其形成的背景，接觸不同的文化提供我們學習如何將言行舉止符合該文化的期待，甚至更進一步比較不同民族間文化異同根基何在。在文化大融爐 (melting pot) 的國家如美國及其他歐洲國家，外來移民多少保有其傳統文化並帶來多樣性，但主流文化還是多數人與他人互動的行為依據。

1. 小寒暄大學問 Small Talk

(1) 該怎麼稱呼呢？

在美國文化裡，與人碰面時打招呼，不僅是友善的表示，也是禮貌的表現。問候時可加上適當的稱謂，正式場合中一般在姓氏前冠 Mr. 或 Ms.，而 Mrs. 及 Miss 則因政治不正確，已較少使用。不知姓名時，先生用 sir，女士、小姐用 ma'am / madam，miss 則通常指相當年輕或十來歲的年輕女性，當然較年長者可以稱呼較年輕的女性為 miss。一般朋友、同學間用名字即可。

(2) 禮貌的做法

打招呼並不僅適用於相識的人，人們在較少人的郊外散步，或在電梯裡、排隊結帳時，陌生的人也有可能彼此打招呼，甚至短暫交談。當然都市人相較於小城鎮的人確實是比較冷漠的。陌生人談的不外乎交通、天氣，排隊結帳時，可能會抱怨一下物價上漲或讚美大拍賣物美價廉等，交換跟當時情境有關的消息。

在戶外、電梯間、走廊上等公共空間，相識的人們都會互相打招呼，簡短一聲「嗨！」或微笑揮手致意皆可。沉默不發一語、面無表情或近距離卻視而不見，難免會被認為是沒禮貌或不友善的行為。說話或排隊的距離以一手臂的距離量丈，注意不要入侵他人個人空間。

(3) 寒暄話題

既然是 small talk，話題當然就不宜深入。天氣、交通、休閒活動、工作動向、旅遊等都是適切的寒暄話題。尤其別問他人隱私 (Don't be a busybody.)，如年齡、體重、婚姻狀況、薪水、價錢、政治、宗教信仰等這些敏感問題。即使是好朋友，某些話題也可能是很敏感的。

還有，問好時回答通常都是正面的。即使對交情不錯的朋友，也傾向「報喜不報憂」。寒暄只是一個形式，經常這些問好的回答是很制式的「好」、「不錯」、「忙啊」。報告生活瑣事，可能反而讓朋友想快點逃之夭夭呢！

好朋友間也喜歡來點好聽的，例如讚美朋友看來很好「You look great!」、衣著很好看「I like your outfit.」、新髮型很好看「I like your new hair style.」等等，所以讚美 (當然要真誠) 也是常用的。對於別人的讚美不要不好意思，大方說「Thank you」即可。

關於較敏感的話題，若對方願與你成為好友，自然會慢慢透露。我們也可主動略提自己的情況，慢慢與對方建立友誼。如果對方說我們該聚聚，別急著問什麼時候，有時這只是禮貌性道別的說法，此時只需附和說好即可。

(4) 忠告與自由

我們常因關心他人，而給予忠告，對個人主義的美國人而言，便顯得極不合宜。忠告他人戒菸、減肥，甚至結婚、生子這些非常個人的事情，某些美國人可能開玩笑地反諷，而回答「Yes, Doc (doctor).」或「Yes, Mom! (You sound like my Mom!)」，意思是「拜託，別管太多了」。

(5) 轉個彎找答案

其實一個人是否已婚，基本上看手就知道了，絕大多數的美國人在婚後就戴著婚戒。若仍想肯定，可以問的安全問題是「Do you have a family?」如果問的是「Do you have a boy / girlfriend?」或「Are you married?」這麼單刀直入的問題，對方可能認為你在暗示對他或她有興趣，或者是要替對方介紹對象，不可不慎。

對美國人而言，詢問他人某件衣物或配件的價錢，等於是在打聽對方的經濟能力，這是很失禮的。所以寒暄時可以先讚美該物品，再詢問在何處購買，例如：「What a beautiful watch! Where did you get it?」對方可能告訴你購買地點，也有可能說是別人送的禮物或太久了、忘記了。這樣轉個彎的問法，可以避掉尷尬的價格問題。

2. 美國駕駛須知 Driving Tips

(1) 美國人的駕駛習慣

美國人十六歲就可以考駕照。在大多數地區，沒車子就等於沒有腳，哪裡也去不了，自己開車作為交通工具可以說是獨立的第一步，因此優良的駕駛紀錄是很重要的。入境隨俗，美國人的駕駛習慣不可不知，才能確保出門平安，且不會拿到罰單。

1. 換車道時要回頭 (過肩) 查看，確定盲點內無車輛。
2. 禮讓主幹線車輛先行，不可爭先。
3. 碰到停車再開標誌 (Stop)，一定要使車子完全停止，確定可以通過再開。
4. 四面都有停車再開標誌時，要讓先到的車輛先停先走，不可爭先。
5. 有行人穿越馬路時，一定要禮讓，不可亂按喇叭或閃頭燈。比中指是嚴重的挑釁行為，不可不慎。
6. 紅燈可以右轉，但要小心行人。若有 No right turn on red. 就要等綠箭頭燈亮，才可右轉。

(2) 被警察攔下怎麼辦？

美國高速公路又寬又直，一不小心就會超速。城市的時速限制通常為 55 英里，多數駕駛駕車時速約在 65 英里左右 (即速限加 10 英里左右)，超過的話就有可能被高速公路警察 (Highway Patrol) 取締，而拿到超速 (speeding) 罰單。違規處罰除了罰款，還可能包括上法庭。如果被警察取締時態度不佳，有可能被戴上手銬，送進監牢，及上法院裁決。在沙漠地區或人煙較少處，速限通常為 100 英里。要注意此時地面警察雖較不常出現，但可能有直昇機警察突然出現取締違規車輛。

酒駕及超速在美國、加拿大及其他地方都是嚴重的交通違規，兩者的罰金都很重且可能要入獄，而且駕駛紀錄差將影響到以後一輩子的保險費。記住車內絕不可以放開過的酒，酒類最好放在後車廂。危險的駕駛行為 (即使沒有超速)，可能會被警察以魯莽駕駛 (reckless driving) 逮捕並起訴，而魯莽駕駛通常是因為酒駕引起的。

臺灣警察巡邏時常開著閃燈，可能導致國人對美國警車閃燈習以為常。「國家地理頻道」曾播出 4 位臺灣在美打工大學生，警察緊追其後閃燈 (加廣播) 還渾然不覺繼續開車，最後被阿拉斯加公路警察持槍攔下。切記在美國萬一被警察閃燈，務必盡快停車。車停好後，靜

坐在車內等待警察。切勿打開車門走出車外或在車內慌亂尋找物品，警察可能會誤認為你在尋找槍械或藏匿毒品而用槍指著你，這是非常危險的。

美國是可以合法買賣槍械的國家，有些州並不要求買槍者註冊登記，因此全國真正槍枝數字無從得知，必須依靠估算。2015 年經濟學人 (The Economist) 估算美國人年人口 3 億 2 千萬人已擁有等同人口數量之槍枝，擁槍比例達百分之百，槍枝氾濫問題極為嚴重，警察因此對違法者執行勤務時非常嚴厲，他們必須防範違法者攜帶槍械，隨時可能採取之攻擊。

因為是執法者，警察過來時通常會很嚴厲，這時可以主動禮貌地向警察打招呼：「Hello, officer. May I ask what the problem is?」警察不喜歡無禮及愛挑釁的人。在國外旅遊因為沒碰過這種情形或不知自己為何被攔下，通常會一時無法反應，但千萬不要裝成不懂英文。警察通常會問外地人是否懂英文，此時要誠實以對：「Yes, officer. I speak a little English.」聽不懂時，告訴警察「I'm sorry, officer. I don't understand.」別裝懂而隨便說「yes」，會給自己帶來麻煩。也可以表示自己是外國人不熟悉當地規則：「Officer, I'm sorry. I'm from another country. I'm not familiar with the rules here.」。

按照警察指示，拿出所需證件 (駕照、行照或租車同意書：driver's license, registration or rental agreement)，雖然已有國際駕照，但是中文駕照也要帶著備查。如需打開前座置物箱或後車廂，要告訴警察因為證件在裡面：「The rental agreement is in the glove compartment / trunk.」保持禮貌，配合警察，對於小的違規，觀光客可能只被口頭警告 (verbal warning)，不一定會被開罰單。

8. 特殊的美國文化體驗
Unique Cultural Experience in America

1. 想賭博嗎?

如果你賭性堅強,就到內華達州 (Nevada) 吧!拉斯維加斯 (Las Vegas) 是沙漠裡最閃亮、紙醉金迷的城市,可以讓你度過整個假期。賭累了就看場秀吧,逛逛超市也可以小試身手。北邊規模較小的雷諾 (Reno) 及與加州邊界的太浩 (Tahoe) 也歡迎賭客,東部紐澤西州 (New Jersey) 的大西洋城 (Atlantic City) 也是賭城,難怪美國是讓旅客花掉最多錢的國家。如果你喜歡特殊的文化氣息,就到印地安保留區的賭場吧!祝你好運!

2. 慢一點!

如果你想邊運動邊欣賞風光,在美、加、澳及其他地方,租腳踏車是既經濟又便利的方式。在旅遊中心及其他地方可以找到腳踏車專用道及特別地圖,你可以用不同的方式發掘旅遊的趣味。

3. 來派對吧!

紐奧良 (New Orleans) 每年一度的狂歡節 (Marti Gras) 的瘋狂程度一定要親身經歷,對許多美國人而言,到了紐奧良等同出國。狂歡節是復活節前四十七天開始齋戒前的街上瘋狂派對,人們喝酒、裸露狂歡、彩繪變裝遊行、從花車上丟串珠、融合爵士音樂與視覺的奇妙感受,是慶祝生命也是享受生命。旅客要注意的是不要撿拾串珠,因為可能會被群眾踩到手指。因為狂歡節太受歡迎,湧入紐奧良的遊客太多,機票飯店都要及早準備。若在夏秋兩季造訪,務必留意美東佛羅里達州及墨西哥灣沿岸的颶風消息,如 2005 年卡翠娜 (katrina) 颶風造成堤防潰堤的重大水災,2012 年桑迪 (Sandy) 颶風讓美東加拿大東部及加勒比海國家受災,連國際大都會紐約的許多地區也泡水斷電數日。對旅客而言,最安全的做法是避免在颶風季節造訪。

註:1. 美國有豐富的自然地貌,經常是世界最多旅遊人數 (The World Tourism Rankings) 排名第 2 的國家,僅次於向來第 1 的法國,第 3-5 名通常為中國、西班牙、義大利。

2. 大小型的嘉年華 (Carnival) 盛行於其他天主教國家,如義大利的威尼斯 (Venice) 與巴西的里約 (Rio),知名賭城如蒙地卡羅 (Monte Carlo) 與澳門 (Macau)。除了典型的觀光活動外,世界景

附錄

觀無論自然、人文或奇風異俗不勝枚舉，旅行者當然也不只限
於歐美地區。

9. 旅遊資訊站 Travel Information

1. World Travel Awards (世界旅遊獎)

　　1993 年創立，每年 12 月頒發各類旅遊服務獎項，堪稱「旅遊界的奧斯卡」獎，有全球性與區域性的獎項，包含最佳航空公司、最佳機場、最佳租車公司、最佳遊輪、最佳機票比價網站、最佳飯店比價網站、最佳廉價航空 app、最奢華飯店品牌、最佳旅遊地、最佳飯店品牌、最佳網路遊輪社群、最佳網路旅行社等。

2. TripAdvisor

　　2000 年成立的 TripAdvisor 已成為網友最常使用也是最大的旅遊資訊網站，提供旅客世界各地旅遊的建議及各種服務的選擇，可下載 app 查詢機票、住宿、租車、遊輪、餐廳、景點等，有大量的評論及意見供旅客參考。

3. Lonely Planet 「寂寞星球」旅遊指南系列

　　除了利用旅遊網站、討論區、論壇的資料外，是不分國籍的自助旅行者及背包客 (backpacker) 人手一本的參考書，被稱為「旅行者的聖經」，是旅遊指南書類的翹楚，無論是觀光大國或是蕞爾小國，每本書的作者不只到訪廣受歡迎之處，更涉足鮮為人知幽僻之地 (off the beaten path)，親臨各地不同等級及主題的住宿、飲食、風光及娛樂活動，不僅提供正確充足有公信力的旅行資訊，並佐以特立獨行的旅行家見解，不受商家及宣傳影響，難怪無論以何種語言出版 (近年已有中文版)、書頁多厚，一直是全球自助旅行者 (world traveler) 的最愛。

4. AAA (The American Automobile Association 美國汽車協會) (簡稱 Triple A)

　　在美加地區旅遊可以參考 AAA 網站的資訊，長期在美者可繳交年費加入會員，該會已有百年以上歷史，會員超過 5000 萬，是全美最大的汽車俱樂部，服務範圍與種類不斷增加，可以上網申請會員及下載 app。申請時會拿到暫時卡，正卡會郵寄到你家地址。AAA 除提供道路緊急救援外，還有地圖、套裝行程、住宿、機票、租車折扣、油價比較等旅遊資訊。許多旅館住宿可享 10% 折扣，即使對短期觀光的自由客而言，省下的錢，可能都已超過年費，很划算。

5. Amtrak 美國國鐵

　　Amtrak 是美國全國性的鐵路系統，經過全美各地大小城鎮，提供類似飛機上的服務，旅客可以透過網路或電話查詢及訂票。

6. VIA Rail 加拿大國鐵

　　提供加拿大境內服務，遍及全國城鎮，與美國國鐵相似。

7. 澳洲國鐵

　　包含 The Ghan、Indian Pacific、The Overland 數家公司，都是歷史悠久，串聯整個大陸，旅客可以上網訂位，前往各景點。

8. Arizona Highways 亞利桑那高速公路雜誌

　　在美國西南地區旅遊時，可以去超市或便利商店購買最新一期的雜誌，內有景點、划算買賣、此區旅遊服務資訊，以及很棒的照片。雖然雜誌看來光鮮，像是為上流人士服務、推薦豪華去處，但其實是亞利桑那州交通局為一般旅遊人士所發行的雜誌。

9. Chamber of Commerce 商會

　　到商會去可以讓旅行者獲得免費地圖及簡介，通常商會時間為週一到週五的 9 點到 6 點。商會不僅可以幫助商務人士推薦當地商品，也很願意對旅行者及度假者提供協助。

10. Michelin Tires 米其林輪胎

　　為什麼要說到輪胎呢？因為米其林出版最有聲望的餐廳指南，世界上所有的餐廳都夢想登上指南的最高星級評比。上榜的餐廳小心翼翼維護得來不易的名聲，如果跌落評比就抱怨不已。如果你期待在旅途中享受一流美食及服務，它會是很好的參考。

　　註：拜科技之賜，旅客使用手機 app 即可購買機票、旅遊國家的各種交通票券、訂房、下載離線地圖、導航、查油價、景點導覽、導航或小費諮詢及計算分攤等，做好各式各樣的旅遊計畫。

10. 五十個今生必訪之地 50 Places of a Lifetime

　　美國「國家地理雜誌」在 1999 年 10 月出版的 National Geographic Traveler 內列出了「50 個今生必訪之地」是出現最早、最知名，也最經典的必訪清單。整個「國家地理」團隊從 500 個被提名的旅遊地，經過一年半的激烈競爭評比後挑出的 50 + 1 地點，雖然難免以美國人的觀點為主，但深受讀者喜愛，流通量驚人的百年雜誌團隊所出爐的結果，可說極具參考價值！(2009 年更新版可供比較)。後來各式各樣的 The Travel Bucket List (The Bucket List 為電影「一路玩到掛」片名)、1000 Places to Visit Before You Die 及 2014 年「國家地理雜誌」50 Tours of a Lifetime 皆受其啟發，許多人也開始列出他們的清單，並計算目前為止去過幾個。

　　正如有關旅行最常被引用的名句之一所言：「The world is a book, and those who never travel read only one page.」(by Saint Augustine) 「世界是一本書，從未旅行的人只讀了一頁 (聖奧古斯汀，古羅馬神 / 哲學家)」。旅行可說是了解自己與這個世界最好的方式，每個地方都是獨一無二。對世界好奇求知若渴的你，今生必訪的地點是哪些呢？

1. 不朽之城 Urban Spaces

- 西班牙－巴塞隆納 Barcelona, Spain
- 中國－香港 Hong Kong, China
- 土耳其－伊斯坦堡 Istanbul, Turkey
- 以色列－耶路撒冷 Jerusalem, Israel
- 英國－倫敦 London, UK
- 美國－紐約 New York, USA
- 法國－巴黎 Paris, France
- 巴西－里約熱內盧 Rio de Janeiro, Brazil
- 美國－舊金山 San Francisco, USA
- 義大利－威尼斯 Venice, Italy

2. 原野大地 Wild Places

- 南極 Antarctica
- 巴西－亞馬遜森林 Amazon, Brazil
- 加拿大－落磯山脈 Canadian Rockies
- 厄瓜多爾－加拉巴哥群島 Galapagos, Ecuador

- 美國－大峽谷 Grand Canyon, USA
- 澳洲內陸－Outback, Australia
- 巴布亞新幾內亞－珊瑚礁 Papua New Guinea Reefs
- 非洲－撒哈拉沙漠 Sahara, Africa
- 坦尚尼亞－肯亞－塞倫蓋提草原 Serengeti, Tanzania-kenya
- 委內瑞拉－德布伊斯高地 Venezuela's Tepuis

3. 人間樂土 Paradise Found

- 義大利－阿瑪菲海岸 Amalfi Coast, Italy
- 美國明尼蘇達州－邊界水域 Boundary Waters, Minnesota, USA
- 英屬維京群島 British Virgin Islands
- 希臘群島 Greek Islands
- 夏威夷群島 Hawaii Islands
- 日本傳統旅館 Japanese Ryokan
- 印度－喀拉拉 Kerala, India
- 太平洋群島 Pacific Islands
- 塞昔爾群島 Seychelles
- 智利 Torres Del Plane National Park, Chile

4. 鄉野地帶 Country Unbound

- 歐洲－阿爾卑斯山 Alps, Europe
- 美國－加州大索爾海岸 Big Sur, California, USA
- 加拿大－濱海諸省 Canadian Maritimes
- 挪威－海岸峽灣 Coastal Norway
- 越南－峴港到順化 Danang To Hue, Vietnam
- 英國－英格蘭湖區 England's Lake District
- 法國－羅亞爾河谷 Loire Valley, France
- 紐西蘭－北島 North Island, New Zealand
- 義大利－托斯卡尼 Tuscany, Italy
- 美國－佛蒙特州 Vermont, USA

5. 世界奇觀 World Wonders

- 希臘－雅典衛城 Acropolis, Greece
- 東埔寨－吳哥窟 Angkor, Cambodia
- 埃及－金字塔 Giza Pyramids, Egypt

- 中國－長城 Great Wall, China
- 祕魯－馬丘比丘古城 Machu Picchu, Peru
- 美國－科羅拉多州維德臺地印地安人古居 Mesa Verde, Colorado, USA
- 約旦－佩特拉古城 Petra, Jordan
- 印度－泰姬瑪哈陵 Taj Mahal, India
- 梵蒂岡 Vatican City
- 網際空間 Cyberspace

6. 未來必訪 Final Frontier

- 太空 Space

11. 各國肢體語言須知
Body Language Speaks Louder than Words

地球村的時代，人們有更多機會接觸不同文化，對於來自不同地區或宗教的人們有些基本認識是必要的。

美國是個大熔爐，在初見面介紹的場合，最常見的是握手禮，將右手空出準備握手。被介紹時不要害羞，眼神要直視對方 (代表自信、誠實)，並且主動伸手與對方握手 (力道須展現熱誠，避免誇張或草率)。朋友間以握手、拍肩表示鼓勵或熱誠，彼此不會稱兄 (姐) 道弟 (妹)，除非雙方都是非裔，男士間不會勾肩搭背，女士間不會勾手表示熱絡，除非是同性戀人。美國人的身體距離 (personal space) 比我們寬得多，說話時不要靠得太近，保持一支手臂的距離，以免對方有壓迫感而往後退。

除了握手禮之外，西方人表示關心與友好的禮節尚有擁抱禮、貼面禮與親吻禮，英國還有吻手禮。但在見面時是否適合要看人們的關係及場合而定，多數人不會在初次見面就與陌生人擁抱、貼面或親吻。擁抱禮可能出現在迎賓、祝賀、道謝、或道別的場合，平輩間的貼面禮與親吻禮是以貼面及親吻空氣 (air kiss) 表示友好。女士們與男女之間貼面與親吻次數各地不一，城鄉有別，男士間是否貼面與親吻也有文化之別。

某些文化如泰國 (Thailand)、印度 (India)、尼泊爾 (Nepal)、柬埔寨 (Cambodia) 等，打招呼不用握手而是行雙手合十 (wai) 的合掌禮，從手放在胸前到眼前的程度表示尊敬的程度，慣於握手的人拜訪這些地區要入境隨俗。

許多亞洲與中東地區，對肢體碰觸相當保守，切記避免趨身向前與婦女握手，女士們可能感到受冒犯。回教文化中男女壁壘分明，異性之間即使是禮貌性的口頭稱讚 (如未婚男士稱讚已婚女士表示有興趣了解對方) 便可能惹惱對方配偶，與已婚女士照相更需取得對方先生同意。回教真主阿拉並無形象，所以保守的回教徒不拍照。

衣著也是肢體語言的一部分，到回教世界衣著要保守，到極為保

守的回教國家 (如伊朗) 旅遊，女士在入境時就要包起頭巾至出境為
止，宗教警察一樣會糾察外國女子的衣著 (不要露出頭髮、手臂、小
腿或身體線條)，男士衣著也要遮住手臂與小腿以贏得他人尊重。進入
清真寺或搭乘公共交通工具要跟同性別的人坐在同一邊，男女有別，
左右不同，不可亂坐。中東地區人民較歐美國家對亞洲人熱情好客得
多，許多古文明與民族風情更是截然不同，對旅行者可謂極具吸引
力。除了解中東地區反以色列與美國的意識外，國人前往時要先對其
宗教、風俗、飲食、社會規範與禁忌多加了解。

此外，印度、尼泊爾、柬埔寨、阿拉伯地區或某些宗教 (如回教)
裡有禁用左手與他人互動的習俗，慣用左手的人一定要記住不用左手
與來自這些文化的人握手、進食、付錢或傳遞物品。

某些文化肢體語言使用廣泛，美國人與義大利 (Italy) 南部人習慣
說話時比手畫腳且表情豐富幫助語言傳達，中東男士間經常彼此碰
觸，但英國人則少用肢體語言。國人經常使用的手勢在世界各地需要
特別注意之處，列舉如下：

1. 豎起大拇指在許多地方是「棒極了」，但在澳洲、大部分中南美
   洲、及義大利南部等於是比中指的髒話。

2. 拇指豎起朝後方比的搭便車 (hitchhiking) 的手勢，在希臘 (Greece) 與
   土耳其 (Turkey) 幾乎等同中指髒話。

3. 我們常比的 "OK" 手勢，在許多地方意為「沒問題」，在法
   國 (France) 代表「零」、「沒價值」，日本 (Japan) 代表「錢」
   或「零錢」(年輕人代表 OK)，但在土耳其 (Turkey) 代表「同性
   戀」(homosexual)，在德國某些地區與一些中南美洲國家如墨西哥
   (Mexico)、巴西 (Brazil)、委內瑞拉 (Venezuela)、巴拉圭 (Paraguay) 代
   表肛門，引申為「混蛋」。

4. 勝利的 V 手勢手的背面要向著自己，如果在英國手背向著他人代表
   髒話，如果是在餐廳要點兩杯咖啡，比錯手勢，侍者不可能為你服
   務。

5. 在希臘 (Greece) 向別人比出數字 5 的手勢是侮辱之意，為歷史上侮辱
   戰敗敵人塗抹穢物的手勢，手掌朝對方臉越近，程度越嚴重。避免此
   手勢，要引起侍者注意、叫計程車或說再見，舉起手，手腕上下擺
   動。

附錄

6. 在馬來西亞 (Malaysia) 、印尼 (Indonesia) 、中東地區 (the Middle East)，以食指指他人是不禮貌的表現，要用拇指代替。

7. 在泰國及中東，人的腳是全身最低的地方，代表不乾淨，所以不要將腳底或鞋底示人，用腳推、指東西，也是不禮貌的表現。泰國人認為頭部最高也最神聖，所以不要摸任何人的頭部上方，當然包括小孩的頭。

　　肢體語言的重要性甚至比真正的語言還重要，尤其在言語不通的情形下，用錯了肢體語言將造成誤會，用對了使彼此心神意會盡在不言中，因此，學習並注意使用適切的肢體語言有助於溝通，超越語言的藩籬。

12. 外交部領事事務局全球資訊網 (急難救助)

Website of Bureau of Consular Affairs, Ministry of Foreign Affairs (Emergency Assistance)

可查詢任何護照、簽證、文件證明、國際駕照 (及各國對我國國際駕照的態度) 資訊及最新出國旅遊資訊及警戒。如在國外有緊急狀況語言又不通的情形,務必出示所攜帶之外交部發出之「緊急救助卡」(上有駐外館電話)。

「緊急救助卡」中英文翻譯:「我來自臺灣,不會說貴國語言,可否提供中文傳譯,要是實在沒有,請聯繫駐外機構,我需要他們的協助」I am from Taiwan (ROC) , and do not speak English (your language) . I wonder if I could have a Chinese (Mandarin) interpreter. If no one is available, please contact the ROC embassy or Taiwan mission in your country. I need their assistance.

旅外國人緊急服務專線:

+886-800-085-095。(諧音「您幫我 您救我」,非緊急勿撥打,以免占線)

外交部緊急聯絡中心:

「旅外國人急難救助全球免付費專線」電話 +886-800-0885-0885,目前可適用歐、美、日、韓、澳洲等 22 個國家或地區。撥打方式如下:

專線電話

國家或地區	專線電話
日本	001-010-800-0885-0885 或 0033-010-800-0885-0885
澳洲	0011-800-0885-0885
以色列	014-800-0885-0885
美國、加拿大	011-800-0885-0885
南韓、香港、新加坡、泰國	001-800-0885-0885
英國、法國、德國、瑞士、義大利、比利時、荷蘭、瑞典、阿根廷、紐西蘭、馬來西亞、澳門、菲律賓	00-800-0885-0885

附錄

護照、簽證及文件證明等問題，請於上班時間撥打外交部領事事務局總機電話 (02) 2343-2888。外交部一般業務查詢，請於上班時間撥打外交部總機電話(02)2348-2999。

註：外交部領事事務局自101年2月29日起提供「旅外救助指南 (Travel Emergency Guidance)」智慧型手機應用程式 (app) 免費下載，結合智慧型手機之適地性服務 (Location-Based Service)，可隨時隨地瀏覽前往國家之基本資料、旅遊警示、遺失護照處理程序、簽證以及我駐外館處緊急聯絡電話號碼等資訊。

國家圖書館出版品預行編目資料

開口就會旅遊英語／黃靜悅, Danny Otus Neal 著.
——三版.——臺北市：五南, 2015.08
　　面；　　公分

　　ISBN 978-957-11-8227-8（平裝附光碟片）

1. 英語　2. 旅遊　3. 會話

805.188　　　　　　　　　　　　　104014018

1AC2
開口就會旅遊英語

作　　者	黃靜悅、Danny Otus Neal
發 行 人	楊榮川
總 編 輯	王翠華
企劃主編	鄧景元、溫小瑩、朱曉蘋
責任編輯	溫小瑩、吳雨潔
美術設計	吳佳臻

出 版 者　五南圖書出版股份有限公司
　　　　　地　　址：台北市大安區 106 和平東路二段 339 號 4 樓
　　　　　電　　話：(02)2705-5066　傳真：(02)2706-6100
　　　　　網　　址：http://www.wunan.com.tw
　　　　　電子郵件：wunan@wunan.com.tw
　　　　　劃撥帳號：01068953
　　　　　戶　　名：五南圖書出版股份有限公司

法律顧問　林勝安律師事務所 林勝安律師

出版日期　2007 年 7 月　初版一刷
　　　　　2013 年 6 月　二版一刷
　　　　　2015 年 8 月　三版一刷

定　　價　380 元整　　　　　　※版權所有・請予尊重※

TIME ZONES OF THE UNITED STATES

PACIFIC
（太平洋時區）

MOUNTAIN
（洛磯山時區）

CENTRAL
（中央時區）

HAWII-ALEUTIAN
（夏威夷-阿留申時區）

ALASKA
（阿拉斯加時區）

WA OR ID MT ND SD WY NV UT CO NE KS CA AZ NM OK TX

HI Honolulu

AK Juneau

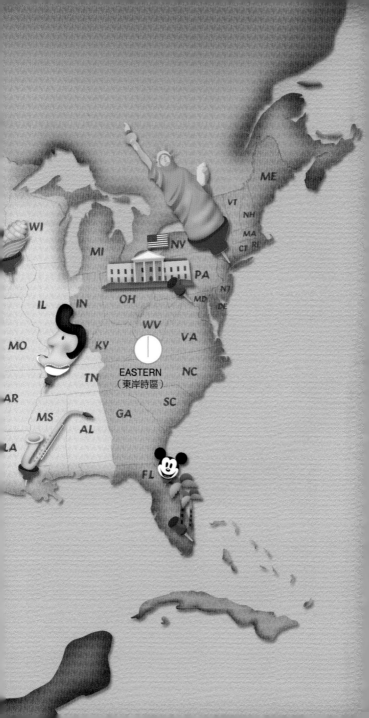

開口就會系列

生活資訊、語言學習、社交禮儀、
經商技巧、疑難解決，全都帶著走

開口就會社交英語
✚
開口就會美國校園英語
✚
開口就會旅遊英語
✚
開口就會美國長住用語
✚
開口就會商貿英語

● 隨書附贈 MP3
讓你隨時聽、隨口說